DEVIL'S CANYON

THE AUTHOR

Buck Stienke is a native Texan originally from Houston. He spent many of his formative years in the Texas hill country, and lived on the LBJ ranch when Lyndon Johnson was president. His love of almost all things Texan extends to movies, books as well as music. He's an accomplished guitarist and singer / songwriter. In fact, a country song he wrote inspired this novel. Buck has an extensive knowledge of guns, modern gunsmithing and ballistics. "Saddle up and hang on tight, pardner. *Devil's Canyon* is a wild ride."

Buck and his writing partner, Ken Farmer, have published eight novels to date. Six have been from a series of best-selling BLACK EAGLE FORCE Military/Techno novels : *Eye of the Storm, Sacred Mountain, Return of the Starfighter, Blood Ivory, Blood Brothers*. They also wrote a pair of historical fiction westerns: *The Nations* and *Haunted Falls* (Laramie Award winner - 2013). *Devil's Canyon* is Buck's first solo effort.

DEVIL'S CANYON

BY

BUCK STIENKE

Cover by Ken Farmer

ISBN-13: - 978-0-9912390-8-5 - Paper
ISBN-13: - 978-0-9912390-9-2 - E

Timber Creek Press
Imprint of Timber Creek Productions, LLC
312 N. Commerce St.
Gainesville, Texas

ACKNOWLEDGMENT

The author gratefully acknowledges Alex Cord, Ken Farmer and Doran Ingrham for their invaluable help in proofing and editing this novel.

Contact Us:
Published by: Timber Creek Press
timbercreekpresss@yahoo.com
www.timbercreekpress.net
Twitter: @cowboybuck
Facebook Book Fan Page:
https://www.facebook.com/TimberCreekPress
940-284-1032

First printing - 4/18/2014

DEDICATION

DEVIL'S CANYON is dedicated to the men who fought in defense of their homes and families in the great American nineteenth century conflict now known as the Civil War. Members of my family served on both sides.

Authors note: My characters speak with different voices as they come from different backgrounds with varied levels of education. I employ a writing technique used by well-known authors for many generations. You probably have seen it done by Louis L'Amour, Herman Melville, Larry McMurtry, Edgar Rice Burroughs and Charles Dickens. This technique is called phonetic spelling in dialogue. I want the reader experiencing the action to see, hear, feel, taste and smell what they do, i.e. "Git yer paws off'n my poke." That intentionally reads differently than "Keep your hands off my possessions." Forget spell check—allow yourself to drift back to 1862 and enjoy the adventure.

OTHER NOVELS FROM
TIMBER CREEK PRESS

MILITARY ACTION/ TECHNO
BLACK EAGLE FORCE: Eye of the Storm (Book #1)
by Buck Stienke and Ken Farmer
BLACK EAGLE FORCE: Sacred Mountain (Book #2)
by Buck Stienke and Ken Farmer
RETURN of the STARFIGHTER (Book #3)
by Buck Stienke and Ken Farmer
BLACK EAGLE FORCE: BLOOD IVORY (Book #4)
by Buck Stienke and Ken Farmer with Doran Ingrham
BLACK EAGLE FORCE: FOURTH REICH (Book #5)
BLOOD BROTHERS - Doran Ingrham, Buck Stienke
and Ken Farmer

HISTORICAL FICTION WESTERN
THE NATIONS by Ken Farmer and Buck Stienke
HAUNTED FALLS by Ken Farmer and Buck Stienke
HELL HOLE by Ken Farmer

MYSTERY/ SCI/FY
DAYS of the HARBINGER by Alex Cord

WESTERN ROMANCE
SURRENDERED by Peggy Patrick
SURRENDERED II by Peggy Patrick

Coming Summer 2014

SCI/FY
LEGEND of AURORA by Ken Farmer & Buck Stienke

WESTERN ROMANCE
SURRENDERED III by Peggy Patrick

MILITARY ACTION/TECHNO
DARK SECRET by Doran Ingrham
BLACK STAR BAY by T.C. Miller

ENDORSEMENTS

Devil's Canyon is one fine historical fiction Western. I grew up reading pretty much every thing I could about the Civil War and the Old West. Buck Stienke has written a great tale of what life was really like back then. Seems most Western writers tend to gloss over the realities during this period of American history. Buck has a keen insight to the harsh life his characters had to deal with daily and portrays it without romanticizing.

I am always disappointed when a author tries to authenticate his work with some random detail he or she failed to research fully. I was pleased to find nothing like this in Devil's Canyon. The bits of what I call color, sound, sights and smells blended flawlessly as the story unfolded.

Serving in the US Marines during the Vietnam War and I know what combat truly is. It's ugly, dirty and gut retching horror. Buck captured that well in his battles. Even a small conflict on the prairie between his protagonist, Eric, and a band of Native Americans after the Civil War is fully vetted in the darkness of death and injury.

Probably should note the underlying search for a lost love carries the tale to a conclusion that will surprise and amaze the reader. I never saw it coming and I usually can.

Devil's Canyon is a great first venture into the Western genre by Buck Stienke! I am anxiously waiting for a second.

Doran W Ingrham
inactive US Marine
Retired Risk Management Specialist
Actor/Author/Screen Writer/ Director
Co-Author of *Black Eagle Force: Blood Ivory* and *Blood Brothers*
Author of *Dark Secret*

TIMBER CREEK PRESS

CHAPTER ONE

SMITH COUNTY, TEXAS
MARCH, 1862

The Yankee's bullet barely missed his forehead as it ripped the black flat-brimmed hat from his head. The sharp report of the soldier's Springfield carbine echoed up and down the wooded lane, scaring the strapping young man driving the wagon as well as his team. He reacted instantly, tossing the woolen blanket off his lap as the horses bolted from the blast. With one hand, he lifted the double barreled scattergun up to his shoulder as the Union private wheeled and beat his mount across the rump with the rifle, using it as a quirt. The wagon bounced and lurched, almost causing him to lose his balance. He extended the shotgun like a massive pistol and fired a round at the retreating soldier.

Buckshot ripped into the blue-clad man's right shoulder—the carbine tumbled to the lush green spring grass.

He pulled the other hammer back to full cock as the cavalryman whipped out his revolver, turned and aimed it at him over his left shoulder. The Yankee's bullet whistled past his ear as he pulled the trigger. From only twenty yards away, the impact of the load of buckshot was devastating. The soldier tumbled out of the saddle and bounced twice like a rag doll— coming to rest lying across the dirt road .

He attempted to miss the body, but the team was already at full gallop—he was pitched into the air and flung his arms wide to try to catch his balance.

"Ow," the tall blonde-haired teen exclaimed as his hand smashed into the log wall in his bedroom, waking him from his nightmare. He was covered in sweat and still breathing heavily. The young man realized he was still lying in his own rustic pine bed. It was dark and cold outside the down comforter and the sounds of wind howling outside made his dream even more surreal.

Tops of the scattered tall slash pine trees surrounding the remote log house swayed with the passage of the last cold front of the season. Nestled in a shallow verdant valley, the house was somewhat protected from the worst east Texas weather. Nonetheless, howling winds made an eerie sound as they blew across the top of the chimney. Rolled glass window panes rattled in concert, creating a cacophony of sounds that made further sleep improbable. Eric Schmidt reached into a small open-topped brass cylinder and fished around for one of the four inch long wooden matches of the day. He withdrew the first one he came across and stuck the lucifer across the roughly planed timber wall, causing the phosphorus and sulfur to ignite with a slight hiss.

He reached for the coal oil lamp on the pecan night table beside his bed, carefully raised the wick and set it alight. The first flames off the charred ribbon of woven linen sent a couple of tendrils of black smoke up the lamp's glass chimney, but in a few seconds, it burned clean and he waved the match quickly to extinguish the fire. Lowering the chimney down to the polished brass base, the yellow light filled half of the small bedroom with a steady glow. He looked at the silver pocket watch lying beside the lamp and saw it was already five minutes after six. *God, what a dream. It was all so real. What in tarnation was that all about?* He shrugged. *Time to get moving anyway.* He could hear his mother in the next room, already stirring around as she began her daily preparations for breakfast.

The smell of strong coffee coming from the kitchen told Eric that his father was up and boiling the acrid black beverage that started his workday. In some ways, the routine of existence in the piney woods in the spring of 1862 was a comfort. All four members of the family shared the workload and the enjoyed the bounty of their labors, but somehow Eric felt an almost undeniable urge to wander, to see more of the land out west that was somehow always beckoning to him.

He pulled a coarsely woven dark blue woolen shirt over his red long underwear, then stepped into a pair of light brown canvas coveralls and finally tugged on a well-worn pair of black riding boots. Turning the wick down in the oil lamp, he headed for the door and turned the handle just before the lamp went dark once again.

"Mornin', Papa. Sleep well?" Eric asked as he strode past he knotty pine table and retrieved a leftover biscuit from the cloth covered bowl in the center of the table.

"Passable," the blonde-haired gunsmith and rancher answered as he opened the cupboard for a mug. "You?"

"I had the strangest dream…Some soldier tried to kill me! I had not done anything…He put a bullet though my new hat." He pointed to a spot just above his bangs.

Herbert lifted a single eyebrow and glanced over at his son. "What did you do then?"

"I shot him twice…with our shotgun. And then I ran over him with the wagon."

"A thing worth doing is worth doing well." Herbert grinned and selected one of the six mugs in the hand crafted cupboard.

"I am serious, Papa. It like to have scared me half to death."

"As it would me, I reckon. Just keep in mind though, it was only a dream."

Eric nodded, but was clear that he was still thinking about his emotional experience.

"We are gonna need some more wood if your mother is to prepare us a hot breakfast." Herbert poured himself a cup of coffee and set the steel pot back on the cast iron wood stove.

He glanced down at the handmade storage box. "Be back in a flash," Eric replied as he sat the buttermilk biscuit down on small plate next to the hive-shaped earthenware jar filled with locally produced honey. He slipped on a pair of leather work gloves he had pulled from the side pockets of the sheared lambskin coat hanging on a wooden peg. He opened the heavily reinforced single door on the south wall of the forty foot long great room and stepped outside. Eric turned left down the covered wood plank porch and filled his arms with dried split oak that was neatly stacked near the east end of the house. Seconds later, the lanky lad of nineteen pressed the toe of his boot against the door and pushed it wide to reenter. Without saying another word, he dropped the firewood into the small box next to the stove and returned to the table to slather a spoon of the golden nectar onto the last of the previous day's leftover baked goods. Between bites, he looked over at his father who was taking his first sip of the strong brew.

"What is on the list today? I think the sidelocks base plates are ready for case hardening. And we still have to temper all the locksprings we made the day before yesterday. The stock inletting is ready for some more oil to seal the grain."

Herbert smiled at his son. Not only did the two bear an uncanny resemblance, but the apprentice gunsmith shared the lack of patience his father had exhibited at the same age.

"Son, what have I tried to teach you about quality over quantity? What we strive for here is precision craftsmanship. Rome was ..."

"Not built in a day," Eric sheepishly finished the sentence with his father.

"Peas in a pod," the young blonde girl quipped as she entered the great room. She was a tall lass for the times, at five feet, nine inches, a trait inherited from her father who stood slightly over six-two. Her corn-silk hair could have come from either parent, but she definitely had her mother's eyes of sky blue. At sixteen, she was actually of marrying age, but the remote family farm's location eight miles outside of the small town of Tyler, Texas didn't seem to encourage many visitors.

"And a good morning to you, too, Baby Hanna," Herbert cajoled his daughter.

"Papa! I am almost seventeen years old...You and Mama were married by this age."

"Right you are, little one," Alyssa Marie Schmidt commented when she reemerged from the center bedroom. She stepped over to the stove, pulled an apricot colored apron off a brass cup hook embedded in the peeled pine log wall, slipped it over her head, and then deftly tied the long strings together behind her back. She leaned in to kiss her husband of twenty-two years. "Are we having a lesson in patience this morning? It is never to early to learn."

"He is a bit stubborn, my dear. Must take after your side of the family," he said with a wink and a twinkle in his eyes.

Hearing that, Alyssa grabbed a spatula off the stove and threatened her husband with mock anger. "My side? Your side is known worldwide for being rock hard in its thinking!"

"Worldwide? My, how our fame has grown...See, son?... Persistence pays off until we are now known near and far, not only for our fine rifles, but also for heads of stone."

They all four laughed. Alyssa lifted the top on a glazed earthenware canister on a shelf beneath the window sill. Only a half inch of milk remained inside.

"Hanna, dear, we are almost out. Could you entice a couple quarts out of Bessy? And it is time to feed the chickens as well."

"Yes, Mama," she replied without protest, as she slipped off her woolen house slippers and pulled on a pair of leather deerskin moccasins. She lit a second oil lamp placed at the center of the table, and then grabbed a hand-woven shawl off the back of a ladderback chair. As she opened the door, the wind tugged tightly at her ankle-length gingham dress. Hanna closed the door and made her way sixty yards over to the barn where a single milk cow and five Morgan horses eagerly awaited their morning feed.

"May as well go out and help her, son. Two can gather eggs faster than one, and we all will be waiting breakfast until it is done."

The first light of dawn was breaking when the freshly sliced bacon and scrambled eggs were coming off the stove. Buttermilk biscuits and coffee completed the usual farm fare. Herbert reviewed the procedures for the color case hardening process and stressed the importance of careful handling of the powdered cyanide, used to create a beautiful as well as weather-resistant finish to the metal.

"For a dozen sidelocks, we will use a heaping tablespoon of cyanide along with two pounds of crushed bone meal…What must we not do when handling the poison?"

"We must not touch it with bare hands or breathe in the vapors," Eric replied solemnly.

"Correct...and how long does the reduction process take?"

"One hour for a light hardening and two for a deep one."

"And what other precautions do we take when we open the canister?"

"We must take it outside of the forge room, allow it to cool completely and stand upwind when the top is removed. The hardened parts must be washed in clear water and then oiled."

Herbert smiled across the table at Alyssa. "Perhaps we shall make a gunsmith of him yet."

She nodded her agreement as she gathered the morning dishes and placed them in the tub for cleaning.

Shortly before noon, a lone rider approached the Schmidt homestead atop a chestnut gelding. A slender and somewhat gangly lad of eighteen—with a nose perfectly suited for someone a foot taller—he rode up to the freestanding workshop situated some ten yards from the house and dismounted. After looping his lead rope around the cedar hitching post, the young man strode up to the closed shop door and knocked enthusiastically.

"Mister Schmidt. Eric?...Anybody to home?"

"Door is open, Karl...Don't knock it off the hinges, boy."

The young man stepped inside and tugged at his oiled canvas jacket. "I do declare, Mister Schmidt, it is hotter than three shades of Hades in here...What are you gentlemen a cookin'?"

"Well, sir, I do not make wagers on the shades of the Devil's domain, but I do believe we have successfully knocked the chill out of the morning air while we were tempering these springs," Herbert said as he held up a V-spring with a pair of wrought iron tongs.

"In addition, we color case hardened these beauties...What do you think?"

Karl leaned over the well-worn shop bench and studied the blue-gray mottled sideplates.

"Mighty fine, Eric. You two do a man proud."

"What brings you out our way?" Herbert asked.

"Dag nab it!...I was so excited, plum near forgot about the shipment."

Both soot-covered men looked curiously at Karl, who stood mute.

"Is it a secret to what shipment you are referring?"

"Oh, no, Mister Schmidt...I was down to the freight office this morning, you see. I spied me a big wooden crate with your name on it. The label said it was from some big steel mill in Birmimgham...Consolidated, I think the name was."

"That would be the barrel blanks I ordered back last January. All our orders from my usual suppliers in Pennsylvania and Massachusetts have been turned down since that war back east got so big last fall."

"Land o' Goshen...That reminds me of the other news. I jest joined up to fight!"

"Fight?...Fight who?...Karl Walterscheid, what have you gone and done?" Herbert asked.

9

"You men are looking at a genuine Texas Volunteer! I am officially signed up to kill Yankees, like the dastardly ones who attacked Jefferson up in Marion County last week…We leave in the morning…"

"Yankees attacked Jefferson? Are you sure?" Eric asked incredulously.

"You folks need to get into town more often. It made the headlines of the Tyler paper…Here, see for yourself," he said as he dragged a crumpled page of newsprint out of his shirt pocket.

Herbert unfolded the front page and read the headlines, as well as the bold request for volunteers. The bottom of the page had inch high letters that virtually shouted the cry, *TO ARMS!*

"What do you know about fighting, Karl? You ever even shot at a man?"

"No more than you, Eric…But the sergeant told us that he will teach us how to mow them bluebellies down like a scythe cuts down wheat…That is what he said, by cracky! Heered him my own self."

Herbert's jaw visibly tightened. "If memory serves me correct, this county voted against secession last year, not that anyone bothered to ask us personally. No Schmidt has ever owed a slave and I do not feel like going to war with my country over something I do not believe in."

"Sir, nothin' agin you personal, but they's a whole lot of folks who think different now…Texas ain't in the union no more."

"We are painfully aware of that," Herbert said pulling his silver timepiece out of the pocket of his bib overalls. "Boys, it is nigh onto time for the noon meal. Will you join us for a meal? Hate to let a neighbor go away hungry…Especially after you rode out this far to tell us about our shipment of barrels."

"Why, sir, it would be my pleasure to accept your kind invitation. Is Miss Hanna going to be joining us?"

"She will, unless she has developed a sudden illness since breakfast."

"Then, sir, that will be jest fine. There is somethin' I have been hankerin' to ask her."

After lunch, Karl asked Hanna if she would walk with him for a while. She agreed, to the consternation of both her parents. Karl and Hanna has known about each other for almost three years, but the young man had never really shown a significant interest in her. But now, on the virge of his imminent departure as a foot soldier in the Army of the Confederacy, the boy had stepped up and popped the question.

Hanna had not been prepared for the marriage proposal but did not turn him down flat. She had merely taken the diplomatic route, batted her blue eyes and held up her hand for him to kiss.

"Oh, Karl…such a gallant young man. It would please me greatly to provide a definitive response to such an enchanting proposition…I shall deliberate forthwith and make my wishes known no later than the first day of June."

He rode off, whooping, hollering and waving his tattered hat high in the air as mud flew from his horse's hooves. Hanna smiled to herself and made her way back inside the log house. Understandably, her curious parents awaited her return.

"Girl, say something…What on earth did you tell him?" Alyssa asked.

"I let him down easy, Mama…I told him *maybe*."

Herbert shook his head and smiled. He turned to Eric. "Son…better get a move on it if you plan to make it back before dark. We can get set up for the job of rifling those new barrels in the morning."

The boy collected a shopping list of other sundries and staples the family needed. "Mother do you and Alyssa want to ride in with me?"

The two looked at each other, and then shook their heads.

"Perhaps next time…There is more than a little chill left in the air," his mom answered.

Once the team was hitched to the buckboard, and Eric had secured a sturdy wool blanket to help keep his legs warm, he embarked upon the journey. It was almost 3:00pm when he pulled up to the freight yard. Two muscular young men helped him load the two hundred pound crate of rifle barrels. A few minutes spent at each of the dry goods and general stores, and he was ready for the return trip. With any luck at all, he would make it back by sunset.

Hidden in the tree line some two hundred yards from the Schmidt ranch house, a twelve man patrol of Union cavalry waited for their commanding officer to finish his observation of the situation. With his seven power binoculars, Lieutenant Buford Anderson had a clear view of young Hanna when she left the main house and walked to the hand-dug well to draw another bucket of water. A pair of hens pecked at the remaining cracked grain scattered around the hen-house. Still others searched in vain for bugs.

"Whoa, boys…we have ourselves a real looker down there."

"Any sign of the men folk?" asked the sergeant.

"Nary a one, Smitty and we did pass over that set of fresh wagon tracks leaving the place. No sign of anybody else. My guess is the man of the house is off to town. We got us some chickens for sure, maybe even snag some hams and sausages in that smokehouse…Easy pickens, boys."

"My belly thinks my throat done got cut, Lieutenant. Ate my last hardtack yesterday…A chicken sure 'nuff sounds good to me, sir," a corporal from Cleveland, Ohio said as he licked his lips.

"Does that gal have light colored hair, sir? Sure looks golden from here," said the sergeant.

"By the Lord Harry, Smitty, you are an amazement to me…You can tell that from this distance?"

"I can dang near smell her from here. It has been a while…"

The young lieutenant's eyes narrowed. "Now hold on to yourself there, Sergeant. I will not be tolerating a repetition of what happened back in Little Rock…The colonel like to have brought us both up on charges."

"No, sir…you have my word. I do not need me no twenty years in the stockade. No siree…That was all just a little misunderstanding, and that is the Gospel truth."

"This time, Smitty, you keep your pants buttoned and your eyes open...Our mission is to destroy the Confederacy's ability to wage war upon the Union. Our spies reported that there is a gunsmith on this here property and we shall take such steps as needed to stop his capacity to produce such. Any weapons we find, we shall destroy...and any foodstuffs we come upon shall become forfeit as spoils of war...Am I clear?"

"Absolutely, sir...All you men just nod..."

The dirty and weary men signaled their affirmation as the lieutenant stowed his binoculars in his black leather saddlebags. He turned to a young wiry private from Toledo and pointed up the hill at the twin bare strips worn in the winter grass by the Schmidt wagon over the years.

"Johnston, you fall back a couple hundred yards and keep a sharp eye on the road to town. Anybody rides this way, you fire off a shot. Understood?"

"Yes, sir!"

"Smitty, take two men and work your way 'round back. Go in easy like...We will come in slow and real quiet behind you. Did not see any dogs, so let us take them by surprise...Get in, complete our mission and we get out clean...Any questions?" Anderson waited a couple seconds for his men to absorb their instructions. Months of constant small raids, with continuous moving and sporadic rations had left the Union cavalry regiment from Ohio looking bedraggled and more than a little scruffy. There had been little contact with actual opposing Confederate ground troops, as the many of the Rebels had, by and large, shipped east for the bigger set piece battles in Virginia,

Pennsylvania and Tennessee. The occasional skirmishes with Confederate mounted forces had been wild melees with pistols and sabers flashing. The lieutenant himself bore a long scar above his right eye from a rebel saber. He was extremely aware of the real dangers of close-in fighting and tried to avoid it whenever possible.

"Move out," he ordered his sergeant and waited for him to move a full hundred yards ahead before he put the remainder of his patrol in motion. "Carbines at the ready...Eyes and ears open, lads...follow me."

The men lifted the barrels of their short Springfield muzzle-loading carbines up and out from their circular leather rings—stabilizing devices called carbine-thimbles that attached to each saddle—and slid the carry slings off their shoulders. They laid the weapons across their laps and checked the security of the percussion primers under the hammers as they walked their horses in a column of two down the dirt road leading to the ranch house.

The first three men tied up their horses fifty yards behind the barn and worked their way slowly past the chicken coop. One of the black and white speckled hens flapped her wings and ran quickly across the yard when the sight of a pair of strangers startled her.

Alyssa was boiling some new potatoes for dinner when the movement of the frightened chicken caught her attention. She peered out the small kitchen window and caught sight of one of the Union soldiers before he disappeared behind the corner of the house. For a moment she froze, not wanting to believe what her eyes had seen. Instinctively, she ran to the front door and slammed the heavy wooden crossbar down into the wrought-iron U shaped brackets bolted into the interior door frame. She looked out the front window and her heart sank at the sight of eight mounted cavalry spreading out across the front drive of the ranch. She reached for the double barreled shotgun that hung above the door for emergencies.

"Hanna! Close the shutters! Soldiers!"

The young blonde girl was sewing a new blouse. She moved with a start, and jumped up to close the heavy wooden shutters on her bedroom window. She screamed when she saw the face of a bearded private appear with his nose only inches from the glass panes.

He reacted quickly as he saw her trying to close the shutters and jammed the muzzle of his carbine through the glass in an hurried attempt to block the window open as the shutter smashed into the carbine's barrel. The private clutched at the stock of the Springfield to keep it from falling out of his gloved hands—his index finger made rough contact with the trigger. The weapon fired, sending a .58 caliber Minié ball blasting through the inch thick shutter and filling the small room with acrid smoke from the black powder.

Once again, Hanna screamed as the round narrowly missed her head and buried itself deep into the interior bedroom wall. Jagged splinters from the pine shutters penetrated her sleeve and buried into her wrist—her blood spurting and staining the gingham a dark crimson. She stumbled backwards and fell to the plank floor, stunned and terrified from the unexpected blast as she called out, "Mama!"

Alyssa ran toward her daughter's voice and spotted her lying bloodied on the bedroom floor. She threw the shotgun to her shoulder, pointed it at the soldier's face peering inside and pulled the front trigger. The man's head exploded in a red mist from a full load of double ought buckshot.

Herbert had reacted to the sound of the first shot fired and dropped his red-hot tongs back into the waiting bucket of water. The hot steel hissed as tendrils of steam rapidly curled up, then dissipated. He grabbed a .45 caliber double rifle he kept loaded and stacked beside the door. Herbert drew the hammer back to full cock and reached for the door handle. He pulled the rifle tight to his shoulder and opened the door an inch or two as the second shot from inside the house rang out. The sight of eight armed mounted men did not deter him at all.

He picked out a man less than thirty yards away—the one wearing the officer's hat—and placed the front sight just in front of his left ear. As the lieutenant raised his saber and pointed at the front door of the house, Herbert squeezed the trigger. The hammer fell, and in fraction of a second, the primer ignited a load of ninety grains of black powder behind the 325 grain cast lead bullet.

Herbert felt the recoil of the heavy load, but didn't pay much heed. Even before the lieutenant's body hit the dirt, the Texan had thumbed back the hammer, unlatched and rotated the top barrel clockwise, and brought the bottom barrel up under it. He swung the rifle to the right and centered a corporal in his sights.

The soldier tried to bring his carbine to bear on the big man, but took a heavy .45 caliber bullet through the chest first. As he tumbled backwards out of the saddle, his carbine fired, striking a nearby horse in the neck and sending it and its rider down hard. Smoke drifted along with the brisk north wind as the remaining mounted cavalry fired at both the house and the tall figure that disappeared back into the shop. Bullets splintered the planks of the door as Herbert placed his back firmly against the thick log walls of the shop. He glanced around, knowing his only way in or out was the single door at the front.

A pair of loaded Colt sample revolvers hung on pegs nearby, one in .36 caliber and the other in .44. With ten shots between them, he had a chance to hold off the remaining cavalry for only a short while. Herbert knew the odds were not with him. He thought about his wife and daughter over in the main house and the mental image of them being killed by these invaders inflamed him in an instant. He grabbed at a duck's foot pistol and stuck it in his pocket before he plucked the two Colts from their pegs. Herbert stuck the toe of his hobnailed boots under the door and pulled it wide and then broke for the front door of the house in a dead run. He fired both pistols to good effect, wounding two more soldiers and killing one outright.

"Open the door, Alyssa!" he yelled out as a staccato of gunfire rang out across the ranch.

***

CHAPTER TWO

SCHMIDT RANCH

The five horses of the dead and wounded cavalry on the open ground facing the house spooked, broke free of the melee and ran in different directions. All of the soldiers had fired their large bore Springfield carbines once and then drawn their Remington 1860 revolvers to return fire at the running man. One of them got off a well-aimed shot just as he reached the barricaded door.

Herbert slammed against the door, only to find it blocked. "Alyssa!...Please!"

She had gotten Hanna to her feet and dragged her into the great room to secure the other window shutters when she heard her husband call out the second time. Her mind filled with panic and fear at the rapid fire sounds of the intense gun battle happening just outside the barricaded door. She crossed the room in a blur of motion to yank at the heavy cross bar. The door opened—Herbert collapsed at her feet. She reached for him as a single .44 caliber pistol ball tore through her apron and into her side. The force spun her halfway around, but she caught her balance, turned and leveled the scattergun at her attacker.

She saw the soldier's eyes go wide with fear just before she pulled the trigger and fired its last load of buckshot at him. The blast tore through one of the black mare's ears before finding its intended mark.

The private grabbed at his throat where five of the lead pellets had severed his carotid artery—his revolver fell from his grasp. The injured horse reared up and bolted—the fatally wounded soldier collapsed forward, slipped sideways out of the saddle and lay still. The frightened mount ran back up the roadway leading into the ranch.

The corporal who had shot Herbert in the back attempted to dismount as his horse danced sideways. The toe of his calf-high black boot hung in the iron stirrup for a split-second too long, causing him to twist and fall hard on the cold bare ground. His heart was pounding in his chest as he scrambled back to his feet, paying little heed to his badly sprained ankle—his mount shied away and galloped out beyond the barn.

"Whoa! Damn you to hell!" he shouted at the frightened gray gelding as it ran out of sight. He turned back toward the house and witnessed the wounded blonde woman roll an injured man over on his back. "I killed him, boys!" the corporal yelled as he limped toward the ranch house, his pistol at the ready.

20

Blood trickled down his left arm from a grazing bullet out of a .36 caliber Colt.

Herbert's leather shop apron had one tiny puckered hole in front where the Union .44 caliber ball had passed through as it exited his body. His left lung was already beginning to collapse and a bright red trickle of frothy blood ran from the corner of his mouth. Alyssa reached for his left hand and grasped it tightly as she stroked his face and looked into his sad blue-gray eyes. Tears streamed down her anguished face as she spoke, "Herbert…Herbert…my love…"

The movement of the corporal hobbling closer caught her eye. She reached for the empty scattergun lying on the floor beside her.

The corporal raised his revolver and fired from only fifteen feet away. His shot struck her just above the heart, killing her instantly. He closed in and tried to peer through the gunsmoke—only to hear a faint click.

As the soldier thumbed back the hammer on his Remington six shooter, Herbert pulled the trigger on his duck's foot pistol. At point blank range, the three barrels stitched a tight pattern across the young soldier's chest—he staggered back two steps and fell dead on the porch.

The light in Herbert's eyes faded—his fingers released their grip on the pistol as his head rolled toward his beloved Alyssa one final time.

Sergeant Smithers cautiously peered around the corner of the ranch house and was dumbfounded by the carnage he saw. Five of his patrol lay dead and two were wounded. Only three of the original eight mounted men who had originally faced the ranch house were still alive.

"Wilson! You see anybody else in there?" he yelled at the trooper at the far end of the house.

"There be a yellowed haired woman inside, curled up agin' the far wall!" came back the reply from the east end of the porch.

"She armed?" Smithers called back.

"Caint tell…She be bloodied up a might."

Smithers eased around the west wall cautiously and worked his way down the porch. He spotted the body of Lieutenant Anderson, missing half its skull. Privates Blaylock and Jones were helping tend to Miller, who ankle had been broken when his horse fell on it after it was hit. He also had a shoulder wound from a handgun ball, but could survive with medical care. Corporal Driggs was another matter. Shot through both kidneys and his liver, he would not make it another hour.

"Help me, Sergeant!" Driggs pleaded. "It hurts sumptin' fierce."

"I know, boy…I will see to what medicines they got inside."

Hanna cowered in a corner along the west wall of the house. She watched a Union soldier step over the bodies of both her parents and turn to face her. She covered her mouth with her right hand to try to stifle the scream that rumbled up her throat.

The soldier grinned as he holstered his revolver and closed the flap over the cross draw rig. His hand went to his belt and pulled a foot-long Bowie knife out of a black leather sheath.

The ol' Lieutenant was right about her. She damned sure is a looker. And ain't nobody gonna stop me from getting what I want now. He approached her slowly, making sure she didn't have a weapon.

Hanna shook with fear and as he closed the distance, she pulled her hand from her mouth and pleaded with him. "No! Please do not hurt me…Oh, God!"

He placed the razor-sharp blade against her throat and grabbed a handful of her hair. "On your feet, wench!" he hissed as he pulled on her golden tresses. She staggered up as he moved behind her and whispered in her ear, "You and me is gonna have us real good time…Ain't that right, goldie?"

Her heart beat as if it were going to burst. She looked down in stark terror at his filthy hand holding on to the bone-handled knife. Tears streamed down her face as they neared the two bodies lying in a pool of crimson near the front door. Hanna began to shake involuntarily as the utter hopelessness of her situation became tangible.

The man led her into the nearest bedroom and spun her around. Smudges of partially dried blood dotted her face. Her right hand was covered from her own blood where she had attempted to pull the wooden oak splinters from her arm. The soldier's eyes were wild when he pulled her close to himself and kissed her roughly. His stale breathe stank of tobacco and his body reeked from weeks in the saddle. She tried to push him away, but he yanked her back to him and tore at the front of her dress with one hand. Hanna slapped his face with all her might. He struck her with a closed fist, hard across her jaw and darkness overcame her.

When she awoke, the sergeant was pulling up his suspenders on his cavalry uniform pants. Her dress had been cut away and she tried to cover herself with her bare hands. She felt a wetness between her legs and raised her hand to see more fresh blood.

"You bastard! My brother will kill you all when I tell him what you did!" she screamed.

Smither's hand went for his knife. He lunged at her, covering her mouth with his bloody hand as he plunged the steel blade deep into her heart. She screamed one last time, but no one outside the room could hear.

"Shame to waste such a fine piece of woman, but you ain't gonna tell nobody nuthin'."

He wiped the bloody blade off on her exposed breasts and slipped it dispassionately back into its sheath. Slowly, he finished dressing and walked back into the main part of the house and over to the kitchen. He grabbed a pot holder and lifted the cast iron lid off the new potatoes. Searching for a plate and spoon, he found what he needed and scooped several of the medium redskins out of the boiling water. He snatched a smoked sausage from the pantry and made himself at home at the table, where he began to fill his ravenous hunger.

Blaylock and Wilson stuck their heads in the doorway. "Sergeant, I thought you wuz a looking for medicine for Driggs. He still is bleeding somethin' awful."

"Forget about him...He has had the biscuit," Smithers replied coldly as he wiped his mouth with the back of his hand. "They's taters in the pot, boys. Git 'em while they's hot."

The two glanced at each other then stepped over the bodies in the doorway. After filling their plates, they joined Smithers at the table.

"This little escapade did not quite go as the lieutenant planned," Blaylock said with a mouthful of potatoes. "Pass me that butter, Jimmy boy."

Wilson passed the crock of freshly churned butter. He slathered it on a chunk of bread he had torn off a loaf they found a nearby cooling rack.

"No, sir...the late lieutenant did not lay this operation out very good," Smitty agreed.

"Well, I reckon that makes you the lieutenant now."

"Dunno 'bout that...We will see what the captain has to say about that when we meet up over by Shreveport...Eat up, boys, we best be grabbin' what we can and gettin' ourselves underway. They done kilt over half our damned patrol here, and we got us one man bad injured."

Wilson gazed over at the woman laying near the front door.

"The crying shame of it all, is that there woman was a good cook...I bet you she could have fried us up some chicken that would melt off the bone."

"That, and she was a fine lookin' woman...Would have liked to have had me a roll in the hay with that one, too"

"Smitty, them women are gonna be the death of you yet," Wilson added.

"Meby so, but a man has gotta die of sumpthin," he said with a crooked grin.

The sun was almost to the horizon as a buckboard topped the rise a half mile from the house. In the trees, some fifty yards away, a very cold and confused Private Elmer Johnston had a decision to make. The squad's commanding officer told him to fire a warning shot if he saw anybody coming. But the man was already so close, that he could shoot back if he were to waste a shot in the air. Johnston wrestled with the dilemma for a couple of seconds before he raised the carbine up to his shoulder. He reasoned correctly the sounds of significant gunfire from the ranch had meant a stronger Confederate response than the lieutenant had contemplated. He would take no chances with this stranger and planned to drop him right off the wagon seat.

He strained to see the brass front sight in the fading light. It disappeared against the dark figure silhouetted against the burnt sienna sunset. He squeezed the trigger as his heart pumped faster and faster.

Eric felt his hat fly off his head as the nearby crack of the Springfield resonated through the piney woods. A cloud of thick gray gunsmoke from the carbine momentarily hid the shooter. He flung the heavy wool blanket off his lap and, using one hand, brought the double barreled shotgun up to his right shoulder as he snapped the reins over the team. "Heyaah!"

The two spooked horses had already broken into a lope and needed no further encouragement. The team responded with a full gallop and the buckboard bounced wildly over the uneven muddy roadway. Eric could see a definite US branded across the left hip of the sorrel horse and the blue uniform was unmistakable as the frightened Union cavalryman wheeled around and tried to make a break for it. The soldier held the empty carbine in his right hand and was beating the cold, hungry horse across the rump as if using a leather quirt.

That son of a bitch tried to kill me! No one had ever even threatened to use a weapon against him before. Eric had been a good-natured lad and—except for a tussle with a bully after church back when both boys were still very young—he had never even been in a fight. But that was not to say he didn't have a temper.

Adrenaline took over and in an instant, Eric forgot the chill of the wind on his cheeks. He stood erect—with legs partially bent to absorb the bouncing of the buckboard—and held the shotgun out like a massive pistol. He thumbed the right hammer back and pointed the thirty inch barrels at the rider only twenty yards away. A load of buckshot ripped into the man's shoulder—the rider instantly dropped the carbine from his shattered arm. It tumbled across the grass and slid to a stop.

Eric watched the man lift his reins to his mouth and grab for his revolver on his left side. He had raised the cross draw holster flap and cleared the leather when Eric steadied the two barrels with his left forearm. Schmidt rolled his other hand around the pistol grip of the shotgun and cocked the other barrel. In a flash, he brought the scattergun around just in time to see the soldier turn in the saddle, look over his left shoulder aim and fire at him.

Eric dodged to his right—the .44 caliber pistol ball just missing his left ear by an inch. He could see the look of disbelief and fear in the private's eyes as he fired. The soldier's mouth dropped open, allowing the reins to fall free from his teeth as the buckshot tore into his forehead. His head snapped back violently—his grimy blue kepi went flying off into the green spring cheat grass. The lifeless body slumped, tumbling off the speeding mount like a rag doll and flopped end-over-end before coming to a halt, face down on the muddy road.

Eric tried to brake the wagon but the steel-rimmed wheels rolled directly over the soldier's body first, nearly tossing him out as the crate of rifle barrels bounced upwards and came back down with a loud crash. He managed to regain his balance and pulled the team to a halt some sixty yards past the slain soldier. Quickly, he tied off the reins on the brake lever before he ran back to check out the man who had shot at him. Eric pulled his .44 caliber Colt from the Slim Jim style holster inside his coat. His heart was still in his throat and beating a mile a minute from the fast-paced events of the previous few seconds.

He cautiously approached the body, not knowing what to expect. The young man had never fired a gun at another human, and yet there in the road before him lay the result of his two shotgun blasts. "Hey, mister!" Eric shouted.

The soldier lay immobile. As he walked closer, the impact of the buckshot on the back of the soldier's skull could be see where it had lifted the scalp at the exit points. Bits of brain and bone were sprinkled across the his greasy black hair. Eric thought he was going to be sick for a moment but pulled himself together and rolled him over where he could see his face.

"Oh, Jesus!...Why did you have to go and shoot at me?" he asked the dead man, trying to comprehend exactly what had just happened. The soldier was not any older than he and Eric could not conceive why a man would try to kill a complete stranger for no reason at all. He tried not to look at the four entrance wounds in the man's forehead, and instead, unbuckled the silver plated buckle on the gun belt and removed the empty holster and two full cartridge pouches. *He does not need of this anymore.* Eric scanned the roadway for the revolver the man fired at him. He walked back a few yards, picked it up and brushed the red dirt off the hammer and conical brass front sight. The Remington was a new model accepted two years earlier in 1858 and one with which he was not very familiar. He stuck his Colt back into his own holster and replaced the Remington back inside the military cross draw rig and snapped the flap closed. Back another thirty yards up the road lay the Springfield Carbine that had come so close to taking his life. He wasn't sure why, but he was drawn pick it up.

He examined the lockplate and eyed the symbol of the spread American Eagle stamped into the plain blued steel. *Ours are much better finished.* The thought of the casehardened lockplates he and his father had just completed jolted him back to the present. *Oh my God. My family!* Eric spun around, sprinted back to the buckboard and jumped up to the driver's bench seat. He snapped the reins across the team's rumps and they lunged forward in the traces. *My God...that happened exactly like my dream this morning.*

"Johnston has contact!" Sergeant Smithers announced as he hurriedly stuffed biscuits down his shirt and grabbed the last half loaf of baked bread. "We got to get the hell out of here! Counted four shots...and the last one was not his."

"Smitty! What about Driggs and Miller?"

"Told you before...Driggs is done for. Miller better get his butt in the saddle if he is going with us. Mount up!"

The three soldiers ran from the house as Smithers barked out orders, "Jones, get Miller mounted! We are leaving!"

"Sarge, his laig is busted up bad. He cain't ride like that!"

"Then leave him with Driggs! Ain't got time to talk."

"Pull me up!...I'll give it a go!" Miller pleaded desperately.

Jones grasped his upraised arms and hauled him erect. Miller stood there with his good left leg bearing his weight. With his right leg shattered and a bullet in his right shoulder, the war was probably over for him. He would be lucky to survive even if the Yankee squad could find a doctor.

"Just get me on a horse, Jonesie, that is all I ask...Don't leave me here!" he begged.

Running to a ground tethered black mare, Jones returned to Miller's side and lifted him from around the waist as the wounded man pulled hard on the saddle with his good left arm.

Miller groaned in pain, but still managed to get his left toe in the stirrup and straighten up enough to throw his splinted right leg over the horse's rump and slide down into the deep McClellan cavalry saddle.

Jones tossed him the reins and swatted the horse on the rump. Miller and the mare departed toward the woods, just a few seconds behind the sergeant and two others. Jones mounted hastily and took one last look up the road, where a team pulling a wagon was just coming into view two hundred yards away. He spurred the brown gelding into motion and followed the other men into the tall timber and disappeared.

Eric slowed as he passed a pair of Union cavalry horses nervously milling beside the road. He stopped, drew his Colt and searched in vain for the men who had ridden them. Darkness was falling rapidly and Eric had a sense he was being watched. Both horses disregarded him, lowered their heads and continued to graze the lush spring grasses. He looked down at the ranch house and sensed something was wrong, very wrong. Light from inside the main house could be seen streaming out the open front door. *It is much to cold to leave the door open like that.* Straining to see as dusk settled in, he could barely make out dark figures splayed out in the front of the log house and shop. With his Colt at the ready in his right hand, he trotted the team cautiously the final hundred and fifty yards to the house—dreading what he already knew he would find.

He could see his parents bodies lying in the doorway, the weak lamp light casting shadows of their profiles out into the yard. Tears fell freely as he dropped the reins and stepped down off the buckboard. He glared at the bodies of uniformed soldiers that had caused this awful calamity, as he worked his way around them and stood over his slain parents. Nothing could have prepared him for the sight of his two lifelong nurturers and role models lying together—blood-soaked in one last eternal embrace. The young man broke down in sobs as he fell to his knees.

For several minutes, he wept uncontrollably, then suddenly remembered his sister. He stumbled back to his feet and yelled out to her, "Hanna! Hanna! You can come out now!"

He called her name toward the barn, turned back and wiped his eyes. Then noticed the door to his bedroom was closed. Forcing himself to lift the lantern off the dining table, he walked to the bedroom with great trepidation. His Colt in one hand, he pulled the door open and shined the flickering light onto his simple feather bed. The image of his angelic sister, so savagely abused, was forever seared into his consciousness. He stumbled back into the living room and threw up.

Minutes later, he thought he heard the weak moan of someone in pain come from outside the door. He gathered himself together and walked outside to where one of the soldiers lay dying. Eric shone the lamp on the man's tortured face.

He responded with a weak plea, "Help me."

Eric stared at him as a rage like none he had ever known before grew inside of him. He grabbed the corporal's yellow cotton scarf and pulled his face closer.

"Why? Why did ya'll do this?" he screamed.

"We had…orders," Driggs replied though parched lips.

Eric loosened his grip on the scarf, allowing his head to fall back onto the barren ground. He pulled his Colt from its holster and placed the muzzle two inches above the soldier's nose and pulled the trigger.

Almost a mile east of the ranch house, the sound of a distant pistol shot echoed off the surrounding hillsides. The five horse soldiers looked at each other in the moonlight.

"Think that was Driggs?" asked Wilson.

"'Spect so. We best keep movin'…Want to put some miles between us and that hell hole before dawn." He smacked his heels against his horse's ribs and the exhausted mount hunched over in pain before it begrudgingly began to move up the wooded hillside.

***

CHAPTER THREE

SCHMIDT RANCH

The new graves were dug by two in the morning—all three member's of the Schmidt family had been laid to rest by lantern light. Three carefully crafted markers had been fabricated, fitted together with precision and painted with the names of the deceased. Eric had bathed and clothed each member with their finest clothes, although plain ones by eastern standards. They were wrapped in a clean cotton sheets and he took pains to read a suitable Bible passage for each. His tears had previously stopped for hours, but the final reading by the dim light of the twin coal oil lanterns had started the flow anew.

Sweat dripping off his brow—his muscles aching from hours of almost nonstop digging with a mattock and shovel—Eric tossed spades piled full of red East Texas clay and loam into the graves and smoothed the resulting mounds down by hand. He stood up, wiped his gloves together to try to clean off the damp leather, and then walked back inside the house.

He built a fire in the stove and heated some water to wash off with a small cloth before changing into a fringed leather shirt his mother had made for him when he turned eighteen. He packed canvas-covered leather panniers with provisions he thought he would need over the next three weeks as he sought retribution on the Union soldiers who had brought about the deaths of his family.

Lead shot, powder, mold blocks to cast additional bullets and a large supply of captured Union weapons made up most of the load. He had scavenged the bodies of the fallen soldiers for equipment and even found the lieutenant's brass framed binoculars and a couple of US Army maps.

The unfamiliar tack that the Union Cavalry had ridden were called McClellan saddles. Purposely made with the horse's comfort in mind, he was at first puzzled by the split seat design. They were extremely lightweight with a wooden tree that was covered with rawhide and then a layer of leather that was dyed a uniform black color. The saddle swell lacked a horn as was common to those found in the southwest. The seat was deep, both front swell and back cantle rose five and one half inches above the narrow seat. A triangular brass shield on the shoulders was embossed with the words *12 inch seat*. The distinctive seat was designed so that the saddle did not make contact the horse's spine and provided excellent cooling for both horse and rider as well. Nothing was fancy, but Major McClellan knew what he wanted in a combat saddle. The four inch-wide wooden stirrups were fitted with a leather hood to keep the rider's boots from slipping through and becoming entangled in case of a fall.

Knives, sabers, handguns and a single Yankee uniform that came close to fitting went into the pannier. He packed an assortment of cooking and eating utensils and added a good supply of jerked and smoked meats, pickled vegetables, canned peaches as well as everyday staples consisting of bacon, beans and flour. Eric strapped the two rifle scabbards his family owned to his own saddle. Finally, all three shirts he possessed and an extra pair of boots and pants his father had worn were folded neatly, bundled with twine and stuffed into the panniers. He walked back to the house for one last look around.

Next to the doorway, he noticed a heavy sheepskin coat that his father had worn for years. He lifted it off the wooden peg and slipped it on. It fit, although it was a tad short in the arms for the slightly taller son—rolling down the cuffs fixed that. He fastened the large buttons—ones cut from cross sectioned deer antlers—thankful to have a coat warm enough to ward off the cold night air as he left the house.

Swinging out the rear doors to the barn he turned the extra horses, as well as the family's milk cow, out into the large pasture behind the house. He opened the door to the chicken coop and blocked it there with a piece of split firewood.

Using lamp light, Eric dragged the stripped bodies of the Union dead and piled them on top of the unlucky Yankee horse carcass, added two dozen pieces of dry firewood for good measure, and doused them all liberally with coal oil. He tossed a match at the pile from the northern upwind side. The flames spread quickly and soon the charred flesh was popping and hissing as the flames consumed them. He looked to the heavens as dense black smoke boiled skyward—tiny red embers danced like demons in the violent updrafts.

"God, please forgive me for what I am doing and what I am about to do. It says in the book an eye for an eye...reckon you were too busy elsewhere to keep my family safe." His voice trailed off—Eric walked his horses around the pyre, staying well upwind as he mounted his favorite, a large buckskin gelding. He rode off into the woods, a single lantern illuminating the tracks of the five surviving cavalrymen.

The damp ground made for easy tracking, even in the poor light. In the dark timber, a thick organic carpet of tree litter—consisting mostly of fallen pine needles mixed with decades of old and new pine cones and decaying branches—showed each hoof print. It did not take a scholar to deduce the Union horses were tired. The debris dragged forward of each track showed that the horses were far from fresh mounts.

The mature pine forest was almost a biological desert underneath the unbroken canopy above. Sunlight never reached the forest floor and no grasses or forbs grew there. They had long since died out from lack of photosynthesis, a process that required sunlight to convert the energy of the sun to food to support plant growth. As a result, only squirrels and a few voles could live in the interior of the dark woods. Deer, rabbits and other herbivores existed on the fringes of the forest and areas where the pine canopy had been broken by fire or intervention from humans. Every half mile or so, Eric would stop and listen for a while. He thought perhaps his ears could tell him something his eyes could not. But in the middle of the night, even the noisy squirrels were fast asleep and the other nocturnal hunters like the owl, coyotes, red wolves, black bear and panthers were off in areas where game was much more plentiful.

The silence was deafening—it only served to make Eric painfully aware of his solitude. He took a drink out of his canvas covered canteen. The cold well water tasted good and reminded him of home. He worked his jaw to attempt to loosen it, after realizing he had been clinching his teeth. His heart ached for revenge, but he remembered his father's many admonitions about the virtues of patience as he jammed the cork back into the canteen.

"Get on up, Bucky. We have miles to go before we are through."

As dawn broke, Eric came up to the Thompkin's place, a small farm ten miles east of his ranch. He had turned off the trail left by the five Union horses and rode along the split-rail pasture fence leading up to the small clapboard house and called out a greeting "Hello in the house! Mister Tompkins? Anybody to home?"

A lone figure looked out the small window and tried to make out who was hollering his name at that time of the day.

"That you, Herbert? I recognize the coat."

"It is Eric Schmidt, Mister Thomkins…Got a favor to ask you."

The slender man, just under six foot tall, with a pointed silver goatee, slipped on his glasses and looked again at the imposing figure astride the thick shouldered buckskin horse. Sure enough, the man was younger than the elder member of the Schmidt clan. He leaned the single barreled shotgun against the wall and opened the door. "Come on in, young man…Sit a spell and knock the chill off'n you."

"Appreciate the invite, sir, but I got some business to attend to."

"As you wish," the old man said as he stepped outside and approached Eric. "Must say…you look like five miles of bad road…You feeling poorly, son?"

"I have had some better days, sir, but I will get to right to the heart it. If you have the time, can you please check on my stock for a couple weeks? If'n I do not come back in three weeks time, consider them all yours."

That there is about the strangest offer as I can ever recall, mused the old man. "What happened to your Pa and the others, son? If you do not mind me askin', that is."

"Yankees murdered 'em all late yesterday…I'm fixin' to hunt 'em down and kill 'em."

Tompkins studied the grim determination in the man's face. He hardly recognized the young boy who had grown up a couple of valleys away. But he completely understood his stoic motivation and nodded his agreement. "My sympathies to you...Good God almighty...what a terrible thing...I would be proud to watch over your place, son. Now, do not go and git yerself kilt in the process."

Eric tipped his hat and turned his horses back to the tracks. Thompkins watched as rode away, bowed his head and said a little prayer for all the members of the Schmidt family. As Eric disappeared into the tree line, the old man shook his head and slowly walked back inside. The east Texas countryside seemed a much lonelier place than he ever felt before.

"Sergeant...Miller is bleedin' agin. We should stop and change his dressings," Private Thaduis Jones announced.

"Jonesie, like a done told you, we ain't a stopping 'til sunset. They could be a whole Reb column on our tail. With all the troopers we lost yesterday, it makes no sense to let 'em catch us now...do it?"

Jones turned to check out their back trail. In much of the rolling hills—with scattered oak thickets mixed with stands of virgin slash and loblolly pine trees—the visibility was seldom over 200 yards. His boyhood friend Ezekial Miller was in a bad way. The eighteen year olds had joined up together back in Ohio in a rush of patriotism. The reality of the war between the states was far less glamorous than either had ever imagined. The sight of his best friend barely hanging on in the saddle was almost more than he could bear. "Smitty, me and Miller are gonna hold up here until I git his shoulder all patched up. We kin catch up with you by sunset."

Smithers reined to a halt and turned the weary horse around to face the two riding at the back of the small group. He spat out a well-worn chaw of tobacco and wiped the dribble from his chin with the back of his riding gauntlet.

"Suit yourselves. We will not be waiting for you if'n you get lost." With that said, he yanked the gelding's head roughly back to the east and spurred horse onward.

Private Jones tethered both mounts to a small youpon holly bush. He helped Miller dismount and was almost toppled by the man's weight as he literally fell out of the saddle.

"I got you, Zeke...I ain't gonna drop you," he said reassuringly as he struggled to tote the moaning man to the nearby trunk of a two foot thick oak. He laid him gently against the rough mottled gray bark and returned to his own horse where he retrieved a canteen.

"Here you go, my friend. You be looking a tad parched."

Zeke drank heavily from the thin bullseye canteen until it was empty. Sweat beads covered his face even though the air was only in the mid-forties. Jones removed his heavy gloves and placed his bare hand on Zeke's forehead.

"Jesus, you done fevered up already! Gotta git you to a sawbones and fast."

"Tad, do you think I am gonna make it? My laig is a throbbing like a drum and my foot's swoll up somthin' fierce...I cain't git my finger inside my boot."

Thadius looked him in the eye and lied, "Sure you are! I bet there be a country doctor in the next town we come to."

"Do really think so?" Zeke replied as he handed the empty canteen back. "That doctor may not fancy up to healin' up a bluebelly."

"Maybe yes, maybe no, but I bet a month's pay he'll do it with my pistol to his haid! Now, you get some rest whilst I go get us some more water. Don't go a runnin' off on me, hear?"

"Do not try and make me laugh, Thadius. You ain't got no comedy bone in you."

Jones chuckled to himself as he retrieved the canteen from his buddy's saddle and checked their back trail one more time. It was a hundred yards or more to the heavy timber behind them. He picked up the Springfield carbine off the ground where he had laid it and turned back to Miller.

"I'm a headin' down yonder and fill up our empties. You holler out if you spy any Rebs coming in."

Miller nodded weakly and laid his head back on the trunk.

The blonde man lowered the brass framed field glasses. He never had used one before, but was quick to discover he could see far ahead into the distance and make out what was transpiring without his presence being known. He tied off both horses and set out to intercept the man with the canteens in his hand. He fastened a latigo strap to the double barrel rifle and slipped it over his shoulder. Eric drew a Union cavalry saber out of the brightly polished scabbard tied to the pack horse's panniers and set off in a course downhill toward the creek.

Moving slowly and deliberately—just as when hunting deer with his father—he closed the distance to his quarry.

Thadius Jones searched for a spot where the creek bank was not too steep or muddy. He finally spotted a promising location with a shallow bend in the brook that featured a sandy bottom and clear cool water. Arriving at the water's edge, he laid the carbine in the lush grass. Jones untied his red bandana, dipped it in the creek and then wiped the dirt and sweat off his face.

After rinsing the dirty cloth as best he could, he bathed the back of his neck where dirt from the previous four days of hard riding had been ground into the inside collar of his blue wool uniform blouse. The private waved the muddy rag back and forth in the creek until it had shed most of its grime back into the slow moving spring water, and then wrung it out one last time and tied it around his neck. *Whew...That feels a heap better already.*

Thadius pulled the cork stoppers out of the stamped metal canteens. He knelt over as close to the creek as he could without placing his knees in the water, submerged the first one and listened as the air bubbled out and refreshing water gurgled in. Suddenly, the hair stood up on the back of his freshly cleaned neck. Call it a six sense, a premonition, but he sensed danger. His hand released the canteen and as he reached for his revolver, the canteen sank to the bottom of the sandy creek. He pulled the flap open on his crossdraw holster, only to feel a shape pain in his back. Thadius Jones looked down, amazed to see a crimson stained silver blade emerge fourteen inches from his chest. His hand went limp as he heard the sickening, sucking sound of the saber being withdrawn from his body. The trees and the creek drifted out of focus as he knelt for only a second and collapsed face down in the water.

Eric grabbed the soldier's legs, pulled him back onto the creek bank and rolled him face up. The young man's lifeless brown eyes stared back at him. He unbuckled the soldier's gun belt and pulled it out from under his body. As had become his custom, he picked up the Springfield, slipped the gun belt and ammunition pouch over his shoulder and made his way silently back to his horses. Ten minutes later, he was standing behind the feverish Zeke Miller when the soldier called out, "Jonesie! You all right?"

"Was that his name…Jonesie?" Eric said as she stepped out from behind a tree. "Keep those hands away from that sixgun," he continued as he cocked the Colt pointed to the soldier's head.

"Don't shoot! I ain't got no money!" Miller pleaded.

"I am not here to rob you, Yankee," Eric spat back as he moved around where Miller could see him.

The way the man said the word *Yankee* made Miller's blood run cold. He had killed several men in battle and on raids in small towns, but now the tables were most definitely turned. Zeke was more scared than any other time of his life. He eyed the Union issue cavalry saber in the man's hand. There was blood on the blade. He struggled to finds his words. "Look, I am hurt real bad, mister…ain't got no quarrel with you. My friend and I will be gone as soon as he gets back up here with some water."

"I got questions to ask you...And your friend will not be coming back."

The words struck him like a thunderbolt. *Jonesie!* His best—and until ten minutes earlier—only friend was gone. His eyes teared up and he sobbed as the utter hopelessness of his situation sank in.

"Which one of you jackals raped and murdered my sister?" Schmidt hissed at the seated Miller.

"Mister, I don't know nothing about no rape!...Where you from? We been on the move for ten months and covered a passle of ground."

"My whole family was butchered last night just twenty-five miles back west of here. I want the name of the animal that did it...you Yankee bastard."

Miller's mind raced back to the jumbled events of the previous night. The nightmare that began as a simple search and destroy mission was continuing the following day.

He moved closer as he lowered the hammer and holstered the menacing Colt revolver and then transferred the saber to his powerful right hand. The tip of the saber was mere inches from the private's right eye.

"You gotta believe me! I had nuthin' to do with it...My horse got shot out from under me...first thang out of the barrel. That broke my laig and then the big man runnin' from the outbuilding went and shot me in the shoulder. I never seen no girl..."

"The name, damn you! I want the name of who did it!...Who went into the house?...Who? Start talkin'!"

"Look, mister!" Miller pleaded. "I was hurt bad. I could not move and…No!…Please!…Ahhh!" he screamed as the man pressed the tip of the saber into the flesh of his forehead, pinning his head firmly against the tree. Blood from the tiny, but bone deep laceration trickled down across his eye.

Eric watched almost dispassionately as dark red blood mixed with the soldier's tears and trailed down his dirt speckled face. He gave the man an ultimatum. "Three seconds! If I do not get the names of who went inside the house, you are gonna be a permanent decoration on this here tree…You hear me, bluebelly?"

The man sobbed and his lower lip quivered as he envisioned the sight of the Texan ramming the saber through his head.

"It was Wilson, Blaylock and Sergeant Smithers! That is the Gospel truth, mister!"

"Which one did it? You rode with the men for some time. His name…last chance…swear to God!"

"Harlen Smithers, he was always after what he could get from the ladies…"

"What does he look like?"

"Dark hair, big mustache, kinda scrawny…average height, twenty-five years old, maybe…"

"And where were you boys headed to? He seems to be pushin' ya'll's horses real hard. From the looks of 'em, you Yanks are short on oats as well as rations."

"He said sumpthin' about a place called Shreeport. I do not know anything more, mister…Honest."

Shreveport? That is 'bout seventy miles, maybe eighty. He pulled the blade off the man's forehead and moved it down to his waist.

The soldier inhaled in terror, expecting to feel the blade sink into his stomach at any moment.

"Unbuckle that belt...slowly...with your left hand."

He nervously complied.

"Now, fling over there," Schmidt said, pointing to his right.

Again, Miller followed the order as best he could, wincing in pain as his wounded shoulder ached a bit when he leaned forward to allow the leather cartridge box to slide between his spine and the tree trunk. He breathed a little sigh of relief when the man eased away to pick up the gunbelt.

The big man backed up, buckled the belt back together and laid the rig across the saddle of the nearest of the pair of horses. He untied them and led them closer to where the wounded private lay.

Miller felt his spirits rise. *Is he gonna take me prisoner and get me to a doctor?*

"Where you from, Yankee?"

"Me and Jonesie enlisted from Toledo, Ohio."

"I suggest you try to make it back there and never come back to Texas."

"Yes, sir," he said as he nodded. "I have had my fill of this man's Army, I can vouch for that." He watched the tall Texan nervously as he lifted his left boot to the stirrup of one of the Army mounts, then swung easily into the saddle. The stirrups on the sorrel were way too short for him, and it reminded him of a huge jockey in a wagered horse race. The man grabbed the reins of the other horse and began to walk the two back to the west. Miller's heart sank.

"Mister! You ain't gonna just leave me here! I cain't walk... ain't got no food...no water!"

Eric stopped some ten yards away and turned the horse around to face Miller, who cried as he pleaded for assistance.

"Show some mercy, mister! Please...For God's sake!"

"I would leave the Lord's name out of it, if'n I was you. I already showed you more mercy than you vermin showed me or my family," Eric said. He removed his flat brimmed beaver felt hat and nonchalantly stuck his index finger through the .58 caliber hole in the front crown. He flipped the hat back in place and tugged it down tight before he locked eyes with the wounded soldier. "'Sides...buzzards got to eat, too."

Miller shook uncontrollably as the man rode off with the two horses. His fractured leg reminded him of his most threatening disability with a searing pain that had him crying like a child. He wiped his eyes and searched the woods for any sight of the man with the mission of revenge, but to no avail. He was all alone, a man without a chance.

***

CHAPTER FOUR

EAST TEXAS

Private Benjamin Blaylock turned in the saddle to take another nervous look back over his shoulder. For the fiftieth time in the last two hours there was no one there following.

"Smitty, you think Miller and Jones are gonna catch up with us?"

"Who the hell knows? Could be that Miller is going to infection. A surgeon could mebe save him, but they's no town near our route 'til Longview. Guess we will just have to wait and see."

"Me, I would feel a bit better, Sarge, with four guns, rather than three…That time they jumped us outside of Murfreesboro, we liked to have taken a lickin' from them Rebs…It was a dicey proposition, if you ask me."

"Nobody is asking you, Blaylock, so keep your trap shut. If I want you to have an opinion, I will give you one."

A full two miles behind them, Eric led three other horses behind him into a large meadow. He had glassed the three Union marauders from the edge of the last clump of pines and waited until they crested a hill to ease out in the open expanse of blue stem grass. The sun told him it was about four in the afternoon and he figured the poorly fed cavalry horses were about worn out.

The fact that he had caught up with them even with the Yankees' substantial head start was all the proof he needed. Their progress had been very slow during the darkness of the previous night and he figured they would be making camp by nightfall.

He had no military training whatsoever, but possessed a lot of common sense and his father's lessons in patience served him well. His skills with handguns and rifles came from many hours spent at a range set up behind the gun shop, where Herbert and Eric competed against one another with guns they bought for resale or crafted themselves. He removed the now empty feed bag from his horse's head, and walked back to retrieve the empty feed bags off the other three.

"Guess these fellas have not eaten this well in a few days, huh, Bucky?" he said to his buckskin who was licking the last few grains of oats off his muzzle. He patted him on the neck and stashed the feed bags back into the almost empty saddle bags on the newly acquired Union steeds. He circled back to pick up the lead rope of his personal pack horse, mounted up and took off into the meadow at a gentle lope.

An hour later, Sergeant Smithers spied a heavy stand of dark timber in the direction in of their travel.

"We kin bed up inside them woods over yonder way," he said as he pointed ahead. "Should be a crik down below where the willows are."

Wilson nodded wearily. The three had no sleep in almost thirty-six hours and were barely hanging in their saddles.

"My tired is a hangin' out, Smitty"

"You and me both," Smithers agreed as he spit a stream of tobacco out the right side of his mouth.

Blaylock turned round in his saddle one last time. "Sergeant…mind if I backtrack up to the top of the last ridge and see if I can spot Jones and Miller?"

"Do as you like, but make it quick. The sun will be down in ten to fifteen minutes. We gonna have us a cold camp tonight, just in case any Rebs have cut out trail."

"I hear you, Sarge," he said as he turned his exhausted mount back up the long rise to his west.

The small cluster of trees near the top of the ridge barely covered an acre of the rolling savanna, but the young man from Texas found plenty of cover inside it. A three year old doe with two very young fawns bolted from the denser brush and ran helter-skelter to the north across the waist high mix of mature blue stem and Indian gramma grass. In seconds, the beautiful spotted fawns disappeared in the vegetation. Eric paid almost no attention to them as he tied up his mount and pack horse and unfastened the lead ropes attached to the pair of Union horses.

He walked the saddled horses to the south end of the stand of trees, tied them securely to one of the crepe myrtle trees and then hurried back to his horse. He pulled the .45 caliber double rifle out of its scabbard, and then reached across his horse for the Springfield carbine. Weighted down by the two rifles, he eased back into the thicket and set up where he could have a clear shot at anyone approaching the cavalry horses.

The sun hung just above the hills to the west, leaving long shadows split by rays of reddish-yellow light cutting through the western third of the grove. Eric had seen the single rider break away from the other two when he last used the Yankee binoculars. Someone had been worried about their tardy friends and was coming back to check on them. He hoped it would still be light enough to see his sights when they arrived.

Two hundred yards from the top of the ridge, Blaylock caught sight of something moving just at the edge of the trees. He raised his left hand to block the red orb as it sat barely touching the horizon. The motion turned into the shapes of two distant horses, but even with the adverse lighting, he could see the familiar colors of Jonesie's sorrel with the white blaze. *Don't camp there, you idiots. We are just down the hill from you boys.* His spirits lifted, he dug his spurs into his horse's sides and forced the nearly wasted mount into a lope.

"Yee-hah! Jonesie! Miller! Mount up, boys!"

Schmidt heard the calls coming in fast. He set the double rifle against the oak tree to his left and thumbed the hammer back to full cock on the Springfield. He had studied the rifle carefully since he first captured it and was confident it would work as designed. The sights were set for 100 yards, but he planned to lure his intended target in closer…much closer. He glanced quickly at the security of the percussion cap, and was reassured by its position. His finger moved to the wide polished steel trigger and waited.

Blaylock's horse breathed heavily at the exertion demanded by its rider as the lope turned in to a ragged gallop.

"Jonesie? Where are you, boy?" he yelled as he closed the distance and reined back on the struggling mount.

A call came from inside the woods. "Wilson?…Blaylock? …Help me…"

The call for help faded away weakly. He swung down from his staggering mount and ran toward the voice. "Where'n hell are you?" he shouted in frustration as he sprinted into the tree line—he never heard an answer. A four-hundred-grain .58 caliber Minié ball fired from a scant twenty yards away crashed into his sternum, tore off the top of his heart and took out two vertebra as it exited. The force of the impact lifted him off his feet and flung him backwards almost a yard, where he landed without fanfare.

"Over here…I am over here," Schmidt said as he stood up. He leaned the Springfield against the oak, picked up the double rifle and walked cautiously to investigate the condition of the prone Yankee soldier. He poked the muzzle against the man's unseeing eye—it didn't blink. Eric rolled him over to see what damage the big slug had wrought on the man. A three inch diameter exit wound spoke volumes. *Jesus! That's some kind of a rifle.* He rolled the body face up and searched the man's pockets for identification. A well worn letter dated the previous Christmas gave up the name Blaylock. *That leaves me with Wilson and Smithers.*

Down the hill a mile away, Wilson and Smithers exchanged nervous glances. The echoes of the far off rifle shot had barely faded, yet both men cocked their ears to listen for the sound of additional shots.

"That was one of ours, Smitty. I knowed that sound better'n my own voice."

"I kin hear, you moron…Question is, who pulled the trigger?"

"Well it cain't have been a Reb patrol. They would have been more shootin' if'n they was a bunch of 'em."

"Figured that all out by yer own self, did you?"

"Dammit, Smitty! What do you think happened? You tell me who done it, okay? I think we need to ride on up there and check it out."

"Boy, you's dumber than a box of rocks if you think I am gonna ride up there in the dark. I am saddlin' up and gettin' the hell outta here, and it ain't gonna be in that that there direction, I guarandamntee."

Wilson watched as the sergeant picked up his saddle and blanket and began to walk toward his horse tied up twenty yards away. "You gonna just leave 'em...all three of 'em?" he asked incredulously.

A worn out Smithers turned to face the panicking private. "Boy, git in your mind that they's dead...All of 'em!" The last of the light in the woods was fading fast as Smithers looked nervously back up the rise behind them. "I do not know what kind of devil we turned aloose yesterday, but it's a comin' after us. Stay if you want, but as for me, I ain't quite ready to join it in hell."

Eric unbuckled the dead soldier's gunbelt and removed his calf-high cavalry boots. They were too small for him, but would hopefully bring a couple dollars in trade for food or ammunition in the next settlement he came across.

He returned to the oak tree and gathered up the Springfield and began the reloading process. He pulled the hammer back to half cock and flicked the remains of the split spent primer cap off the nipple. Next, he pulled open the cartridge box he had added to his gunbelt. Eric grabbed a paper wrapped cartridge and bit off the twisted paper on the powder end, exposing a pre-measured 60 grains of FFg black powder. He held his left hand in a tight ring around the muzzle of the rifle as he quickly poured the charge down the barrel. Lastly, he squeezed the hollow based Minié ball out of its paper cover and into the bore. He yanked the ramrod out from under the barrel and drove the ball and powder the full length of the barrel and seated it firmly.

He replaced the ramrod securely in the gun stock. Pulling a leather capping flap out of his shirt, he pressed one of the percussion caps over the exposed nipple and pulled down on the leather flap. The leather yielded up its primer, stored in a precision punched hole along the perimeter of the thick material. The Springfield was once again ready to fire, so Eric pulled the hammer back off its half-cock position, engaged the trigger and gently lowered the hammer onto the percussion cap, securing it in place.

As dusk settled in, Eric had gathered up the fifth horse just acquired from the late private and tethered the starving animal with a feed bag hung on its head. He had hidden all the critters well out of sight and kept a watchful down the hill for any signs that either one of the remaining two Union soldiers had gathered the nerve to try to backtrack and engage him.

He emptied a jar of pickled beets his mother and sister had laid up and sliced off bite-sized pieces of smoked dry sausage. The beef tasted good, but the meal served only as another grim reminder of the great loss he had suffered only twenty-four hours earlier.

The crescent moon rose higher in the sky—he finally concluded that the two Yanks were not coming and moved to a secluded spot inside the grove. He spread out his bedroll and pulled a homemade blanket tightly around himself. He forced himself to stop thinking about his family some time around midnight and fell into a deep sleep.

Sergeant Smithers nodded off in the saddle a third time, allowing the reins to fall from his hands. Several minutes later, the bone weary horse carried him under a low hanging limb. The jagged pine had a smaller tapered side branch—dry and dead from the work of borer beetles—that caught him under the chin and impaled him for just a second as the horse wandered forward.

He woke with a fright to searing pain and the sound of the pine branch cracking as it broke. Smithers tumbled backwards out of the saddle, but not before unintentionally spurring the horse. The startled mount broke into a run in the pitch dark. Only fifty yards away, his horse collided with a three foot thick loblolly pine and died instantly from the resulting broken neck.

Private Wilson roused to the screams of Smithers, who thought he had been bayoneted in his dreamlike state. His horse reacted to the screams and spun around, not knowing where to run in the almost complete darkness. Wilson almost tumbled from the saddle, but after a couple jumps, was able to calm the horse with soothing talk and strokes to its neck.

Suddenly, he realized he did not know where he was. And he didn't have any idea where his sergeant was. A wave of panic overtook him for a moment. Then, he remembered he had followed the older soldier into the dense pine forest just as the sun went down. Neither had any idea which direction they traveled after a while, but Wilson had assumed that his NCO possessed some fantastic innate sense of direction or internal compass. He called out in the darkness, "Smitty? Where in hell are you?…Smitty? You hurt?"

The hapless sergeant got to one knee and struggled to talk, but, something was terribly wrong with his mouth. It hurt like fire to move his jaw. He tore off his gauntlets and felt his neck. The broken end of a three-eighths inch thick branch had punched up under his jaw and impaled his tongue. Only two inches of the smooth barkless remnant of a pine branch protruded below his jaw. He grabbed the stub and pulled. His fingers slipped off the slippery blood-coated wood. A panicked, garbled scream somehow made it past his lips.

Wilson fumbled in the blackness for a tin of white phosphorus parlor matches he kept in his coat pocket. He scratched the tip of the match across one of his uniform buttons, igniting it with a hiss and quickly had the yellow pine shaft of the match burning. Shading his eyes from the direct flame of the match with his off hand, he scanned the area in the direction of the garbled scream.

A tiny bit of light reflected off Smithers' white forehead, where the sun had not had the chance to burnish his skin to the color of cured tobacco. Wilson swung out of the saddle, causing the leather rigging to creak as the saddle rolled slightly in response to the uneven weight distribution.

"I see you, Smitty!" Wilson called out as he got his both feet down on the thick pine needle carpet of debris covering the forest floor. "What happened?" he asked as he moved slowly, trying not to extinguish the match.

Smithers did not answer, but pointed frantically to the small stick protruding from his neck.

In the private's hand, the tiny flame of the pine matchstick reached the juncture of Wilson's thumb and index finger, producing the expected results. "Ow! Dammit!" he responded to the burn as he flung the smoldering sliver of match stick away and then stuck his wet tongue to the burns. Wilson blew on them for a second, and then dug back into his pocket for the match tin. "Hold on there, Sarge! I will hep you out in a jiffy!" He struck a second match and moved in closer where he could see the senior man's predicament clearly. "Jumpin' Jehosafat! How did you do that to yerself?" Wilson asked incredulously.

Smitty's eyes flashed angrily as he tried to tell him. *Just pull the damn stick.*

"What? I cain't make out what you are sayin'!" a confused and not-too-bright Wilson asked as the mumbled and completely indecipherable command emerged from the sergeant's mouth.

Smithers leaned his head back and moved his hands from the bloody stub and pointed at it, and then motioned with hand signals to try to tell Wilson to pull it out.

"Why didn't you jest say so?" Wilson asked as he eyed the half-burnt match. He transferred the match to his left hand and grabbed at the dead pine stub. He tugged at it, but it was too slippery to gain a good purchase on the small exposed end. He tried again, but was just getting his first two fingers and thumb in good position when the match seared his left hand. The second burn in less than a minute frustrated Wilson, who cursed his bad luck. Something in the pitch blackness that followed jogged his brain and reminded him a fire could provide more light than a match. "I will git it! Do not fret yourself, Smitty. Got me an idee!"

He lit a third match and pushed a small pile of pine needles together and cleared a circle of bare earth around it with his bare left hand. He touched the half-burnt match to the dry brown needles and was reassured by their rapid ignition. "Here we go. Now gimme a look at what is ailin' you," Wilson said as he positioned himself beside Smithers in the flickering light. "Tarnation, Sarge...If I did not know better, I would say an Injun done shot you in the throat. This here looks like an arrow broke off in ya!"

Smithers glared and pointed at him, and then back at his throat and motioned for him to pull the stick out.

Wilson nodded. "I git it...Hold yer horses. I am a fixin' to yank it plum out of you," he said as he pulled a yellow handled Barlow knife out of his coat.

The sergeant's eyes grew wide as he opened the three inch blade. He shook his head vigorously and waved his hand. The movement of his head sent waves of pain shooting up his spine, taking his breath away.

"I ain't a gonna cut it out, you sceerdy cat! Need me sumthin' to grab on to that damned stick...It be slicker'n owl shit on a door knob," Wilson exclaimed as he grasped the knife in his hand with the blade edge squarely against his thumb.

Smither's nodded slightly in agreement, but moaned as even the smallest movements pained him greatly.

The private held the knife under the stick and his thumb on top it while he placed the heel of his left hand against his forehead to stabilize him. "On the count of three…Ready?"

He blinked in agreement.

"One…Two" As he spoke the word *Two*, Wilson yanked forcefully. The jagged shaft of wood came out, along with a small spurt of blood. Smithers' eyes rolled to back the top of his head and he passed out cold, falling backward to the thick bed of pine needles.

"Three." Wilson examined the crimson colored pine branch.

A warm breeze from the southeast pushed into the cluster of trees atop the grassy ridge top as a warm gulf weather system overran and pushed out the weak cold front—typical Texas spring weather. The buckskin gelding inhaled the warm moist air, shook his head and then snorted, causing Eric's eyes snapped awake at the sound. For a moment, the darkness under the wool blanket disoriented him—then he painfully remembered where he was and why he was camped there, almost forty miles from home.

He flipped back the covers and got to his feet—still fully clothed from the previous night. The sky to the east was beginning to show the first signs of dawn, although a line of low gray clouds was obscuring the stars back to the southeast. Well rested from the almost seven hours of sleep, Eric picked up the double rifle laying on the bedroll and eased through the scattered trees between himself and the clearing. He looked downhill to where the two Yankees had entered the tall timber the previous evening. The woods were an endless dark band in contrast to the mostly light gray of the winter-killed seed tops of the blue stem of the meadow. Responding to nature's call, Eric unbuttoned his pants and relieved himself against the base of a small redbud tree.

As he finished, he noticed what looked like a small star below the horizon off to his left. In the distance, the band of mature loblolly pines extended to the north to the far hilltops and presumably beyond. Their darkness was unmistakable in contrast to the grassland, and yet he detected a light coming from inside the trees. As he looked on, the light went dark. Eric rubbed the sleep from his eyes. *Was I just making that up?*

He fastened his trousers and looked again. *There! That is a definitely a light.* He turned and made his way to the horses, retrieved the binoculars and quickly worked his way back through the thicket. He focused on the light and could detect the unmistakable triangular shape of a campfire. When someone walked between his position and the fire, the light again disappeared. He could not determine who the person was, but immediately began to develop a strategy to find out.

Eric located a unique landmark to identify the area from which the campfire emanated. A single tall pine tree with the top split wide by a lightning strike years earlier stood out some twenty yards from the densely packed edge of the tree line. Noting it was an estimated 100 yards south of a direct line to the campfire, Eric lowered the glasses and hurried back into the trees where his saddle, blanket and bridle awaited. Three minutes later, the anxious buckskin was saddled up. He slid both the double rifle and the Springfield into their respective scabbards, and strapped his Colt and a Remington six shooter on with his heavily laden belt. Two more holstered Remingtons went across the withers before he hopped into the stirrup and swung easily into the saddle.

"Be back for you boys in a while," he promised the former Union mounts and his pack horse before he spurred the buckskin on. "Let's go, Bucky. We got us job to do."

Eric started down the hill. As he felt the big gelding warming up, he led the big horse into a moderate lope at the bottom. He didn't want whoever was tending the small fire to be able to see him riding in from the tall grass, so he chose to rapidly close the distance to the nearest woods before the sun came up. The light of the campfire disappeared in the dense timber off to his left as Eric slowed the buckskin to a walk.

Once they reached the edge of the pines, Eric turned Bucky parallel to the tree line and kept the lightning damaged landmark tree in his field of view. Some one hundred yards south of the lone split pine, he reined into the trees and dismounted.

He pulled a feed bag out from his saddle bags and scooped several hands full of whole oats into it before he hooked the bag over the horse's ears. He patted him on the neck as it began to eat. "Enjoy your breakfast big boy...you earned it. Now, keep quiet...all right?"

With his horse's needs met, he tied the lead rope to a tall, skinny sassafras. He drew the two rifles out of their scabbards and slung the double barreled .45 over his left shoulder. Almost as an afterthought, he pulled one of the extra Remingtons out of its holster and stuck it securely inside his pants waistband. He took one last look at his horse, quietly slipped into the dark timber and disappeared.

The hungry Union private swallowed the last piece of sausage he had liberated from the Texas ranch house then washed it down with a few remaining drops of water from his canteen. The fire was beginning to go out again, so he stoked it with a couple pieces of dead pine limbs he had gathered from nearby. Only a couple of yards away, the prone figure of Sergeant Smithers cast a shadow against the rough gray bark of the innumerable mature pines. The chatter of a dozen nearby gray squirrels—irritated with the two uninvited guests—was almost constant.

Wilson looked overhead, wishing he had a squirrel rifle to provide the fixings for a stew once the sun got a little higher. The light from the coming day was visible at the edge of the woods, some fifty yards from the campfire. Wilson could tell it was cloudy, as the stars were not visible but he was still uncertain which direction was north. He hoped against hope that the distant light he could see in the trees was the direction east.

Wilson was without a map of the Confederate State of Texas, as the only ones their patrol had possessed were left on the lieutenant's body in their haste to depart the ranch. He glanced over at Smithers. *Still breathin'*. Earlier, the private had thought the man died when he pulled the pencil-sized stick out of his throat. He hadn't stirred much since, but at least the bleeding had stopped. A sound came from the forest floor beside him, scaring him enough to cause him to pull and cock his revolver. His heart beat wildly as he searched the darkness beyond the campfire. Another similar sound from a different direction caught his ear. *Sounds like a footstep!* Wilson swung the muzzle in that direction. Nothing. Another pine cone toppled from the heights and bounced just ten feet from the fire. He spun and pulled the trigger as the motion caught his eye.

The blast from the revolver woke Smithers, who instinctively scrambled to pull his weapon. With his adrenaline pumping, he searched the firelight for a likely target. "Whutha hell you shoothin at?" he mumbled, his tongue badly swollen from the pine branch puncture.

"Pine cones…Them squirrels been a bombin' us and got me jumpin'," Wilson sheepishly responded.

"Thammit! You mowon!" cursed the sergeant as he scrambled to his feet. "Wherth my horth?" he demanded as he holstered his revolver.

"Sarge, your horse runned off when you tangled up with that there branch."

"You dennet go twy and fine him?"

"Golly, Sergeant, I did not want to leave you all alone in the dark…bad hurt like you wuz. Thought we would wait 'til daybreak and round him up together."

"Whut I tell you about hinkin'?" a frustrated Smithers spat back. "Ga any wa…er?"

It took a couple seconds to decipher Smitty's impaired speech. "Oh, water...Fresh out, Sarge. Maybe still some in your canteen. Want me to go look for old Ned?"

He gave Wilson a hard look. *How the hell did I get stuck with the biggest fool in the Union Army?* He shook his head. "How long wath I out?"

"An hour...maybe two. I ain't got no watch."

Smithers looked around the campfire and found a large pine cone and searched for a dead branch with a Y at one end. After a couple minutes, he found one and wedged the pine cone into the fork to make it secure. He walked back to the fire and held the cone over the flames until it ignited and made a passable torch. The two men began to follow the tracks left by his horse during the night. In under a minute, they stood over the stiff body of the sergeant's mount.

"Thammit," cursed Smithers.

"Well, at least you got yore saddle and riggin' back. A man has gotta be thankful for little things, ain't that right?"

"Shu-up, Wilson. Jus han me tha wa...er, and geh my gear," he grumbled.

Five minutes and six pine cones later, the pair stumbled back into the light of the campfire. Wilson dumped the saddle, bags, blanket and bridle off his shoulder into the thick bed of pine needles. He leaned the single shot carbine against a nearby tree.

Smithers nursed a mouthful of water from his canteen and tossed the almost burnt out pine cone torch into the fire. A dozen red embers rose up like fireflies and mixed for a couple of seconds with the thin column of gray smoke climbing into the branches of the surrounding evergreen trees. Wilson sat down dejectedly.

"How we gonna manage with only one horse, Sergeant?" he asked as he looked up at the injured Smithers. He knew his own mount was almost played out. The prospect of both of them riding double was almost an impossibility. He glanced around to gauge the condition of his mare. His heart skipped a beat, She wasn't where he had left her tied up. He sprang to his feet and looked for his saddle and Springfield. Both were gone. "Where the hell is *my* horse?"

An imposing tall man with a frontiersman fringed leather shirt and a wide-brimmed hat stepped out from the shadows of two thick pines. He had an equaling imposing rifle pointed at the two soldiers only twenty yards away. "Lookin' for something?"

Wilson glanced at the carbine Smithers had laid against the tree and lunged for it. The sharp crack of the .45 caliber rifle was followed almost instantly be the *thwak* of the bullet striking home. Blood sprayed from both sides of the soldier's chest and he slid to a halt, face down, with his outstretched hands within inches of the carbine.

Smither's dropped the canteen from his mouth and reached for his holstered revolver with both hands. His left lifted the black leather flap cover while his right grabbed the wooden stocked grip frame and withdrew the Remington from the crossdraw holster. He had not taken his eyes off the stranger with the cold blue eyes. After firing the rifle, the man had swung the rifle away with his left hand and gone for the Colt on his right hip. Smithers thumbed the hammer back and was still trying to swing the muzzle around to aim when the stranger's Colt fired. The .44 caliber round ball shattered his right forearm and lodged in his liver. The impact spun him around and sent his service revolver flying—he staggered from the pain and shock of his wounds, but reached across his blood stained belly and pulled the stag handled belt knife out with his left hand. A scream had just begun to fill his throat when a second shot from the Colt tore into his left shoulder. The knife blade dropped harmlessly onto the pine straw as the sergeant fell onto his back. He tried to sit up, but a huge right hand crashed down on his jaw, and everything went black.

When Smithers awoke, he found his shoulder and abdominal wounds had been cauterized. Bits of charcoal and ash still clung to the puckered charred flesh. A tourniquet had been applied to his right arm. Both arms were tied tightly behind him, wrapped around the base of a large hundred-year-old pine. He legs were splayed wide open with ropes leading to other pine trees. It was much colder than he had remembered and he looked down to find himself completely naked from head to toe. The stranger had taken him belt knife, cut off his long john underwear and tossed it into the fire. The man sat cross-legged only ten feet away, watching him closely.

"You must be the one named Harlen Smithers," the man said with almost no emotion.

"It waddun me who done it…Wilson over 'ere is the one! You gotta lemme go."

"Done what?" the man asked.

"He ha…had his way with her and kilt…er," Smithers struggled to get the words out.

"Who did he kill?"

"Da yellow haired girl. Your sis…ter."

"How did you know she had a brother?"

"She tol …" Smithers stopped in mid-sentence. "She tol him and he tol me."

Eric stood up and drew the stag-handled knife out of its sheath. He tossed the knife up gently, then caught it by the eight inch blade. He threw it forcefully toward Smithers, the knife sticking blade first in the bare earth with a *thunk*, only inches from the soldier's exposed genitals. He screamed as he tried to move back, but found himself hopelessly bound to the tree.

"The problem with your pack of lies…is that Wilson there did not have a knife big enough to cut my sister like she was…That one between your legs is the one that killed her…ain't it?" Eric hissed at the bound man.

He moved closed and pulled the knife out of the ground and wiped the rich organic dirt off roughly on Smithers' leg. A thin line of blood appeared, ran down the inside of his pasty white thigh and disappeared in the soil. Eric smiled as he stuck the stag-handled knife in the scabbard behind his Colt.

"Wha are you doin'? You not a Reb!" Smithers cried out.

Eric picked up armfuls of pine cones he had collected and dropped them on Smitty's lap, completely covering the naked man's shriveled manhood. He gathered some pine straw that he had previously removed from the base of the tree as a firebreak and piled it on top of the pine cones.

The purpose of the man's actions hit Smithers like a bolt of lightning. His stomach cramped and if there had been any food in it, he would have vomited it outright.

"Doncha do it! Jus kill me!" Smithers pleaded though the pain from his swollen tongue and jaw.

Eric picked up a smaller pine cone, grabbed hold of the Yankee's chin, forced his jaw open, and then stuffed the wide end of the rough conifer seed bundle into his mouth.

Smithers could no longer talk or scream. The Texan picked up a burning stick out of the campfire and walked slowly back to him. He looked directly into the terrified man's eyes.

"Their names were Herbert, Alyssa and Hanna Schmidt... She was only sixteen years old...You scum sucking Yankee bastards killed my folks, and raped and murdered my baby sister...I was no Rebel before today, but I am one now...Swear to God, I will spend every day protecting my people from animals like you...And you, Harlen Smithers...you sorry son of a bitch...You ain't never gonna rape nobody again."

Eric touched the burning branch to the dry pine needles. The flames quickly spread to the pine cones and burned with great intensity. He added the stick onto the blaze and turned away to gather his horses. He couldn't hear the silent screams and he never looked back.

***

CHAPTER FIVE

EAST TEXAS

Half an hour later, Eric topped the rise north of his campsite from the previous night. He could see for miles to the north and east. Turning in the saddle, he lifted the flap on his leather saddle bags and retrieved the maps he had taken from the dead Yankee lieutenant. He tried to match the contours of the terrain that he could see to those shown on the map. As best as he could determine, he was somewhere just south of a line between Longview and Marshall, Texas. The map showed a road connecting the two. He could work his way up there and see if there was a market for the Yankee horses and gear. *The money would sure go a long way toward food and equipment to get me a new start out west somewhere.* He remembered the ranch and a fresh pang of sorrow came rumbling up from his heart.

His immediate motivation of revenge for his family's massacre was somewhat satiated by the deaths of all those Yankees directly involved. Eric's future plans were a nebulous cloud floating out on the horizon. He could not quite stomach the thought of returning to the home place—at least not yet.

The image of the three new wooden crosses was permanently etched in his memory. Someday, perhaps he could live there, but for the present, the ghosts of his father, mother and sister would be a constant reminder of all he previously had and all he had lost. It just hurt too much to contemplate.

Sounds of a distant church bell ringing drifted softly to his ears. He cocked his head one way, then another, to try to locate the source. *What day is it? Sunday? I went to pick up those damned barrels on Friday.*

Eric turned in the saddle and tried unsuccessfully to find the sun to gauge the time of day. Low clouds covered the sky from horizon to horizon. He thought for a second and remembered his father's timepiece in his shirt pocket. He fished it out—a wedding present from his maternal grandfather—and opened the embossed silver cover. *1201...Church must be just letting out.* Eric wound the stem—somehow, the simple act connected him to his beloved father and the slightest hint of a smile came to his lips. Snapping the cover closed, he returned it to his leather fringed shirt and nudged Bucky north.

He crossed a stream a mile or so down the valley and led the pack horse and his four new acquisitions down a well-used cattle trail on the other side. After another fifteen minutes, he came across a field with several milk cows grazing inside a split rail fence. In the distance, he could see a solitary unpainted frame farm house with a small barn out back. He reined the buckskin in that direction.

A woman with three small children was tending to a quarter acre garden as he neared. His approach had not gone unnoticed. The woman gathered up her offspring and hustled them into the house. The door was closed when he rode up and removed his hat.

"Hello the house!…Ma'am? I do not want anything…I just need to ask a question."

The door creaked open and a single barreled shotgun poked out, pointed at him.

"I ain't got nuthin' to share! Move on! I know how to use this here gun!"

Eric raised his hands and his hat high in the air.

"Yes, ma'am…I am most assured you do. But can you tell me where the nearest town is? I would like to sell some of my horses."

The door opened wider. The woman, in her late twenties, kept the scattergun pointed at him. She studied the man for a few seconds before she spoke. "Longview is eight miles west. Marshall is east 'bout a half day's ride. The road between 'em is a just north of here."

"Thank you kindly, ma'am," Eric said as he lowered his hands slowly and reined his horse to leave. He pulled up and looked back at the house. "Which town had a church? I heard the bell a while back."

She lowered the muzzle slightly, not exactly sure of the stranger, but no longer feeling an immanent threat. "There is a small settlement 'bout a mile down the creek where it crosses the main road. They call it Beaver Creek, and there is a little church there. It ain't much, but it is all we got in these parts."

He tipped his hat and wheeled to follow the creek.

"What's you name, mister?" she called out before he moved off.

"Schmidt. My name is Eric Schmidt, ma'am," he replied. "Thank you for the directions."

She watched him until he and the train of horses disappeared across the field, and then she checked the back trail from which he came. Seeing no one else, she lowered the hammer on the shotgun and closed the cabin door securely.

A moderately sized two room log trading post and a small one room church were the featured buildings in the town of Beaver Creek. Muddy roads and a couple of small farms spread out over a half mile radius completed the settlement. Lying along the road between Longview and Marshall, travelers could stop by the trading post for supplies and partake of a meal and have a drink if they were so inclined.

Eric rode past the store and up to the church, which did not have the luxury of a steeple or tall spire to declare its purported use. A plain whitewashed wooden structure, it did have a six foot tall cross affixed to the eve of its pitched roof. In Eric's mind it could use another fresh coat of paint.

He bypassed the hitching post in front and instead rode to the side of the building, where he left his string of horses and allowed them to graze between the building and the side street that ran north and south. A single blue roan was tied to one of the four hitching posts set parallel to the main road through town. A one horse Stanhope buggy tethered to another of the four led him to believe there was more than one person still inside. He walked underneath a tarnished brass bell hung from a ten foot archway set over the flagstone sidewalk leading to the entrance door. He reached up and touched the thick rope attached to the bell and wondered just how loud it would ring if he were to pull the rope in earnest.

The Schmidt family had not attended formal services regularly, but had made the trip into Tyler at least once a month, weather permitting, for Sunday services. Herbert had argued that there was no place open to do business in Sunday, and preferred to travel in only on weekdays, but Alyssa had insisted on broadening the children's religious training. As usual, they compromised, with Eric and Hanna enjoying the visits with other children their own age.

Eric approached the door and a sudden awareness of his dress and unshaven face made him uncharacteristically self conscious. He removed his hat and, sticking it under his arm, tried to comb back his hair in some semblance of neatness. It really didn't help. His face was covered with a two day coating of trail dust, mixed with splattered dried blood and sweat. No one was going to mistake him as a Beau Brummel.

He opened the door and stepped inside. When his eyes adjusted to the darker conditions he saw several rows of roughly sawn benches on each side of a narrow isle. In front stood a simple pulpit constructed of knotty pine. An impressive large white cross, flanked by several pairs of candles filled the far wall. A tall thin man in a black frock coat and matching trousers sat on the front bench talking to a young woman dressed in solid black. She wore a black veil and held a white handkerchief under the veil, dabbing at her eyes. The man stood when he became aware of Eric's presence. "May I help you, sir?" he asked with a deep southern drawl.

"I just stopped by to pray for a while, if it is all right with you...Did not mean to intrude. I will come back some other time," Eric said as he turned to go.

"Sir, the house of the Lord is always open to those in need. Missus Johannsen and I were just finishing a special prayer for her husband. Please stay."

Eric turned and took a seat in the back row. He felt strangely out of place and uncertain what to do. Nothing came to his lips when he tried to pray.

The young widow rose and, with the help of the pastor supporting her with his caring arm around her shoulder, made her way toward the back of the church. Schmidt stood as she approached and nodded his condolences. She recoiled at first from his unkempt appearance, then was consumed again by her own heartache, tears flowing across her fair cheeks. As she reached under the veil to attempt to dry them, Eric could not help notice her bone structure resembled that of his own mother. Tears rolled down and dripped onto the hat brim he unconsciously crushed and released. For several minutes he sat there alone. He stared at the cross trying to remember the Lord's prayer, then felt the steady hand of the pastor on his left shoulder.

"You want to tell us about your troubles, son?"

Eric was confused. "Us?"

"The Lord and I share this space, my boy. We are both are here to listen…when you are ready."

For nearly thirty minutes, Pastor John Standridge sat and listened as Eric spilled his heartfelt tale of personal loss and revenge. He did not judge or interrupt.

Finally, when the young gunsmith had finished, he looked at the preacher. "Am I going to hell for what I done?"

The solemn man looked at him and shook his head. "Son, the word of God tells us *Vengeance is mine, sayeth the Lord.* But it also says *An eye for an eye.* Someday…in God's own time, you will stand before him and find out, but it would be a blasphemous presumption for me to tell you what He is going to say…These are terrible times, my son, thrust upon us by forces out of our control. That young woman that just left…she lost her husband a month back fighting in Virginia. She just found out by letter received last night, but has no body to bury in her time of sorrow…I cannot in good conscious tell you that what you did was wrong, as I was not there to suffer as you did…There but for the Grace of God…"

"Thank you, Brother John. My folks always tried to teach me right from wrong, and I just can not sit still while evil men afflict those too weak to defend themselves."

"Perhaps God has anointed you, my son, like he did David, to slay the Philistines in righteousness."

"Well sir, I do not think ..."

Suddenly a man burst into the church. From his attire he was likely a blacksmith.

"Reverend...Some soldiers are outside wanting to know who owns these here horses!"

Eric's hand went instinctively to his sidearm.

Standridge placed his hand on top of his and turned to the blacksmith. "Blue or Gray?"

"They's wearing gray, Reverend."

The pastor stood and offered his hand to Eric. "Come on, son, let us go meet our friends."

The two men exited the church only to see almost twenty armed volunteers milling around the Union horses and fondling the gear. Three wagons were parked between the church and the trading post and had benches for the soldiers along each side, but several men had their own mounts. It was apparent that many of the newly minted soldiers were destined to be infantry, as they lacked horses. When some of them saw Eric, they leveled their rifles at him as if he was the enemy.

Standridge raised his hands and spoke out and loud clear, "Whoa there, boys, ya'll have the wrong idea. Put down those smokepoles...This here is a genuine Hero of the Confederacy! He and his paw wiped out a Union patrol all by themselves."

Not sure of what to think, some of the volunteers slung their rifles. Others were still cautious, holding their rifles at the ready.

"My name is Eric Schmidt, I come from over Tyler way," he said in a strong voice.

In one of the wagons, a familiar voice called out. "Eric…It's me…Karl Walterscheid!" The brand new Confederate private bailed out of the wagon and came running over to him to excitedly shake his hand. "Glad you changed yore mind, Eric!" He turned to several of his fellow soldiers and motioned for them to come closer. "Hey, boys! This here is the brother of my bride-to-be…Hanna's big brother…The one I told ya'll about on the ride over."

The mention of his sister's name hit Eric like a knife to his heart. Tears began to well up and he released Karl's hand to wipe his tears off his face.

"Whatsamatter? She did not go and change her mind did she?" he asked as he tried to picture what had come over him.

The Reverend stepped forward and placed his arm around Walterscheid's shoulders. He looked the anxious young man in the eye. "Son there has been a terrible tragedy."

His eyes jumped anxiously from John to Eric and back.

"Yankees attacked the Schmidt ranch on Friday last."

"What?…No!" Karl screamed.

"All the family died from wounds, except for young Eric here who was in town when the attack occurred. I am so sorry for your loss."

"It cain't be! I just asked her for her hand on Friday! Eric, tell me she is all right…"

Eric partially regained his composure and wrapped his arms around the devastated suitor in a compassionate bear hug. "I am so sorry, Karl…Hanna is…gone…My baby sister is gone."

After a while, the commander of the Tyler Company approached Eric and extended his hand. "Good day, sir. I am Captain Marcus Aurellius Matson, Confederate States of America. My most sincere sympathies for your loss."

"Thank you, Captain. With a name like that, you would have thought they would have made you emperor."

Matson laughed. "I see you have an education, sir."

"Yes, sir. My mother taught us the classics, plus mathematics and history, you know."

"You know how to read and write, I take it?"

"In four languages, though my Latin is a little rusty, Captain."

"In you own words, can you tell me how you came to personally defeat a superior force of Union cavalry?"

"Well, sir, I tracked 'em down and took 'em on one by one, except the last two…Oh, and the first one. He missed…I did not," Eric said pointing at his hat.

The captain apprised the young man. "Fascinating! Private Walterscheid said you are a trained gunsmith. Is that right?"

"Yes, sir. I learned the trade from my father, Herbert. He is…or I guess, was, well known in the area for custom gun work."

"I see. Now, how did you end up here in Beaver Creek? I would not think the Yankees would travel by main roads."

"No sir, that is for certain. Once they were down to only five of them, they avoided contact. I managed to find out they were headed back to Shreveport. I saw this here road on the map I took from the Yankee lieutenant. I figured to collect some money when I sold their horses and tack."

The captain was impressed. The young lad had all the qualities he could ask for in a subordinate. "Sir, it is within my power as Company Commander to offer a commission to you in the Tyler Volunteers. It is customary in the forces of the Confederacy for the men to vote on who serves as their officers. I will make the nomination to the men…It would be my honor to serve with a man of such caliber."

"In plain talk, Captain, you want me to help you kill Yankees…Is that the long and short of it?"

The captain grinned. Of the entire company of men assembled in the small village of Beaver Creek, only he, the sergeant who recruited most of the volunteers and now Eric Schmidt had ever seen actual combat, killed an enemy soldier or fired a weapon in anger. *Our mission is no glorious quest.* "I like a man who speaks his mind. That goes a long way with me…And, yes, that is exactly what I am asking you to do, Mister Schmidt…What is your answer?"

Eric's mind raced. The mental picture of his family was still ever to the forefront of his daily thoughts. He placed his hands on his hips and felt the stag handle grip of the knife he had taken off Smithers and remembered exactly why he wore it. It reminded him of Hanna and he would never let it out of his possession. He extended his right hand and looked Matson squarely in the eye. "Looks like I am your man, Captain."

***

CHAPTER SIX

MARSHALL, TEXAS

The Seventh Company of the Second Brigade of Texas Volunteers bivouacked just outside of town at the county fairgrounds. Captain Matson took Eric—now officially known as Lieutenant Schmidt—to the general store downtown in the bustling community where the unit quartermaster had set up shop. The facility had a tailor who fitted the new lieutenant for his officer's uniform and hat. Eric had been able to sell the Union horses to some of the soldiers who had preferred to become cavalrymen and the pack horse to the quartermaster. The national demand for horses was at an all-time high as the needs of the two warring armies were growing every month.

"Come back in the morning, Lieutenant, and we shall have the uniform ready for final fitting. I am truly sorry we did not have a ready-made one in your size," the tailor said, as he wrote down the last of Eric's measurements on a lined tablet with a stubby pencil. "We do not get many men as tall as you are…you understand."

"I would not know. My father and I were almost the same size and my mother made all our clothes."

His hat was a different story, as was his cape. Both were available, so he picked them up as Matson showed him where to draw his footlocker. As an officer, he was authorized a wooden storage box to store and transport his personal items, such as shaving razor, extra shirts, socks and sundries. The lockers would be carried in wagons accompanying the cavalry units operating in conjunction with the infantry.

Enlisted infantrymen had only their knapsacks and as a result, carried much less gear along with them. The same could be said for enlisted cavalry, who were restricted to what their saddlebags could tote.

Back at the camp, Captain Matson turned to Eric as they walked between row after row of tents in the sprawling bivouac area. "Did you ever read any books on military history or tactics?"

"Can not say as I ever even heard of a book on either of those subjects."

The captain smiled. "I suppose not everybody wanted to go to West Point."

"Where is that?"

"You have never heard of West Point?"

Eric shook his head.

Matson merely grinned and laughed. When the two reached the tent assigned to the junior officers of the Second Brigade, he pulled two well-worn books off his personal writing desk and handed then to Eric. "You might find these interesting...This one is from a famous European strategist, the other is from a Chinese philosopher."

"Von Clausewitz? Must be German..."

"Prussian, actually...A part of eastern Germany."

"*The Art of War*? This must be the Chinese one," he said as he opened the book.

"Right. English translation, of course...You didn't mention you could read Chinese."

It was Eric's turn to laugh. "No, not yet. But I think it will be interesting reading what a Chinaman has to say about warfare...Sun Tzu...Funny name. Never heard of him, neither."

"After you finish those two, I have an Italian book about the philosophy of projecting power militarily."

He nodded as he perused the two titles. "No American authors?"

"You must realize, Eric, our nation is a young one...The Chinese have been a culture for almost four thousand years."

"Never thought about it like that...Suppose I should get crackin'"

"Read while the light is still good...I want to see that you get some instruction this week on the proper techniques for sabers, both mounted and afoot. Here in the cavalry, we often have to fight with them extensively."

He nodded and took a seat on a three-legged camp stool. He opened the Von Clausewitz book entitled *On War* and noted the date of first publication was 1832. It book covered the Prussian viewpoint of warfare as it existed in the early part of the nineteenth century and reflected lessons learned from the defeat of French Emperor Napoleon Bonaparte at the battle of Waterloo.

Two hours later, his head was swimming. Never had he considered the possibility of war as an extension of politics. His family had hardly discussed the subject—he had grown up taking personal freedom as a natural state of being. His father and mother did as they pleased, following the guidance in the Holy Bible, and had been very happy.

The only manner in which the war had affected them was in the interruption of Herbert's supply of materials, at least that was what Eric had perceived. Now the book from the Prussian military philosopher had him thinking about words like audacity, asininity and decisiveness.

"Learning anything, Lieutenant?"

The words shook him from his reverie. He looked up and saw a stranger gazing down at him. The older man—an imposing figure in his Confederate gray uniform with three gold stars embroidered on the upturned collar—wore a full beard. His lined and tanned face bore witness to months spent outside, but nonetheless reflected an intelligence and compassion in his eyes. Eric turned the book face down on the small wooden table and rose to his feet.

"Afternoon, General."

"Colonel, son…Generals have a wreath around their stars," he replied before he extended his hand. "William Stephens, Commander of the Second Brigade."

Eric took his hand and shook it firmly.

"Pleasure to make your acquaintance, sir…Oh, and to answer your question…yes, sir…there is so much I have to learn about military operations and tactics. These books have opened my eyes quite a bit."

"Pleased to see you admit that you can learn more. That is a sign of intelligence…The main reasons I dropped by, is twofold…First, I wanted to meet the man who single handedly decimated a marauding enemy patrol. Second, I wanted your input about the intelligence aspects of the maps you captured."

"Colonel, I cain't take credit for killing all those Yankees…My folks shot a few before…before I could get back home." His voice cracked slightly as the raw images of the scenes of devastation came rushing back. He fought through the waves of emotions and took in a deep breath.

"Modesty and honesty are virtues too often overlooked by the young…I only wanted to inquire if you have anything to add about the maps."

"Well, sir…one man I questioned did say they were headed back to Shreveport to regroup with a larger force…You see, I did not know I was going to be joining up with the Confederates at the time, or I would have questioned him further."

"I understand…So, you do not know exactly when or where the rendezvous was to take place?"

"No, sir, but…I might make an observation…if you would permit me."

"By all means, Lieutenant."

"Judging from the rations I found on the men that I encountered, or rather…the lack thereof, I would say that there is a good chance that they are planning a raid in force on the supplies at Shreveport. I have never been there myself…Is it a town of any size?"

"A population of four thousand or thereabouts. It is an important shipping depot on the Red River."

"From what I gather, the Union Army does not have a secure supply line in Louisiana or Arkansas, therefore they must forage for supplies from Confederate and civilian sources…Is that your assessment, Colonel?"

"Yes, I would have to agree. We have not been able to engage them in any decisive manner to stop their raids on small towns spread out all over east Texas. If we placed a larger defensive garrison in Shreveport, it would tie up our combat forces for an unknown period of time based on a supposition."

"But you still would like to bring your weapons to bear to defeat the enemy in a decisive engagement…is that not so, Colonel?"

"Of course, son. What would you suggest to make that occur?"

"My father used to set out traps for foxes and wolves, when they would become a nuisance around the livestock…especially with the chickens. What would you say if we were to paint up some empty boxes and barrels on their outside like they were full of food and supplies?...We could leave them where they were plainly visible and place some experienced sharpshooters in nearby buildings to wait for an attack. That way, we would not need more than thirty men to wreak havoc on a much larger force caught between them."

Eric could see the wheels in the older soldier's brain begin to turn as he mulled over the suggestion.

Colonel Stephens nodded, smiled and extended his hand. "I shall have my staff make up a list of three dozen of our best and make plans to move out with them tomorrow. Splendid idea, Schmidt. Let us see how it works out."

Eric saluted him as he had seen other men do in the camp. The Colonel returned the gesture and strode out purposefully. After a few seconds, Eric sat back down and began to devour another chapter of Von Clausewitz.

As the sun neared the horizon, Captain Matson returned to the tent and found Eric almost through with *On War*.

"My God, boy, you are almost through with that?"

He held his place and looked at the thin layer of unread pages remaining. "Appears so. My mother taught me to read without saying the words with my mouth...It really flows faster when you do not do that."

"Yes, I could imagine where that would be possible, but can you possibly comprehend a serious work such as Von Clausewitz at that speed?"

"I can read the Bible cover-to-cover in under six hours."

"My, my...That is simply astounding, Lieutenant."

"Guess I kinda take it all for granted. My folks were something real special to me...but I reckon everyone feels that way."

"Be thankful that they wanted you to learn. Some families only seem to want more kids to work around the home place...Rather like hired hands they do not have to pay....But enough of that...You hungry?"

"Could eat half a steer."

"Let us then make haste to the mess tent. Do not want to be last in line."

"Mess tent?"

"I keep forgetting that you lack any formal military training." Matson chuckled. "A mess is what we call our dining facility. On permanent posts, there are structures called mess halls, but in the field, we use tents. Enlisted personnel have theirs and officers use another."

"I shall just follow you, Cap'n. You seem to have all this soldiering stuff down pat."

They walked past row upon row of four and six man tents until they came upon a much larger white canvas one with the sides rolled up, on account of the warm muggy afternoon. Inside were rows of tables with benches alongside. Metal pots containing the beef stew hung on chains suspended from three thick black iron rods, each six foot long and joined at the top to form a tripod.

Enlisted cooks served the hearty stew to the officers who moved through the line and picked up tin plates, forks and a large piece of crusty bread. With plates filled, they approached two men from the Seventh Company that were already seated. Matson spoke to the senior officer, "Major Timmons, mind if we join you, sir?"

"Why, certainly Marcus...and who is your mountain man friend here?"

Matson laughed. "Pay no attention to the buckskins, Major. This is the newest lieutenant in the Seventh, Eric Schmidt from down Tyler way...Eric, say howdy to Joshua Timmons and Arnold Abrahams."

The two men shook hands with him and took their seats. They had barely sat down when Timmons caught Matson by surprise.

"You have not even got the man a uniform yet and he already has a fire lit under the old man."

"What?...I do not understand," Matson said as he dipped his bread in the thick brown gravy surrounding the stew.

"That ambush over in Shreveport...the Colonel has us putting together a special team of crack shots to bushwhack the Yankee cavalry when they come for the bait."

"What in tarnation are you talking about? I left Eric in the tent reading all afternoon...You must have gotten the story wrong."

Captain Abrahms shook his head. "Nosiree. I saw Colonel Stephens myself...He is certain this young whipersnapper's gonna carve up a Yankee company, maybe a battalion over there."

All three turned and looked at Eric, who felt his face flush slightly.

"All I told him was I think those Yanks are half-starved because their logistics are not in place. They are presently overextended and with an appropriate diversion as a target...or trap, in common parlance...we could draw them into a field of crossed fire from which we could exact a terrible toll."

Matson's jaw fell slack. He sat for a second studying Eric, then glanced at his contemporaries. They were equally stunned by his grasp of the situation.

"How old are you, Lieutenant?" Major Timmons asked.

"I turned nineteen last December, sir."

"And where did you learn your military tactics?"

"Uh, sir, they are not just my tactics...Some of the ideas came from my father...others from General Carl Von Clausewitz...some from me," Eric shrugged.

"That is incredible...Marcus, where in blazes did you find a man of such vision? Regardless his age...the young man has himself some depth."

"To answer your question, Joshua, Eric and I crossed paths over at Beaver Creek. I was bringing back a couple wagon loads of raw recruits and we saw a string of Union cavalry horses grazing next to a church...Turns out, our young Schmidt and his family killed off a whole Yankee patrol."

"Is that true, Eric? How many bluebellies were there?"

Eric instantly became more somber and introspective at the turn of the conversation. "Twelve of em...They killed my family…I tracked 'em east towards Marshall…After the last one was properly dealt with, I headed north," he said coldly.

By then, a number of other officers had gathered around the table to get a better look at the young man in the buckskins. They had so many questions about tracking and the tactics he had used to defeat a superior force that his dinner became cold. One captain asked to see the Remington revolver Eric wore on his left hip and he spoke for fifteen minutes about the relative merits of both the Colt and the Remington, relying on his background as a gunsmith.

His calm, but authoritative manner, enhanced by his technical knowledge and physical presence did not go unnoticed by the senior officers in the mess.

Colonel Stephens leaned over to Lt. Colonel Bobby Don Smith and whispered, "See what I mean? That young buck is a natural leader of men. If this thing in Shreveport works out like he says, we may have to give him a company of his own."

"Are you not rushing it a little, Colonel? I think the boy's a little too wet behind the ears to put him over a hundred men…particularly since he has absolutely no actual experience as a cavalry officer."

"Call it a gut feeling, Bobby Don, but I have seen a few men who can make others want to follow them right into the jaws of hell itself," Stephens said as he leaned back on the bench. "They cannot teach that in school and we do not have the luxury of time or infrastructure here in the south…I will take leadership and brains when and where I can find them…I want you to lead the expedition tomorrow and let the boy have his own head...You can command the Shreveport detachment to support the operation as required...Understood?"

"Oh, yes sir...I will give the boy enough rope to hang himself...if that is what you want."

"Dammit, Bobby Don, that is not what I said and you bloody well know it...Something about the way he thinks might just give us the edge we need to fight a numerically superior Union Army. I am not one to slog it out like Napoleon tried to at Waterloo...A shameful waste of humanity...Besides, that is why I joined the cavalry in the first place."

"I will watch out for him, Willy...Just like to get your goat from time to time." Lt. Colonel Smith grinned.

"Come on...I have some Brandy and cards in my tent. Gotta let you have a chance to get even."

The two rose and disappeared from the mess without another word. A dim yellow glow from the street lights of Marshall was visible off in the distance as they walked the eighty yards to the command section tents.

After breakfast the following morning, Eric reported the Brigade Command tent as he had been ordered. Colonel Stephens announced the duty roster of the officers and enlisted men assigned to the Shreveport expedition, then turned the meeting over to Lt. Colonel Smith, who briefed the assembly on the mission objectives. Eric was happy to see that three wagons had been assigned to carry the faux cargo designed to serve as bait for the Union cavalry. Finally, he was introduced as the Executive Officer for the mission. The announcement came as a surprise to both him and Captain Matson—one of the platoon element leads in the mission. Nonetheless, Eric stood before the men and kept their rapt attention.

"Gentlemen, it is my honor and privilege to serve with you on this operation. Our mission, as has been well stated, will be to lure Union forces into a trap and spring it shut with such ferocity and overwhelming concentrated firepower as to destroy their ability to conduct offensive operations in this theater. In addition to the usual items assigned to all cavalry, the mission requires that each man be issued a second Enfield carbine or rifle and two additional revolvers...Furthermore, each soldier shall carry the amount of forty rounds of fixed ammunition for his rifles and an additional sixty rounds for his pistols."

A murmur went through the crowd, as most cavalry engagements were short-lived charges with a single rifle shot, followed by a cylinder full of pistol rounds and a reversion to the saber as the wild melees usually went. The fresh-faced young man in buckskins with two guns and two knives on his belt had stirred a hornet's nest.

Eric raised his hand, and the crowd fell silent. "I know what ya'll are thinking...I understand. What we are about to attempt is not what is considered business-as-usual for mounted troops...Now here is what we are going to do..."

Fifteen minutes later, Eric had laid out his plan. Colonel Stephens glanced over at Lt. Colonel Smith, who shrugged his shoulders and smiled. Both were impressed by Eric's detailed operational concepts of communication and planning and optimistic about the chances of success. Stephens stepped forward.

"There you have it, men. Gather the gear you need and assemble back here at eleven o'clock sharp. Colonel Smith is anxious to get under way."

The men dispersed as directed by their brigade commander.

Eric began to depart to make ready when Colonel Stephens called him over. "Lieutenant...a word please."

"Yes sir?" Eric turned to face him.

"Fine presentation there, son. I did have one question."

"Yes, sir, and what would that be?"

"What was the purpose of having the men bring a change of civilian clothes? You do realize that we are an actual combat arm in the service of the Confederacy?"

"Oh, absolutely, sir...I am very much aware of our position."

The colonel looked at him for some further revelation as to his intentions.

It took Eric a moment to understand the man's concern. "Sir, I was talking with Captain Matson about the size of the garrison in Shreveport. An additional forty or so of our men would effectively double our strength. My plan is to use our troops in a defensive escort until such time as we reach Shreveport. That will serve the function of implying a value placed upon the good in the wagons...We can, of course, expect to be seen by Union spies and sympathizers. Once we get the false goods delivered to Shreveport, we shall make a show of most of the detachment departing. At that point, the apparent lack of a securing force will make the bait appear to be vulnerable to any opposing forces."

"I see. Your point is a valid one. Now, what about the mufti?"

The word had Eric stumped.

His young face read like book to Colonel Stephens. "Regular civilian clothes, Lieutenant...Non-uniform items."

"Oh, sorry...I never heard them called that. When the departed troops reenter town and take up their assigned hidden positions, I would like them to be dressed in...mufti...That way, a spy riding through town would not know our true strength."

"Well, by Hannah, that is one trick they do not teach at the Point!...Learn that from that book you were reading?"

"No sir, my dad taught me how to blend in with the countryside for hunting turkey and deer from a ground blind."

"I suppose it would work for critters, too. One point I would be remiss not to make concerns combatants wearing uniforms. What you have planned is acceptable in the States of the Confederacy...However...should you attempt a similar ruse above the Mason-Dixon line...your capture by Union forces would result in an automatic finding of your being a spy...Death by firing squad is the punishment."

Eric swallowed hard. That bit of information was news to him. "I will keep that in mind, Colonel."

"Do not let it bother or slow you down in the least, young man. I have assigned Colonel Smith here to keep you out of troubles of that nature...He and your own Captain Matson will advance your schooling the intricacies of military arts and protocol. I am more interested in results and, as I told you before…I like the way you think."

"I will take that as a compliment, Colonel. My father strove to give me a sound foundation in logic and my mother…well, sir, she taught me to read and you could say gave me a thirst for knowledge."

"A man could not have asked for a better start, my boy. My deepest sympathies for their loss…I am sure you were proud of them both," Stephens said as he placed his hand on Eric's shoulder and looked him straight in the face.

Tears welled in Eric's eyes. The pain of his loss was still too fresh, too close to the surface to deny.

Captain Matson caught sight of them and spoke up, "Sir, we have a few things to make ready for the mission…so if you will permit me to drag Lieutenant Schmidt away, we will get to them."

Matson snapped a salute, followed by Schmidt. The two senior officers returned the gesture.

"Carry on, gentlemen, and good luck," Colonel Stephens said.

Matson wheeled away with Eric right behind him.

He wiped his eyes once and drew in a deep breath, then exhaled slowly. "How do you think it went?"

Marcus laughed. "If it went any better, they will have you on the General's promotion list by sundown."

The forty mile trip to Shreveport would take two days. After only three miles, Eric shifted uncomfortably in the saddle.

Marcus noted the look on the younger man's face. "Having second thoughts about switching to the McClellan saddle?"

"My butt's thinking it was a big mistake. I kept the biggest one that I found, and I really like the all rings for the gear."

"The cavalry saddle rides a little different than the western and Mexican ones do. Did you ever hear of posting."

"You mean like mailing a letter?"

"No." Matson chuckled. "Posting is a style of riding where you put a significant part of your weight on the stirrups in tune with the horse's natural rhythm. Watch me."

Matson pulled out of formation and nudged his horse to a road trot from the walk they had been using while keeping pace with the slower wagons. Eric pulled up along side and was bouncing slightly on each step while Marcus seemed to glide along. The captain reined back to a walk.

"How did you do that?" Eric asked.

The senior officer grinned. "Magic..." He shook his head. "...Not really...Here is the secret...Watch you horse's right front foot...When it comes off the ground and starts to come back at you, put a little more of your weight on the balls of your feet. When it goes forward, relax and let the saddle come up and touch your backside. Ride with your legs slightly bent. Feel the rhythm, use your balance and stay in the center of the horse."

"Seems like you would get tired without sitting down."

"It takes a while to get used to it, but believe me, it is a lot easier on both your butt and the horse's back. After a while, you will be able to see the foot come up out of your peripheral vision and it just comes naturally."

"I will try anything right about now. Thought I was gonna need a can of horse liniment just to make it till dark."

The first night, the wagons were pulled up close together in a grassy field where the tall pine trees had taken over. Scattered dogwood and redbud trees as well as a few "Christmas tree" cedars lined the edge of the clearing. Twenty small field tents were laid out in a row parallel to the dirt road—most of them glowed with small oil lamps and tallow candles as night fell. Captain Matson gazed over at Eric, lying on his back with his hand clasped behind his head. He could see the younger man's eyes were open.

"What are you thinking about?"

"I should be tired, but I cannot get my mind to relax. Are you sure four sentries are enough?"

"That should be sufficient unless that rider Colonel Smith sent to Jonesville comes back with information about recent enemy activity in the area. We will send a man out in the morning to scout ahead to Waskom and Greenwood. There is not much going on between Marshall and Shreveport."

"Hope I am not sending everybody out a wild goose chase."

"Eric, do not keep second guessing yourself. Your basis for arriving at the decision to launch this mission has not changed. Until we get information to make a better one, stay with what you have…The men get nervous if command is wishy-washy."

"I do not know…It is just that…I never was responsible for other men's lives before. What if the Yanks are much stronger than we think? We could get a passel of these men killed…"

"Did you not listen to what I just said? These men are volunteers, right down to the last man...they know what might be out there, and they trusted your judgment and your plan to work...Stay the course."

"Suppose you are right."

"Of course I am...That is why I am a Captain." Matson chuckled. "Now go to sleep."

"Night, Marcus."

Eric said a silent prayer for his family and his men and soon drifted off.

Dawn broke with a bustle of activity. Two men assigned to kitchen patrol had built a sizable fire in the rock-lined pit. Black cast iron tripods supported pots for the ever-present beans and flat cast iron griddles sizzled with fresh cut bacon rashers laid out in rows. The aroma of coffee boiling could be smelled in half the camp—a slight east breeze robbed the upwind soldiers of the pleasure.

Eric pulled on his pants and boots, and then rolled up and tied his bedroll in a neat tight cylinder. Marcus was sharpening his saber with a pale white Arkansas stone. He turned to Eric who was about to pull on his buckskin shirt.

"Hold on there...Almost forgot that you never got to attend that saber drill I was going to schedule for you today."

"You mean, now...before breakfast?"

"I mean even before you get dressed. Go ahead and draw it out of the scabbard."

He pulled the thirty inch blade out by its gilded steel handle, then tossed the brightly polished stamped steel scabbard back on his saddle.

Marcus visually checked the saber as he flexed and warmed up his wrist.

"That is the wrist-breaker you captured from the Union officer?"

Eric nodded.

"It is the latest one from the Ames company, I see. They make a good saber, with sharkskin on the hilt and wire wrapping to keep it from slipping in your gloves. Note that only the bottom of the blade is sharp…Its real purpose is for breaking arms and collarbones. It can be thrust into a person's body to inflict a mortal wound, but do not try it when you are riding past. It will only break your wrist or get jerked out of your hand…If you do not let go, you can get pulled out of the saddle. With me so far?"

Eric nodded.

"Follow me. We will use those small cedars over there for our enemy."

"All right…But I have to say, the saber is a poor substitute for a good firearm."

"Afraid I have to agree with you. But, when you are in close contact with enemy infantry or cavalry…there may be times when this hunk of steel is all you have between life and death."

"I am listening…Which one of these here trees reminds you of a Yankee?"

"This eight footer should do...Now the first lesson for fighting with sabers is to impress upon you that it is not a sword...nor is it a foil. The saber is only sharp on one side and cannot cut on the top at all. The tip is sharp to allow it to cut...and it can inflict a fatal wound on a single thrust."

"I saw that right off...on the first Yank I snuck up on."

"Right...It also is relatively silent, and that may be useful if you happen to be on foot and have more than one opponent." Matson extended his own saber to demonstrate. "Grip the hilt firmly...like so. Insure your knuckles are well inside the guard, here...If they are not, a blade from an opponent is likely to take your fingers off the first time you cross swords."

"That would not be good."

"Exactly...You would then lose your saber...and your life, in short order. So, make the saber an extension of your arm."

"Like this?" Eric asked as he pointed the saber with his wrist slightly cocked.

"No...Straighten the wrist. It takes muscle power to keep the wrist cocked over like you had it. Your hand would tire quicker and your grip fail sooner."

Eric made the adjustment Marcus asked for.

"There you have it. Now watch as I move to make a back hand horizontal slash."

Matson started a move with his right hand just above his left shoulder. The shiny silver blade flashed through the air, the whistling sound was unlike anything Eric had ever heard. Small green limbs flew from the cedar where the forward eight inches of the blade had made contact. Marcus continued with the blade until it was well behind him.

"Note that I followed through with the attack and did not try to stop the blade early. That would have slowed the blade down and lessened its effectiveness...Like in boxing when you throw a hook."

Eric nodded.

"Your turn...Set up here like I did, feet shoulder width apart."

"Like this?"

"Of course. Now start from the position I showed you. Choose the spot you want to strike and focus your attention there as you bring the blade around...Whenever you are ready."

He picked his target and, in a glint of silver, the saber flashed in a semicircle and sang out as it made contact with the cedar tree. Eric's blade struck the tree slightly higher than where Marcus' blade had, but with similar results.

"Very good. How did that feel?"

"A little strange...but it felt as if the blade would have been a lethal weapon."

"That it was...There was a reason I showed you the backhand slash first. Most people want to use their forehand naturally. Can you guess why?"

"More reach or more power?"

"Correct...But what happens when you make a forehand slash?"

Eric thought hard for a moment. "You have to extend the arm first before you get any blade motion."

"Right…And what can your opponent do when your arm is hanging out there motionless?"

"Chop it off?"

Captain Matson grinned. "Maybe they will just break it, if you are very lucky. Otherwise, folks can start calling you Stumpy."

"That is not really funny."

"Perhaps not, but I will wager you remember this lesson. So…go ahead and make another backhand slash and follow up instantly with your forehand…Let me see how you do."

Eric complied. The cedar tree suffered more damage. Matson continued with the lesson, and instructed him on the downward slash—a lunge and an upper cutting vertical stroke where the wrist was rolled palm up. He spent several minutes on parries and blocking techniques, combining boxing and grappling with the use of the saber. Finally, he turned to Eric who was starting to glisten with a light sweat, despite the cool spring air.

"Now, I want you to show me a combination of all the offensive maneuvers I have shown you. Keep going until I say stop…Understood?"

"Like falling off a log," he said enthusiastically.

"Begin."

He erupted with a flurry of slashing attacks on the newly chosen tree. Bit of green cedar limbs and leaves flew in all directions for several seconds, but as Marcus counted slowly in his head, the blows became less frequent and less effective. He smiled as Eric grasped his saber with his left hand and reacquired a better grip. His breathing became more labored and louder.

"Stop," Marcus commanded as the saber slipped though the young man's fingers.

Eric grabbed at his right hand and rubbed it hard, and then followed suit on his forearm.

"Forty seconds," Matson announced dryly.

"What? That had to be at least three minutes...Look at that tree."

"Oh, you killed him, all right. Would not want you after me, if I was a tree."

"Are you makin' sport of me?"

"No...well...maybe just a little. I counted to forty for a reason. Did you see how quickly your hand and arm tired?"

"Yeah, and I thought I was stronger than that."

"Oh, but you are. When we did that drill at West Point, I only lasted twenty-two seconds...the first time."

"They did it more than once?"

"It was required to be able to last a full minute to pass."

"So, you are trying to teach me something else, are you not?"

"Some of the men we may come up against can go on for several minutes. They have developed their hand and arm muscles over years and years of practice. Plus, they now have had some recent combat experience to boot...Just want you to know what your limitations are at this point. You will get better and stronger...believe me."

Eric flexed his hand open and closed several times, trying to get the circulation going in it again. He reached down and picked up his saber, the blade covered with the sticky sap from the cedar.

"Thanks for the lesson, Captain. I believe I learned lot."

"You pick it up fast. Let us go see what the cooks have got for us...All this tree killin' has made me hungry."

Matson took a seat next to Lt. Colonel Smith and motioned for Eric to sit beside him.

"Any word from the scout you sent to Jonesville, sir?"

"He got back around ten last night. No one had seen any enemy patrols...My guess is there was not much of military significance there to make a foray to such an out-of-the-way location."

"We should reach Shreveport by late afternoon, if travel conditions remain good."

"That would be my best estimate, also. I see you took young Schmidt out for a lesson...How did it go, Eric?"

"Fine, sir...if we get attacked by trees, I will be ready."

All three laughed. Eric cut up his ration of bacon and mixed it with his beans before he downed them. Suddenly a thought crossed his mind. He remembered the binoculars stashed securely in his saddle bags.

"Colonel Smith, do many of our men have field glasses at their disposal?"

"I have a collapsible brass telescope for scanning at distances. But in answer your question, I would have to say no. Why do you ask?"

"Just wondering…I appropriated a pair from the Yankee officer killed at my ranch. Thinking about it made me wonder what our capabilities are within the units of the south."

"Glass making and lens grinding are more prevalent up north, as are steel mills and sword makers like the Ames company that built that saber you carry," added Captain Matson. "I think Ames Sword is from Ohio."

"That is where the Yankees I encountered were from."

"They died a long way from home," observed Smith.

Schmidt sat silent for a minute. He contemplated the ramifications of disparate industrial production capabilities between the states in the Union and those in the Confederacy. His conclusion did not bode well with him and it reflected almost immediately in his face.

Bobby Don Smith caught the look instantly. "Anything wrong, son?"

"I was thinkin' about the North and the advantages it possesses in manufacturing at this point in time."

"And what did you conclude?"

"Well, sir, the first thing is we have an uphill fight ahead of us. The second is we need to make every good use of captured enemy equipment, from boots to bullets and binoculars…And the third is we need to start planning to intercept the Yankee supply trains, boats and wagons."

Smith and Matson stared at the young man, then exchanged glances.

"You came up with all that while thinking about a pair of binoculars?" Smith asked.

He nodded, looked out past the camp at the edge of the woods, and then pointed over his shoulder with his thumb.

"I get this feeling that somebody is watching every move we make. They could be out two or three hundred yards out...maybe we cannot not see them, but they can see us, using those binoculars or telescopes."

"Make you nervous?"

"Not exactly nervous...but, call it...concerned."

"That is good. Men need to listen to their gut instincts when in combat...Sometimes, we need all the help we can get. After this mission, I will pass what you said on to brigade. I happen to agree with you."

Matson mused over the conversation. *Trains, boats and wagons? How were cavalry troops going to intercept boats?*

"Here is a question for you, Eric. If we get to Shreveport and find the Yankees are planning to arrive by river barge or sternwheeler, how would you go about stopping them with just the resources of cavalry?" he asked.

"How wide is the river at Shreveport? I have never been there."

"I would imagine some four hundred feet...what would you say, Colonel?"

Bobby Don nodded and sopped a bit of bean gravy from his plate with the corner of his cornbread ration. "About that."

Eric chewed a bit of hickory smoked bacon as he contemplated his answer. "A thick rope, suspended between pilings or trees would do. Or a stout wire rope or cable if we could find one big enough."

"Could not the enemy cut a rope with a knife?" Captain Matson asked.

"Of course...but only if they could see it. I would leave it a foot or two under water, weighted down with rocks, then use sharpshooters to keep anyone from the approaching the bow of the boat. If the company assigned to protect the town had a cannon, I would reinforce a position overlooking the rope and blast the boat to bits when it got hung up. They could certainly hit a large stationary target, at a distance of less that 200 yards...I would imagine."

"You imagine correctly...Matson, I think you have an additional job to do when we get to town. See if we can find us a suitable amount of rope. If they can not provide it in Shreveport, perhaps Alexandria will be able to meet our needs."

"But, Colonel, that was a just hypothetical question I proposed to Lieutenant Schmidt. There has been no sign of Union Naval activity as far up river as Shreveport."

"No, but they have made forays up the Arkansas River into the Little Rock area and are threatening towns up and down the Mississippi. I have seen reports that Vicksburg is particularly vulnerable."

"I read where that river is over a mile wide in places," Eric added as he took a sip of the strong black coffee.

"That is a fact, Eric, but your idea could work wonders in smaller waterways. But, for now, gents, we must focus our attention on this mission. Let us get packed up and under way."

Lt. Colonel Smith stood up and headed back to his tent. Matson glanced at Schmidt and grinned. "Things are always going to be interesting with you around, I can see that."

"I trust you mean that in a positive way."

"Oh, I do…Grab yourself a couple of corn dodgers for the road…We may keep rolling through the noon meal if the Colonel has a mind to."

By two in the afternoon, the morning's scout had ridden back from Greenwood and reported scattered sightings of small Union forces from around the Shreveport vicinity. No contact had been made with the small garrison from the town proper, but conflicts with locals had resulted in several deaths of residents and a couple of dead Yankee mounted troops.

Lt. Colonel Smith called Schmidt and Matson to his side and then handed the young Lieutenant a folded piece of paper tied up with a short piece of twine. "Eric, I want you to ride ahead and make contact with the Shreveport garrison commander, Major Robinson. Give him this paper to identify yourself. Tell him we shall arrive an hour or so after you and to make a visible show of making preparations for protecting our load of supplies."

Eric took hold of the small missive and slid it into a small flap pocket sewn into the front of his buckskin shirt. "Yes, sir. Any other orders?"

"Scout out any locations you deem suitable for our sharpshooters to utilize while they lie in wait for the Yankees. I feel you have a keen sense about these things, and will allow you considerable latitude, despite your acknowledged lack of military experience. Do feel capable of carrying out my orders, Lieutenant?"

Eric wasted no time in mulling over the answer. "I am ready for whatever awaits us in Shreveport, sir. I already feel personally responsible for the Army making this trek to another state, and I am therefore the one to make good on my suppositions. If the Yankees fail to show up, we shall have to pursue them elsewhere."

"That, sir , is the attitude I want to see in my men…Keep a sharp eye out for Yankee stragglers. There may be some hereabout and I want you to travel alone." Colonel Smith glanced to Matson, who was at first slightly surprised at the senior man's decision. "The less you look like an infantry officer, the less attention you will draw to yourself. In fact, I do not want even you to salute when you depart. I have a gut feeling we are being watched, even as we speak," he said as he looked uneasily over his left shoulder.

The senior officer's admission only reinforced the same feeling Eric had felt since breakfast. He took a quick glance around as the last of the wagons slowly rolled past. Sixteen mounted cavalry followed, with the more experienced among them keeping alert for any sudden attack from the dark timbers lining both sides of the road. Eric extended his hand to the commander and said, "I suppose then that we shall meet in three hours, sir."

Smith shook his hand firmly as he spoke from the heart, "Go with God."

Eric nodded first to him and then to Matson. He wheeled his horse back toward the head of the column and lightly squeezed his legs against the gelding. Bucky responded without further urging and broke into an easy lope past the visibly laden wagons and the escorting cavalry. Matson and Smith watched him disappear around the next bend in the then narrow road.

"I surely hope the young man knows what he is doing," Matson remarked as he cut a small plug of tobacco from his twist and popped in his mouth.

Three Union Cavalry soldiers assigned the task of monitoring the wagon trainload of Confederate supplies waited for two full minutes after the last of the mounted men providing rear guard rounded the shallow bend in the road.

Corporal Eldon Evans collapsed his brass telescope and slipped it inside his saddlebag. He looked back west toward the town of Greenwood and made sure there was no more traffic eastbound before he spoke to his two privates, "Mitchell, I want you to carry a message back to brigade HQ. Tell them the Reb convoy has done passed our present location and should git into Shreveport no later than five o'clock. The convoy was too heavily guarded for us to make any attempt to intercept...You got all that?"

The smooth-faced private from Cincinnati nodded. "They gonna be in Shreveport at five and they wuz too many for us to try and take 'em."

"Close enough...Now, the brigade is supposed to meet together up north of town between the road to the Indian Territories and the Red River early this evenin' or tonight. Me and ol' Stu here are gonna bird-dog them wagons all the way back to town. Tell the colonel they is chock block full of victuals. I seen the markings on them boxes, plain as day. We need 'em lots worser that than them Johnny Rebs do. Hate to see all that food floated down river to Alexandria a'for we could get our hands on 'em."

The young private looked back in the direction the Confederates had departed. He had not had a full hot meal in almost three days. The thought of fresh eggs, bacon and perhaps a bowl of beef barley soup surely made his mouth water. "You can count on me, Corporal...Chock block full of victuals. I will tell him."

"Boy, I know you will do us proud. Try not to get yourself killed on the way. Understand?"

A small flash of uncertainty passed over the boy's face, then vanished as quickly as it came. "No, sir. I ain't gonna let them see me a'tall." He spurred his black mare from their hidden vantage point fifty yards inside the tall timber and dogwoods. In just a few seconds, he was out onto the road and trotting toward the town of Shreveport.

"Dang yore hide, Evans. Thought you were gonna make the kid piss his pants."

He shook his head and frowned. His dark wiry mustache formed a horseshoe shape above his pursed lips. "Not my fault he ain't got no more balls that what he has. Boy ain't even shaving yet and the lieutenant wants me to make him into a regular fightin' man."

Evans grinned, exposing a gap where one of his upper front teeth was lost in a barroom brawl three years earlier. He let fly a stream of tobacco juice in the direction of the rapidly departing private. "Me, I do not give a hoot in hell if'n he lives or dies...Damn fool kid is the lieutenant's nephew or sumthin'...He should have stayed to home, nursin' on his momma, if'n you ask me."

Stu just stared back at his slightly disheveled corporal, then took a drink from his canteen. He took the cork and smacked it tight into the opening on the canvas-covered metal vessel. Looping the leather strap through a large brass ring attached to the front of his saddle's forward skirt, he let the canteen drop into the loop and slide to rest against the neck and shoulder of his sorrel gelding. "Do what you want, Eldon, but if you let that kid git hisself kilt, the lieutenant ain't never gonna let you make sergeant."

The frown returned to Evan's face. He wiped his stained leather riding gauntlet across his mustache to clear away a dark drop of tobacco spittle hanging there. He glared at Stu, a rough looking man of twenty-two—only a year younger than himself. "Sez you. Who asked you, anyhow?" Evans spurred his mount, chuckling to himself.

Buck Stienke

Stu let the slightly cantankerous corporal ride out for almost fifty yards before he urged his own horse into motion.

***

CHAPTER SEVEN

SHREVEPORT

Eric slowed the big buckskin gelding to a walk as the traffic on the dirt streets of Shreveport got heavier. He knew the road leading into town passed by the CSA headquarters, but he was still surprised by the amount of hustle and bustle a town of only 4,000 could generate. Wagons of every shape and size as well as surreys, buckboards, drays and countless individual mounts crowded the main thoroughfare called Texas Street.

A half mile east of his location, the broad avenue dropped down to the Red River crossing where a ferry would—for ten cents—transport a person across the slow moving river. Eric studied the mostly wooden structures as he passed by and tried to imagine which would be useful in the implementation of his trap. The tallest building, a four story hotel called Le Pavilion, had a dual purpose balcony around the second floor, which also served as a cover for the eight foot wide boardwalk surrounding the elegant structure. His mother's lessons in history, art, and architecture came to mind as he identified the design as French, undoubtedly an influence from the earlier days when Louisiana was a colony of that western European nation.

A buggy passed in front of young Schmidt as the driver turned left onto Cypress Street as Eric approached the intersection. He stared at the jet black Standardbred gelding in the harness, appreciating the long sleek lines and obvious care and conditioning lavished on the animal. Almost as an afterthought, he glanced at the occupants of the shiny new barouche open carriage seeing a well dressed middle-aged white man holding the reins, his charcoal colored frock coat sporting a black satin collar that bespoke of his wealth.

Beside the driver sat a strikingly beautiful young lass of eighteen or so. Her long red hair was stylishly piled up atop her head and covered with a fashionable hat imported from France before the war began. She wore a jade green tightly fitted ankle-length dress—one that was custom tailored for her.

Eric locked eyes with the gorgeous woman for a brief second before she turned her nose up at his rustic attire and mud spattered boots. Her features were fine, with a heart shaped face—the combination of fair skin, red hair and emerald green eyes pleased him to no end. He reined his horse to a stop and watched as the buggy continued south on Cypress. "Bucky…did you ever see such a sight?"

His reverie was short-lived. A cranky forty year old teamster cracked a whip over his four mules pulling a heavy load of molasses barrels as they passed beside him. The sound of the whip echoed like a pistol shot, jarring Eric back to the task at hand. His hand flew to the Colt on his right side and he somewhat sheepishly let go of the leather flap covering it. The wagon creaked and groaned down the street as Eric pulled in behind it.

He watched curiously for a few seconds as a small wooden bucket with a metal hoop handle swung lazily back and forth from a steel hook screwed up into the wagon bed near the heavy tailgate. He could see a the handle of some sort of wooden utensil sticking out of the bucket and finally determined it was for axle grease. His father had made sure Eric lubricated the hubs of the family buckboard every second or third trip into Tyler. However, his dad had never sent the small can of grease along with the wagon. *Good idea.*

Eric sidepassed to the side of the busy street and let his buckskin drink from one of the numerous wooden plank water troughs lining it.

The almost random thought about his dad and the axle grease had unexpectedly brought a wave of sadness to him. He dismounted, wrapped the lead rope around the six-inch-thick peeled hickory hitching post and walked a few yards to a public water pump set next to another horse trough. Eric took off his black broad-brimmed hat and pumped the handle several times until the crown was half full. He dipped his hand into the cool water and brought it to his mouth, rinsing trail dust from his lips and mouth before he spit it back onto the dirt street. He splashed another handful on his face and then poured the remaining water over his forehead and let it run back into his dirty hair. He started to pull the hat back into place when a shouted command froze him.

"Don't move or I will blast ye to Kingdom Come!"

Eric blinked several times as the water continued to slowly drain from the soggy hat. The sight of three Confederate soldiers with their rifles leveled at him was not one he had anticipated. The tallest of the three—an infantry corporal as indicated by his rank—stepped off the wooden plank boardwalk and into the street, all the while keeping his weapon pointed at his chest. Eric heard the two clicks of the heavy sidelock's mainspring as the rebel soldier brought the hammer back to the fully cocked position.

"It's a Yankee cavalry sword all right!" came a call from behind him. "He has got a Yankee issue carbine in the boot on one side, too. Boys, guess we got us a Union spy right here in Shreveport."

Eric turned slightly to see a shorter young man in a private's uniform standing beside his buckskin gelding, with his captured Ames saber pulled out from his bedroll. The handle had been partially visible and had attracted attention from the four soldiers as soon as they walked out of the small cafe located three doors down from the hotel.

"Keep your hands off my equipment, Private...I am Lieutenant Schmidt, here on orders to see your Major Joseph Robinson."

"How come ye ain't in uniform? And where did ye come by the Yankee gear?" the corporal demanded.

He and the two other soldiers closed the distance between themselves and the tall man wearing the fringed leather shirt. None had lowered their weapon.

"I killed the Yanks who murdered my family back in Texas...All of 'em. That is where those weapons came from," Eric said as he let the words sink in for a second. "I joined up with the Confederate cavalry out of Tyler...Seventh Company. I got a message in my right front pocket from Colonel Smith for your Major Joseph Robinson."

"Somebody claims to have a message for me?" said a forty-year-old man who had just exited the cafe.

By his uniform, Eric could tell instantly that he was most likely the man he was seeking.

The corporal lowered his rifle. "This here man claims to be one of ours, Cap'n. But he is carrying Union gear...Meby he is a spy."

The major scrutinized the young man with his hat and hands in the air. He let his own left hand rest on the hilt of his Union issue saber. "Who did you say your commander was, son?"

Eric began to breathe a little easier. "Colonel Bobby Don Smith is commanding the supply train...Colonel William Stephens is our leading our brigade...My immediate superior officer is Captain Matson, sir."

"Marcus Matson?"

"Marcus Aurellius Matson...Did you go to West Point, too, sir?"

121

The grave look disappeared from the major's face at once. "Men, lower your weapons. That is no way to treat an officer of the Confederacy."

He extended his hand and Eric gladly took it.

Thirty minutes passed as Eric briefed him on his plan and the two, along with the detachment senior enlisted man, discussed suitable sites for the Texan reinforcements to lay in wait for the Union cavalry.

"So, Colonel Stephens agreed to your idea to have the men wear civilian clothes?" Robinson asked as he lit a yellowed carved Meerschaum pipe.

"He and the general thought it might be the right way to get the Yankees to show themselves. They both have been trying to make contact with them for some time…but to no avail."

"I agree that they have been quite illusive in nature. We, of course, have received reports of sporadic sightings across much of the northwest corner of the state. As, you are probably aware, by the time we get the word and move to engage them, the enemy is long gone…We ourselves lack the manpower to cover the entire territory, as most of our men have presently gone east to fight with Lee."

"I discussed that probability with my brigade commander when I came up with this idea. The supply column should arrive within another hour and a half…two on the outside. The accompanying cavalry escort will pretend to depart town to the south, then double back shortly after sunset…They will have changed clothes and plan to filter back in singles and pairs."

"A bit unorthodox, Lieutenant, but it could damn well work...All it takes is a little cooperation from the enemy. You did say you never actually laid eyes on anyone trailing the supply train?"

"No evidence, sir, I must admit...but I am certain I felt their presence a time or two."

Corporal Eldon Evans reined up inside the tall timbers just west of town. The Union cavalryman and his compatriot watched the line of wagons until they were well inside of Shreveport before he turned to his slightly younger private. "I seen all I need to see. We stick around here any longer and somebody is like as not to spot us."

He nodded his head to the north and Stu tugged on his reins to head for the planned rendezvous location with their brigade. Evan followed a couple seconds later, after checking the road back to the west one final time to insure no one had come into view. The pair melted into the dense underbrush and vanished with hardly a trace.

It was almost 6pm when the two were challenged by a blue-clad sentry that stepped into the trail leading to the Union encampment. "Halt! Who goes there?" The seventeen year old volunteer was steadfast in his duty, and kept the Springfield rifle pointed at Evans' chest as the corporal raised his right hand.

"That is about enough of that crap, boy...Cain't you recognize two of your own?"

"Yeah, I sees ye real good...but I got to ask ye anyhow...who goes there?"

"Corporal Evans and Private Sheffield, scouts reporting to the colonel."

The young private returned his rifle to the port arms position and nodded slightly. "Clear to pass." He stepped aside and never cracked a smile as the two scruffy looking horsemen rode by.

"Bucking for promotion, that one is," Stu noted as they passed out of earshot.

"Little piss-ant would wet his pants if'n somebody were to taken a pot shot at him. I guarandamntee you."

Row upon row of dirty white canvas tents appeared in a clearing a few hundred yards off the road to the Indian Territories. Lines of soldiers queued up to the mess tents as a evening meal was being served. Stu caught wind of the weak stew that the cooks had cobbled together out of the meager rations and game brought in by foragers.

"Looks like we are in time for the chef's surprise tonight."

"Hate to think what's in it...probably snappin' turtles, coots and coons."

"Naw, I mind I smelled me some sowbelly...Just greasy 'nuff to slide on down and drown the worms in yer gut."

"Yer makin' it sound real inviting like...Meby I will soon stick to hardtack and jerky."

"Suit yer own self. We better unsaddle the nags 'fore the sergeant catches us eatin'. He would just as soon put a boot in yer ass if he thinks yer slackin' off on the mounts."

"Yup...Cavalry noncoms are funny like that."

They drew rein next to a picket line of underfed Union horses that were straining at their lead ropes to graze on the remaining spring grass. Each swung down and ground tied their horse as they loosened the girths and stacked their tack next to a couple of other saddles. They folded their damp square saddle pads—outside in, neatly in two—and lay them across the sweat-stained black leather of the military issued rigs.

Stu stepped quickly to the back of the line and tried to catch a glimpse of the gray, slightly gelatinous mass being spooned over a portion of boiled white rice in the well-worn metal plates. He could see slices of bread were being placed in the bottom of the bowls before the serving of the daily mystery meat was ladled on top. "Hey, what's in the kettle?" he asked a scrawny pimple-faced teenager from Poolville, Ohio.

"Do not ask me…nobody tells me nuthin'."

A corporal in front of the young buck private called back to Stu. "Heard they got some possums last night. The cook says it tastes like pork…but what does he know?"

Several of the men grumbled as Stu made a face. Rations had been dwindling for the previous three weeks, with long term provisions being limited to hardtack and beans.

"Guess I was jest a dreamin' 'bout that sowbelly…A man cain't even trust his nose no more."

Eldon and Stu sat cross-legged on the ground about sixty yards from the mess tent. Evans sopped up the last of the greasy gravy with the stale bread and forced it down as he reached for a canteen. "Them cooks could learn a thing or two 'bout spices and cookin' in general. That is about a pitiful excuse for gravy as I can recall." He wiped a dab of gray off his black mustache covering his lower lip onto the back of his left hand. The corporal glanced down at his hand and wiped it clean on the grass.

"Know what you mean…They's plumb outta pepper and salt…I heared one say."

"We best go give our report to the colonel…Meby he will be excited enough about that supply train we seen to jump up and take it from them rebs."

"You been in longer'n me. He does not seem too all-fired keen on getting into it with them southern boys. That is why we ain't go no provisions…he just keeps us a movin' all the time and our own supply wagons cain't keep up."

Evans took a swig from his canteen and sloshed the water around in his mouth long enough to cut the grease out before he spit. He pushed the cork home and reached down in his tunic for a chew. Using his belt knife, he cut a small plug off the twist of tobacco and popped it into his mouth. "Well, guess now is as good a time as any to let the old man know what we seen."

Inside the command tent, the two scouts couldn't help but notice the china plate set to the side of the colonel's desk. A thick slice of smoked ham, appropriated during the raid on Jefferson, lay beside a half loaf of fresh bread.

"Now where exactly on this map did you two see this supply train?"

"Sir, like the private we sent ahead should have told you, we wuz just outside of Greenwood...right about here," he said placing his finger on the map. "With their bigger numbers, the three of us did not stand no chance in taking them supplies by ourselves. So, we kept on their tails until they reached the outskirts of Shreveport and then we came back here to report, sir."

"Colonel, I think I can take a company, perhaps two and make a reconnaissance in force to secure those provision for ourselves," a twenty-eight year old junior officer suggested.

"Captain Humbolt, I appreciate your offer. But you, sir, have no idea of the rebel force's disposition and strength within the confines of Shreveport...Bear in mind, inside town our ability to maneuver is greatly limited, taking away one of the greatest strengths we, as cavalry, possess."

"Sir, thank you for reminding me, but I would like to advise the Colonel that I have taken the liberty to dispatch a pair of good men to reconnoiter the enemy for exactly the reasons you have spoken."

The senior officer raised his eyebrows at the news. It was clear that he was not pleased. "And have you considered the possibility that they might be seen or captured? Their presence could cause an alarm, making the Confederates reinforce their position."

"That is true, sir, which is why I made the decision to utilize two volunteers who grew up in Virginia, sir. I equipped them with captured horses and ensured that they wore no uniforms, nor carried any identifying papers or even union currency."

127

"Are you telling me you authorized these men to act as spies, without my knowledge?"

"Yes, sir…I take full responsibility for my actions…The men were aware of the punishment for being caught as spies. But, in light of our current logistical challenges, I thought the action a prudent one…sir."

The colonel's eyes narrowed—the tension inside the tent was growing by the second. He looked up at the two majors and one lieutenant colonel attending the briefing. "Hal, what do you think of this? Are we in a position to mount an offensive operation against a rebel garrison inside a town the size of Shreveport?"

The light colonel took a long draw on his cigar, and then blew a small cloud of blue-gray smoke across the tent. Private Sheffield stifled a couple coughs as Evans shot him a hard look.

"Colonel Hatfield, my gut instincts tell me our mounted troops are worth three to one against a poorly trained and equipped bunch of slave holders. Your young Humbolt here has shown exactly the kind of resourcefulness I would expect from an Ivy League graduate…Let us see what his scouts have to say and make plans post haste to grab those provisions before they can be loaded on a boat and shipped out of reach."

Hatfield nodded agreement. "Shreveport is a transshipment port vital to their cause. Interception of supplies accomplishes two goals…supplying our needs and denying theirs…Captain, when are your men due back?"

"Sir, I instructed them to return not later than an hour after dark."

"In that case, I want you to have your men of the fifteenth ready to ride by 10pm...Major Collins, your twelfth will do so as well. Both of you will report to Lieutenant Colonel Hal Wilburn, who will serve as commander of the two companies. A midnight attack will not be expected as the rebs have no idea we are within striking distance."

Captain Humbolt beamed at the opportunity to lead his men into a real battle...It was just the thing he needed to impress his father-in-law and former college fraternity brothers back north.

Major Collins took the assignment more somberly. A nighttime raid into a rebel town was not his cup of tea. His eyesight was fading as he had passed his forty-third birthday the month before. However, he was not going into battle alone. Each company was staffed close to 110 men and most were young enough to be his children. He, like all the others, saluted crisply when the commander dismissed them.

"Well, I hope you are satisfied," Stu said glumly to Evans.

"What are you bellyachin' about? You said you wanted to get your hands on all them victuals."

"Meby I did, but I did not think we wuz gonna have to go into town and fight for 'em."

SHREVEPORT, LOUISIANA

Two men stepped off the sidewalk and into the street as the city lamplighter went about his business and began the tedious process of igniting the coal oil lamps atop the freestanding posts every hundred feet or so down the central business district. He paid them little heed, as did the platoon of Confederate cavalry that had accompanied the wagons laden with boxes of foodstuffs from Texas. The men, each dressed as a common farm hand, watched as the young captain passed the command to his sergeant and signaled with his gloved hand.

"Columns of two...For-ward...ho!"

His command was repeated, the sound echoing down the lightly traveled street as the two dozen mounted soldiers fell into two lines and urged their horses into a road trot. The usual sounds of horses snorting and whinnying almost drowned out the creaking of their leather tack and the rhythmic thumping of full canteens against the swells of their saddles.

"Saddle up," one of the two said to the other.

His partner acknowledged the command with a single nod of the head. They followed the soldiers, but stayed a couple of hundred yards behind them, until the platoon crossed the road leading south to Alexandria or north to the Indian Territories and kept heading west back to Texas.

The leader of the two reined north and bumped his heels into his sorrel gelding's sides. It began a gentle lope that was matched by the bay mare the other man rode.

In less than a mile, the houses and commercial buildings gave way to scattered small farms, then quickly to gently rolling densely forested lands unsuitable for either grazing or the plow. As darkness settled in, the men turned off the road and make their way back into the Union camp.

UNION CAMP

"Captain Humbolt, suh. Sergeant Anderson and Corporal Calhoun reporting as ordered," the senior man said in a deep southern accent.

"At ease, men…What did you find out?"

"We can confirm the shipment, suh. Just like the private said, they wuz a bunch of heavily laden wagons with a lot a food on 'em. Does seem that them Johnny rebs got no problems with supplies."

"I see…Now what about sentries and gun emplacements? Did you have the opportunity to reconnoiter those as well?"

"We spent over forty-five minutes walking around, Cap'n. They was not no cannon in sight and the soldiers that brung the wagons in done rode on back…headed to Texas," the corporal added with a crooked grin.

"Really? You certain of that?"

"Absolutely, suh," Anderson agreed. "We tailed 'em out of town…rekon as how they had to get right back. But that garrison in town?…Them boys is not much punkin'…Never seen no more than eight er ten tops…And they only left three men guarding the wagons."

A smile came to Humbolt's face. "And where are the wagons located at this time?"

"They's just outside of the detachment headquarters on Texas Street. Seen us a wagon yard down by the ferry landin' and that there will be where we can get us some teams."

"Gentlemen, you have done a fine job here today and I

would think that the colonel would be inclined to accept my recommendation for a commendation for each of you. Get yourself a little rest and a bite to eat. We shall depart at 10pm."

The two enlisted men snapped salutes and stepped outside the smaller wall tent and walked away.

Humbolt glanced over to his company first sergeant. "You know, if this little operation comes off like clockwork, we both may be in for a promotion." He smiled as he pulled a bottle of bourbon out of his personal canvas kit bag and poured two fingers worth into a pair of blue enameled coffee cups.

"Here is to you…Major," the master sergeant said as they toasted their impending victory.

***

CHAPTER EIGHT

SHREVEPORT, LOUISIANA

Eric checked his timepiece in the dim yellow light from the street lamp below his window and quickly snapped it closed. *Eleven fifteen. If they are coming, I would think they would be here before midnight.* He gazed across the street at the darkened windows above the general store where he knew four sharpshooters were positioned.

Beside him, an empty whiskey barrel served as a makeshift table. Upon its top lay six Remington .44 caliber revolvers with their ready-made paper cartridges. Leaning against the plank wall next to the window were his father's double rifle and a pair of Springfield .58 caliber rifles. Ten feet away, one of the local detachment privates sat in a chair with a double barreled shotgun in his lap and a brass framed Colt .44 revolver hanging from his hip.

"Say, Lieutenant…What time is it gettin' to be?"

"Quarter after eleven. The bar downstairs should be closing right about now. Think I heard the barkeep holler something about closin' time a while back."

"Uh-huh. They shutdown early on weeknights, but stay open until two on Friday."

Several men walked out of the bar below and headed to their horses tied up along Texas Street. Two others stopped outside and carried on a final conversation. Neither were visible under the covered walkway.

"Do you really think there is…"

"Shhh." Eric responded, holding a raised finger to his lips. He pointed down to the unseen voices just feet below their position.

"Sorry," eighteen year old Bradley Smithson mouthed.

Across the street and down several doors, Captain Matson sat in a ladies millenary shop with three of the other Texas volunteers who had changed clothes and doubled back after dark. Their mounts were hidden inside a wagon yard a couple blocks north of Texas Street, and the men had walked in pairs and groups of three to where their weapons had been stashed earlier.

The last two customers from the bar mounted up and departed for home, leaving the street mostly deserted, save the six loaded wagons and three brave, but very nervous guards. Matson looked over at the company's senior NCO.

"I think there is a good chance that if there are any Yanks nearby, that they might take the bait. The supply wagons looked good coming into town and I would imagine news of their arrival spread pretty quickly."

"It would do us all proud to get into a donnybrook with 'em, Captain. The younger men are aching to do something besides drill day in and day out."

"That may be so, but after they have a taste of real combat, they may be wishing they had kept their thoughts to themselves...Glory is a fleeting thing, once the bullets start flying."

One of the youngest men of the expedition, a private from the town Corsicana listened intently. The strain of the hours of waiting was beginning to take its toll on him. He began to question his own bravery as he watched for the first sign of an enemy soldier. He looked out in the dimly lit street and saw the shoe shop across the deserted boulevard. The sign was painted with a large black boot centered in a field of white. It reminded him of the calf-high cavalry boots the CSA had issued him.

The local Confederate commander had made the suggestion to stagger the soldiers' disposition so that they were not directly across the street from each other. In that manner, they were far less likely to suffer from friendly fire if the Union forces made a move to steal the supplies.

Captain Matson, and Lieutenant Schmidt had heartily concurred the move, as had their commander, Colonel Smith. Wagons laden with tightly packed bales of cotton—each of which weighed close to four hundred pounds—were stationed a couple of blocks south of the ambush site as well as down at the main livery and wagon yard. When the first shots rang out, the teamsters were instructed to drive the rigs into the choke point at each intersection, effectively blocking the Union cavalry inside.

The twin columns of mounted troops slowly walked their horses down the dark unpaved side street, their revolvers at the ready. Faint moonlight from the waxing orb cast ghostly shadows across the plank sidewalks and hitching posts in front of the simple wooden homes.

Captain Humbolt led the second company of hungry Union cavalry toward the lantern-lit Texas Street six blocks ahead. He could feel his heart rate begin to pick up in anticipation of the brief skirmish. This was to be his first taste of real battle and he was starting to get nervous. Nighttime raids were always dangerous—unseen holes and obstructions could cripple a mount or knock a rider out of the saddle. If the rider's horse spooked badly, it could be nearly impossible to find it again before sunrise. However, the darkness did allow a significant element of surprise for which most military commanders would be willing to accept the greater incumbent operational risks.

A Confederate corporal, sitting in the bell tower of the First Baptist church, waited until the last of the enemy riders passed beyond his location. He carefully struck a match and then lit the sooty wick of the lantern awaiting on the belfry floor. He closed the rectangular glass door and snapped it shut before he raised the light twice behind the wooden louvers designed to keep the frequent Louisiana rains from pouring into the tower. The corporal checked the security of the percussion cap on his rifle before he blew the lamp out and waited. The trailing riders quickly disappeared in the moonlight a couple of blocks away, but the signal man would be ready if they passed by his way again.

"That is the signal!" Eric whispered excitedly as the second spot of light disappeared from the distant church bell tower. He pursed his lips and whistled a call from the meadowlark. Across the street, the call came back and was repeated several times up and down the street. The young Texan could feel a lump in his throat begin to grow as the grim reality of the situation came to rest on his broad shoulders. He glanced over at the young private seated near him. "Be ready…Hell is about to happen."

Lieutenant Colonel Wilburn held up a hand and brought the raiders to a halt a hundred feet before the intersection with Texas Street. Faint yellow light from the nearest street lamp cast a shadow across the roadway, but left the Union troops in near darkness. As briefed earlier, a dozen troopers from the rear of Major Rollins' A Company pealed out of the main column and lined up on the left side of the street. Their task was to secure draft horses from the wagon yard near the Red River ferry crossing.

Captain Humbolt brought his C Company riders forward to close the gap. He watched closely as the senior operational commander pulled his saber and squeezed his horse up into a trot and headed toward the corner.

Rollins' company followed suit with Humbolt's close behind. In a few seconds, four columns split, the shortest one turning left onto the broad expanse of eastern Texas Street and the main attack force—totaling almost 200 cavalry—rolling right, breaking into a gallop as the buglers sounded the charge.

The three Confederate guards stationed near the wagons filled with the empty boxes of provisions turned as one to the sound of the bugles echoing off the storefronts. A corporal from Alexandria leveled his rifle at the lead trooper still some one hundred yards distant and yanked the trigger. The shot went wide of its mark, but caught another soldier in the throat, sending him sprawling out of the saddle and under the hooves of a half dozen of the Yankee cavalry.

Instinctively, the horses jumped to try to avoid stepping on the man and caused even more confusion as horses collided—one of them stumbled and flipped end-over-end, with its rider taking the brunt of the fall.

The two other guards fired quickly and dove for cover of a small alley between a couple buildings as they had been briefed.

A rapid volley of handgun fire emanated from the cavalry's front ranks as the Union soldiers closed in on their objective, splintering the unpainted wooden posts supporting the balcony over the boardwalk. A pall of black powder smoke drifted behind them as they thundered unaware into the ambush kill zone.

Eric leveled the front sight of his over-and-under double rifle the Union officer as the cavalry commander was barking orders to his troops. He squeezed the trigger, sending the man backwards out of the saddle as the .45 caliber slug ripped through his chest and spine. Even in the pale light of the coal oil street lamps the dead man's saber glinted as it fell with him and stuck point first into the dirt street.

As if ignited by a single short fuse, the night air erupted into a calamitous cacophony of sound as the other Confederate soldiers began to fire accurately into the milling mass of cavalry that filled the street. Eric rolled the lower barrel up and under the fully cocked hammer. He snapped it back to his shoulder and took quick aim at an enlisted man with several stripes on his sleeve.

The man's horse spun slightly beneath him as Eric touched off the round, but it still passed though both lungs and sent the mortally wounded trooper to the ground, never to rise again. Around him, other Union cavalry fired back wildly at the smoke from the hidden sharpshooters. Terrified horses screamed in pain as some of the shots taken at their riders missed their mark and found them instead.

A long series of rebel yells—the likes of which Eric had never heard before—began to sound off as the southerners fired again and reloaded. He set the custom rifle down and picked up one of the .58 caliber smokepoles. He lined up the closest troopers in his sights as the man took aim at him as well. The trooper's pistol shot went high and shattered the glass window pane above him. Lieutenant Schmidt's shot connected with the corporal's left shoulder, nearly severing the man's arm before he tumbled out of the saddle.

The second shot from Private Smithson took down two men simultaneously—one shot high in the forehead and another on the gut. The heavy load of double ought buckshot worked as planned. "Did you see that, Lieutenant? I got me two fer one!"

Eric glanced over amid the noise and excitement to congratulate the young man on his marksmanship. "Nice shooting, Pri..."

His word were cut off when a Yankee pistol ball came through the open window and stuck the young man from Monroe Louisiana square in the temple. His head snapped over, his facial expression melted from obvious jubilation to a blankness that immediately reminded Eric of his father. The soldier slumped to the floor right before his eyes.

The sight steeled him—he turned to the empty whiskey barrel and grabbed up a pair of the Remington sixguns. Firing deliberately from either hand—one shot every second—he rained death and destruction down on the companies of cavalry.

Captain Humbolt didn't take long to realize that Shreveport, Louisiana was not going to be the ticket to fame and glory he had hoped to share with his college fraternity brothers over brandy. The carnage he had witnessed in the first few seconds scared him beyond words. "Ambush!" he yelled in a much higher than normal voice. "C Company...retreat!" He wheeled his mount around, dug his short spurs into the terrified horse's ribs and swatted it on the rump with the flat of his saber.

The company bugler brought his brass instrument to his lips but took a shot to the neck and tumbled to the blood-spattered street. The company commander continued east for a few yards through his oncoming troops before he caught sight of a couple of heavily laden wagons being driven across the roadway at the next intersection—effectively blocking it.

He reined his horse back viscously, and spun it around in pure panic. Humbolt beat his sword across the rump with his saber once again, but this time took little care about it—the flashing steel left streaks of crimson across it's coat.

Eric set the two empty revolvers back atop the barrel and grabbed up the last loaded long gun. He fired a shot at a fast moving soldier that had decided to make a break for it the west. Leaning out of the window as the man passed by close to the sidewalk—his lead was good—but in his haste, the shot was a tad low. The slow moving slug dug into the man's left side, passed through his pelvis and into the horse. The two tumbled from its impact and rolled up just past the entrance to the bar. Eric leaned the rifle against the window sill and turned around to the whiskey barrel one last time. Two of the Remington revolvers were already stashed butt forward in his belt holsters—he snatched up the other pair off the lid and ran downstairs to the bar, taking the steps two at a time.

He unlocked the front doors and swung them both open wide. Without even stopping to look first, he strode out into the street and stood like a man mountain in the melee. For a second, he just picked out nearby targets of opportunity—dropping soldiers from the saddle, one after the other, as they tried to reload. A couple of them tried to run him down or slash at him. He fired both pistols simultaneously at close range with great effect. When the two revolvers ran dry, he simply dropped them and went for the pair on his hips.

Captain Matson looked out the shattered front window of the millenary shop and marveled at the action. *My God...I have never seen such utter calmness under fire.* He stepped out of the front door after Eric passed by and wove his way though the carnage that was once Union cavalry. A few shots rang out at the ends of the street, where Confederate soldiers picked off those who had tried to break past the blocking wagons and teams.

A single Yankee rider was left mounted in the ambush kill zone. He was an officer who had changed directions a half dozen times and was frantic to escape at all costs. Matson watched curiously as Schmidt holstered his two sixguns and drew his saber.

Eric began to close the distance between himself and the lone rider. He stopped when the man pointed his saber at him and commenced a charge. A slight smile came across his face.

Captain Humbolt pushed his bloodied mount on in a last ditch effort to prevent his capture—his ego would accept nothing less. The rest of the Confederates had already reloaded and moved to a vantage point to watch the crazy lieutenant from Texas as he faced the Union officer. The Yankee holdout held his saber high as he galloped at the man in buckskins.

Eric held his saber high with his left hand wrapped firmly around his right one inside the guard. He was absolutely motionless as the rider thundered down on him.

Matson anxiously looked on as his apprehension grew. *No! Dammit! That is not the way I showed you...*He inhaled deeply to yell out a warning as the rider's arm cocked back and slashed down at the motionless man's head.

Eric pressed down on his toes at the last second, forcing his body to fall backwards, still holding his saber overhead. The Yankee was already committed to his swing and his blade went high as the big man rolled to his right. Eric stuck with blinding speed at the horse's right front leg. The muscles in both his forearms rippled as the heavy saber made solid contact, ringing out as it severed the horse's leg just below the knee. The horse stumbled badly and nosed over onto the street—sending its stunned rider sprawling.

"I'll be dammed," Matson said as Humbolt staggered to his feet.

Eric had already jumped up and was closing the distance between him and the Union captain. "Give it up, Yank. It's all over," he said as he walked up.

"Never, you southern scum..."

The lieutenant didn't even honor the verbal slight with a reply. He made a series of feints with his saber that the Union officer handily parried. Then he began a series of harder, faster blows that gave the Yankee much more trouble and staggered him back almost to the sidewalk.

Suddenly, Eric lowered his sword tip to his left and appeared to be getting winded as he was panting heavily.

Captain Matson watched with horror. *You were not ready, son...I told you that.*

Humbolt cocked his arm back and let go with a mighty crossing blow at his opponent's neck and was astounded when the big man easily rocked down and it passed over him. When the captain attempted to recover—using a backhand—he spotted too late the trap the younger man had set.

Eric's backhand slash rocketed up like rattlesnake striking. It caught the Union officer's forearm just above the wrist. The power and energy he gave to the Ames saber severed his opponent's hand as the razor sharp blade *pinged* once more.

Instinctively, Humbolt grabbed at the bloody stump to staunch the copious spurts of crimson. The rebel's blade flashed once again in the glow of the street lamps and buried itself to the hilt in his chest.

Eric grabbed the man's uniform collar and pulled him close as his opponent's knees bean to wobble. He spoke clearly and plainly, "DamnYankee...go home."

With a mighty shove, he pushed the dying man off the blade and stood there alone in the middle of the street as a series of cheers began to ring out from the victorious Confederates.

Scattered shots rang out from down by the wagon yard on the east end of Texas Street as the last of the raiders were either killed or captured. Captain Matson and a half dozen Confederates carefully checked the status of the Union soldiers lying in the roadway as terrified residents of Shreveport began to get themselves dressed and walk outside to see what had transpired downtown.

Colonel Bobby Don Smith and several of the Texas volunteers rode up from down by the river where they had supervised the entrapment of the Union cavalry and successfully engaged those who had tried to escape. The commander surveyed the devastation as the last of the severely wounded Yankee horses were put down with single pistol shots behind their ears.

"Marcus…by God it worked," Smith said as he swung out of the saddle and ground tied his horse. "Have you talked to Major Robinson and discussed our casualties?"

"No, sir. I believe he is just coming out of the dry goods store now. Looks as if they have at least one dead…or pretty badly wounded."

Smith glance back over his shoulder as three men carried a limp body out and lay it on the sidewalk. Another man in front of the next building was sporting a blood-soaked bandage on his thigh. "See that they get proper medical attention. Where is young Schmidt?…Suppose he gets the lion's share of the credit for this operation."

"He went back into the bar a couple minutes ago, Colonel. I have not had a opportunity to…" Matson turned to see the young lieutenant walk though the swinging doors with the body of a private in his arms. "Aw, dammit…There he is, sir… carrying out another casualty."

Eric knelt and gently laid the teenager on the street at their feet. He had tears in his eyes as he tried to make his report. "His name...was Bradley Smithson...Came from over Monroe way, just a couple day's ride east of here...Took out three of them Yanks before..."

Colonel Smith placed his hand on his shoulder. "He died a soldier's death, son...I wish I could say it got easier...losing one of our own...but I cannot lie to you. We shall make certain his people know that he died bravely."

"Thank you, sir. I would appreciate it if you extended me the honor to write a letter to his parents...I was with him when it happened."

"By all means..." He noted the fresh blood on the young man's buckskins. "Are you hurt, Eric?"

He looked down at his badly stained shirt front and sleeve, "Not mine, Colonel...Must have belonged to that Yankee captain. I have to collect my weapons, sir. If you two will excuse me." He turned and walked briskly back to the saloon.

Smith watched him as he strode away before Captain Matson spoke,

"Colonel, let me tell you what I saw..."

He began to recount the Lieutenant's actions leading up to the final saber duel with the recently departed Union commander of C Company. Other members of the Texas volunteers who had likewise witnessed the display of bravery under fire crowded around and added their comments as well.

By the time Eric made it back downstairs—laden down with an armful of long guns, extra paper cartridges—Major

Robinson and his troops from the Shreveport detachment had rounded up the last Union survivors and were herding them to a temporary stockade adjoining the Confederate headquarters.

The freshly commissioned young officer headed to talk his commanders as one of the Texas volunteers spoke up.

"Hey there, Lieutenant. Lemme give you a hand with all that there gear."

Eric held out his arms as the corporal and another private reached for the guns. "They all need cleaning and reloading…however, the double rifle stays with me."

"Anythin' you say, sir…We will get right to it."

They soldiers moved over into the light of the nearest street lamp and quickly pulled up the leather covers on their ammunition pouches and reloaded the three rifles. The double barreled shotgun, used so effectively by the late private, was handed off to another soldier who was similarly equipped.

Schmidt approached Colonel Smith as he continued to debrief with Matson. He grabbed his over-and-under rifle by the checkered pistol grip and rested the forestock back over his left shoulder as he looked down at Bobby Don.

"What got into you out here tonight, young man? Marcus tells me you danged near cleaned 'em all out, all by your lonesome."

A curious look came across Eric's face. "What do you mean, sir?…I just got…" He glanced back to Captain Matson who was also grinning like a jackass eating persimmons.

"Am I missing out on the joke?" he asked. "I do not understand, Colonel…We set the trap as planned, the Yankees came in and took the bait, hook line and sinker...We tore into them with all we had...Thought that what we were supposed to do."

Smith held up his hand. "Whoa there, Lieutenant. I am undoubtedly the happiest man in the whole brigade tonight. Your idea of an ambush has made it possible for us to do something even our brigade commander has, of late, been unable to accomplish...and that is to engage the enemy en mass and inflict heavy losses upon them."

"Initial count of enemy casualties is one hundred sixty-four dead, thirty-one wounded and almost a dozen captured...We lost four dead and another eight men wounded," Matson added.

Schmidt slowly shook his head. "I do not know what I expected...All this...all this death..." His voice trailed off as he watched a couple of soldiers from Louisiana drag a Union soldier's corpse to the side of the street. A buckboard, followed by a heavier freight wagon, were being driven down the street as other Confederates grabbed the vanquished soldiers by the hands and feet, swung them up over the sideboards and stacked their limp bodies like cordwood.

"It is a pitiful sight, indeed...Why could not they all have just stayed home and let us live in peace?" Eric asked.

"That is a question you will have to ask Mister Lincoln. He is the one who refused to accept the fact that the Southern States were no longer willing to live with the underhanded fiscal policies and legislation that favored the industrialized north," Matson replied.

"You should tell me about all that some time. I thought the war was supposed to be all about slavery..."

"Not at all," Smith said. "Not by a long shot."

"This cannot be all the Yankees that came into Texas and Louisiana. Surely they have some men left in reserve..." Schmidt observed.

Bobby Don exchanged a glance with Marcus. "Now that you bring up the matter, they certainly did not travel all the way down here without some sort of a supply train of their own."

"Not to mention cooks, mess tents and all the like. They have to be somewhere close by...I would imagine," Matson agreed.

"Of course," Colonel Smith agreed. "If we only knew where."

Eric's eyes narrowed in the dim light as he watched the last of the captives being herded into the local Confederate headquarters building. "Those Yankees we took as prisoners know where the rest of them are. And I know how to make them tell us." He turned without a word and began striding eastward toward the Confederate headquarters.

Smith and Matson watched him for a second, stunned by Eric's audacious actions. The colonel grabbed the junior officer by the sleeve.

"Come on, Marcus. I swear I do not have the foggiest notion as what that boy is up to now...but, by God, we at least have to go down and watch him."

Lieutenant Schmidt held the lamp high with his left hand as he eyed the Union prisoners being held in the windowless storeroom that had been converted into a temporary stockade. For their part, most of the vanquished soldiers looked askance at the man clad in blood-stained buckskins and refrained from making direct eye contact with him out of fear. He looked nothing like any real soldier they had ever faced—even though he wore a pair of Union issue sidearms and a Federal Cavalry officer's saber hung on his left hip.

Eric walked slowly past the line of men seated against the clapboard wall and came to a halt in front of a prisoner wearing corporal's stripes. Schmidt studied the man's face for a second, noticing the gaunt soldier had tobacco stains on his horseshoe shaped mustache. He had suffered some minor gunshot wound to the upper arm, but apparently the round had missed the bone, as he wore a bandage but no sling. "What is your name, mister?"

The Union soldier glanced nervously over at his compatriots but said nothing.

In a flash, Eric drew his sword, the blade hissing as it cleared the shiny steel scabbard. He brought the tip of the blood stained blade to rest a quarter inch from end of the prisoner's nose. "I asked you a question...I will have an answer. Now, then, let us try this again...what is your name?"

The prisoner swallowed as he looked cross-eyed at the saber's menacing blade. Even in the lamp's flickering yellow glow, he could not miss seeing the blood on it. "Eldon Evans, Corporal."

"On you feet, Corporal. You and I are going to have us a little talk."

Evans pressed his back hard against the wooden wall as he pushed himself to his feet. He stood only five feet eight inches tall and the fearsome man with the sword was a good eight inches taller, even before the uncreased hat was taken into consideration. The corporal could feel his heart pounding in his chest.

"Put your hands up and do not try anything stupid," Schmidt said.

Eldon shook his head vigorously. "Was not plannin' on it, mister...Honest."

"You will live longer if you do not. Out the door and into the hallway with you."

The prisoner nodded and moved that direction past a pair of armed Confederate guards. Following Eric's directions he walked to Major Robinson's private office where Matson and Smith were waiting, along with local detachment commander.

"Have a seat," Eric ordered. "You can put your hands down now."

Eldon quickly complied, but looked around nervously at the four men.

"Where are you from, Corporal?"

"I do not have to answer that. They said all I have to give is my name and rank."

Eric smiled. "That is what they told you back in Toledo? According to the map, Ohio is a long way from here, would you not agree?"

The mention of Toledo sent a shiver through Evans' spine. *How in tarnation did they know I am from there?* He reacted visibly to the question, but said nothing.

"Never been there myself," Eric continued. "Although I did meet a few men from up that way recently." He smiled as he studied the Yankee prisoner for any sign of a personal connection. " Ever recall anyone named Benjamin Blaylock or a private named Wilson?...Does the name Jonesie ring a bell with you?"

"A lot of people have names like that...Could be people I know from back home, but I doubt it."

"I suppose you are right...Like I said before, I never have been up to Ohio. How big a town is that Toledo, anyhow?"

"It is real big. I 'spect it must be...hold on! I told you I do not have to give you nothin' but my name and rank."

"Of course, Corporal Evans from Toledo...Maybe you know another man from up that way. He kinda favored you with that mustache of yours. Let's see...Smither's was his name... Harlen Smithers. He was a sergeant as I recall, and his men called him Smitty...Ever run into him?"

"Of course...everybody in the whole company knows Smitty." Evans looked hard at the man in buckskins. *Who the hell is this guy and how does he know so much about our outfit?* "How is it you came to know all them folks? You some kind of spy or somethin'? Ain't wearing no kind of uniform..."

"Lieutenant Schmidt is an officer in the service of the Confederacy. His new uniform was being tailored for him

152

before we were ordered to leave camp abruptly on this assignment," Matson interjected.

Evans' eyes darted from Matson to the others and then back to Schmidt. Eric only smiled, confusing the captive even more.

"So, tell me, Lieutenant…when did you come to meet those men you named?"

"I met all those friends of yours just this past week."

"And where are they now?"

"Oh, they are still back there in east Texas," Eric replied. He casually reached around and casually pulled the stag handled knife from its sheath and began to nonchalantly clean his fingernails.

Colonel Smith watched on as a cloud came over Eric's face for a second, and then quickly dissipated. *My God…This young man has got some incredible control on his emotions, I will grant you that.*

The prisoner studied the unique pattern of the ridges in the stag grips. *Jesus, that there is Smitty's knife! How did this jasper come to have hold of it? He would not have taken anything for it.* Finally, after a couple minutes of silence he could not hold his curiosity and longer. "How did you come by that knife? I know you did not buy it from him."

"Funny you should ask, Eldon…Let me tell you the story 'bout that. Think you might find it…interesting."

Several minutes later, Eric had finished recounting how he came to trail all the Yankees involved in the murder of his parents and sister. Major Robinson had not heard the entire tale before, at least not in gory detail and almost lost his dinner. Corporal Evans stomach churned but he was able to re-swallow his last meager meal.

Schmidt leaned closer to the prisoner as his eyes narrowed once again. The affable Texas smile was nowhere to be found and Evans felt a chill that had nothing to do with the springtime temperatures.

"So, you see, Eldon that is why you have to make a choice…It is rather a simple one at that. You talk to me, and tell me where your reserves are encamped, or…" He paused and studied the eight inch blade in the light for a few seconds. "…you get to die a long, slow…painful death by Smitty's pride and joy…Your choice."

The blood ran out of Evan's face, his eyes crossed and he felt as if he were going to faint. He glanced at the senior officers and was not reassured in the least by their stony silence. "You cain't let him do this to me! It ain't right!"

Bobby Don nodded his agreement. "I know son…but believe it or not, our the battalion commander has placed him in charge of this whole Shreveport operation. I am afraid that I cannot lift a finger to help you…Suggest you tell him everything he wants to know."

Matson leaned in closer and whispered, "Would not take too long in making your decision if I were you, Corporal. I saw what he did to your company commander out there with his saber…Took his arm off with one stoke and ran him all the way through with another. That man there…whoo boy…he is 'bout as close to a being a wildcat if I ever saw one."

Evan's breath became shallow and more rapid. He licked his parched lips as visions of getting skinned alive—or worse—raced across his mind. One last look into the icy blue eyes of the man in bloody buckskins convinced him the threat was no bluff. "What is it you all want to know?"

***

CHAPTER NINE

WOODS NORTH OF SHREVEPORT

It was almost dawn when the teams pulling the supply train turned off the main road to the Indian Territory onto an infrequently used trail as they approached the Union encampment. Behind the wagons were columns of cavalry, all at a walk. The moon had just set, leaving little but starlight for the teamsters to use for navigation.

The sleepy sentry stepped into the rutted wagon tracks of the secondary roadway and brought his weapon to port arms as he issued the prescribed challenge, "Halt! Who goes there? Advance and be recognized."

A soldier clad in the uniform on a Union private held the reins of the first wagon. He spat out a stream of tobacco juice and said the one word countersign the Yankees had briefed before the raid on the Confederate depot, "Abraham…Now get the hell out of the way…We got done all the food we wuz sent after."

The sentry grinned and thought about how good the morning breakfast was going taste. He stepped back to the edge of the road and watched as the first wagon creaked past. He never heard the man walk up behind him or felt the steel rifle buttplate that crashed into the back of his head with a sickening thud—he slumped forward in a heap.

Eric reached down and lifted the body out of the path on the next wagon. He heaved it into the deeper grass lining the trail, retrieved the man's weapon and handed it up to one of the soldiers crouching down in back of the freight wagon. His face and hands had been darkened by the use of a copious amount of crushed charcoal mixed with lard. He turned quickly to lead a squad toward the Union cook fires already burning in the distance.

On the east side of the camp, a master sergeant—who had previously served in the US cavalry before hostilities broke out between the states—led a similar patrol silently taking out a series of Union sentries with clubs and knives. Behind him, a company of mounted Confederate cavalry, led by Major Robinson from Shreveport moved into position and waited.

The first orange rays of the breaking dawn began to radiate across a magenta sky, quickly turning the eastern horizon a myriad of colors from peach to apricot. Songbirds greeted the day with a chorus of mating calls as they regularly did in mid-spring.

Inside a dingy white cotton pup-tent, a young Union private awoke to answer a call of nature. He threw off the blue woolen blanket from the canvas sleeping pad and slipped into his black cavalry boots—not even bothering to pull on his uniform pants over his cotton knee-length night shirt. Walking quickly to the slit trench dug alongside a head-high row of hemlock brush, he fumbled with the excess material of the undergarment for a second.

"Whew," he said when he finally found relief for his condition. Suddenly, he noticed a pair of white eyes looking at him from the brush. He squinted in the scant light to make out a human form and then the dark outline of a almost jet black face.

"What are you lookin' at, darky?" he demanded.

In the blink of an eye, an twenty-seven inch cutlass style bayonet, affixed to an .577 Cal. Enfield rifle flashed across the foot wide trench and ripped into his torso. The fatal gash through his liver sent a searing wave of pain through the unprepared trooper—his dying scream echoed throughout the camp.

From the east and west, bugles sounded the charge as the teamsters slapped their reins at the horses patiently waiting in their traces. The cavalry had been dispersed in two tight semicircles, with ground skirmishers firing from covered positions to the north and south.

Robinson's mounted men hollered out their frightening rebel yells when the attack commenced, quickly dropping

startled Union soldiers with deadly pistol shots as they emerged from their tents. Many Yanks never even made to it their rifles, stacked in neat pyramids a few yards from their canvas abodes.
Others fumbled for a second trying to disconnect the stacking swivels in the pre-dawn light. In that precious time, the rebels closed in and fired at point blank range, often leaving the residue of a smoky powder burn surrounding a bullet hole in the face of an unprepared trooper.

The wagons loaded with heavily armed riflemen—thanks to the hundreds of US Army issue carbines captured in the earlier ambush—careened though the camp, pouring accurate close-range fire at the panicked cooks and any troops that made it out of their tent.

A gray pall of sulfurous black powder smoke hung over the encampment as the senior Union officer raised up a white towel on his saber. He held up both his hands as he stood thunderstruck from the intensity of the surprise attack. One of the Confederate cavalry NCOs noticed the gesture from the older man clad in a nightshirt and striped uniform pants and yelled out in a loud southern accent,

"Cease fire, boys! They give up!"

It took several seconds for the word to get passed down as men on both sides continue to fight in the heat of the brief battle. Many of the Confederate mounted troops had exhausted their handguns and reverted to saber, slashing at targets of opportunity with deadly effect. Likewise, the skirmishers relied on their bayonets and rifle butts after their revolvers ran dry.

Calls repeating the cease fire order finally ended the melee. Lt. Colonel Smith reined up to the NCO who was holding the Union commander at gunpoint. He returned his saber to its scabbard, stepped from the saddle. He took a moment to look around at the carnage his men and those of the local Louisiana detachment had inflicted. Smith slipped his right off-white leather gauntlet off as he approached the officer who had offered to surrender. Saluting, he said, "You can put your hands down, sir…I take it you are the man in charge."

He nodded, returned the salute as he lowered his hands and tossed the towel off the tip of the blade. "Otis Hatfield, Colonel, US Army," the bearded man said in a firm voice. "You, sir, have taken us quite by surprise and I respectfully request you accept the surrender of my unit under the rules of war." He laid the saber's blade across his open left palm and proffered it to Smith.

Bobby Don received the saber with his left hand and extended his right. "On behalf of the Confederacy and the men of the Fighting Seventh, I accept your surrender, sir. Your men fought honorably and you, sir, made a wise decision to spare their lives. I will so note it in my report."

"Thank you, sir. May I have the name of my esteemed adversary?" replied the obviously relieved Union officer.

"Of course, sir…I am Lieutenant Colonel Bobby Don Smith, from Nacogdoches, Texas."

Eric stepped up from the shadows to witness the transfer. It reminded him of what must have happened following much larger famous battles such as Waterloo, where Napoleon was defeated by Wellington.

Smith noticed Eric's presence. He grinned and motioned him closer. "I would be remiss if I did not introduce my new executive officer, Captain Eric Schmidt." He handed the captured saber to the young man in black face. "This victory is yours, son. You earned it."

He took possession of the saber as he noted the astonished expression on Hatfield's face. *Captain? Did he say Captain? What in the world is an executive officer?* "Thank you, sir. I shall put it with the others I have collected."

The Union prisoner of war eyeballed Schmidt closely from head to toe, not remembering ever seeing a fighting man that looked quite like him. He finally turned back to Smith. "Now, sir…with your permission, I would like to see to my dead and wounded."

"Absolutely, Colonel Hatfield…Captain Schmidt, escort this gentleman to his tent to allow him the opportunity to get properly dressed. Then I need you to assist him in making the necessary arrangements…I would like to have this camp packed up and ready to move out no later than ten o'clock."

He took another look down the line of tents at the dead sprawling in their grotesque final poses and sighed. "Sergeant Major, collect all the enemy's weapons. Assign prisoners to a burial detail as needed."

The burly NCO snapped a crisp salute. "As you wish, sir. Jenkins…Anderson, you two are with me." He and his chosen team moved out on foot.

Several of the Confederate cavalry dismounted to help segregate the barefooted survivors of the dawn raid. With picks and shovels, the Union solders set about the solemn task of laying their slain comrades to rest in shallow graves.

Several hours later, the last red dirt mound was patted down smoothly and one of the Confederate corporals—a lay preacher—spoke the appropriate words over the Union fallen.

Two Confederates—one a sergeant from Texas and another a private from Louisiana—had died from gunshots suffered in the engagement. They were placed into a wagon once the empty boxes were removed. Another pair of seriously wounded rebels rode in the same freight wagon bed, but a handful of less seriously injured men chose to ride back to town on their own horses.

Major Matson, also promoted on the spot by Lt. Colonel Smith, supervised the binding of the prisoner's hands using short lengths of cotton rope. They were allowed to ride mounted, rather than being jammed together in the freight wagons, but their reins were tied back to a saddle ring and the horse's lead ropes were cleverly tied to a longer one that created, in effect, a walking remuda.

"Do not get it into your head that escape is a possibility," Matson said in a booming voice. "These scatterguns on either side of you will cut you down before you get twenty yards…and the Colonel had assured me that we will not stop to bury anyone shot while trying to escape…Do I make myself clear?"

162

The men grumbled an acknowledgment as the teamsters up ahead snapped their ribbons to begin the journey back to town.

Eric was mounted again on his favorite buckskin horse. Using only slight pressure from his knees, he gently urged Bucky into a slow walk. He used a white cotton handkerchief he had appropriated from the kit of one of the deceased union troops to wipe away the black charcoal dust and lard. It quickly became a lost cause as the black streaks of camouflage coating fouled every inch of the cloth.

Marcus rode up beside him and smiled at the sight. The younger man's forehead checks and neck were relatively clean, but his eyes were both still surrounded by black. Matson reached into his tunic and retrieved a relatively clean kerchief.

"I know you cannot tell without a mirror, but you look as though some prize fighter gave you two monster shiners."

"I thought my idea to darken our faces was a good one. Now I am not so sure."

"The notion was sound...you and the boys made it into camp undetected did you not? Raccoon eyes are a small price to pay, I would wager."

Eric nodded and took another swipe at his eyelids. The cloth streaked black again. He turned in the saddle to face the major. "How is this?"

"Still a little under your left eye," he replied as he pointed at the smudge.

"Thanks." Eric rode silently for a couple minutes after he wiped himself clean. Fatigue was definitely setting in on both

163

men as neither had slept at all. "Marcus, can I ask you a question?"

"Why yes, of course. That is how we learn."

"Uh, I noticed back there after the Yanks surrendered that the Colonels were all...well, all gentlemanly acting. I am not sure what am trying to say, but they acted like they were trying to be nice to each other and it rather surprised me."

"I think what you witnessed was called respect...not being nice. You have not been a member of the profession of arms...as we call ourselves...for a very long time, have you?"

"No...just a few days...But, you already knew that."

"I did...Being a career military man is not based on personal revenge or hatred...rather a desire to do what is right to protect the society as a whole...Do you see where I am going with this?"

"I am not sure I understand..."

"War is a nasty, violent business that can bring out the absolute worst in a person." Marcus paused for a second to allow his words to sink in. "However, when the shooting stops, and the battle is over, we must try to remember what our civilization is all about...why we were fighting in the first place...That is why Colonel Smith treated the Yankee commander with respect. In other words, he did it so that he could respect himself after killing all those young soldiers."

"So what you are saying is that he did not kill them because he hated them, but because he felt it was his duty?"

"Right...Now, sometimes in the heat of battle, a man's emotions can get away from him...whether it is fear, excitement or some primordial passion that is in play, it can be somewhat hard to differentiate those feelings from hatred...But one thing I want you to remember...Someday, this war, like all wars, will be over...I cannot tell you who will be on the winning side, only that it will be over. And at that time, those of us who survived will be required to lay down our arms and learn to live side-by-side with those who felt differently."

Eric thought for a few minutes about what his friend had said. He pulled the cork from his canteen and took a swallow of the strong black coffee he had filled it with before he and the others had left Shreveport. The brew had long since cooled off but still had the caffeine kick he needed to stay awake. He wiped the dribble off his chin with the back of his gloved hand, and then replaced the cork and tamped it tight. "Marcus, do you think I was wrong to threaten that prisoner like I did?"

The major smiled before he answered. "As the Machiavellian precept goes...the end justifies the means. It is all covered in another one of those books I want you to read...Do you really think that the Colonel and I would have allowed you to skin that Yankee alive?"

Eric hung his head slightly and shook it. "No...Suppose not...but I did not know it that at the time."

"Neither did that Yankee...I am sure you took ten years off his life, at least. We went along with the show to see what he would tell us. You believed you would skin 'im...and so did he. We certainly did not want to leave a capable Union force roaming free around our territory."

"Neither did I...But, now...now, I am a little ashamed at how I acted, looking back at it. I have to say I was not raised like that...My mother would have been mortified."

"People in wartime do things that they normally would never even consider possible. It is all part of the terrible tragedy that is war." Marcus turned around and took a look at the grim faces of the prisoners they had taken in the raid. "Those boys back there are very likely the victims of geography as well as you...God, I wish Lincoln would have allowed us the opportunity to go our way in peace. But there is no turning back now...too much blood has already been..."

"What is going to happen to these prisoners now?"

"I imagine that they will be shipped down to New Orleans, or maybe, even over to one of the bigger prison camps over in Georgia or Alabama. They will sit out the war and be sent home once a peace treaty is signed."

"I imagine that is preferable to being killed on the battlefield."

"That it is...It will be interesting to see where we get sent next. Colonel Smith will write up a report detailing the particulars of the engagement and send a dispatcher back to Texas. I cannot see the division staying in Longview for longer than is needed to whip the new volunteers into shape."

"The others who joined up in a fit of patriotic fever may have a rude awakening in store for them."

"That, my young friend is true...War changes men. Some for the better...some for the worst. None come out the same."

Matson stared of into the distance as if he was looking at something at least a thousand yards away.

Eric glanced over at his friend a few more times as they rode side-by-side in silence. He had never seen exactly the same kind of curious blank expression on a man's face. It was as if some of Matson's life force had been somehow lost overnight. Both men were understandably fatigued, but that didn't account for what he sensed intuitively. *This business of making war is a lot more complicated than I thought.*

Two hours later, the slow moving procession reached the main streets of Shreveport. Curious town folks lined Texas Street where workmen had boarded over the windows shattered by gunfire during the ill-fated late-night raid. They glared at the prisoners as the Confederates marched them into a nearby cotton warehouse for holding.

Eric tied Bucky to the hitching post outside the Le Pavilion hotel and loosened the cinch. He unstrapped his saddle bags, tossed them over his shoulder and then patted his horse on the neck while he slipped the double rifle out of the well-worn scabbard. "I'll be back to get you fed once I get myself some place to wash up and bed down...Do not go anywhere, you hear?"

He trudged wearily up the two broad steps into the lobby and glanced around at the well dressed patrons who cast disapproving glances at the filthy and bone-tired fighting man. He looked around the room until he spotted the balding man behind the desk. *That must the clerk the major was talking about.*

Laying the rifle on the counter, Eric spoke up, "Major Robinson told me he made arrangements with you for our accommodation."

The clerk shook his head. "Sorry, but we are all full up. Officers of the Confederacy have been assigned all our spare rooms."

"That would be me...I am Captain Schmidt...Eric Schmidt. I see my name is already written in the ledger." He pointed at the large hard-bound book lying open on the polished oak counter.

The clerk didn't look as if he believed him, but noted the dried blood covering most of the man's fringed leather shirt. He decided quickly to accede to the request for a room. "Yes, sir...room 304. First room on your left from the stairwell." He swallowed nervously. "Will the gentleman be requiring a bath this afternoon?"

"Absolutely...May I inquire as to a laundry as well? And I shall need someone to stable my horse...Big buckskin tied out front."

"Certainly, sir." He turned around and reached for a skeleton key nestled in a marked cubbyhole matching the room number. "I will send a boy up to notify you when the bath is ready, sir. We have laundry service as well...I shall have the bellman take care of your horse right away."

"Appreciate it, mister," he replied as he took the hold of the key.

He walked slowly toward the stairs. When he arrived at room 304, he leaned the double barreled rifle against the flocked wallpaper as he slipped the key into the polished brass lockplate and turned it.

The door swung open to reveal a brightly lit room with two six foot tall windows that allowed the afternoon sun to stream in past lace curtains. *Whoa. Never would have guessed this place was so fancy.* A four-poster mahogany *rice tester* bed dominated the room. Eric marveled at the well executed carvings in the dark wood. A pair of matching tall night stands, each with a small crystal candelabra flanked the raised headboard. The bed itself had four down-filled pillows with an ivory colored duvet atop the high tread count sheets. *Man, oh man. Mama would have really liked this place.* Her smiling face flashed through his mind for a couple seconds, but the pain of her loss was too intense—he pursed his lips and willed it away as tears rimmed his eyes.

Looking around, he spotted a fancy chest and armoire beside a marble-topped wash basin. A matching ceramic pitcher of water was already filled and waiting for the room's guests. He laid his saddle bags atop the satinwood chest and opened one of the two large pouches. Pulling the flap back he reached in and grabbed the pairs of canvas pants and hand-sewn white cotton shirts he had packed the night he left home. He slipped the pants into the top drawer of the chest and stacked them neatly. The shirts, he hung in the armoire.

Eric unfastened the saber hanger followed by the heavy gunbelt and placed them beside his saddle bags. Lastly, he pulled the bloodstained neckerchief and leather shirt over his head and laid them across the back of the single chair in the room. It was a rather dainty looking one of obvious French design—the slender cabriole legs were made of a hardwood that Eric identified as walnut.

He carefully sat down on the elegantly embroidered seat and was greatly relieved it supported his weight. Using one of the cavalry boot's heels as a blocking wedge, he pushed the other one off—spurs and all—and let it fall to the hardwood floor. *That feels better.* He flexed his toes in his dirty socks and marveled at the amount of trail dust that had collected on his trousers in the thirty-six hours since he left the Confederate wagon train back in east Texas. It took a lot more work to get the remaining boot off without assistance or the use of a boot tree. He set back up, taking care not to put too much aft pressure on the chair and then finally stood erect and stretched the toes wide on both feet.

Slipping the leather galluses off his shoulders, he removed his trousers and laid them on top of his filthy shirt before he unfastened the tabs from the eight buttons sewn fore and aft onto the waistband. Suddenly, there was a knock at the door.

"Mister Schmidt, sir, your bath is ready," came a young black man's voice from beyond.

"I shall be but a minute," he replied as he reached for the pants in the top drawer.

"Sir, I has the bathrobe and slippers for you to wear to the bathhouse in my hands."

It took a couple of seconds for Eric to understand what the man had intended for him to do. He had never stayed in a fancy hotel, although he and his family did spend a night in a Tyler boarding house after a friend's wedding once. He opened the door part-way to see a fourteen year old boy dressed in a uniform much like the hotel porter had worn downstairs—a black pair of pants with a matching vest over a starched white shirt. The young boy held out the robe and fabric slippers for him. Over his arm was folded a green cotton sack with a rope closure on one end. He smiled when he saw Eric eyeing the sack.

"Mister, they say you need some clothes laundered. If'n you wants, you can puts 'em in the sack and I be totin' 'em down there for ya."

"I understand now. This is my first visit to Shreveport...I am a little new to all this."

"Yessir...Takes your time. If'n you got boots to polish, I do a good job on them my own self, sir. They be ready when you gets through wit the bath."

Eric took the items and closed the door. He shimmied out of the long underwear tops and bottoms and chunked them into the laundry sack. Once he had checked his pants pockets for any personal items, he stuffed them and the rest of his dirty items in as well. He slipped into the long bath robe, wrapped one side over the other and tied off the sash to hold it. He grabbed up his boots and headed for the door.

The bath house was segregated for men and women. Eric stepped into a high-backed brass tub filled with very warm clear

171

water. A nearby stand was placed so that the long-handled bristle brush and bar of lye soap was in easy reach. He lay back and allowed the hot water to melt away the soreness from three days in the saddle. After a while, he made good use of the brush, some scented lye soap and a small washcloth to take away the grit and grime of the previous few days.

After he finished the bath, the lone attendant's offer to shave him was unexpected. However he slipped the robe back on and sat back in the barber chair and, for the first time in his life—someone else shaved his face.

Once he had returned to his room, the decision to go to sleep or get something to eat was a toss-up. He finally decided his empty stomach was rumbling such that it would interfere with his desire to sleep. He dressed with a clean pair of khaki colored canvas duck pants and a high-collared white cotton shirt. Eric took the only clean cravat he owned, a shiny black one, and tied it into a bow in the mirror over the wash basin. *Looks like I am ready for church.*

He had noticed that many of the townspeople dressed much differently that they had back in Tyler. He placed the flat-brimmed hat on his head, but frowned at the reflection of the ragged bullet hole in the looking glass. Besides, the hat was very stained from perspiration and trail dust. He remembered the deerskin money pouch he had left stashed in the saddle bags. *Ain't broke...Least not yet. Suppose I could buy a new one.* He pulled the pouch out of the bag and stuffed it into his pants. Almost as an afterthought, he grabbed the gunbelt and strapped it on. For several days, he had not gone without being armed and although it was a new addition to his wardrobe, he felt somewhat naked without it. Eric adjusted the sheath knife back behind his right hip, walked out and locked the door.

He strode quickly across the lobby of the bustling hotel, gathering admiring glances from the women folk and jealous looks from the men. His blue eyes sparkled once again with the renewed energy from his bath, and he managed to smile as he nodded to a couple young women he passed.

"Evening ladies."

"Same to you, sir," the braver of the two replied.

The more reserved one merely tittered and tugged at her friend's sleeve.

"Have you a place nearby you would recommend for dinner?" he asked the desk clerk.

"Antoine's is west on Texas Street only two door's down, Mister Schmidt. It specializes in fresh fish, but does an excellent job with steaks."

"Many thanks," he replied. "Oh, by the way…where can a man buy himself a new hat?"

Marcus waved Eric over to join him and the other senior officers who had just set down for drinks before dinner.

"You clean up well, pilgrim."

"Thank you, Major. I feel better after washing up."

Colonel Smith offered him a seat next to him. "Glad you could join us. We all got the same recommendation from the hotel…either it is really good or he gets a kickback. We'll find out soon enough."

"Kickback?"

The others laughed. "Finder's fee…uh, a percentage of the gross."

Eric's face relayed his confusion as he took a seat.

"Never mind…Be happy such shenanigans never crossed your path," Matson added. "Can I buy you a drink?"

"They charge for a glass of water?"

Again, the others began to laugh, only slightly louder the second time.

Marcus placed his hand on the young man's shoulder. "I see we have a true neophyte on our hands. 'Buy you a drink' generally refers to an alcoholic beverage of some form. Have you a preference?"

Eric shook his head. "Papa made some blackberry wine one time…We made some muscadine grape wine several years ago, but it was not really all that good…as I remember."

"How old were you then?" Bobby Don asked.

"Twelve?"

"No wonder…a person's tastes changes as they get older. Do not think I would have even appreciated a good Bordeaux at that age. May I interest you in a bourbon, rum or perhaps some Scotch?"

Eric shrugged.

"Bring this young man some of Kentucky's finest," Marcus called over to the waiter.

When it arrived—an amber liquid an inch deep in a shot glass—Eric eyed it suspiciously. He lifted it to his lips and inhaled the raw fumes of the lightly-aged sour-mash whiskey. "Whew...Ya'll really drink this on purpose? Kinda reminds me of turpentine."

"Sure we do, son. Rare back and toss it down. The taste will grow on you," Smith assured him.

Eric inhaled deeply and then let it out before he glanced at the other officers seated around him. All eyes were upon him, as he brought the shot glass to his lips and tossed the 100 proof bourbon down. He swallowed and gasped three times to try to catch his breath. His eyes watered as he pointed to Matson. "Son of a..."

"Smooth, huh?" Matson said as he smiled broadly.

"Gun," Eric finally croaked out.

"Maybe we better start you out on beer," Bobby Don said as he patted him on the back. "Do not want to kill off my Executive Officer on the first night...That would not do at all."

***

CHAPTER TEN

SHREVEPORT, LOUISIANA

Dinner was almost ready to be served to the weary officers when a middle-aged man entered the front door of the restaurant accompanied by an elegantly dressed young woman. She was obviously much younger than he, her flaming red hair and sea green eyes caught the attention of all the men who gazed upon her, regardless of their marital status. The Maître d' greeted the couple warmly and escorted them to a table only a few feet from were Eric and his senior commanders were dining.

The young Texan's jaw hung slightly slack as he watched the head waiter pull out the chair and seat the young lady. Marcus immediately noted the lad was obviously transfixed. He subtly elbowed Major Robinson and nodded first toward Eric and then at the radiant young woman.

"I believe we have witnessed a prime example of the *goddess effect* in action…would you not agree, Joe?"

"That we have, Marcus…that we have," he said with a grin.

"Pray tell, that is not an case of robbin' the cradle, is it?"

"Oh, no," Joseph replied. "That gentleman is her doting father. Her mother, Elouise…God rest her soul…died in childbirth. Angelina takes after her quiet remarkably…I am told. There is a painting in the mansion's parlor of the lady and those who have seen it say there is no discernible difference."

A curious look came to Matson's face. "Mansion?"

Robinson nodded as he continued to look at Eric. "Ya'll are not from 'round here…I keep forgettin'…Mister Augustin LeBlanc owns over three thousand acres of cotton fields…south of town along the Red River…prime bottom land…They are quite well-to-do, I can assure you."

Marcus leaned back in his chair and blew a giant smoke ring from his imported Cuban cigar. It floated lazily upward before gradually dissipating in the haze. He then turned back to the local army commander and whispered, "Do you know him well enough to finagle an introduction for our illustrious young Executive Officer?"

"Absolutely, sir. I would think he would be proud to meet young Schmidt here. After all, he did engineer a tremendous victory for us against a much larger force and that is definitely in the interest of our local businessmen such as the esteemed Mister LeBlanc." He slid his chair back, stood up and then leaned over speak. "Excuse me gentlemen, I shall return shortly."

A waiter approached the men and offered a freshly prepared yeast roll to each of them. All gladly accepted and slathered the golden baked goods with butter from a small china bowl set near each place setting.

"There is honey in the center of the table...if anyone cares for it," Bobby Don announced.

"I believe I will," Marcus replied.

"This place is living up to its reputation, I would say," Eric commented as his attention was momentarily diverted from the nearby table.

Joe approached the couple and formally reintroduced himself. "Mister LeBlanc, I am Major Joseph Robinson, commander of the local army detachment here in Shreveport."

LeBlanc—dressed in a fancy linen frock coat with a ruffled silk shirt underneath—smiled up at him. "Good evening, sir. It is a pleasure to see you again...My congratulations on your victory. It would appear we are deeply in your debt...The reports I have heard say we were badly outnumbered by the Yankee invaders."

He nodded. "That is true, sir. We were most fortunate to have had a number of heroic volunteers from the great state of Texas to come to our aid...If you would permit me, I would very much like to introduce few of them so that you may personally convey your gratitude. They lost some fine young men defending our homes and businesses in the process...as did we."

"By all means, sir…I would love to shake the hands of those brave soldiers."

Robinson turned around smartly and returned to his table. "Gentlemen, one of Louisiana's finest citizen's would like the honor of meeting the men who assisted us in the glorious defeat of the Yankee interlopers…"

Eric looked up from taking a bite of his roll. A small golden drop of fresh honey dribbled down his chin. "Huh?"

"Wipe your face, young man. Time to meet the goddess," Marcus said with a huge grin.

"What?"

The three Texans stood straight and tall and Robinson made the introductions. He waited until it was Eric's turn before he really poured out the flowery expressions. "And lastly, it is my great pleasure to introduce Captain Eric Schmidt, Executive Officer of the battalion and architect of both the entrapment maneuver and the surprise attack early this morning that so soundly defeated the Yankee invading forces in northern Louisiana."

Eric's face reddened slightly as the introduction brought a round of applause from other patrons seated nearby.

Angelina gazed up at him admiringly, smiled and then batted her green eyes—slightly increasing his discomfort and embarrassment even more.

He sheepishly grinned and nodded his acknowledgment to the other diners before his eyes were drawn inexorably back to hers. *I cannot believe I actually got to meet this magnificent young woman.*

179

"Proud to make your acquaintance, Captain," LeBlanc said as he extended his hand to the much taller man. "To tell you the truth...I did not think you were a soldier...You being so young and not wearing a uniform like your compatriots."

"I understand completely, sir. I just recently joined up and my uniform was not ready before we departed on this mission."

"I see."

"You look quite familiar, Captain Schmidt. Have I perchance seen you somewhere before?" Angelina asked demurely.

"Yes ma'am. That is entirely possible...I was dressed in mufti so as to not attract attention to myself when I arrived late yesterday afternoon. I distinctly remember seeing you and your father in a buggy behind a coal-black Standardbred...that emerald dress bought out the color of your eyes very nicely, if you do not mind my saying so."

It was her turn to blush. She glanced nervously over at her father, who simply smiled as he nodded his head. He was well accustomed to the affect her beauty had on suitors.

"A man with a sharp eye for detail...Colonel, I see why you chose this one as an Executive Officer. He would be a valued asset to any organization."

"Thank you, sir. It was our distinct pleasure to meet you and your daughter. Now, if you will excuse us, we shall retire to our table and allow you to dine in peace."

Augustin held up his index finger. "Sir, I would appreciate the opportunity to discuss your military endeavors in a more private setting...Would the four of you do my daughter and I the honor in joining us for dinner tomorrow night at our home...if that is not imposing on your good nature?"

Bobby Don bowed slightly and smiled. "Mister LeBlanc, we shall look forward to it. What time shall we call?"

"Six o'clock would be perfect. We could watch the sun set from the verandah and get to know one another better."

"Until then, sir...Miss LeBlanc." Smith and the others nodded politely and returned to their table.

Eric whispered to Marcus. "She is absolutely the most gorgeous woman I have ever laid eyes on. And now we are invited to dinner with her and her father...I do not have even a coat to wear..."

"Calm down, there. I am certain Joe here knows a tailor who can suitably alter a jacket before tomorrow night...You still have some money left over from the horses and gear you sold, do you not?"

He nodded as the waiters brought out the first course, a tomato bisque in fine china bowls and began to place them in front of the four men.

"Just sit back and watch, Eric. We will show you how a gentleman dines. You do want to be able to make a favorable impression on the young lady?"

"Uh huh."

"Sit up straight and pay attention. This soup is the first course and should be partaken slowly as the main course is being prepared..."

Four riders approached the elegant French style mansion on a private road lined with mature red oak trees forming a canopy. Several wood frame houses and what appeared to be warehouses were visible off the southwest. Beyond those were flat plowed fields, where Eric noted a half dozen mules—each pulling a single moldboard plow—were turning under the stubble of the previous fall's bountiful harvest of cotton. In closer was six acres of garden that helped keep the family and plantation workers fed.

As they neared the first major building—the stables—a young black man dressed sharply in dark colored pants and a crisp white cotton shirt rose from his seat on a bench set near the side of the building. He approached them with a welcoming smile as they reined to a halt.

"Welcome to the Chateau LeBlanc, gentlemen. I will see to your horses. Please follow the path on the right to the side gate. Someone will meet you there to escort you to the main house."

"Thank you, young man," Colonel Smith responded as he stepped easily out of the saddle and handed him the reins.

"Nice place they have here," Marcus remarked as he gazed at the huge paddocks connected to the stable itself. Four sleek Standardbreds were in the first enclosure, a half dozen Tennessee Walking horses occupied the second and a bevy of draft horses and mules milled about in the far one.

"I have never seen the like," Eric said as they turned toward the gravel path.

Another black man, much older that the first—dressed in white cotton pants and a matching loose fitting top—was

182

herding a small flock of sheep from the well manicured, fenced lawn into an adjoining pasture on the far side of the house. He cajoled the fleecy four legged critters though the gate and closed it.

A third man in a much more formal attire—a black morning coat over a cream colored shirt and striped cravat—smiled broadly as he swung open the gate under the gracefully curved wooden arch. "Pleased to have you all join us this evening. Mister LeBlanc has been anxiously awaiting your arrival." He closed the gate behind them and walked briskly to lead them down a hand-laid red brick sidewalk that gracefully wound its way around the three story home.

Eric's eyes grew wide as he tried to gauge the square footage. At over six thousand feet, it dwarfed the home his father had built back in Texas. The design was French Empire with a mansard roof, common in the former colony bought by President Jefferson only six decades earlier. They walked to the portico on the west side and climbed the steps to the first level—a sixty foot wide porch with eight white painted wooden columns. A dozen rocking chairs with cane seats had been arranged there, all facing the majestic view over the vast fields to the west.

The escort opened the twin nine foot tall leaded glass doors to the home and beckoned them to enter. Stepping inside the huge room, Eric could not help but notice a large chandelier illuminated by more than two dozen candles. Their light was refracted by hand cut French and Austrian crystals—the overall effect dazzled him with its intricacy. He turned toward the elegantly carved marble fireplace and gazed at the life-sized portrait of Elouise LeBlanc above the mantle. He immediately thought of Angelina. However, his thoughts were short-lived. The booming voice of his host shook him from his reverie.

"My friends, I am so very happy to have you join us this evening. May I interest you in a small libation to wash away the dust of your ride?"

Seated in the rocking chairs, with the sun hanging low on the horizon, the soldiers and LeBlanc discussed the local Confederate campaign against the Yankees. Eric kept looking over his shoulder for a glimpse of the red-haired beauty, but she was obviously not inclined to discuss such manly matters as maneuvers and firepower.

Just as the sun touched the horizon, the doors to the house swung wide and a glorious figure appeared. Clad in a ivory colored satin dress, with a full skirt that flowed all the way to the inlaid rosewood parquet floor, Angelina was a vision to behold. Her hair was pulled back and up in a French twist, with a couple of her flaming locks curled tightly and dangling from her temples. She had applied a modest amount of rouge to her cheeks, adding a touch of red lip paint and a relief carved cameo broach with her mother's profile to finish off the look.

"Father, I am told dinner is almost ready. May I join you men to watch the sunset? It is so nice and clear tonight."

"Of course my dear…we have finished our discussion of the unsavory subject of armed conflict. Your presence is most welcome."

"May I offer you a seat?" Eric stood up as she walked out on the porch.

The other guests were only a second behind him in rising for the lady of the house.

"Such a gentleman...I graciously accept your offer, kind sir." She took her seat as one of their servants hurried up.

Eric stepped quickly to another adjoining chair and sat back down.

"Would Miss Angelina care for a beverage?"

"Perhaps a small glass of our Bordeaux would be nice."

The servant nodded and disappeared back into the house. Moments later, he returned with a stemmed crystal filled with a dark bluish-purple wine. She lifted it off the silver serving tray and took a sip.

"Thank you, Cyrus."

"My pleasure, Mistress," he said before he disappeared back into the house.

"I would imagine your place is quite self-sufficient, being so far from town," Eric said as he, too, sipped on a glass of the aged wine.

"It is a matter of necessity, my father says. We have our own mill, vineyards and garden. We do travel to town often and from time to time, stay over when needed. I do like seeing all the different people..."

Eric nodded. "My thoughts exactly. I grew up on a small place several miles from Tyler, Texas...however, I have a burning desire to see what the wild country out west is like...snow covered mountains...majestic vistas..."

"Wanderlust is what Father calls it. He always reminds me of our roots here in Louisiana. I have never seen mountains either…except in books and art."

"Has your family been here long?

"Almost since the beginning…the early seventeen hundreds…Some of our fore-bearers help found Natchitoches."

"I did not know it was lost."

The young beauty broke into a quick laugh, the sight of which pleased him to no end. His smile was genuine but had a disarming quality nonetheless.

"You are very quick…I shall have keep my eyes on you."

"Please do, I promise I will not mind…Look there, is not that sunset gorgeous?"

The scattered cirrus clouds took on a multitude of reddish pigmentation as the burning celestial globe dipped below the distant tree line.

"It is indeed, sir. I love the way the light changes colors… sienna, burnt orange and crimson."

He glanced quickly back at her. "You sound like an artist, Miss LeBlanc. Do you paint?"

"I have a tutor who is attempting to teach me that skill… Please call me Angelina."

"As you wish. Anything to please a beautiful lady."

As the last bit of chocolate mousse disappeared off the Colonel's plate, he glanced up to the head of the table where Augustin was lighting a post-meal cigar.

"Anyone else care to join me in a smoke?"

Anglelina made a disapproving face. Eric noticed it and quickly demurred, although the other male guests gladly partook the offer.

She dabbed at the corner of her mouth and lay the linen napkin beside the plate. "Father, if you will excuse me, I would like to show Mister Schmidt the boat docks before it gets too late."

He waived his hand somewhat dismissively. "I am sure he will be bored to tears, but whatever suits you, dear. Be sure to take a lantern and watch out for the water moccasins."

Eric watched carefully as she leaned over and gave her dad a peck on the cheek. He was not certain but he thought he caught a brief wink from her as she stood back up and extended her hand.

"Come along, Eric. I think you will find the river most interesting."

He took the lit coal oil lantern from the servant and lifted it up to illuminate the way across the lawn. "Lead on, because I do not really know where we are going."

"Silly, there is only one river on our property. It runs behind the house."

"I gathered that, but I did not see any dock."

"Of course you could not, because the water is much lower than the bank near the house. We would not want the house to be flooded every year, now would we?"

"That make sense, now that you mention it." He could see the lawn continue for another fifty yards where it disappeared over the gentle embankment. Once they reached the edge, a wooden stairway descended the slope to a flattened area where a narrow roadway was built to gradually ascend the river bank and join with the main road. They used the stairs and walked out onto the heavy cypress timbers of the dock.

"We ship our cotton out from this dock and send it down to New Orleans. A river boat comes up and ties off alongside here," she said pointing at the T shaped section of the dock that lay parallel to the shore.

"Steam powered boats, I assume. Are they side paddle or stern wheeler?"

"We have had both…have you ever been on one of them?"

"No, just saw their pictures in books that I read."

"Once I went to Baton Rouge and then to New Orleans on business with my father."

Eric chuckled. "Red stick…what a funny name for a town."

A smile came to her face. "You speak French?"

"Oui, merci beaucoup, mademoiselle," he said in passable attempt that the language.

"Not bad," she said with a smile. "Did you learn that in school?"

"No…my mother taught me…At home on our ranch."

She noted a change in his eyes, but in the lantern light could not quite place the reason for it. He blinked once, turned and stared out toward the dark sluggish moving water of the river.

"I never got to meet my mother…Father says she and I look alike."

"I saw the resemblance in the painting. You are as beautiful as she was...I am sorry you did not get the opportunity to know her. I cannot imagine..." His voice trailed off

"Thank you. That is very kind of you to say."

"A place this large...it must take a lot of slaves to work it," he replied, changing the subject.

"Oh, we do not have slaves. My father personally abhors the practice. What he decided to do was to was to buy slaves when he could, and let them work off their cost in wages. Once their debt is repaid in full, they are free to remain here and work for us or leave. He gives them a signed copy of their freeman papers either way."

"Do many of them just pack up and leave?"

She shook her head. "Not many...Sometimes they want to go and try to find a family member or loved one who got sold elsewhere, but his system has made for really loyal employees."

Eric pondered her answer for a moment. "It makes me happy to hear that. I looked at all that your family has accumulated and somehow got the notion it was built on the backs of the slaves..."

"Many of the other local planters still use them, I am told. Your assumption would be correct in most instances." She pointed at a bench built on the side of the broad dock. "Would you mind if we sat for a bit? I love looking at the stars."

"Not at all." He took her hand and held it as she swept the hoops in her full skirt forward and gracefully took a seat. He sat beside her and then set the lantern underneath the bench to allow them to enjoy the night sky to its fullest. Eric glanced to the east and spotted a familiar constellation. He pointed up above the three bright stars lined up in a row. "Are you familiar with Orion? Those three big ones make up his belt."

"I studied them a couple of years ago, but classroom diagrams are quite not the same as being out of doors."

"Here is another easy one." He turned around and searched for the north star. "This one looks like a big dipper…in fact, that is what it is called. Now…if you take the two stars on the outside of the dipper…draw an imaginary line from the bottom to the top, then go about seven times the distance between the two stars and you will find the north star…Look, it is right there." He pointed to its location and turned to see if she was paying attention. Her eyes were locked on his face. "Its name is Polaris…"

She raised her index finger to his lips. "I know." Angelina leaned in closer until he could feel her breath.

His heart began beating faster as he realized what she wanted was what he wanted as well. Tilting his head ever so slightly to the right, he gently touched her cheek and brought his lips to hers. Softly at first, they kissed until passion began to grow. He slid his hand to the back of her head and pulled her closer to him as they seemed to melt into each other.

After almost a minute, he broke off the torrid kiss and began to draw in quick ragged breaths. "Forgot to breathe," he finally was able to blurt out.

"My goodness…" she said as she also inhaled and then exhaled deeply. "I don't think I've every been kissed like that."

"Did I do something wrong? I do not have much experience in…"

She cut him off as she placed both of her graceful hands on his face and pulled it down to hers for a second helping.

Eric handed the lantern to the servant as they entered from the portico. The others had moved to a formal sitting area where Colonel Smith and Augustin LeBlanc were laughing at some tall-tale one of them had concocted.

They turned to watch the young couple walk up.

"No poisonous snakes on the dock tonight, I trust?"

"Not a one, Father…Eric thinks it is too early in the year for them."

"That so?"

"Yes, sir," he replied. "Reptiles are cold blooded and it still cools quickly off after sunset."

"I see."

"Father, he is also a whiz at celestial navigation…and he speaks French."

Augustin grinned. "I am so glad to know that. Would you like to join us? I have invited our esteemed guests to remain overnight, as that ride back to town can be so tedious in the dark…They gladly accepted."

Eric and Angelina briefly exchanged glances and nodded nervously.

Waving at a servant, Augustin called out, "A glass of sherry and one of port for these two youngsters. They must be half frozen to death by the sudden onslaught of the cold."

After breakfast the following morning, the LeBlancs walked the four officers out to the stables and bid their farewells.

"You gentlemen are welcome here any time. We enjoyed your company immensely."

"Your hospitality is legendary, Augustin. Until we meet again," Colonel Smith said as he tipped his hat. "Miss LeBlanc."

"Fare thee well," Eric said as he looked at Angelina one last time.

Marcus and Joe Robinson both waved as Smith reined his mount north and nudged it into a trot. Eric backed his buckskin up for several feet, not wanting the angelic image of her smiling face to disappear. Finally he waved his last good-bye, and wheeled Bucky about.

For a minute they watched the riders as they grew smaller and smaller in the distance. Angelina reached for her father's hand and held it tightly.

"Father, I think I really like that one...A lot."

He looked over at her and smiled broadly. "I can tell, my child...he is not the same as most of the other young men who come courting."

"He is not rich, if that is what you mean. Did you know he lost his whole family recently? I cannot imagine..."

"Yes, Marcus told me the story." Augustin placed his hand on her shoulder as they headed back to the house. "Do you know what Eric told me before breakfast? He pulled me aside and said that he was proud of me for my policy to make freemen out of slaves. Can you believe that? Most men are too jealous of our money and holdings to tell me that they are proud of me."

"He has...I cannot put my finger on it, exactly...but something about him that makes me want to be with him...Is that wrong, Father?"

Augustin grinned and took in a deep breath and then let it out slowly. He took one last look up the drive at the four riders. "No, my dear," he chuckled. "That something is probably just a little thing called love."

***

CHAPTER ELEVEN

**HOUSTON, TEXAS
TRANS-MISSISSIPPI
CONFEDERATE ARMY HEADQUARTERS
MARCH 17TH, 1864**

A young Confederate cavalry colonel led his battalion into the open field near the converted schoolhouse. Surrounding the headquarters in a series of semicircles were hundred of tents of the infantry assigned to defend the southeastern part of the state. He raised his hand to signal a halt, the order was relayed visually and verbally back to the four hundred battle hardened veterans.

The colonel turned in his saddle to face the lieutenant colonel and first sergeant of the unit. "See to your men and take care of the mounts. While we are here, try to get your hands on any supplies they may be able to spare. I shall go see what the good general has in mind for us."

"Aye, sir," the executive officer replied as he snapped a weary salute. "The boys can certainly use a rest." He spun his mount around and called out the command. "Second Battalion...dis-mount!"

The colonel nudged the jet black stallion down the road another hundred yards past a field hospital and blacksmith shop to the white clapboard two story headquarters building. He dismounted, and tied off the spirited horse to a hitching rail outside before he stretched out his back and trudged up the stairs.

Two enlisted guards snapped to attention as he reached the top step. They eyed the big man's bushy blonde handlebar mustache, his long hair hanging down over his collar as they snapped to attention and brought their rifles to a present arms position. "Good afternoon, sir," they said in unison.

"At ease, men...What kind of mood is the old man in today?"

The guards eyed each other for a second. "We are not at liberty to say, sir," replied the braver of the two.

"That good, huh?" the colonel replied as he shook his head and grinned. He removed his hat and stepped inside. Walking over to a senior enlisted aide, he announced himself, "Colonel Schmidt reporting to General Matson."

The man escorted him upstairs to the appropriate office and knocked on the closed door before opening it. "Colonel Schmidt to see you, sir."

Matson was huddled over a large desk with a handful of maps spread out before him. Two other officers—a colonel and a brigadier general—were standing beside him. A small wood-burning stove warmed the room, as spring was still a week away. Matson's eyes lit up at the sight of his old friend. "Eric, great to see you again."

"You too, General," he said as he snapped a salute. "Your telegram said urgent...what have you got for me and the boys?"

The major general returned the salute. "Make yourself comfortable, this is going to take a while...Have you met these gentlemen?"

"I know Colonel Bigsby here," he stuck out his hand to the stranger. "General, I am Eric Schmidt, commander of the Second Battalion."

"Your reputation precedes you, Colonel Schmidt. I am General Nathan Lane...I will taking over the division from General Stephens."

"I had heard he was wounded...is he..."

"Not yet...the doctors had to take his leg and an infection set in," Matson replied.

Eric shook his head. "He is a good man...It distresses me to hear of that. Our situation, gentlemen...how bad it is?"

"It has been almost two years since New Orleans fell and nine months since Vicksburg surrendered. The loss of those two cities effectively cut us off from the rest of the forces of the south."

"I got letter from Angelina a few months back telling me that her father was forced to ship his cotton via railway to

Marshall. Then they put it on ships down the Sabine River to try and make it through the union naval blockade. Their only other option is to ship overland to buyers in Mexico and brigands have taken over in the Texas hill country."

"Union forces have even cut off the southern Rio Grande, and occupied the port of Corpus Christi. We retook Galveston and you and your men held the Yankee's encroachment at Matagorda, protecting our southwest flank along the coast," General Lane said pointing at the map.

"I take it we are having supply issues getting past the blockade," Schmidt said

"The word *issues* is an gross understatement...I am afraid. The only real cash export we have is cotton, and faith in our currency is waning precipitously. Foodstuffs are in short supply, out troops are scattered in political gambits into New Mexico and are suffering defeats from the Union forces in south Texas as well."

Eric watched closely as Marcus described the challenges facing them. "Do you think the Yanks will make another push up the Sabine? We thrashed them pretty hard the last time they tried that."

"No," Matson replied. "The river is far too narrow to get past our gun emplacements. Here is the reason I recalled you and your cavalry...Reports from Louisiana tell us General Nathaniel Banks is leading the Union Army of the Gulf...accompanied by several gunboats...up the Red River. Major General Richard Taylor, commander of the Confederate forces of Louisiana has asked for reinforcements to help defend

Shreveport from the south. He remembered our little exploits there two years ago and asked for you by name." Marcus smiled a crooked smile. "Fame and fortune await thee."

"When do we leave?"

"I have arranged steamships and barges to take you and your men up the Sabine to Marshall. From there you will travel by rail to Shreveport and meet up with..." He looked down at the page long handwritten disposition-of-forces memorandum. "...Twenty-seven other Texas brigades...You will then proceed south with Taylor's army."

"If the Union takes Shreveport...the war is essentially over for Texas," Eric said somberly. "We cannot allow Louisiana to fall."

"I am happy to see that you grasp the importance of this action," General Lane said. "Of course, these discussions are to be held secret. We cannot allow anyone outside our immediate command structure to know where we are going...Is that understood?"

"Yes, sir," he replied. *Twenty-eight brigades? I have never seen that many soldiers together at one time. This is really a huge battle they envision.*

Marcus watched Eric bend over, study the maps and then follow the Red River backward from it confluence with the Mississippi. His finger stopped just short of Shreveport.

"Have you seen her since we left the plantation?"

He stood erect. "I got to spend a couple of days there on the way back from Arkansas...Plus I get letters from time to time...when they can catch up with me."

"I am told they have a mail sack for your battalion downstairs. I had them hold it awaiting your anticipated return. Your men would appreciate them, I would imagine."

"Thank you for your consideration, Marcus."

He shook his head. "I wish I could do more…I know your boys are bone tired, Eric. You and your men will have to depart within three hours. We have your transportation set up for pickup in the town of Orange the day after tomorrow before sunset."

"I understand the urgency of the mission, sir. It would be nice if we could get a hot meal into these troops. They fought hard against the bluebellies along the coast. You would have been proud of them."

"I will see what our quartermaster can rustle up. Our own supplies have been getting more meager month by month…By the way, you may have to bivouac near Shreveport for a day or two. Some of the outfits involved are repositioning from Wichita Falls, Fort Worth and Waxahachie. You may get a chance to pay your respects to Mister LeBlanc."

A slight smile came to Eric's suntanned face. "There you go, sir…the old carrot and the stick routine…I hope she still recognizes me."

"I think she will…Just make sure to take a bath before you drop by." Matson chuckled at his little joke. "Remember that fancy hotel back in Shreveport?…The Pavillion?"

"We were sitting in high cotton and did not know it, General. If I can swing a room there again, I will do so for old times sake."

"Good luck to you, my friend. I wish I was going with you, but the senior brass wants me here providing security for the Port of Galveston and overseeing the defense of the mouth of the Sabine. We cannot let the Union get a foothold down here either."

"Until we meet again, General." Eric shook hands with him and the other two officers and departed.

"Glad to have him on board," Lane said to Matson. That boy looks big enough to take on a whole company all by himself."

"We got enough time before you depart...Let me tell you all about his first engagement with the enemy," Marcus said as he rolled up the maps.

ORANGE, TEXAS

The steamboat's whistles echoed across the slow-moving river on the east side of town. A flock of brown pelicans lifted off the upper decks of the Cajun Belle and swooped low across the still waters at the noise. Ancient cypress trees with their characteristic flared trunks lined the far bank and a half dozen mottled green and brown turtles sunned themselves on a couple of half-submerged logs slowly rotting in the shallows. The Belle and her sister ship, the Sabine Queen, each towed a large shallow-draft barge behind them with two hundred horses closely packed into makeshift corrals.

The captain of the steamer gave the order to depart, and the crew responded quickly, untying the heavy hemp hawsers that had kept her fast to the wharf. She pulled tight on the tow line and as the massive paddles churned up the green waters, the vessels began to inch forward and gradually picked up speed. Black smoke billowed up from the twin smokestacks as the firemen down in the hellish hold shoveled coal into the hungry furnaces.

Eric swatted at a persistent mosquito that had drawn blood from his neck just below his right ear. His reactions were quicker than the insect's and the contact left a small smudge of blood on his gray uniform collar. "Little early for these to be a bother...is it not?" he asked one of his company commanders.

"I am not sure, Colonel. We had some down by Matagorda...or were those things called sand flies?"

"Those were biting flies...I hate 'em a whole lot more and the horses do not care for them much either."

"Nor do I...Do they have alligators in the Sabine? That is Louisiana on the far bank, if my memory serves me well," Sergeant Major Mark Peterson asked.

"I believe they are found up and down the length and breadth of the Sabine river basin, particularly in the southern end. We might do well to remind our men not to be tempted to go for a swim if they feel the need for a bath. Now, being cold-blooded reptiles, they might be a mite slower than usual this time of year...But I would not bet my life on that."

"Colonel, I do not think alligators use calendars...How would they know what time of year it is?" Captain Rob Tucker joked.

"If I see one, I shall make it a point and ask him." He smiled, and then took out his gold pocket watch and wound the stem a few times before he flicked open the cover. "It is almost six o'clock, gentlemen. We should see that the men get a chance to eat...The captain said all they had to offer was and Johnny cakes tonight...Bacon and cornbread tomorrow. We are already running low on salted beef as you saw back in Houston."

"Colonel, I hope they have better supplies up in Marshall. We cannot expect these men to put up much of a fight if they get sick or weak from hunger...Napoleon said an army travels on its stomach."

"I am aware of that, Sergeant Major...That is one reason I want our men fed before the officers eat...They need to know we are concerned for their welfare. It does not make the food any better, or more plentiful, but I will not have my men thinking I have it easier than they do...That kills morale faster than anything."

The men made their way down from the observation deck and into the crowded passenger level. Weary soldiers were tightly packed onto unpadded wooden benches. Several were trying to sleep and a couple were playing cards—a few scribbled notes with stubby yellow pencils to loved ones using scraps of rough brown paper. The smell of tobacco smoke drifted from corn cob pipes as the ships churned steadily north. One homesick trooper was trying to console himself with a upbeat tune on a mouth organ.

Eric smiled as he recognized the familiar tune, *The Yellow Rose of Texas.*

DEVIL'S CANYON

SHREVEPORT, LOUISIANA

With a chorus of squeaks from thirty sets of well-worn brakes, the troop transport train lurched to a stop. Eric and the rest of the officers rocked forward and then slammed back against the wooden benches.

"And I thought we were gonna make it here in one piece."

"Come on, son. Beats two weeks in the saddle and bein' up to our ears in swamp water," replied Colonel Bigsby.

"Let us get off this noisy contraption before is catches fire," added General Lane. "Will do us some good to stretch our legs."

Looking outside, Eric was struck by the differences he saw. Hundreds of new buildings had been built and level of enterprise was many times over that of his first visit to the town. "So much has changed since I was here last time. Hardly recognize the place."

"Things can change in a couple years," General Lane added. "Hell, they can become almost unrecognizable in a matter of hours. We are bringing in nine thousand men to reinforce the five thousand already deployed here. Just look at all those caissons stacked up in rows. I am unsure as to who's command they belong...maybe Randal's...or they could be some of Maul's boys..."

"Command and control will be a considerable challenge with fourteen thousand men," Eric said as he and the other officers made their way to the front of the car.

"Challenge? From what I heard from commanders back east, it is almost an impossibility. With the noise and the smoke, things go to hell in a hand basket...Opportunities are often missed because time and distance take their toll on critical information…Runners and messengers on horseback sometimes get themselves killed before they even get close to their intended commander."

"This is my first battle with heavy artillery support," he replied. "Anything I need to be particularly aware of?"

The general nodded. "Sure…Do not get in a hurry. Artillery barrages are often set to begin and end at a certain time. Those shells do not know friend from foe…You ride into the target area before the barrage stops, we might not find enough of you to bury."

"Thanks for the pointer." Eric grinned. "I hate it when that happens."

"We all do…Plus, stuff cotton in your ears…You'll see why." Lane replied. *Young charger is not too proud to ask for advice. That is a good sign. He might make it through the next few days after all.* "My next stop is the headquarters. I shall see you men at the rally point."

"Some of those replacement mounts are more than a little bit green. I do hope they settle down before we have to take them into combat."

"Colonel, I shall keep and eye on them for ya," Sergeant Major Peterson replied. He spat out a well used chaw of tobacco to the dirt. "Cain't say I cotton a buckin' horse when the bullets are flyin'." He pulled a twist out of his pants and gnawed off a chunk with the few teeth that still remained on the right side of his mouth.

Eric nodded and squeezed his knees against the sixteen hand stallion's sides. "Come on, Thunder...let us get this gaggle moving."

Long columns of infantry marched doggedly southward on Market street. Half of them wore issued uniforms, the other half were dressed in a hodgepodge of homespun shirts, Confederate and even Union uniform items, especially hats called kepis. Slow moving wagons packed high with foodstuffs, cooking gear, ammunition and tents brought up the rear.

Eric moved to the head of the two columns of cavalry. Glancing over at the first sergeant, he reined back to match pace. "A company...report."

"Two men missing and unaccounted for, sir."

"Any idea where the hell they are? Are they missing...or did they desert?"

"Colonel, at this point, I have to say missing. Have not checked all the bars in town yet."

"Assign two men to look for them...I want you to take the company out to the rally point and get the horses grazed out. I will rejoin you after I get briefed from the headquarters command section."

"Yes, sir!" He snapped a crisp salute. Sergeant Carter pointed to two corporals near the front of the procession. "Wimberly, Simmons go look for Baker and Ash...drag their asses back to the rally point on the double."

They peeled out of line and headed back into town as he barked out a order to his men, "A Company, in a column of twos...forward...ho!" He motioned with his gauntlet covered hand and sent the group in motion. An eighteen year old guidon bearer rode second in line with his unit standard snapping in the breeze atop a seven foot pole.

Schmidt rode back to his other three companies and repeated the check-in and dispatch procedure before road trotting his horse up to Texas Street. Hundreds on people milled around, including dozens of wounded soldiers—many of them missing limbs.

One shop specialized in artificial legs and a bench outside was packed with former infantrymen on crutches, all waiting to be served. Eric touched the brim of his hat and nodded an acknowledgment of their sacrifice. The Trans-Mississippi Confederate Army Headquarters occupied what was formerly the parish courthouse.

He tied his horse to a wrought iron rail set into concrete. Inside the bustling headquarters, he looked around to see if he recognized any familiar face from two years earlier.

A sergeant looked up from a desk spoke right up, "Colonel, may I help you, sir?"

"I hope so…I am the Second Battalion Commander under General Lane. Would be looking for the current intelligence briefing."

Another colonel with his back to the center of the room heard a familiar voice and turned around. "Eric!…Son, I never thought we would cross paths again."

He glanced over at the one speaking and immediately recognized Joe Robinson. He quickly stepped up and extended his hand. "Great to see you, my friend. Still running the show around here?"

"Not anymore…They brought in a major general when New Orleans and Baton Rouge fell. I see you are still in one piece."

He nodded grimly. "Not for lack of trying, I can assure you…Most of those Yankees draftees are not worth their salt. They cannot shoot well under pressure…therefore we always make damned sure they do not get a chance to breathe during any of our engagements."

"I kept up with some of your exploits via dispatches. Nice job down toward Corpus Christi, I might add. What was the name of that place where you boys stopped them?"

"Matagorda Bay. It was far too shallow for their gun boats to provide adequate support to their ground forces…We let the cavalry get out way ahead of the infantry and once they were out of range, we attacked in them strength…For some reason, the Yankees decided to return to the safety of the port."

Joe grinned. "You always had a way to look at the big picture."

"We selectively use our strengths to defeat the enemy's weakest points. That is why I am here…to try to avail myself of the latest information."

"Come on, I will let you hear it from the old man himself."

The two colonels made their way upstairs to a spacious, if sparsely furnished, office. The door was already open, but nonetheless, Robinson knocked on the jamb before he and Schmidt entered. On the walls were framed maps of Louisiana,

Arkansas and Texas as well as black and white photographs of Robert E. Lee and confederate President Jefferson Davis.

A major general with a full head of brown hair, a matching bushy mustache and goatee was seated, discussing something with Brigadier General Lane. The senior man looked up and waved them in. "Who do you have with you, Joe? Damn, I feel old...these colonels are looking younger every day..."

"Eric Schmidt, sir. Second Battalion cavalry from Texas, under General Lane's command."

"Schmidt? The same wildcat that whipped up on a Union brigade here a couple of years back?"

Eric extended his hand as he glanced over at Robinson. "Guilty as charged, sir...Now, I have to tell you that Joe Robinson and his Louisiana boys played a big hand in that fracas. Honored to meet you, General Taylor. Your reputation speaks for itself."

The son of former general and President of the United States, Zachary Taylor stood up and shook the young man's hand firmly. He himself was the youngest major general in the Confederate Army and had been an extremely wealthy plantation owner before Union forces had overrun and sacked his home in St. Charles Parish, Louisiana. "I am honored to make your acquaintance, Colonel. I assume you came to ascertain the disposition-of-forces, am I right?"

"Absolutely, sir. This is shaping up to be a decisive engagement for the entire Trans-Mississippi Army and I wanted to be apprised as to when and where we could reasonably expect to engage General Banks."

Taylor moved to a wall map of the area. "Overwhelming Union forces have defeated us at Baton Rouge and Alexandria. With their gun boats in support, they have proceeded up the Red and will arrive here in Shreveport no later than the tenth. My plan is for us to cut them off south of town before they reach this far…We have to keep Shreveport out of artillery range at all costs."

"What is their strength and where is Banks at this time?"

"The last telegraph message we had out of Natchitoches before it fell yesterday put him right there with around nine thousand men and several gunboats." Lane remarked and pointed at the small town less than eighty miles south southeast.

"That gives us less than a week to prepare." Eric's head was spinning. *9,000 men…how many will we have ready?* "If I may, sir…" He stepped over to the huge sepia-toned map.

"I, sir, am intimately familiar with the topography south of town. It is very open and essentially consists of plowed cotton fields for much of this countryside. Farther south, starting about six miles from the Chateau LeBlanc…" Eric said, pointing at the chart. "…past the town of Mansfield, the stagecoach road to Natchitoches wanders away from the Red River. These tall trees and rolling hills will preclude direct fire support from their gunboats…Have not been down that way for almost a year, but I seem to recall an area near the Sabine Crossroads where it might be possible erect some breastworks for your defensive artillery and concentrate the Yankee infantry between the wooded areas along here…See, sir?"

His hands made a sweeping motion across an hourglass shaped clearing on the map. The stagecoach road ran in a fairly straight line from northeast to southwest and was intersected at right angles by the lesser traveled Sabine Crossroads.

"These heavily wooded areas will act like a funnel if Banks tries to move overland. They will preclude his moving artillery, massed troops and supplies in a flanking maneuver…While they are not completely impenetrable…due to vegetation's density and the presence of extensive swamp-like conditions…most commanders will not want to become bogged down inside them. There is, to my knowledge, no other direct route to our position and I am not aware of him possessing a navy flotilla adequate to move his entire force."

Taylor nodded his agreement. "I remember that place well …back when we were forced to move up here from Bayou Teche. You are correct…The only two ways north through there are on that Natchitoches stage road or by the Red."

Taylor and Lane studied the map for a full minute then looked back at Eric.

"Colonel, I do not know where you went to military school, but you learned your lessons in strategy quite well," General Taylor said with full sincerity. "How long have you been contemplating the defense of Shreveport?"

He shot a quick glance over to Robinson before he responded, "I had a week to mull it over as we traveled up from Houston, sir…however, I did not know where we would expect to engage them."

"I respect your input, Colonel. Many men allow themselves to be far too parochial in nature…They know what they know and choose to let that be enough."

Another knock came from the doorway and two brigadier generals entered. The younger of the two was around thirty-five and wore a dark full beard and had wavy hair—the older officer appeared to be at least fifty, was clean-shaven and was tanned from months in the field. Eric could tell by the yellow trim on the older man's uniform that he was a fellow cavalryman, but the other was an infantry officer.

"Would you gentlemen care to join us for dinner? That is if you are not in the middle of something…" the bearded man said.

General Taylor answered quickly. "I think we could break away for a bite…However, some introductions are most definitely in order before we go. Gentlemen, these two scoundrels are a pair of my most trusted commanders…General Alfred Mouton from down by Opelousas, Louisiana way and the equally famous General Thomas Green, recently of Houston, Texas."

All five shook hands and introduced themselves. Eric was well aware of the exploits of both men. Green was a genuine hero of the Texas Revolution—having served as a gunner on the only two cannons used by the victorious Texans at the battle of San Jacinto. He even had a county in Texas named after him.

Mouton spoke English with a decided French Arcadian accent and was the son of a former Governor of Louisiana before the war. His accent and background immediately reminded Eric of Augustin LeBlanc.

Eric traveled alone down the tree-lined dirt road to the Chateau LeBlanc. His mind raced at what he would say to the fiery redhead once he got the chance. Unlike his earlier visits, he was not expected this time and was not met by a stable hand. He stepped out of the saddle and loosened the girth after he tied the lead rope to the corral fence. Using his broad-brimmed cavalry hat as ersatz whisk broom, he tried to knock off as much of the sandy trail dust as he could.

Walking up the red brick steps outside the front portico he remembered clearly the first time he and the others had watched the sunset from there. Eric lifted the solid brass knocker and firmly rapped on the door. After a few seconds, the door opened and a familiar black servant greeted him.

"Mister Eric! How nice to see you again, sir. They did not tell me you were coming."

"My return was unplanned, Cryus. Are the LeBlancs at home today?" Eric felt uncharacteristically nervous, for reasons he could not quite lay a finger on. "It is very important that I speak with them."

"Why, yes sir, Mister Eric. Please come in…Mister LeBlanc, he is outside overseeing a trade on some cattle. I will send one of the boys out to fetch him directly. Miss Angelina is in the study…I will be happy to notify her of your arrival…"

"That will not be necessary, Cyrus. I know the way…think I will just surprise her, if you do not mind."

Cyrus smiled broadly as he turned to find someone to notify Augustin. Eric stepped quietly across the parquet floors to the hallway back down the center of the elegant home. The library was on the east side of the mansion and its three ten foot tall windows took full advantage of the early morning light and avoided the hot afternoon sun.

Thousands of books were stacked neatly in floor to ceiling walnut bookcases. A rolling ladder allowed the LeBlancs to easily access the higher volumes. He stopped short of the doorway and leaned around the white painted frame to catch a glimpse of Angelina seated in Chippendale camelback sofa.

She was wearing a light yellow cotton dress with long mutton sleeves, a lacy tight-fitting bodice over a floor-length full linen skirt. She had her back to the window and was engrossed in a gothic love story called *Wuthering Heights*. Sunlight streaming through the shear silk curtains creating highlights in her hair cascading down in soft curls.

He tiptoed across the room and finally stopped a few feet from her. Eric stood silently for a moment, listening to her breathe. "Must be a great book," he said softly, breaking the silence.

"Oh!" She was startled and slammed the book closed. Her eyes flew wide when she saw him standing so close, his blue eyes focused on hers and a big grin upon his tanned face. She sprang to her feet and leapt into his arms. "Eric!"

He wrapped his powerful arms around her, pulled her close to him and their lips met in a prolonged passionate embrace.

Eric tossed his officer's hat onto the embroidered chair next to the sofa.

"Why did you not tell me you were coming? I look awful…"

"Shhh…You are a vision from heaven…Helen of Troy would hang her head in shame to find herself in the same room as you."

"I thought you were never going to come back."

"What?…I told you…nothing can ever keep me away from you…Nothing."

Angelina's green eyes lit up and her smile dazzled him as it always did. He kissed her again and again, each one more passionate than one before.

***

CHAPTER TWELVE

CHATEAU LEBLANC

Augustin and Angelina listened closely as Eric explained the situation pertaining to the approaching Union army.

"As we have seen or have had reported, the Yankees respect no boundaries when it comes to taking private property from captured territories. I really wish I had better news to share with you, but the grim fact is almost anything that is not nailed down can be expected to be carted off as spoils of war."

She was obviously frightened and glanced to her father and then back to Eric. He had a serious look on his face.

"You will not let that happen to us, will you?"

"Sweetheart, you know I will do anything in my power to protect you and your home. It is just that…" His voice trailed off and he was forced to turn away.

"You have got to do something!" she pleaded.

"I am doing something, my love...I came here with a whole army of Texas volunteers to fight the Yankees coming up the Red River valley. We have chance...a very good chance...to stop them, but I would be remiss if I did not warn you both of what might happen if we fail."

"How many days did you say we have?"

"Four or five...I will be leaving in the morning to attempt to slow down General Banks as best I can. There will be a decisive engagement, I can promise you that...Of course I cannot tell you the exact nature of our battle plans...To do so would put all of us at risk. As long as you know nothing, you cannot be forced to divulge information should spies or outriders show up here before the main battle takes place."

Eric could tell the news was hard on his young angel. She didn't cry but her tears were not far from falling. She held on to her father's hand tightly.

"I do not want you to go, Eric. We need you here to protect us."

He took in a deep breath—his blue eyes seemed to pick up the color of his gray tunic. "Angelina, honey...If I thought I could do any good by myself, I would...you know I would. But there are thousands and thousands of troops marching up here as we speak. They also have gun boats, and if we cannot stop them, they will be steaming right up into your back yard by week's end...do you understand what I am saying?"

She nodded as a single tear rolled out of her left eye.

"I shall see if we can get our most treasured possessions packed up and ready to be shipped into town," Augustin said soberly. "All of our cotton crop from last season is already sold and delivered. I just traded for some breeding stock and we still have a considerable number of horses to consider."

"I understand, sir. I only wanted you to have the opportunity to be prepared. You may not actually have to transport your valuables unless the battle goes badly against us. The proximity of the Union forces will make time very critical if that unfortunate event occurs."

"How long can you stay?"

"I begged General Lane to allow me a twenty four hours furlough...Thankfully, he agreed."

Angelina wiped the tear from her cheek. "In that case, I will do my best to be of cheerful demeanor during our time together. You always say life is too short not to savor the moment."

That night after dinner was finished, Augustin, Angelica and Eric retired to the parlor sipping on their preferred aperitifs. Candlelight provided the only illumination as the sun had long since set.

Augustin settled back on a burgundy leather wing back chair. Eric escorted her to a gold silk brocade settee, took a seat beside her and tenderly held her hand. They talked of the upcoming planting season for a few minutes.

"Sweetheart, would you mind terribly if I could spend some time alone with you father? There is something we need to discuss."

Her eyes darted from his to her dad and back. She had no inkling of what that discussion might be, but smiled sweetly and began to rise. He stood first and helped her to her feet, giving her hand slight squeeze as she turned to the door.

When the drawing room pocket doors clicked shut behind her, Augustin sat his cigar down in the cut crystal ashtray atop the freestanding mahogany table. A wispy column of pungent gray smoke snaked upward and wound its way through the brass candelabra on the pie crust table top. He locked eyes with Eric as he asked, "What is on your mind, son?"

"Sir, in the two years since we first met, I have come to have strong feelings for your daughter."

"Is that a fact?" Augustin's face showed no emotion whatsoever.

"Yes, sir, it is. And I think it is safe to say that she has developed a fondness for me as well."

"Really? My what a suprise…What are you intentions in regards to her feelings? As her father, I am obviously most concerned…her well being is utmost in my considerations."

"I understand, Mister LeBlanc. As you know, I do not come from a wealthy family…my means are modest to say the least. My parents died when I was in my teens and I have not even seen our ranch in years. Not even sure it is still there…"

"Go on…"

"Sir, the crux of the matter is that I love your daughter very much and I am seeking your permission to ask Angelina for her hand…I promise to love her, and cherish her and do my absolute best by her…forever."

The older man settled back in the overstuffed leather chair, his face not giving away anything as he contemplated the request. He said nothing for a moment, then leaned forward as Eric became more nervous with each passing second. Resting his elbows on the arms of the chair, he brought his hands together as if to pray and then placed his fingertips against his lower lip.

Seconds passed as the two men studied each other carefully. Eric was certain he saw tears start to rim Augustin's hazel eyes.

Finally he spoke. "Son, for twenty years that young daughter of mine was all I had left to love after her dear mother passed on...I knew this day would come and I was..." He stopped and took a deep breath before continuing. "For many years, I was afraid I would lose her as well...But knowing how happy you make her gives me greater joy than you can possibly imagine...I cannot think of another man so deserving of her love and devotion...You are brave, intelligent, considerate, and trustworthy....she and I both sensed that the first time we met. I feel now that I am not losing a daughter...rather I am gaining a son."

Eric sprang to his feet and extended his hand. "Thank you, sir...I promise you will not regret it."

"Call me Augustin...or father." He took the colonel's hand and shook it firmly.

They walked together to the mahogany doors leading to the formal dining room. When Eric slid them open, Angelina was standing right outside, smiling from ear to ear with tears running down her cheeks.

"Were you eavesdropping, my dear?" he asked.

She threw her arms around him and hugged him with all her might. "Yes...Of course I was! Did you think for one minute that I was going to let you get away from here without me?"

"I suppose not," he said as Augustin chuckled.

She released her bear hug and stepped back slightly. Angelina had a smile somewhat reminiscent of Mona Lisa's as she arched one eyebrow, as if to say, *I'm waiting.*

It took him a second to comprehend the meaning of the look. "Oh, right...Almost forgot..." Eric dropped to his knee and reached for her right hand. "Angelina Michelle LeBlanc...I love you with all my heart and soul. I promise to forever cherish and protect you, as long I shall live. Will you grant me the greatest honor on earth and marry me?"

Her green eyes sparkled in the candlelight as a huge smile came to her face. "Eric Schmidt, nothing would make give me more joy than to be your wife."

He rose to his feet and kissed her passionately as Augustin beamed his approval.

Moonlight filtered though the ivory colored linen shears lining the tall bedroom windows. Eric rolled over in the four poster bed and wondered what time it was. Sleep had been sporadic at best as he was still very excited from Angelina's ready acceptance. Suddenly, he heard the faint noise of the bedroom's hallway door handle being turned. He reached to the night stand for the Remington revolver he always kept nearby. The door swung open slowly, almost without a sound.

Light from a single candle flickered over the form of a young woman, clad only in a diaphanous silk nightgown. She tiptoed into the room and carefully closed the walnut door and turned the skeleton key to lock it. Her bare feet padded silently across the finely woven oriental rug as she approached the bed. She glanced down at him and was only slightly surprised to find his blue eyes wide open and looking up at her. He smiled.

"I could not sleep," she said.

He shook his head. "Neither could I."

She set the brass candle holder on the night table closest to the door. Her red hair was no longer piled fashionably above her head. Angelina and taken it down and brushed it with one hundred stokes—as was her nightly custom—before retiring earlier. It fell in long, glistening strands across her breasts and was rising and falling with every one of her rapid breaths. "I thought about it for hours..." she said as she raised the covers and slipped between the sheets.

"Thought about what?"

"How empty my life would be if I never got to love you...I know...you cannot stay...even if I asked you to." She laid her head on the down pillow.

Eric rolled over on his side to face her. "God knows...you are the most beautiful woman I have ever seen...But I cannot risk your reputation with my desires to have you right now."

She giggled. "Why did I have to fall in love with Sir Galahad?...Kind sir, my reputation is intact...you asked for my hand and I gave it willingly. As far as I am concerned, we are already married...anything else...is merely a formality." She slipped her hand under his nightshirt and ran it up between his legs.

He gulped as her fingers wrapped around his turgid manhood and squeezed it firmly.

"At least part of you agrees with me."

"You know what I mean…" he said as he softly brushed her cheek. "We should wait until we get married after the battle."

"Or not," she said. Angelina released her intimate hold, then tossed back the covers as she slid her over on top of him and quickly sat up. She crossed her arms and tugged the silken nightgown past her head and tossed it on the floor. Leaning down, she pressed her ample breasts against his muscular chest and kissed him passionately.

He wrapped his arms around her and held on tightly as they both began to feel their passions rise.

She sat up again as they both were again gasping for breath.

"Let us get you out of this night shirt. I want to see everything that I am getting myself into…"

He readily complied and pulled the cotton flannel garment over his head. "You are becoming somewhat bossy, now that I have proposed…are you not?"

"I know what I like and I usually get my way…you can ask my father."

"I will have to take your word for it."

Angelina ran her hands over his chest and traced the chiseled outline of his pectoral muscles before drifting down to his washboard abdominals. "Just like one of those Greek statues…"

His hands drifted up from her hourglass waist to caress her breasts tenderly. "You are even more gorgeous than Venus de Milo…with arms, of course."

They spent time exploring each other's body by the flickering candlelight. Eric lifted her up and laid her down beside him. The two young and inexperienced lovers finally joined together and felt the culmination of their years of passion for each other. He kissed her one more time and rolled over on his back. Angelina snuggled up against his chest and listened to his heart beating strongly.

"Have I told you lately that I love you?"

He grinned. "Not in the last five minutes."

"I am so sorry…I could not catch my breath…"

"Nor could I." He grinned and stroked her silky locks back from her face. "No matter what happens next week, my love…we will always have this moment."

A single tear fell. She brushed it awau and forced herself to smile. "Do not go off and get yourself killed, Eric Schmidt…I absolutely forbid it."

"Yes ma'am…I promise."

Angelina closed her eyes and gave a silent prayer for his safe return as she held on tightly.

SHREVEPORT-NATCHITOCHES STAGECOACH ROAD
April 8th, 1864

Eric scanned the road where it made a slight bend a mile and a half south of the Sabine Crossroads. Using his binoculars, he could easily count the Union cavalry sent that morning to probe the Confederate positions ahead of General Banks and the main body of the Army of the Gulf. He continued to watch as the two columns—each over fifty horsemen long—came into view. He waited until they were both fully exposed and insured that there were no others coming right behind them "Boys, looks like we have a full company coming at us. Ya'll know the plan...time to get it done."

His major and captain commanding the first two companies in his battalion saluted and returned to their hidden positions in the dense foliage. Eric sent hand signals across the dirt road to his first sergeant. That soldier acknowledged the number of enemy cavalry approaching and sent a young corporal messenger with the latest word to the reserve company hidden in a narrower choke point a quarter mile up to the northwest.

Colonel Schmidt stowed his field glasses in the well worn saddlebags and lashed them tight. He could feel his heart rate beginning to pound faster as the Yankees trotted into the trap. A slight southern breeze blew the Spanish moss back and forth in the oak trees above him and his mount stamped somewhat nervously as he could hear the approaching hoof beats. A flock of white herons flew overhead in a westerly direction in search of a quiet stream. *Must be gunboats on the river.* He pulled the double barreled shotgun from his scabbard. At close range encounters, he had learned it was just as deadly as a rifle and sometimes took out two adversaries with one shot at the head level.

The Second Battalion had become well-versed in the art of mounted ambush. Schmidt preferred to use overwhelming force in rapid attacks. Some of his men were hidden in the ferns and underbrush lining the main stage roadway. Their horses were tied off twenty to forty yards back into the woods, ready for an advance or retreat as needed.

Eric glanced to the left at his bugler, Wyman Scoggins, a young corporal from Athens, Texas. He had his slightly tarnished brass instrument at the ready, and he was already nervously licking his parched lips in preparation for his bit of disinformation and confusion he would add to the Union Army woes.

Finally the Yankee company moved into the killing zone Schmidt had selected. Their commander was riding a full row behind the unit's standard bearer as the guidon flag fluttered in the wind. Eric noted the major was on the far side of the column, so he picked another target that would still do some damage. He lined the brass bead sight of his shotgun up with the union private with the shiny bugle hanging by a yellow cord around his neck. Pulling a slight lead to compensate for the six miles per hour trot, he squeezed off the first round...

With the shotgun's blast, an acrid cloud of gray gunsmoke obscured the target momentarily, but a riderless horse appeared a half second later as a couple of hundred shots rang out in the next few seconds.

Wyman blew the Union Army signal for *charge* twice as the confused and decimated columns spun around and attempted to react to the onslaught. A thick pawl of gunsmoke filled the woods from both sides of the road and began to drift upwards and filter into the treetops.

Most of the Yanks pulled their pistols and fired blindly into the haze out of desperation. The handful that dismounted and ran for cover quickly met their fate when a half dozen pistol shots fired from pointblank range found their marks.

Only a dozen of the Union soldiers—five of them wounded—responded to the commands to charge. They were galloping ahead, brandishing their sabers when a couple of bugle blasts of the signal to *retreat* were sounded. None of them knew that their commander had died of multiple gunshots in the first volley. Four of the mounted survivors ignored the signal in their panic. They rode helter-skelter into the Confederate reserves awaiting them where intense rifle fire cut them to pieces.

"Wyman, give me *Dixie*...loud and clear, if you please."

"Yes, sir!" He took in a deep breath and sent forth the unit's signal to *recall*.

Like gray ghosts from the swamps, the men of the first and second companies moved out to take the remaining Yankees prisoner.

"Get 'em back up in the saddle if they can ride. Prepare them for transport back to Camp Ford in Tyler. Otherwise, leave 'em for the Union doctors. We are gonna have plenty for our own surgeons to tend to."

"You heard the colonel!" bellowed the first sergeant. "Collect all their arms and pile 'em over here...Ain't got all day!"

Eric rode up and down the lines, but kept one eye on the road to the southeast. "First Company, report."

"Two wounded, one dead sir."

"Second Company…"

His command was cut short by a quick reply, "Two dead, three wounded and one unaccounted for, sir."

"All right…get moving. If they try to escape…shoot to kill!" he called out in a loud voice so that all the prisoners could hear.

Using Union horses to carry the captured weapons tied up in bundles, the Second Battalion headed north as another Yankee patrol appeared around the distant bend in the road. It was quickly apparent that the force was much larger than a company size. Eric didn't bother trying to count the oncoming hordes. It was obvious that they numbered in the hundreds of cavalry and were being followed closely behind by the infantry, artillery and a complete logistic train.

"Third Company…fall in!" the young colonel ordered as they rode up along side his reserves. He pointed to a trusted sergeant. "Thompson…I want you to ride ahead and report directly to General Taylor. My suggestion is to set up our artillery for an impact area on that rise just before it opens up into the big meadow. You know the place?"

"I do. Right past that choke point on that ridge."

"Good. Let him know that Bank's main force is only a couple of miles behind us. Got all that?"

"Yes, sir. Anythin' else?"

"One more thing…If the Yankee cavalry makes a run for us after they find out what happened to their scout company, have Gray and Daniels prepared to fire over our heads. We will try to draw them into cannon range as best we can. There is no way in hell the Yanks can get their artillery into position to cause us a problem on the retreat."

"Colonel…a short round from our side…"

"I know…A calculated risk I am willin' to take…Now get going."

Thompson nodded agreement, and saluted. He extended his hand. "Gook luck to you, Colonel. Think you are gonna be a needing it."

"Appreciate it." Eric shook his hand and the sergeant wheeled around and spurred his horse into an extended lope.

Schmidt rejoined the column and rode to the lead as Thompson's mount increased the distance between him and the remaining members of the Second Battalion.

Elements of the 14th Cavalry from New York under General Lucas arrived first at the scene of carnage in the road. Dozens of bodies littered the ground and a few severely injured fellow troopers called up for help.

A fresh faced Lieutenant Colonel named Beasley from Albany reacted quickly. "First platoon! Fall out and assist the wounded. Get this road clear…The rest of you are with me!" He waved his hand forward and took the balance of the company onward at a canter. He could see the Confederates retreating ahead and wanted nothing more than to give them a taste of their own medicine.

His first platoon dismounted and began the unpleasant task of pulling the dead clear of the dirt road and offering medical assistance and water to the severely injured.

"Get a doctor up here! Pass it back!" one enlisted man called out.

His request was relayed back down the line until a young physician riding with the 18th Cavalry—also from New York—responded and rode up to see what was needed. He was only twenty five years old and straight out of medical school. Without a team of surgeons and a field hospital at his disposal, he felt completely inadequate to deal with the sucking chest wounds and gunshots to the gut.

He cut open a grizzled sergeant's tunic to find a dime sized hole oozing dark red blood on the side of the abdomen. The injured man's eyes were glazed with shock as he rolled him over and looked for an exit wound. The doctor found a ragged half dollar sized hole where the bullet had mushroomed and exited through the lowest rib in the back.

Jesus…Liver shot. There's nothing I can do…

He rolled the man onto his back as a death rattle emerged from the NCO's throat. Taking his thumb and middle finger he closed the soldier's eyelids and looked around for another survivor.

Approaching the rise in the woods, Captain Doran Ingrham took a glance back at the pursuing battalion. *They have cut the distance to 800 yards.* "Colonel, they are still out of rifle range but are closing in mighty fast."

Eric turned in his saddle. "'Bout the way I planned it. What do you think we should do?"

"You are asking me for advice?"

He smiled. "Actually, I want to see if you learned anything in the last few months...just in case I go and get myself killed."

Doran looked somewhat perplexed but plunged ahead. "We are coming up the big wide meadow. We have nine thousand men set up on the far side of the clearing and another five thousand in reserve. Artillery support should be available if Thompson made it through."

"That is true...What I am asking you is what should *we* do."

Ingrham locked eyes with the big colonel, who gave not a hint of what he was thinking. "We do not want to stand here and fight toe-to-toe with a full battalion. That would be a waste of good men...I say we should slow down the retreat and let the Yanks think that they are catching us...Suck them into cannon range and let our boys tear 'em all to hell and gone before we counterattack."

Eric grinned. "By God, I think you will make a cavalry officer yet." He spurred his horse forward and the two men rode to the front of the column. "Bring 'em back to a walk, Major Farmer. Do not want those bluebellies to lose interest in us before we get across the ridge."

"Aye, sir." He raised his hand. "First Company!...Forward at a walk."

Shouts repeating the command echoed back down the columns. Some of the replacement men looked nervously back at their pursuers. Others who had fought with Schmidt for years, merely grinned.

"Oh, hell. Just be damned glad that you ain't with them Yankees a followin' us," one commented. "I get the feelin' our Colonel has already done kilt 'em all and they just ain't heard old Gabriel blow his horn yet."

Eric conveyed his orders to all three of his company commanders then pulled his own horse to a halt near the crest of the hill. The columns resumed a trot and continued to move northwest. Huge mature moss-covered trees covered the ridge line in both directions and created a natural funnel through the large meadows on both sides of it. He retrieved the binoculars from his bags and checked the rapidly approaching Union cavalry before he urged the stallion up the crest.

From there, he could see the massed formations of Confederate infantry in the distance and did a quick survey of the various artillery unit emplacements. Most were well behind the lines of men and had significant amounts of earthen breastworks and sawn logs installed to help protect the cannon crews.

He turned around to check on the Union cavalry that had been pursuing him and the men of the Second. They had closed the distance and were under five hundred yards away and moving up fast.

Colonel Beasley eyed the lone Confederate officer suspiciously. He, too, relied on his field glasses and could see the sun glinting off the silver stars on the man's uniform. *Hell's bells...we have ourselves a rebel colonel out there, just taking in the view.*

"Watson! Fall out and get that rifle of yours ready!"

The sergeant, one of the better marksmen in the battalion, did as he was ordered. He pulled out of the line of trotting cavalrymen and reined up beside Beasley and his executive officer. He slid his Sharps carbine off his shoulder and checked the security of the primer seated under the hammer. "Yes, sir...what be the target?"

"See if you can knock that reb colonel off his horse before he gets over that ridge."

He squinted at the distant rider. "I will do my best...It is a almost a quarter mile away, I reckon."

"You did it at Chickamaugua...Tell you what, take him on the first shot and I will throw in a five dollar gold piece."

Watson grinned as he pulled the front ladder sight up to 450 yards. "Get your money ready, Colonel," he said as he brought the rifle up to his shoulder.

Eric watched curiously as the man took aim at him. *Bit out of range for the average shooter...*A cloud of whitish smoke belched out of the .50 caliber rifle. The young Confederate colonel pressed his left knee slightly against the well-trained black stallion—it immediately side-passed two yards to the right. Eric stuck his left hand through the leather strap on his binocular and let it fall free as he quickly yanked his Springfield from its boot. A heavy slug whistled past him and ricocheted off the road at the crest. *Damnation! He is a good one.*

He thumbed up his rifle's sight for the distance to the target and drew a fine bead. He let out half his breath and squeezed the trigger. The rifle bucked into his shoulder as the .58 caliber slug arced through the air.

Schmidt pushed his mount back to the left as another cloud of smoke erupted from the Union shooter. *How in blazes did he reload that fast?*

"You are gonna have to try harder…" the Yankee colonel began to say when the chunk of hot lead ripped into his chest and knocked him out of the saddle.

It was clear the distant rebel could shoot accurately. The executive officer looked down in horror as the blood spurted from the ragged hole in his former commander's chest. The wounded man's mouth was open and frothy bright red blood streamed from his nose—it was instantly obvious that the shot was fatal. The major looked back up the road where the rebel was disappearing over the crest of the ridge.

"Dammit to hell! The murdering bastard is getting away! Forward at the gallop…ho!" He hastily drew his saber and leveled it, pointing at the road ahead.

The two columns of cavalry broke into a ragged surge forward as the unit's three buglers sounded the charge.

Eric put his stallion into a rocking horse lope and then spurred him into a gallop when the sounds of overlapping bugle calls of the rapidly approaching enemy drifted over the ridge. Three hundred yards north, his Second Battalion was arrayed in a blocking formation in a series of three shallow arcs. One platoon had continued north with the Union prisoners and captured weaponry. He pulled up alongside Captain Ingrham and reined to a sliding stop. "Looks like we have a whole battalion coming in hot."

"If I know you...you had to do something to aggravate them."

Eric grinned. "Just playin' their game...They took a potshot at me."

"I heard a couple from them and one from you. Who did you shoot?"

"I think he was their commander. Rolled his butt out of the saddle, whoever he was."

"How far?"

"Far enough...quarter mile maybe...Did Sergeant Thompson make it through to General Taylor?"

"You bet, Colonel. He is over there in the Third Company with Major Means...Said the general was happy as a kid in a candy store and he would be right proud to make the Yankee's arrival a special one."

"Glad to hear that. Like you said, we would not like to fight it out toe-to-toe out here in the open...We are not God's own fools."

At that instant, the lead elements of the Union charge crested the hill. They focused on the Confederate cavalry deployed immediately across their path and began to hoop and holler their war cries. The men of the Second Battalion responded in kind as they readied their rifles.

Colonel Schmidt had briefed a maneuver derived from studying naval warfare. In a straight line convoy, a string of ships was limited in firepower due to the range of its guns. The lead ship would be in range long before the trailing ones. Therefore the optimum tactic for engaging a strong, even superior force, would be to *cross the T*. A commander could arrange his fleet to sail or steam perpendicular to the incoming enemy force and have all of his ships fire simultaneously in a tactic known as *maximum broadsides* at the oncoming lead vessel. In that manner, he could take advantage of all his firepower while the enemy was limited with his.

Eric bellowed out his command, "First and Second Companies...dismount and ground your horses!"

Over two hundred men swung out of the saddles and forced their mounts to kneel and then lay down. They crouched down behind the prone horses and took aim at the oncoming Union cavalry.

Several hundred yards behind the Second Battalion, General Taylor watch through brass telescope as the enemy thundered closer—an almost solid snake of blue squeezing through the narrow gap at the ridge top. *Got to hand it to those Texas boys...they are showing me some backbone out there.*

Almost half of the Yankee battalion had entered the meadow when he gave the order. "Signal the artillery to commence firing."

The lanky sergeant quickly complied, "Yes, sir!" He waved the semaphores briskly and then repeated the flag signal. The second was not really needed as the rapid cascade of cannon blasts ripped the morning's silence from the northern reaches of the kidney shaped meadow.

Eric saw the lead Union element was crossing the two hundred yard stake that his men had placed alongside the stagecoach road. "Take aim and make them count, boys! Fire at will!"

The roar of a hundred rifles in the first row of dismounted cavalry was deafening. After firing, each man bit off the end of the prepared paper wrapped cartridges and dumped the load of black powder down the muzzle, and followed it up with the .58 caliber Minié ball and rammed it home.

The first volley of cannon fire arrived in the target area simultaneously with the bullets from the cavalrymen—the results were catastrophic for the men from New York. Shrapnel and rifle ball tore into the column, ripping into man and beast indiscriminately. A handful of soldiers rode on through the carnage and emerged from the dust and smoke, as the men in the Second Company picked out individual targets and fired in unison. The closest Yankees fell under a hail of accurate bullets, but behind them, others were ready to press on as they crossed over the ridge, unaware of the threat of the deadly gauntlet of fire that they soon would face.

Eric rammed home another round in his rifle, stuck the rod in the ground close by and a placed fresh musket cap on the sooty nipple. He rolled back onto his belly as a second round of cannon shells shrieked low overhead. He could actually see the black 3.55 inch diameter balls in flight. Using a timed fuse, the shells detonated the powder charge inside once the round had traveled the calculated distance to target and exploded among the columns of Union cavalry. Troops from Eric's third company knelt and fired over the heads of their prone compatriots in the other two companies—creating an almost constant volume of fire at the Union forces.

***

CHAPTER THIRTEEN

MANSFIELD, LOUISIANA

The smoke and rifle fire was absolutely incredible as the combination of concentrated small arms and the artillery barrage wreaked havoc on the vanguard of Bank's Union cavalry.

Colonel Schmidt caught a glimpse of a mounted sergeant trying to cut to his left. He placed the front sight a good five feet in front of the horse's nose, maintained the lead and squeezed the trigger as a shell from a six pounder detonated fifteen yards behind the Yankee. The rifle bucked back in recoil—a fraction of a second later the rider pitched off the horse as if catapulted. Eric reloaded again as he heard distant Union buglers sound the charge.

The breeze drifted the rifle smoke away and unveiled a scene of almost unimaginable carnage. Riderless horses—some of them badly wounded—stumbled and scattered from the killing zone. Scores of dead and wounded covered the roadway and surrounding ground from a hundred and fifty yards out from Schmidt's battalion almost all the way to the wooded ridge line.

The last of the ill-fated Yankee unit from New York cleared the shallow rise and continued the charge amid the carnage and chaos that lay before them. The words of Lord Tennyson came to him as if in a dream :

> *Cannon to right of them,*
> *Cannon in front of them,*
> *Volley'd & thunder'd;*
> *Storm'd at with shot and shell,*
> *Boldly they rode and well,*
> *Into the jaws of Death,*
> *Into the mouth of Hell*
> *Rode the six hundred. ...*

He looked on as shell after shell tore them asunder. *My God...Did they not learn anything from the British in the Crimean War? Why in hell cannot you stupid bastards just give up and leave us alone?*

Eric waved and hollered at his guidon bearer, "Signal the artillery to cease fire!"

"Yes, sir!" he responded and raised a red four foot square cloth flag attached to the long pole.

The troops in the back two rows behind him began to hold their fire as the young trooper rose up on one knee and briskly waved the distinctive banner back and forth.

Half a minute later, the big Confederate guns fell silent.

"Second Brigade! Mount up…Stand at the ready!"

Schmidt's men scrambled up, tugged on their horse's reins and forked their saddles once the mounts had gotten themselves to their feet. Only three of the troopers had been wounded during the brief firefight, and five of their horses and been hit. He shoved his rifle down into the waiting scabbard and drew out his saber.

"Buglers! Sound the charge!"

Leading off with his big black stallion, Eric took his men across the open meadow toward the remnants of the shattered Union force. Those stunned survivors who did not surrender immediately were cut down by a volley of pistol shots as the rebels closed in. A few of the remaining company of Union cavalry noted the huge numerical advantage of the advancing Confederates and initiated a retreat without waiting for an order to do so.

Others, including a burly former lumberjack from upstate New York, didn't break and run. The huge master sergeant was sporting a gash across his left check where a piece of hot shrapnel had flayed him and he wanted a chance for some personal payback. He spotted the colonel leading the charge and spurred his big blue roan to intercept. He cursed at the rebel commander when their sabers crossed and clanged—sparks flew as they passed.

Both men reined right to quickly re-engage their opponent, keeping their weapons between themselves and the other rider. The screams of wounded and dying men echoed across the battlefield as the Confederates skillfully defended their home turf from the blue clad invaders.

Eric figured correctly that he was not likely to overpower the six-foot-six Paul Bunyan in the flesh. He parried the Union soldier's thrust and countered with a backhand slash at his neck. The sergeant instinctively leaned away from the blade and it missed by only inches. Before he could regain his balance, Eric followed up with a forehand to the man's thigh. The razor sharp blade cut through fabric and muscle alike and laid open a six-inch-long gash. The New Yorker's right hand went to the wound without thinking.

Schmidt had learned to anticipate his opponent moves three or four in advance. In a lighting fast thrust, he jabbed through the soldier's bulging triceps and buried the first ten inches of his saber's gleaming blade deep into the man's chest.

The Yankee's back arched as the intense burning sensation of the saber racked his body. He felt his right arm was pinned and used his massive shoulder muscles to free it.

Eric looked on as the blood gushed out of the man's severed triceps and the dumfounded soldier dropped the saber from his hand. He yanked his blade clear and made another crushing backhand...this time to the sergeant's neck, just below the skull.

The Yankee's head snapped back violently—his blue forage cap tumbling and bouncing off the roan's rump. His body slumped and slid out of the saddle, landing across the lower torso of another soldier ripped in two by cannon fire.

Eric spurred his horse forward to a melee where three Union troops were engaging a pair of Confederates. With one mighty blow, he severed a Yankee private's right arm. *That should even out the fight a bit.* He sheathed his bloody saber and drew the Remington revolver from his right hip.

He chased a couple of retreating stragglers back over the crest of the ridge as of the last union troops still attempting to fight were cut down by pistol fire. One of the retreating soldiers turned in the saddle and took a shot at him. The .44 caliber ball tore into the silver star braid on the right side of his collar, but failed to actually penetrate the wool uniform. He leveled his well used sixgun and returned fire at forty yards, striking the man in the lower back several inches from the spine.

The Yankee hunched over and managed to stay in the saddle, even with a probable fatal kidney wound. He and his friends continued to gallop southeast as fast as their horses could run—clods of red Louisiana clay flying up behind their hooves.

Eric looked past the handful of retreating troops and saw a sight that caused him rein back on his sweaty mount. His well-trained horse responded instantly, sliding to a stop with his back legs carving a perfect pair of elevens in the packed dirt. Both he and Thunder were breathing heavily from the adrenaline of the noisy battle as he studied the approaching Union force. A long uninterrupted line of blue stretched out as far as he could see down the road.

Oh, my God...Got to be at least nine thousand of them. That is what the reports from Natchitoches had said. He spun Thunder around a couple of times to check for any nearby threats. Finding none, he holstered the revolver, reached into his saddle bags and pulled out the binoculars. Adjusting the two eyepieces to focus on the far distances, could see cavalry leading several brigades of infantry and intermixed with them were field artillery, caissons and supply wagons of all sort.

So this is what it is like back in the east. None of the battles Eric had participated in before had involved much more than a few hundred men. It was obvious that over 20,000 men would be engaged in the day's fighting in what would be known as the Battle of Mansfield. He stowed the field glasses, turned back to the ridge and rode back down into the killing field. Coming upon one of his buglers, he called out, "Mister Tomkins…sound recall, if you please."

Crossing the meadow with his entire battalion and two dozen prisoners of war, Eric glassed the northernmost recesses for the flags of each unit. Directly to the north were those of the Louisiana Brigades under General Mouton. Almost a mile away were the distinctive swallowtail Lone Star banners of the Texas units under Generals Bagby and Lane comprising the left flank of the Confederate's defensive positions.

"Sergeant Major," he said pointing to the northeast. "That should be Lane's boys set up way over yonder. Take the men up there and see that they get fed. Designate a squad to escort all the wounded to the hospital tents and turn the prisoners over to the security section. The company commanders will accompany me to debrief this morning's action with General Taylor."

"Yes, sir. Be my pleasure."

As the top enlisted man executed his orders, Eric pulled out of formation and collected the three junior officers he needed and rode ahead to meet with the major general.

Arriving at the command section, they dismounted and proceeded to the front of the large white tent. A sentry snapped to attention and blocked their entrance.

"Sir, the General is having commander's call at this time. You will have to wait here."

Brigadier General Lane looked out and saw the four men standing at the far end of the tent. He quickly made his way to the sentry. "It is all right, son. The general will want to hear what they have to say."

The sentry moved aside. "Sorry, sir."

Eric extended his hand. "Appreciate you help, General. Got some news that will not wait."

"Came a little close there, did they not?" Lane asked, pointing at the frayed sliver thread on the Colonel's collar. "That your blood?"

Schmidt's gray wool was spattered with red from the two saber encounters with the Union cavalry. His right thigh was particularly drenched.

"No, sir...Guess the good Lord is looking out for me."

The back of the command tent featured a large table with detailed map of the battlefield painted on it. Wooden blocks with various unit designations were placed to replicate the actual disposition of forces at that time. A dozen senior officers crowded around it as Taylor discussed the situation as he saw it.

"General, sorry to interrupt, but this is Colonel Schmidt, the commander of the Second that made such a fine showing out there this morning."

Taylor broke into a huge grin. "Gentlemen, make way. I have to congratulate this man. By Hannah...he gave the Yanks *what for* on this day." He stepped past a couple of brigadiers and extended his hand. "Great to see you again, Colonel."

"Same here, sir. I need to advise you that Banks and the rest of his main force are less than two miles out...a line of blue as far the eye can see."

Taylor nodded. "I had some spotters in the treetops along the ridge. I understand you made good contact earlier today."

"Yes, sir. We killed or captured a company-sized force a few miles to the south and then had that fracas in the meadow...About fifty of 'em got away."

"But your plan went like clockwork...Where did you learn that trick about laying your horses down?"

"One of my company commanders, Captain Ingrham here, is a former Texas Ranger. He learned that tidbit fighting Comanches...works well if you can keep them out of range."

"Whatever works, I say...I do want to commend you and your men for their bravery and discipline in that firefight...Calling for artillery fire over your heads...That showed some sand."

"My unit commanders deserve all the credit for the training of our men. I will be sure to pass on the complement to the troops. They held fast when needed and, by the way...your accurate artillery was the primary factor in the battle today. If we can keep Banks from breaking out past this ridge line..." He moved to the table map. "...we can bottle him up good. This road is narrow as ya'll know and it forces them to concentrate right here. That should afford our artillery an advantage. If they try to cut another path through the woods, we can target that spot as well."

"You men surely see why we picked this spot to set up our defenses," Taylor said to his commanders. "Colonel, I want you and your men to take a breather for a while...You certainly deserve it...General Lane here will place you in reserve, to be called upon as needed."

"The men will appreciate that, sir. My first sergeant is seeing to it that the troops get fed as soon as they can...but we will be ready to fight again when necessary."

"Cannot ask any more of you. We are off to a great start, thanks to you and the men of the Second...Get yourself some rest and plan to be deployed later in the day."

Eric stepped back and saluted smartly. Taylor returned the gesture. Lane patted him on the shoulder as he and his subordinates passed and gave him an appreciative wink.

"You done good, son."

By noon, the Union commander Banks had dispersed his men in a tightly packed *L* shaped arrangement—the long arm of the *L* was in the tree line in the eastern end of the ridge, while the short arm was back a quarter mile from the ridge with a small meadow providing a good field of fire for his artillery if the rebels tried to used the road to attack. Units from Illinois, Ohio,

246

Iowa, Kentucky, Indiana, Massachusetts, Missouri and New York faced the Confederates.

Banks ordered his cavalry to attack and search any weaknesses in the rebel defenses. All the probing actions did was confirm his worst fears—the capable Major General Taylor had laid out a formidable crossfire with cannons and made the Union cavalry pay dearly with each advance. All of the well-defended rebel infantry units were able to beat back the Yankee forays.

Taylor made a decision to attack Banks before he could strengthen his position. He had Brigadier General Mouton engage with his infantry as units of the Texas Cavalry attacked from both flanks. Mouton bravely led his men forward but was picked off and killed by a Yankee rifleman. His men continued forward, but took heavy losses—almost a third of the unit were casualties.

General Taylor was personally hit hard by the loss of his friend and forced to transfer command of the Louisiana detachments to another brigadier general descended from French nobility. Camille Armand Jules Marie—known better as Prince de Polignac—was a French Army veteran of the Crimean War. His aristocratic grandmother had been best friends with Queen Marie-Antoinette, but the men of the Texas Infantry Brigade knew him simply as Prince Polecat.

Eric watched the savage battle unfold from the left flank. *How the hell did those Yankee riflemen inflict such a high casualty rate at such a distance?* The rate of fire surpassed that of the muzzle loading Springfields and Enfields that his men were issued.

A young rider came in fast from Taylor's headquarters. He rode directly up to General Lane and handed him the leather dispatch case containing the written orders. The brigadier quickly pulled the message out and read it aloud,

"Mouton killed in action. Polignac leading frontal assault on Banks' center. Require all available cavalry to attack flanks. Most urgent. Advise your intentions." He folded the missive. "Tell the General we will be engaged by the time he hears this reply."

"Understand, sir...Right away, sir," the young corporal replied. He saluted and wheeled his mount to deliver Lane's response.

Colonel Schmidt had been standing nearby awaiting the expected orders. The brigade commander turned to him and grinned. "Looks as if your lollygagging days are over, Colonel...Taylor wants us to support Polignac and the Texas Infantry in the center."

"Will do, sir. I saw General Mouton as he fell. His boys are getting ripped apart out there...I sent one of my company commanders on a scouting expedition two hours ago. He found a small meadow located just east of the Yankee's lines...Apparently, it is not visible from their position. I believe we can work our way through the woods and regroup there to attack them in force from behind."

"I trust your judgment, Eric...Do not take too long. We have to support the assault on the center or all those brave men died for naught."

"I understand, sir...Luck be with you." Eric extended his hand instead of saluting.

The two shook hands firmly and Eric broke away and hurried to his horse.

Arriving back at the reserve encampment, he sought out Captain Ingrham. "Saddle up...You are leading us to that hidden meadow you found. Make it snappy, but keep the noise down, if you can. I want our arrival to be a complete surprise."

"Column of twos at the max, Colonel. Kinda tight in them woods, but it is dry between the creeks. We will be on top of those Yankee bastards before they know what hit 'em."

"That is the general idea...now get the lead out." Eric hollered to the closest bugler, "Sound assembly!"

As the notes echoed across the campsite, 290 men scrambled to get mounted.

Doran stepped to his dapple gray gelding and untied the lead rope off the metal hook on the picket line. He grabbed the near-side heavy horsehair cinch and pulled it tight enough to push the tongue of the latigo through the large brass ring looped it off. He jumped up, stabbed his dusty squared toed boot into the metal stirrup and then swung his right leg over the big gray's rump. He pulled the slack from the reins and sat back in the saddle. "Settle down, there, Jack. There will be plenty of time to get nervous later."

Horrendous sounds of the battlefield penetrated the woods as the Confederate troops maneuvered between the centuries old stand of loblolly pines. The forest floor was barren of green growth and littered eight inches deep with dead pine needles. Overhead a dense canopy precluded the sun's direct rays from ever reaching the ground.

Ingrham weaved his way through, entered the two hundred yard wide oval-shaped clearing and then continued until he was only forty yards from the south end when he drew rein. He motioned to the men of his company to continue to file past and take up their positions.

Eric came through with the second company and took a spot in the western edge. When the last of the troops had made it to the meadow, he pulled one of his four revolvers. All his men followed his signal and drew their weapons as well. He could feel his pulse begin to quicken as he nudged Thunder into a walk, directly toward the sounds of the Union cannons.

The incessant crack of rifle fire from the front lines of the Yankee soldiers let him know that there were still plenty of Confederate troops and cavalry engaged. Acrid gunsmoke from the battle drifted through the last hundred yards of woods separating the advancing rebel horsemen from the Union-held position.

Eric tried to keep sight of all his units as they attempted to kept abreast of him, but the smoke made that nearly impossible. He could see only a hundred or so of them as they eased though woods like silent gray ghosts on a rendezvous with death. His bugler hung tight beside him as the only means to communicate with so many men with the cacophony of noise from the enemy lines ahead.

General Banks listened to the report detailed to him from the young captain. He was situated in a command tent a full half mile behind the last line of cannons and almost a mile from the forward rifle positions.

"So you say they that have killed at least five hundred infantry with less than a hundred lost on our side?"

The young officer nodded. "Yes, sir. We think they might start to retreat as they cannot sustain those kind of losses indefinitely. Our lines are holding firm, sir."

Banks looked own at his own paper map with his units laid out in numbered flags representing the units deployed. "We cannot win a battle from a defensive position. Tell General Dudley I need him and the 31st Massachusetts to attack in force in fifteen minutes. Advise Al Lee to send out the 16th Indiana as well. I want Taylor's rebs to be on the defensive...We shall find out if he is willing to take three thousand casualties to hold this scrub pasture...That will tell us what kind of man he really is."

The captain snapped to attention and barked his reply, "Yes, General." He made an about face, strode quickly to his waiting horse.

No one was watching behind the Union lines as nearly three hundred mounted Confederates broke free from the trees on the eastern flank. Most were far too busy firing at the massive numbers of troops advancing from the north. Eric pulled the hammer back on his pistol as the bugler's charge sounded.

A gunner from one of the many artillery units positioned well back behind the Union lines caught sight of the movement out of his peripheral vision. He tried to yell a warning to his commander, but was cut down by a .44 caliber ball.

Holding his reins in his teeth, Eric fired well-aimed shots from each hand as he and others charged through the canon emplacements, decimating the Union gun crews and spreading terror and disarray among the survivors.

Other members of the Second Brigade closed on the Union's infantry right flank, creating panic in the troops from the 14th and 18th brigades from New York under Brigadier General Albert Lee. Hit from two sides by fierce rebel attacks, many of the men—weary from the long march—chose to surrender.

Mounted Yankee infantry, belonging to the 16th out of Indiana and the 2nd from Iowa were likewise caught in a crossfire as the Texans swept in from the east.

Eric fired both his Remingtons until they were dry. He stuffed them quickly inside the flapped holsters and pulled the two spares from the custom-made open-topped ones on his stallion's withers. He continued the attack and soon found himself near a clapboard frame structure along the stagecoach road—known locally as the Fincher House. A Union officer was riding back toward the front at gallop. Pushing his pistols back into their simple, but effective rigs, Eric drew his Springfield from the scabbard and thumbed the hammer back to full cock.

The young officer was riding almost directly at him as he centered the front sight blade on the man's chest. Eric noted the captain had drawn his sidearm and was bringing it up to eye level when he sent the round down range. A cloud of sulfurous smoke belched out as his rifle cracked. He nudged his horse to the right to allow him to see his opponent. The body of the young messenger was laid back over the cantle, but still seated in the saddle as the horse galloped past.

He heard a thunderous volley of fire erupt on the western flank as General Bee's Confederate cavalry units—the 26th and 1st—led a charge ahead of the infantry from General Scurry's 16th, 17th and 19th. The iconic Texas Lone Star flags as well as the Stars and Bars fluttered on the staffs born by brave infantrymen at the lead.

Union General Dudley never received the order to advance—thanks to the sharp shooting of one young rebel colonel. His flank folded under the onslaught as more Union soldiers began to surrender or simply ran away from the onrushing rebels. Some of the mounted units from far away Massachusetts attempted a counterattack, but were beaten back by accurate rifle fire and made a hasty decision to withdraw. They rode past the infantrymen from the Wisconsin 23rd that were abandoning the field in a near panic.

General Bates could hear something different was going on at the front. The sounds of distant enemy artillery had ceased and his own cannons were no longer pouring a murderous fire onto advancing Confederate infantry. He spun around and glared at his staff. "Colonel...Who the hell gave the order for the artillery to cease fire? I want to know the man's name and have him brought up on charges!" he bellowed.

"I will get things back under control, sir," the staff officer from Ohio promised as he turned to leave the command tent. He made it out to his horse and swung into the saddle as the first of over a hundred retreating cavalry galloped past. He held up his hand and halted a sergeant. "What's the meaning of this? No one gave any order to fall back."

"Meby so, Colonel, but them rebs have a say-so in the way things are a goin'...Right now they's a couple of thousand of 'em broke through on the flanks..."

The colonel stood up in his stirrups in order to see a bit better up the road. Looking over the heads of the mounted troops, he could see a wave of blue pouring into the road from both sides. Some of the caissons were hitched to teams and were falling back as well. "Dammit to hell!" He stepped down, ground tied his horse and ran back into the headquarters.

Banks looked up at the agitated man.

"General, the lines have been broken up front...The rebels outflanked us and everyone is falling back...It's a Godawful mess out there..."

"The hell you say..." Banks muttered. He looked at a location on the map a few miles south that looked promising. "Here is a spot north of Pleasant Hill...Get the word to Ransoms' 13th Corps to fall back there and make a stand."

The colonel nodded.

Banks pointed over to a major. "Head south and bring up all of Cameron's reserves. Let them know we intend to fight it out…but this location is no longer tenable…understand?"

"Yes sir."

Both men took their orders and departed in haste.

General Taylor listened to the reports coming in from the front. Another messenger rode up from the north. "Sir, the reserves under Brigadier Generals Churchill and Parsons have arrived. They asked me to advise you that they have five thousand troops available."

"Thank you, Corporal. Stand by…I think we will be using them directly." He studied the maps as his aides pushed the wooden blocks around on the board. "General Walker, your flanking maneuvers have done the trick it seems. It would not hurt your feelings if I sent the reserves in to push Banks on down the road a piece, now…Would it?"

"No, sir. My boys paid a heavy price in this afternoon's battle. They could use the rest."

"General Lane, do you feel the same?"

"Absolutely, sir. We lost too damn many brave soldiers out there…We have already taken over a thousand Yankee prisoners and captured twenty cannon and a hundred and fifty wagons, I am told."

"That settles it…Have you men hold where they are and we shall move up the reserves to continue to dog old Banks and his boys all the way back to New Orleans."

Eric gazed across the lines formerly held by the Union cavalry. Dead horses and men were strewn about in grotesque shapes as their bodies began to bloat. Flies buzzed incessantly as the stench of death became more nauseating by the minute. He reached back into his saddlebags and withdrew one of the spare revolver cylinders he had reloaded and primed during the lull earlier in the day. He pulled the cylinder pin out on the Remington and dropped the empty back into the saddle bag.

The full one—kept in a suede leather drawstring pouch—was slipped into the frame and the cylinder pin replaced.

Captain Ingrham rode up and offered him a drink from his canteen. "She ain't cold any more, but she is still wet."

"Thanks," Schmidt responded as he took a swig and handed it back. "How many did we lose?"

"Fifteen dead...and another eighteen wounded. The other companies were about the same."

"Damnation..." was all that Schmidt could muster for a reply.

"Gave a lot worse than we took, Colonel...For what it's worth...it is not your fault. We sent those blue bastards packing and captured five hundred or more...plus horses, cannon and supplies. I figure our artillery has just about doubled."

Eric nodded. "See that the men get fed well. I saw some tins of bully beef in the Union wagons. All of us have been living on short rations for some time now...Anything else?"

"Almost forgot...We found a couple of new type rifles on the New York regiment...one loads from the buttplate with a fixed brass cartridge and can hold seven rounds. And then there is another type rifle with paper cartridges. It loads from the back and has a sliding block that lifts up and closes off the barrel."

"Assign a detail to collect as many of those rifles as they can. I want to get my hands on them and see if they will give us any kind of advantage. Do not know which one was used by that trooper that popped at me this morning, but he dang sure surprised me with the speed of his second shot."

"Consider it done." Doran wheeled away to put together a scavenging team.

Eric lead his horse to a clear spot and dismounted. He untied and pulled a feed bag off the saddle skirt, and then filled it with the last of the oats he carried. He slipped it over Thunder's muzzle and secured it behind his poll. "Here you go, old sport. You earned it."

The sounds of the distant battle far to the south of Mansfield began to wane as darkness fell. Eric sat around the campfire with several of his men, many who were enjoying a relaxing cigar. He sat the tin cup on the ground beside his saddle. "You know, I almost had forgotten what real coffee tastes like…those blasted burnt acorns never even came close."

"You ain't lyin', Colonel. Some folks like the way the Cajuns down here boil up some of their chicory roots and call that nasty stuff coffee as well. My pappy says it tastes like seed ticks smell."

Eric nodded as he looked over at the young captain. "Well, never smelled a seed tick, so I'll take your word for it...Were you able to get together that list of our men killed in action?"

"Yes, sir...Each one of the companies wrote down the bad news as best they know. Some of the wounded no doubt will not make through the night...them sawbones all been overwhelmed by the casualties...I hear tell."

"Understand we will need a new commander for the Third Company..."

"He got shot out of the saddle and was jumped by a handful of 'em early on. Major Farmer put up a hell of a fight, his men said."

"Did you get a chance to ask them who they want to lead?"

"I did not want to push the issue earlier this afternoon, sir. They were still pretty shook up by his passing and had not decided where to bury him just yet. Some wanted to ship him back home...Others were thinking about laying him to rest where he fell."

"I shall talk to them shortly. We have no idea how quickly we will be put back into the lines. Need to have a commander in place when we do." He looked over at Captain Ingrham who was studying the falling block breech loading rifle that had been captured. "What is the verdict on that one? It looks fairly well made from here."

Doran got to his feet and moved closer to his battalion commander and handed him the rifle butt first with the action open. "Looks first rate to me. Eliminates the need for a ramrod, except for cleaning. You take your paper patched bullet with the

258

powder charge attached and slip in into the rear of the barrel...The act of raising the lever lifts this block, shears off the excess paper and exposes the powder charge to the flame hole from the nipple. It is called a Sharps."

"Nicely machined...well balanced...maybe a tad muzzle heavy." Eric dropped the lever, exposing the chamber. He pointed the rifle at the fire and studied the bore for a few seconds. "You know, the rifling is pretty deep. It should hold a good group. I'm betting these are what the Yankees used on Mouton's division...they were dropping like flies out to three hundred yards or so."

"You are probably right about that. I know those little Spencer carbines played hell on our flanking attack. They just kept a shootin'."

"How much ammunition did we capture for those?"

"We took at least eighteen caissons that I know of...Now, some of them carried kegs and ball for the cannons, but I saw some wooden crates that were marked as rifle cartridges...I will check it out at first light."

"Good...If we get a chance, I want to test the two rifles in the morning...at a distance."

***

CHAPTER FOURTEEN

CONFEDERATE CAMP
PLEASANT HILL, LOUISIANA
APRIL 9TH, 1864

A young messenger rode in from the north on a chestnut gelding with a white blaze. He quickly dismounted and was cleared to enter the command tent. Lifting the flap on his leather communiqué pouch that he had strapped across his chest, he produced a stack of letters, reports and orders and handed them to the administrative NCO. "The latest from Shreveport headquarters," he said.

"Stand by for a return trip," the burly man answered. "Get yourself some coffee if you like." Master Sergeant Blakely sifted through the stack quickly and distributed the reports to the appropriate departments. The letters addressed directly to Major

General Taylor, he left intact and passed them to the general's aide.

Originally from Kentucky, the major reached across the desk and picked up the letter opener with a carved ivory handle. He slipped it under the flap and cut through the envelope's top edge and handed it to the general. "From General Edmund Kirby Smith, sir."

"Let us see if he accepted my resignation, after all," he said with a frown visible even with his huge mustache. Taylor didn't trust his superior in the Trans-Mississippi campaign. He slipped his finger inside and pulled out an official looking parchment. He read it and began to chuckle. He handed it to his aide. "Billy, boy, if that does not take the cake! Not only did he ignore my resignation…but the son of a bitch promotes me to Lieutenant General…effective yesterday."

The aide read the proclamation and smiled. "What are you going to do now, sir?"

"I am going to kick General Banks and his band of cutthroats all the way back to the Mississippi…that is what. Get me General Green and call up the reserves from the Sabine Crossroads."

Eric lined up the sights on the Sharps rifle on a paper target hastily tacked to a distant pine tree. He controlled his breath, exhaled partially and gently squeezed the trigger. The rifle bucked and its report echoed off the trees surrounding the clearing. He picked up his glasses and watched intently as the spotter approached the target and then held a pointed stick at the bottom of the deep *V* cut in the top half of the six inch wide strip of white wallpaper.

"Looks like three in row, sir…right smack dab in the middle," Doran remarked.

Eric got to his feet from the prone position. "We need to check this out. I cannot recall ever shooting better." He led the way—followed by several of his soldiers—to the tree over one hundred yards away. They discovered three dime-sized holes overlapping each other in a rough cloverleaf. Eric knelt down and covered them with the top half of his left thumb. "That dog will hunt," he said with a big grin.

"What would you take for that old smoke pole?" one of his sergeants asked. "Being a used gun and all, I would offer two-fifty Confederate."

"Not today, Jedediah."

"Three dollars and I got the cash money right here…"

"Old Susie…she may be used, but she is not for sale. Go pick yourself out another one. Think I will hold on to her."

"Named her already Colonel? Dang, you must in love," Doran chimed in.

"My papa always said 'only accurate rifles are interesting'. This one has my full attention for now."

"Did you want to try that Spencer out as well?"

"What I would like to do with them is see what they will do from the saddle. If they are as fast handling as I think, we may want to make some changes to our tactics."

"I will put together a small squad of men who can shoot well…Let me know what the target will be."

"I was looking at some of the captured empty food crates we had left over. Stack a few of 'em as high as a man and see how many hits we can get at one hundred fifty yards in ten seconds."

"Easy enough to do." The captain barked out orders to his men who scurried to set up a man-sized target.

The five selected soldiers were given a few minutes to familiarize themselves with the new cartridge firearm. Doran showed them how to load the weapon from the tube under the buttplate. Each man filled the magazine with seven of the stubby .56-56 Spencer rounds. The rimfire cartridge featured a pointed lead bullet of .546 diameter that weighed 350 grains over forty-five grains of black powder. At 1200 feet per second, it was comparable to the .58 caliber muzzle loaders used by both the Union and the Confederates.

"Mount up, boys. See if we can give the colonel a run for his money."

Eric and a flag man stood off to the side some thirty yards from the stacked wooden crates. The young commander of the group pulled out a gold watch he had recovered from the body of a Yankee train engineer that had objected to his train being captured by the rebels up in Arkansas the previous fall. His final mistake was to pull a sidearm.

The six riders faced the target at a distance of one hundred yards. Captain Ingram waved his hand when they were ready.

Schmidt waited until the second hand swept across the Roman numeral XII at the top and ordered the flag man to give the signal to fire. The first round of shots rang out, followed a couple of seconds later by another—slightly more ragged in duration. Another two volleys of sporadic fire filled the air with a billowing cloud of smoke.

The second hand reached the II mark. "Cease fire," Eric called out.

The flag man waved the staff again as a few final shots rang out. The smoke from the six repeaters began to drift clear.

Eric checked up range to see the riders raise their muzzles. "Let us go see what they did." He and his signal man stepped closer to see the stack riddled with bullet holes. The crate sides and backs were splintered by the soft lead slugs.

Doran rode up and dismounted. "Cain't see crap from back there. Tell you what…a high volume of fire does create a smoke cloud you can hardly see through…How did we do?"

Eric grinned. "Word to the wise…do not try to hide behind empty crates…you will find yourself leaking in a bad way. How man rounds did you fire?"

"Got off four myself before I lost sight of the target."

"Well, sir, there are close to twenty holes in the boxes…ya'll did not miss very many."

"If we were moving as we shot, the smoke would not be as much of a problem. Or, perhaps, if we were dispersed more. What do you think?"

"Believe you are on to something. Get the men some familiarity training with these Spencers. I think the little carbine's advantages will outweigh its disadvantages…at least until we run out of ammunition." Eric began to walk back

264

toward the area where the remainder of his battalion were still camped.

"We have plenty for a couple of major engagements. After that...well, we will cross that bridge when we come to it."

"I like the way you think, Major."

Doran looked at him curiously. "Major? You mean to say I just got promoted?"

The colonel nodded. "Yep...Been meaning to tell you. I talked it over with the men in the Third Company. Told 'em I recommended Captain Johnson take over command...at least until we get this fight with Banks over and done with...They agreed with me."

"But who will take over as Executive Officer in Johnson's place?"

"I was kinda hoping you would...you have come a long way, and if something happens to me, I reckon you could do an outstanding job."

"Can I have a while to think about it? I feel responsible for the men under me in the Second."

"They will still be your responsibility...along with everybody in the First and Third. It does not get easier as you go up in grade."

Ingrham mulled over what Eric told him. "Guess not...I would pick Lieutenant Simpson to take my place. I will get the men training on the Spencers and put him up for a vote."

"You do that...I have got myself about fifty letters to write. Not looking forward to it, I tell you. But their families deserve to be told."

A hour later, a courier arrived with a message. Schmidt read the missive and sent the man back to Taylor's headquarters before he barked out an order.

"Bugler! Sound Assembly!" He folded up the letters, stashed them in his saddlebags, rolled up his bedroll and then strapped it down tightly behind his cantle. Eric watched with some satisfaction as his subordinate commanders assigned troops to drive some of the captured supply wagons—they tied their mounts to the back. In fifteen minutes, the battalion was assembled into its three companies and ready to deploy south into combat.

General Richard Taylor defeated the forces of Union General Banks at Pleasant Hill, forcing him to continue his retreat all the way to the Mississippi. General Thomas Green, hero of the Texas Revolution and commander of the Texas cavalry under Taylor, was killed while leading an attack on the Union gunboats at Blair's Landing on April 12th, 1864 during Bank's retreat.

APPOMATTOX COURT HOUSE, VIRGINIA
April 9th , 1865

On Palm Sunday afternoon, a silver-haired general astride an impressive light gray horse named Traveller made his way to a two story red brick private residence belonging to Wilmer McLean. The home featured six square wooden pillars supporting a full length front porch with a balcony above. General Robert Edward Lee wore what appeared to be a new uniform, impeccably tailored with a very ornate sword attached to a sash around his waist. His boots were highly polished and were mated with spurs that had large shiny rowels. He and his aide-de-camp, Colonel Charles Marshall, tied up outside the fence and walked silently up the steps to a first floor room where General Ulysses Simpson Grant awaited their arrival.

In contrast, Grant wore the non-distinctive uniform of a private, and it, as well as his high riding boots, were splattered with mud. Other than two small epaulettes with three stars on each shoulder, there was nothing to indicate the rank of the man wearing it. Lee speculated, quiet correctly, that Grant had learned to give Confederate marksmen a great amount of respect for their long range sniping capabilities.

The two Confederate officers were escorted inside and Lee was seated at a small oval writing table near a front window. Grant took a seat about ten feet away at a marble topped desk. The two opposing generals had actually met years earlier when they served together in the Mexican War, and discussed their common history before they got around to the subject of the surrender of Lee's Army. After four long years of death and destruction wrought by the two opposing armies, the actual discussions of the two were remarkably amicable.

Lee finally brought up the topic that the two had seem hesitant to discuss. "Would you be so kind as to put your terms in writing?"

The Union General nodded. "Very well, I will write them out." He turned to his aide. "Hand me my order book, if you please."

The colonel produced the leather satchel and Grant took out four blank sheets of stationary separated by carbon paper. He laid them out on the table top and began writing quickly. Grant looked up and noticed the fancy sword that Lee wore. He was compassionate enough to add another few lines to the articles of surrender—a special short sentence allowing officers to keep their side arms, horses and personal baggage. When he finished, he had his aide pass the document to General Lee.

The older officer reached into his pocket, pulled out a crisp white linen handkerchief and slowly but thoroughly, he cleaned his reading glasses. He adjusted them until he was satisfied and then picked up the two page document.

General R.E. Lee,
Commanding C.S.A.
APPOMATTOX Ct H., Va.,
April 9,1865,

General; In accordance with the substance of my letter to you of the 8th inst., I propose to receive the surrender of the Army of Northern Virginia on the following terms, to wit: Rolls of all officers and men to be made in duplicate, one copy to be given to an officer to be designated by me, the other to be retained by such officer or officers as you may designate. The officers to give their individual paroles not to take up arms against the Government of the United States until properly and each company or regimental commander to sign a like parole for the men of their commands. The arms, artillery, and public property to be parked, and stacked, and turned over to the officers appointed by me to receive them. This will not embrace the side-arms of the officers, nor their private horses or baggage. This done, each officer and man will be allowed to return to his home, not to be disturbed by the United States authorities so long as they observe their paroles, and the laws in force where they may reside.

Very respectfully,
U.S. Grant,
Lieutenant-General

General Lee carefully perused the handwritten letter and noted a word was likely missing. "After the words *until properly*, the word *exchanged* seems to be omitted. You doubtless intended to use that word."

Grant looked perplexed of a moment. "Why, yes. I thought I had put in the word *exchanged*."

"I presumed it had been omitted inadvertently," replied Lee, "...and with your permission, I will mark where it should be inserted."

"Certainly," agreed Grant.

Lee pressed his hands on the pockets of his apparently new general's uniform and fumbled around for a second looking for a writing instrument. One of the Union brigadiers handed him a pencil, which he gladly accepted. He made the interlineation and then nervously tapped the pencil on the table as he continued to review the document. Finally, his face relaxed as he grasped the generosity of Grant's surrender terms. "This will have a very happy effect upon my army."

General Grant nodded. "Unless you have some suggestions to make in regard to the form in which I have stated the terms, I will have a copy of the letter made in ink and sign it."

Lee hesitated for a brief moment. "There is one thing I would like to mention…The cavalrymen and artillerists own their own horses in our army. Its organization in this respect differs from that of the United States."

Several of the Union officers noted how Lee still considered the states of the Confederacy to no longer be part of the union and glanced around uncomfortably.

"I would like to understand whether these men will be permitted to retain their horses," Lee said.

"You will find that the terms as written do not allow this," General Grant replied. "Only the officers are permitted to take their private property."

Lee read over the second page of the letter again, and then remarked, "No, I see the terms do not allow it. That is clear." His face showed plainly that he was quite anxious to have this concession made.

Grant noted Lee's discomfort. He responded quickly before Lee was forced to speak. "Well, the subject is quite new to me…Of course, I did not know that any private soldiers owned their animals, but I think this will be the last battle of the war…I sincerely hope so…And that the surrender of this army will be followed soon by that of all the others…and I take it that most of the men in the ranks are small farmers and as the country has been so raided by the two armies, it is doubtful whether they will be able to put in a crop to carry themselves and their families through the next winter without the aid of the horses they are now riding, and I will arrange it in this way…I will not change the terms as now written, but I will instruct the officers I shall appoint to receive the paroles to let all the men who claim to own a horse or mule take the animals home with them to work their little farms."

Lee's weathered faced conveyed his relief. "This will have the best possible effect upon the men. It will be very gratifying and will do much toward conciliating our people." He handed the draft of the terms back to General Grant.

Grant motioned to Colonel T. S. Bowers, a member of his staff. "Make us final copies in ink."

Bowers was a little nervous, given the great import of the proceedings. "Colonel Parker, you have the most legible handwriting in the staff. Would you do the honor?"

Ely Parker readily agreed and moved to the table near the back of the room. He opened the top of the conical shaped inkstand on the table and found it was dry.

Colonel Marshall, Lee's aide stepped over pulled a small boxwood inkstand out of his pocket. Parker gladly accepted the use of it and wrote the official surrender papers using Confederate ink.

As Parker made the official copies, Lee directed Colonel Marshall to draw a letter of acceptance of the terms of

271

surrender. He wrote out a formal sounding draft with pencil and hand it to the general.

Lee took it, and, after reading it over very carefully, frowned. "This is far too formal. Make is shorter and to the point."

Parker complied with his wishes and revised the draft. Lee simplified the second draft even more and directed him to complete a final in ink. Using paper borrowed from Grant's aide, he composed the final letter.

HEADQUARTERS, ARMY OF NORTHERN VIRGINIA,
April 9th, 1865
LIEUTENANT-GENERAL U. S. GRANT

GENERAL: I received your letter of this date containing the terms of the surrender of the Army of Northern Virginia as proposed by you. As they are substantially the same as those expressed in your letter of the 8th inst., they are accepted. I will proceed to designate the proper officers to carry the stipulations into effect.

R. E. LEE,
General

GALVESTON, TEXAS
TRANS-MISSISSIPPI
CONFEDERATE ARMY HEADQUARTERS
May 26th 1864

General Edmund Kirby Smith glared across the table at the Union Major General Edward R. S. Canby. It had been almost two months since General Lee signed the formal papers surrendering the Army of Virginia to Grant. President Jefferson Davis refused to allow other Confederate armies to lay down their arms, as his primary military leader had, even though his remaining forces had been surrounded, outmaneuvered and were starving. Davis and his wife Varina were captured on May 10th near Irwinville, Georgia as he tried to escape to Florida en route to Cuba.

The Confederate army under Smith had begun to unravel since Lee's resignation, with countless desertions, a mutiny in Galveston on the 14th, riots in Houston on the 21st and 22nd. A state of general lawlessness was growing in many areas of Texas. Governor Pendleton Murrah stuck to his secessionist views and discouraged surrender by his generals. What turned out to be the last battle of the Civil War had occurred far to the southwest on the banks of the Rio Grand at a place known as the Palmito Ranch almost two weeks earlier.

"General we will have to make a formal inquiry into the disappearance of Confederate stores in both Houston and Galveston. My people tell me that the warehouses have been looted," Canby stated with a someone arrogant tone to his voice.

273

"You think I do not know that?" countered Smith. "Hell's bells, man. Half of my army has already been dismissed or deserted…We have no money to pay them and some were nearly starving. Your naval blockade has worked only too well for you, sir."

Canby sat back and took in a deep breath. He had hoped the surrender process would go along in a gentlemanly manner, but he could see the Confederate four star was becoming agitated. He glanced at the other rebel officers in the room, Major General Marcus Matson and Brigadier General Eric Schmidt. Both of the younger men were grim-faced and appeared somewhat gaunt. He had, of course, heard of each man's military record and was appreciative of the fact that he would not be facing them in battle any more.

"I am quite certain that the civil unrest was outside of your ability to contain, given the unfortunate circumstances in which you find yourself at this time, sir. I have take the liberty to write these conditions of surrender as we discussed via communiqué beginning on the ninth of this month. You may review the papers to see if all is in order, General."

Smith stoked his coal black beard casually, as if it were a subconscious action. "That would be the appropriate thing to do, I presume."

Canby waved to an aide who presented the papers before the rebel commander. Smith read the two pages carefully as Marcus and Eric looked over his shoulder. The terms were essentially the same as those given to Lee by Grant back in April. Smith was happy that they did not vary at all and sighed a breath of relief. Former Confederate President Davis was being held prisoner by a vengeful US President Andrew Johnson, who had assumed office after Lincoln's assassination on May 10th.

President Davis had been charged with treason and was shackled twenty-four hours a day as Johnson considered him to be complicit in Lincoln's murder.

Kirby Smith lifted up his pen and signed both copies of the surrender. He passed them back across the desk that he had occupied for that last few months. "I suppose that does it...We will make every attempt to comply with the administrative requirements, but as I discussed earlier, many of the men did not wait for the formal dissolution and have already headed home by any means available...Cain't say that I blame them much."

Canby nodded. "It is an unpleasant business, sir...Your men fought hard, and now is time for all of us to come back together."

He stood up and extended his hand. General Smith begrudgingly took it as he and the forty-seven year old West Point graduate finalized the surrender of the last major command of Confederate troops.

Marcus and Eric walked toward the line of horses tied outside the headquarters building. "What are you plans? Gonna hang around for the final ceremony where we haul down the flags?"

Eric shook his head. "No, my friend. I have enjoyed about all of this soldiering I can stand in one lifetime. We killed thousands of them...maybe hundreds of thousands and for what? Our fellow Texans are on starvation rations, the deep

275

south is in ruins and damned Federals still think that they are our lord and master."

"Cain't say I disagree with you. The bastard politicians who forced our secession in the first place are still up there in Washington, sitting on their fat asses and passing one-sided legislation that enriches them and their crooked cronies...It will get worse before it gets better."

"I can only imagine. The sorry bastard Lincoln started all this. He would not let the southern states go their own way in peace. Now that he is gone, Yankee historians are gonna make him out as some kind of God damned hero...Mark my words." Eric's eyes drifted away to the horizon in what is known as a thousand yard stare. "Right now I have two things to do...Call one last brigade assembly and personally thank those brave souls who stood with us...And get myself back up to Shreveport."

Marcus smiled. "She is gonna be the most beautiful bride you ever saw. Please give her my warmest regards...I wish the two of you many years of happiness."

It was Eric's turn to smile. His solemn look melted away as he imagined Angelina in a wedding gown. "We have not set a date as yet. I wanted this war to be over before we wed...Say...I never got a chance to ask you...would you do me the honor or serving as my best man?"

"You let me know when and where...wild horses could not keep me away."

"Where will you be once this army is disbanded? I will send a telegram..."

"I think Austin might be the next place for me. My younger brother is up there with his law practice. His name is Hortatio Matson."

"I do not imagine your mother named any of her children after normal people." Eric chuckled.

"Was not her style, I suppose. Maybe she wanted us to live up to our names."

"That you did, sir...that you did." Eric stepped back and saluted his friend smartly.

Marcus Aurellius Matson snapped to attention and returned the salute. He stuck out his hand and Eric took it. "Take care of yourself. Knowing you has been like finding another brother."

Eric nodded, released the hand shake and both men gave each other a huge bear hug.

"Fare thee well, my brother." Eric said as he stepped back, and untied his black stallion. He stepped into the stirrup and threw his right leg over the high cantle one more time. He wheeled around and urged the Thunder into a trot. The young cavalry general never looked back as a tear ran down his cheek.

Two hundred tired and hungry men milled about the bivouac area following General Schmidt's impassioned speech. It was not designed to raise the men's moral, but nonetheless, it accomplished the task. Some stood weeping at the finality of the surrender. Others were happy to be released to return to whatever life they had before.

Colonel Doran Ingrham followed Eric to his command tent. The general took off his tassled broad brimmed hat and tossed it on the table. "Have a seat, my brother. I believe I have just what the doctor ordered in my footlocker."

Doran sat down on the ladderback chair and pushed his own cavalry officer's hat back on his head. He watched as Eric unrolled a large towel from the corner of the locker and pulled out a bottle of amber liquid. He recognized the label.

"How long have you kept that in there? I did not know anyone still had Tennessee sipping whiskey..."

"Little over a year. It was compliments of one of Bank's generals back at the battle of Mansfield."

"Oh, I remember, now. That case of bourbon made our boys real happy."

"Yep. I saved this one last bottle for a special occasion."

"Wish it was a happier one, General."

Eric poured two fairly clean glasses about half full. "You do not need to call me general any more." He handed one to Doran. "When we finish this drink, I am going to take off these grays and put 'em in a pannier along with all my other gear in that locker...From now on, I am plain old Eric Schmidt."

Ingrham laughed. "Somehow, I doubt that...Bet you'll be livin' high on the hog over in Louisiana."

Eric shrugged. "Do not know 'bout that. Things are tough all over these days. Who knows what the future will bring?" He sat down across the plain wooden table from his former battalion commander.

"To the future..." Doran raised his glass.

The two men clinked their glasses together. "To the future...and all those who have fallen," Eric finished the toast.

278

He took a sip of the straight 100 proof liquor. It burned as it went down. He gasped slightly and blinked his eyes.

Doran took two swallows and shook his head quickly as he took in a ragged breath. "Smooth, ain't it?" he wheezed.

Both men laughed until they had tears in their eyes.

"Why the hell is this supposed to be fun?" Eric asked.

"Guess that by the time you get to the bottom of the bottle, your mouth is plum numb. Then, when you are drunk as a skunk, you can call it fun."

"Everything would be numb if I finished the whole bottle by myself. I must be a lightweight when it comes to drinking."

"There are worst things in life than not being a hard drinker, my friend. Seen me a bunch who did not know when to say when…Some of 'em died way too young."

"Uh huh." Eric took another sip and began to unbutton his uniform coat. He stood up and slipped it over the back of his chair. A cameo broach was hanging from a dainty gold chain on his neck and rested on his sweat-stained undershirt.

Doran caught sight of it for the first time. He leaned in closer for a better look. "Is that her? God…she is beautiful."

"Actually this was her mother, Elouise LeBlanc. Angelina bears a remarkable resemblance. She gave it to me for good luck."

"Well, it worked, did it not? You, sir, are one lucky man. How long has it been since you saw her?"

"Almost eleven months, now…On the way back from kicking old Banks' ass down to the big muddy."

Ingrham grinned. "I seem to recall a morning when you rolled back into camp smiling like a possum eating persimmons."

"Guilty as charged…not to change the subject, but what are you going to do with yourself…now that we are officially out of the Yankee killin' business?"

"That is a quandary, is it not? You taught me a hell of a lot about guns and tactics over the last few years. Cain't see myself behind a mule any more…bustin' sod." His whole body shuddered. "It is a little too…too…what is that two dollar word you like to use?"

"Plebeian?"

"Yessir…It would be plebeian to go back to what I was a doin' before I became a cavalry man. Maybe I will mosey on down south and see if the Mexicans will pay real money for a hell-on-wheels hero of the Confederacy." He downed the last of the bourbon and set the empty glass down with a thud.

"If you need references, you can always use my name…that and a penny will get you a cup of coffee most places I know."

Doran laughed. "It is a deal. By the way, what are you gonna use to haul those panniers? Not Black Thunder, I hope…"

"Oh, hell no. He would not stand still to be a pack horse. Too much fire in that big boy…I gave the quartermaster sergeant a hundred Confederate dollars for a nice five year old gelding. He handed back the bill and said 'Forget it, that money ain't worth spit anyway.' He insisted that I take him."

"Another reason I need to get down to Mexico. I got me five hundred in Confederate to my name and no job. How 'bout another three fingers of that whiskey? Does not look like I will be buying any drinks any time soon. But I cain't feel my lips…"

"The bar is still open." Eric filled the glass another time and poured himself a smaller one. He turned back to the footlocker and began to root around. He pulled a pair of civilian pants and slightly stained fringed leather shirt and tossed them on his cot. Finally he found what he was looking for—a nondescript leather pouch with a drawstring. He stuck his index fingers inside and pulled it open. Pulling a pair of shiny US gold $50 pieces out, he tossed them to Doran.

He caught them in his hand and looked back to Eric. "What in tarnation is that for?"

"Call it Mexico money…call it whatever you like. You earned it, believe me."

"Where did you get it?"

"Found it on that Yankee supply train we derailed north of Little Rock."

"And you kept it a secret all this time?"

"Did not want any of our potential deserters to help themselves before they took off."

"So that is how you kept *finding* all those extra supplies for our men for the past year…"

He grinned. "Yep. I could not see myself just confiscating food from our own civilians to help feed the boys. Those folks had to eat, too. Real money was short and the gold seemed to

281

make things come out of haylofts and cellars…Like magic."
Eric grinned.

"You are a sly one…You know that? Listen…I appreciate the loan. If I am ever in your neck of the woods, I will pay you back. I promise."

"No, by God, you will not. I ain't no banker. But if it helps you get on with your life…may it bless you and keep you safe…Now drink up. I gotta get changed, packed up and then ride on over to see when the next boat sailing up the Sabine departs."

Eric dusted off the black broad-brimmed, uncreased low-crowned hat. He pulled it on as Doran cinched up the last of his belongings on the pack horse.

Ingrham turned to see his friend take one last look around the tent. Eric walked out with a pair of pistols and a stag handled knife on his gunbelt. "You look kinda naked without your saber."

"Feels a little different, too, but reckon I will get used to it."

"Got your scattergun and the Sharps in the gun boots, I see. Expecting problems?"

"Yep…Things have gone to hell in a hand basket 'round here. Do not want to find myself unprepared on the road…you neither."

"I will be out of here in a day or so. Promised to help with the rosters, but that is about all. Do not want to make it too damned easy on the yanks."

"Best of luck, brother Doran. You know my door is always open to you." Eric gave him a big bear hug.

Doran patted him on the back. "Take care of that pretty lady of yours...God be with you."

Eric felt a lump in his throat begin to build. He nodded and lifted his old hobnailed boot into the left stirrup. He couldn't bring up a single word, so he forked the saddle and reached out for the pack horse lead rope that his friend held. Eric touched the brim of his hat and tugged on the rope as he nudged his mount into motion.

Doran stood silently watching as the big man rode away. He dabbed at his eyes and turned to walk back to his own tent. For the first time in years, he suddenly felt alone.

***

CHAPTER FIFTEEN

SHREVEPORT, LOUISIANA
JUNE 1865

The whistle announced the arrival of the eastbound noonday run. Eric checked and noted that they were a good fifteen minutes late and pocketed the gold watch in his fringed leather shirt as the train began to slow, amid a high pitched squeaking of the brakes and a light cloud of ashes from the wood-burning steam engine that drifted down like dirty snow flakes. He eyed the other passengers in the car—an eclectic mix of active duty US Army soldiers, some former rebel enlisted troops—still in uniform, a few scattered farm folks and a smattering of businessmen trying to make a living.

For some reason, the mood aboard the train had been edgy, with few people making eye contact and only those people traveling together bothering to speak to one another. Eric let it pass as what would be expected so closely following the bitter conflict. He held on to the seat back in front of him as the engineer brought the assembled cars to a jolting stop, complete with a series of clashes of the metal couplings.

"Shreveport!…Shreveport! End of the line! Watch your step getting off," barked the conductor as he moved from car to car. Eric stood up and offered to help a lady traveling with a small child get to her feet. She eyed him cautiously, then finally accepted his gesture—almost begrudgingly.

What is wrong with people these days? Cannot a man do a kindness without being suspect of something? He tipped his hat nonetheless and decided to drop the matter from his mind. *In an hour or so, I will be at the Chateau LeBlanc and in my sweet Angelina's arms once more.* That happy thought put a bit of spring in his step as he shook off the tightness in his lower back from the unpadded wooden benches.

He made his way to the back of the car and stepped down from the train onto the passenger platform. In less than a minute, he was back at the livestock car and walked up the gangplank to retrieve his two horses.

"How you doin' there, Thunder? Ready to get off this noisy contraption I wager." He tightened the cinch on his saddle and then did the same for his pack horse's panniers. "Easy there, Dollar. I will get you boys some water once we get into town."

He led Thunder down the sloped walkway and ground tied him as he went back for the gelding. He didn't take a chance tying the two together and possibly getting on or the other injured on the narrow wooden planks.

"All right, you two…that is enough for now. Do not want you water foundering on me and leaving me afoot eight miles from our destination." He tugged back on the reins and lead rope to pull both of his animals away from the trough. With a little pressure on his right knee, he turned the stallion eastbound on Texas Street and then gently urged him to an extended walk.

Shreveport had changed a lot in eleven months. No longer the headquarters of the Trans-Mississippi Confederate Army, the street traffic was fraction of what he remember from his last visit. Dozens of unemployed blacks—recently freed from their bonds of slavery—milled around on the town's boardwalks with nothing to do and no money to live on. Eric passed a squad of US cavalry riding in the opposite direction. *Guess it will take a while for that sight to not get my blood pumping.*

He saw the Pavillion Hotel and a couple of other familiar sites before he turned south on the Natchitoches stage road. Approaching the edge of town, he squeezed his legs and brought Thunder up to a full trot. Dollar fell back a little, making the lead rope coil tighter around Eric's gloved hand. "Come on up, boy. You do not want to get on my bad side, 'cause I will drag you I have to…'Sides…you ain't got forty-five pounds in those canvas bags. You oughta be happy I am not on *your* back."

Dollar picked up the pace as if he actually understood, but mostly because the lead rope had pulled his halter tight and held his head up higher than was comfortable. The well-trained horse matched the stallion's pace and they began to cover the packed ground quickly.

Eric turned off the main road and down the tree shaded lane to the Chateau. He looked out at the fields and noted that the cotton had not been weeded like it was the previous season. In fact, there were no hands out doing the labor-intensive chopping and in the distance, he could see some fields left fallow. *Augustin must have not been able to get enough seed this year.* He rode on and was surprised that the garden was a tenth the size of the plot he first saw in his initial visit. Eric began to get a bad feeling in the pit of his stomach. Something was wrong—terribly wrong.

He caught sight of the barns, but didn't see any livestock or horses in the paddocks. Coming to the end of the majestic oaks lining the entry, he saw a sight that shook him to his core. Where the majestic French mansion once stood, only a half dozen blackened chimneys jutted starkly into the June sky. *Oh my God...Oh my God.* He spurred Thunder to a gallop and released the lead rope. Dollar followed along in the trail of dust, not wanting to be left behind.

Eric reined to a sliding stop and dismounted. His heart beat wildly as he sprinted to the side gate and flung it wide. He raced around the hedges and caught sight of the charred timbers, bricks and tiles that once stood as an aristocratic sign of wealth and culture. He slowed when he saw a row of whitewashed pine crosses set at the heads of freshly mounded earth. He mouth fell open wide as he formed the word *no*—but no sound emerged.

"Hold it right there! Do not come no closer!"

Eric heard the unmistakable sound of two hammers being cocked on a scattergun. He slowly raised his hands and turned in the direction of the voice.

"Mister Eric? Is that you?"

A frightened black man stood up from his hiding place in the singed shrubbery. He was pointing the shotgun directly at the heartbroken man in buckskin.

"Cryus?…What?…" He glanced over at the row of crosses. "What happened…Is she…?"

"Oh, Mister Eric…I wish you could have been here…" the former head of the household staff began to weep.

"Oh my God, Cyrus…I did not know," Eric stammered. "…When?…How…?" His tears streamed down his tanned face, soaking his handlebar mustache.

Cyrus lowered the shotgun and walked slowly to his side. "I am sorry Mister Eric…you misunderstood. She is still alive, at least I think so."

Eric grabbed him by the collar of his shirt. "What?" He looked over at the graves. "What did you say?"

"Those deserters that rode though here…They killed Mister LeBlanc and some of the others and looted the house…I had taken Miss Angelina over to tend to Misses Hebert…see, she was having a baby and they was no doctors about…"

"She's alive?…I thought…Where is she?"

Cyrus shook his head, a deep sadness etched on his face. "When we gots back over to here after birthing that baby, the house was already burned and Mister LeBlanc…he was dead…laying out there in the yard…Miss Angelina, she went to pieces. She say they was nothing here for her no more." Tears ran down the black man's face as his voice cracked. "We cleaned him and the others up best we could...and laid them to rest right there in the yard."

"What happened to her? Where did she go?"

"That is what I am tryin' to tell you, Mister Eric...Honest to God, sir...I do not know...she dug up a little trunk that was buried down to the cellar and had me put it in the buggy for her. Then, Miss Angelina...she up and drove away."

Eric tried to collect himself as best he could. His mind raced to all the possibilities that could have befallen her—most of them bad. Since the south's surrender, the countryside had become rife with violent criminals of all persuasions. The economy was in shambles, with jobs few and far between. "Tell me, my friend...how long has she been gone?"

"Nigh on two weeks, I think. Most of the folks round here on the plantation done took off...Me, I stayed here in case she change her mind and come back. Got me a place over in one of the cabins and tend to what is left of the garden...A man has to feed hisself somehow..."

"Stay as long as you wish, Cyrus. I am sure she would want that...I will find her...I...I can never stop looking..." his voice trailed off.

Cyrus nodded. "Good luck to you, Mister Eric...Cain't think 'bout nothin' bad happenin' to her...Hurts my heart..."

Eric placed his left hand on the servant's shoulder and stuck out his hand. "Thank you for staying...Tell me, where does that Hebert family live? I shall start over there…Mayhap she went to stay with them."

Cyrus shook the big man's hand and then pointed south. "You go back to the main road and head like you was goin' to New Orleans. "'Bout four miles or so, they is a side road to the west. Take it for another mile and you will see the house…It be the only one you can see from the road."

"It is a start…I will send word when I find her."

"Bless you, Mister Eric. May God watch over you and Miss Angelina."

Tyler, Texas
August 1865

Eric crested the hill looking down at his family farmhouse with a feeling of great sadness. For almost two months, he had scoured the Louisiana countryside, stopping at every city and town and asking questions about a red-haired young woman in a buggy. He always got the same answer. He had checked with LeBlanc distant cousins in the Natchitoches area and ridden all the way to New Orleans and not one person had seen or heard from her. It was as if the earth had opened and swallowed her up without a trace.

Johnson grass grew waist high in the private road leading to the ranch. *Guess nobody wants to come out this far from town without a reason.* He pulled up outside the log house and tied off to the hitching post. Native bluestem and even some small shrubbery had overtaken the hard-packed driveway and the graves were overgrown with three year's worth of weeds. A

290

small dark mound was all that was left where he had burned the bodies of the marauding Yankee patrol and their dead horse. Coyotes and other small mammals had dragged the charred bones off and gnawed on them for the calcium they contained.

He unsaddled both horses and turned them out in the pasture to graze. Moving back to the house, Eric straightened the cross over his mother's site and knelt and said a prayer for each member of his family.

He walked to the barn and opened the door. He was surprised and somewhat happy to find the wagon still inside, with its cargo of rifle barrel blanks. A thick layer of grit and dust covered the lid and the metal straps binding the crate together were rusted, but from experience he knew the barrels themselves would be slathered in cosmoline and most likely still useable. He checked the rigging on the wagon. Some critter had chewed through the reins four feet back from the surcingle. *Rats, I suspect. No problem. They were goin' for the sweat salt. I can stitch that back together in nothing flat.*

He closed the barn doors and walked back to the house. With no small amount of trepidation, he lifted the latch and pushed the heavy entrance door wide. Other than a thick layer of dust, the front room looked much like it had when he left on that fateful night. He tried not to think about blood stains near the front door as he walked over to the kitchen table.

A handwritten note caught his eye. *That was not here when I left.* Eric picked up the brown craft paper and blew the dust off of it. Sunlight streaming in the east window lit up the tiny filaments and they danced in the air as they drifted slowly down.

Dear Eric Schmidt, Esq,
If you are reading this here note, then you survived the war, I guess. I read where you were fighting over to Louisiana and helped lick the Yankee aggressors under Banks. I took care of your animals best I could. Some soldiers of the Confederacy came by and offered money for the horses and I sold them for you. I kept the milk cow for two years, but she took sick and died anyway. Come by the cabin and I will give you the money I am holding in your name.

Thadius Thompkins
Fifth day of October, 1864

I'll be dipped. I never knew old man Thompkins' first name. Eric read the letter again and chuckled. *Eric Schmidt, Esquire! If that is what you think, then more power to you, sir. I will have to drop by before I pack up.*

He checked the kitchen for utensils, pots and pans he could use and stacked them in an empty apple crate on the table. He was starting life over, but not from scratch. A few household items would be needed when he got to wherever he was going.

He eased the door open to this parent's room. The wooden shutters were closed, so he lit a match and lifted the oil lamp chimney to access the wick. When it was burning, he waved the match to extinguish it and lowered the glass. *That is more like it.* Looking around the sparse accommodations, the thought hit him. *We damned sure did not have much, but we were happy.*

He pulled open the pine wardrobe that his father had crafted out of wood from the farm. There were only three shirts and two pair of pants that had belonged to his father and four dresses and two aprons that Alyssa Marie had worn. He pictured his mother in the familiar print apron. A pain of heartache shot though him. *Dammit. I told myself I was not gonna do this,* as tears welled in his eyes. He pulled his father's wooden hangers out of the small stand-alone closet and quickly shut the door. Looking at the feather double bed, he took his free hand and wiped back the tears. *It is bigger than my single bed and I darn sure do not want to sleep on the ground any more. Had enough of that to last a lifetime. I can roll it up and cover it with a tarp.*

He walked to the next room and checked it out. He had already packed all his clothes before he left home three years earlier. He picked up the lamp from the table beside his single bed and sloshed the base around to check the level of coal oil before bringing it out and setting it down. Moving to the last bedroom, he hesitated for a minute before opening the door. He knew he really didn't want to see that blood stained bed again and bring those memories flooding back.

Eric took in a deep breath and steeled himself as he pushed the door open. He was not prepared for the sight of an empty bed frame. The mattress was gone and a short note lay on the peeled pine frame.

I took care of it for you.
Thadius

Eric felt a lump form in his throat. *Bless you, old man.* He closed the door and turned to the bookshelf. There were far too many titles to take on his journey, but the decision on which ones to keep took almost an hour. He picked *Moby Dick; or The Whale* by Mevlille, *Robinson Crusoe* by Dafoe, The Works of William Shakespeare, a *Tale of Two Cities*—Charles Dicken's classic tale that had been the last book purchased by Alyssa Schmidt and lastly, an account of the explorations of Meriwether Lewis and Lieutenant William Clark earlier in the century. Eric was always fascinated by the true tale of heroic adventure and particularly intrigued by the Girandoni air rifle—a .46 caliber repeating weapon capable of killing deer-sized game. He stacked the five books on the table and made his way outside to the workshop where he had his father had spent so many hours honing his craft.

Tools left on the workbench were covered with a fine patina of light rust. *Papa would be livid if he saw this. Have to clean 'em the best I can and get some oil on these.* He moved to the anvil. *If I can lift it by myself, it goes. Otherwise it stays put.* He placed one hand under each end. *Papa could pick this up all by himself.* With a deep breath, he grunted and easily moved it a couple of inches and set the 150 pounds of forged steel back down.

Dad gum...Army life must have made me stronger than I figured. But I would not want to carry this very far. I will wait 'til I get the buckboard in place. He looked down at the forge. *Cain't take it all with me, but I can dang sure use the bellows. They do not weigh much.* He looked up on the shelf above the workbench and spied his father's bound notebook. Pulling it down, he batted off the cobwebs and untied the latigo string holding it closed. The pages with his father's handwritten notes were a bittersweet treasure. He felt the love and connection between himself and his father and the gentle warmth of that emotion was a good one. "Papa you taught me well. Hope I make you proud on me someday," he said in a low voice. Eric closed the book and slipped it under his arm.

Eating a plate of salt pork and beans on his family's dinnerware was a time of remembrance for him. He could hear his mother's voice and almost see his sister's face again. Eric had learned to make cornbread, watching his mother and her gentle hands stirring the buttermilk into the flour and cornmeal mixture. With no milk or eggs available, he had passed on that staple, because it just didn't taste right without them. *God, I wish we had some pictures taken of our family. I miss them so.*

After dinner, he wandered out to the pasture with a couple of quarts of whole oats and two feed bags. He whistled and then called out, "Hey, you two! If you want it, better come and get it." Thunder and Dollar trotted over. After grazing on the abundant summer grass, they were almost sated, but no horse turns down a good ration of grain.

He slipped the bags on and watched as they finished. The presence of the two horses helped make it not quite as lonely as it otherwise would have been. The house and modest ranch had been the only home he ever knew, but the memories of his lost family were far too oppressing to make him want to stay. His hand went to the broach under his shirt, as it had many times in the past year.

Eric could see Angelina clearly when he closed his eyes. Her lips, that special smile she gave only to him and the mischievous sparkle in her green eyes—it was all there. But so was the pain. *Maybe that is why she could not stay at the plantation. Too many ghosts of her father. I think I understand now.*

He opened his eyes and turned toward the three crosses. Wishing he had been there to help her though the pain didn't make it so. He knew that night would most likely be the last he would ever spent in the house. Eric pulled the empty feed bags off Thunder and Dollar. He walked slowly to the house and brought the saddle, panniers and tack inside for the night.

TEXAS HIGH PLAINS
AUGUST 1865

In the week that had passed since Eric had resupplied at a small town known back then as Eagle Springs, Texas, the scenery had not changed much…Miles and miles of rolling prairie, broken by the occasional creek and a few scattered clusters of mesquite or live oak. The trail he had picked was not a well traveled one, often little more than a single animal track wide.

He had seen his first mule deer and was curious about how the animal developed its unusual bounding gait. They could run like a whitetail when forced to, but often chose to spring forward on all four feet simultaneously. The bucks sported velvet covered horns featuring a bifurcated main beam and the both the male and females alike had large mule-like ears, that gave the animal its iconic name.

Eric had bought a horse collar in Wichita Falls to ease the chaffing Dollar experienced with the heavily laden wagon. The sorrel grew accustomed to it quickly, but Eric often wondered if he should have made a trade for a mule to do the heavy work, back when there was the chance. He had not laid eyes another human being for over two days, but often felt the presence of the unseen Comanches that roamed the area along the Red River and much of the Texas panhandle.

Topping a shallow rise, he stopped to let the horses take a blow. In the distance, a dark, almost black stain on the knee-high grassland piqued his attention. *Is that a burned area?* He pulled the brass framed binoculars out of the small open topped wood box on the buckboard seat beside him and unwrapped the bandana he wrapped around them. He blew forcefully to clear the trail dust that had nonetheless accumulated on the lenses. *What in tarnation?*

As he focused for the distance to the far-off phenomenon, he could see it move, undulating over the open terrain. Suddenly, a part of the monolithic mass separated for no apparent reason. He could see a string of dark objects leading a small group. *Buffalo!* For the first time in his life he experienced the wonder and majesty of hundreds of thousands of the wild beasts in their native environment.

The herd was over a mile wide and almost three miles long, covering the ground as they moved from one feeding area to another. The Texas summer sun was high overhead and temperature was already climbing into the low nineties, but he sat there from his vantage point and watched the sea of giant bison pass by. *Wonder if the Sharps would take one cleanly? Probably would but I do not want to waste the meat…Too damn hot to try to cut it up and jerk it before most of it spoils anyway. I should have bought more pepper. It would keep the flies off of it while it dries.*

He snapped the reins over Dollar's rump. "Get on up there, boy. Cain't be lolligagin' all day." The horse complied and set the wagon in motion again. Five miles later, Eric encountered an area where the herd had grazed the blue grama and buffalo grass down and the impact of tens of thousands of sets of hooves had the sandy ground packed firm. The trail he had been following disappeared completely. "Never saw the likes of this. Good for makin' the miles roll by pretty darn quick."

After a half hour, Eric stopped and scanned the endless horizon looking for a reference point to assist in maintaining his west-northwesterly direction. There was none. "Aw, hell, now I know what a ship captain feels like out on the ocean." He turned around and stared at the wagon tracks in the dirt. They created a gradual crescent shape across the terrain. "Would you look at that? If we do not watch out, we could well be goin' round in circles. How could you let happen, Dollar?"

He chuckled at his joke and dug in the box for the lensatic compass he owned. The well-worn piece of military navigation gear had served him well many times before. He held it out away from his gunbelt and any other metal items and checked his heading. "Dammit to hell! Two hundred sixty degrees?" He looked up at the sun's position. "You are no help either...Go find a cloud to hide behind."

It was then he remembered the history lesson about the staked plains. Early Spanish explorers had severe trouble navigating the featureless terrain in search of the fabled Seven Cities of Gold. They had come up with a system of using tall stakes driven into the ground to maintain a course. As long as they could see two staked behind themselves, they could do so. They named the endless prairie the Llano Estacado, or staked plains. *Ain't got any stakes and there is not a tree in sight. The old compass will have to do.*

Eric tugged on the ribbons and popped them lightly over Dollar's rump. "Gee on up, there." The horse had begun moving and pulled the buckboard about forty degrees right when the sound of a distant rifle shot drifted over a nearby hill. He reined back to a halt as he listened intently. The crack of another shot broke the sound of the wind passing by. Three quick pistol shots followed in rapid succession. Eric reached for the Spencer laying on the buckboard seat as he stared at the hilltop.

A lone rider's head appeared just above the closely grazed grass. His broad-brimmed hat was slid back on his head, held only by the stampede string tied tightly under the man's chin. Another figure appeared slightly behind him and offset to the left. That man turned in the saddle and fired a pistol shot at something or someone that was pursuing him. *At least they ain't shooting at me. Wonder what the ruckus is all about?*

It didn't take long for the answer to his question to become apparent. A dozen Indians—half of them riding painted horses and the rest aboard tan or black mustangs—topped the ridge in hot pursuit of the two cowboys.

Eric made a rapid assessment of his priorities. He knew instantly that the wagon was slower and less maneuverable than being mounted on his stallion. He set the brake and tied the reins off on the handle. He already had the Spencer repeater in his hands, so he jumped from the wagon and raced to the back to untie the lead rope. The horse nervously stamped his feet as the war cries of the advancing Comanches drifted down on them.

"Whoa, Thunder. Hold on…Let me get this cinched up."

Cradling the rifle in the crook of his arm, he pulled the girth tight and forked the saddle. He turned in the direction of the pair of incoming cowboys and spurred the big stallion right at them.

On of the two cowboys looked ahead. "If we can get behind that wagon, maybe we can make a stand…what the hell is that crazy fool doing?" He was even more puzzled when the man lifted the rifle at a full gallop. "Christ! Is he pointing that at me?" He ducked as the rifle fired from only fifty yards away and the bullet whistled past. The solid *blap* as the lead slug hit his intended target came from close behind him. He looked back over his shoulder as the nearest Comanche warrior, with a hole in his chest, tumbled off the paint horse.

Eric snapped the lever down and up, chambering another round. With practiced precision, he thumbed the hammer back and lined up the front sight on another of the attackers and quickly pulled the trigger. Thunder galloped ahead through the cloud of gunsmoke as a second rider went off to the happy hunting grounds.

Eric exchanged a quick glance at the black cowboy who rode past with a lathered-up pony, but didn't have time to pay his respects. He levered in another round as one of the pursuers let fly an arrow from his short bow. Seeing it in flight, Eric flipped the muzzle slightly at the last second, deflecting the thirty inch long shaft away. He brought the hammer back as the Indian nocked another and fired at the red man from a distance of only ten yards. The bullet went through the Comanche's jaw and took the back of his head off in a cloud of red mist.

Another warrior leapt from his pony as he passed the big man. Eric smashed the man across his neck with the rifle dropping him instantly, but he lost control of the Spencer in the process. The carbine tumbled to the ground as the two separated and he went for his two sidearms. Three of the war party had decided to make a break for it after seeing four of their fellow braves fall, but the remaining four began to encircle him from a distance. He dropped one with a shot from his right hand and another with a left handed shot before an arrow found its mark in his left forearm. It passed through with the bloody stone point sticking out several inches. Try as he might, he couldn't maintain his grip on the Remington and it tumbled from his grasp as another Comanche began to draw back his bow.

Eric swung around as his blue eyes locked with the dark eyes of the much smaller native, but before he could fire, the man's head snapped back violently—the arrow poised on the warrior's bow slipped off when he clutched at his throat.

The sound of another horse coming up fast behind him caused Eric to wheel his horse around. That's when Eric spotted the black cowboy with a steel framed Henry rifle at his shoulder. The man fired and the last of the Indians who had chosen to stay and fight hunched over and grabbed at his stomach. The painted warrior spun his horse around and began to gallop off, but soon slid from the horse's back and flipped end-over-end twice before lying still.

As quickly as the attack had begun, it was over. Eric was breathing heavily and looked down at the shaft sticking out of his arm. Blood began to drip from the sleeve of his bucksiin shirt. "Dammit to hell! Three years I fight and never get hit and now this!"

The black stranger called over to him, "Hey mister! Many thanks...You all right?"

"Took one in the arm, but it is a long way from my heart."

"Lemme give ya'll a hand. Done this before, I have." The man turned his weary mount closer to the big man that had just saved his life.

Eric holstered his Remington and began to look around for his two lost weapons. *Must be losing my edge.* He spotted the rifle laying thirty yards away, close to one of the Indian's bodies.

"Hold still and I will cut the arrow in two, then you can pull it out. Do not brake the shaft if'n you can help it. Splinters, they get infected sumpthin' awful. Might lose that arm."

Eric eyed the sweaty man closely as he slipped the Henry into its scabbard and pulled a large Bowie knife out of a sheath on his gun belt. The cowboy appeared to be around thirty years of age, and built solidly with broad chest. He held out his injured arm and the stranger took hold of the slender shaft near the feathers.

Putting the blade against the pencil-sized shaft, he looked at Eric for a moment. "Try not to move, this may smart some."

"Just do it."

The man nodded and pushed against the arrow at a sixty degree angle as he held tight on the sinew wrapped feather fletching. The knife sliced it off cleanly.

Eric gritted his teeth as the flexing pressure on the shaft stung like fire for a second.

"You can pull the rest out by the arrowhead now, just do it quick, is all."

He complied with the instructions as the second cowboy rode up to join them. "Ah…ah," he moaned as the shaft exited the arm. Blood began to flow even faster. He dropped the arrow in his lap and wrapped his hand around the wound. Eric looked at the arrowhead that had done all the damage and started to throw it away but quickly changed his mind. *Hell…might make a souvenir out of it. First time I ever got shot.*

A younger white man with a long stringy brown hair and a bushy mustache rode up on his right side. "Mister, we owe you for savin' our bacon out here. If you had not come along when you did…"

"That be right. Them Comanch bucks wuz on the warpath for sure. Lookit all that paint."

Eric gazed at the bodies strewn about them. Each had red and yellow pigment smeared in broad stripes across their cheeks and foreheads. "Ya'll are welcome. Those boys looked like they would have tried to kill me as well if they had run across me first."

"I know that is right," said the black cowboy. He stuck out his hand. "Name's Jefferson...Nathanial Jefferson, but most folks calls me Nate."

"Howdy, Nate." Eric shook it with his right hand. "Pleased to make your acquaintance. I am Eric Schmidt....Sorry 'bout the blood."

"Do not pay it no never mind, pilgrim. It will wash off...This here's my partner, Cletus Montrose."

"Cletus," Eric said acknowledging the introduction. "What were you gents doing out here so far from civilization?"

Nate broke into a laugh. "Well...You see, it wuz like this...I came up with the big idea 'bout roundin' up these wild cattle that be roamin' here about. Me and Cletus wuz gonna be in the cattle bizness. But them Comanch...they done had other ideas, if'n you know what I mean."

Eric was puzzled. "I have not seen any cattle to speak of for several days."

"They's out here, believe me. Mostly over in the Palo Duro canyon, but we found a couple dozen up on the Canadian and few on the Salt Fork of the Red."

"Nobody claims to own them?"

"Nosiree…That there is the beauty of my plan. Ain't nuthin' cheaper than free and it ain't stealing neither."

"Nope…we ain't never seen no brands on any of them beeves."

"Must be descended from those that got away from the Spanish explorers I read about," Eric offered.

"May be right…Say, friend…we best be tending to that arm. Got anythin' to wrap it in?"

"Back in the wagon. Cletus, can you fetch my rifle for me? Tryin' to keep from bleeding too dang bad. It dropped over yonder a ways." Eric nodded in the direction where it lay.

"Happy to help you out. I seen it when it fell."

***

CHAPTER SIXTEEN

TEXAS PANHANDLE

All three men sat on the back end of the buckboard. Texas summer sun beat down mercilessly as Eric gritted his teeth and poured the warm water from his canteen onto both the entrance and exit wounds. The arrowhead had left a three quarters inch wide gash on each side.

"You be lucky it missed the bone," observed Nate.

Eric grimaced slightly as the water stung the exposed flesh. "To tell the truth, I ain't feeling exactly lucky right this minute. If I was *really* lucky…that damn arrow would have missed."

Nate and Cletus laughed. "Man's gotta keep a sense of humor in times like this."

"Ya think so, do you? Can you tear me off a couple pieces of that sheet?"

"Sure thing…What you gonna do with that there honey?" asked Cletus as he ripped a long narrow strips off the end of the cotton cloth.

"I plan to put it on the wound…Helps with infection."

"Huh?…Never heard that. Where did you learn 'bout honey and wounds?"

"In the war…Ya'll know that Roman soldiers used to use it the same way?…A long time ago."

Both shook their heads. "You gonna stitch it up, too?" Nate asked, eyeing the sewing kit in the cigar box—marked with the flowing script of the late Alyssa Schmidt.

"Planning on it…Otherwise, the wound keeps on oozing for days. Kinda makes a mess out of things."

"Uh huh…Guess you saw a lot of wounds in the war."

Eric nodded as he patted the two gashes with a dab of the golden nectar. His tone turned markedly colder. "More than I ever wanted to see." The blood quickly turned the sticky goo to a bright pink color. Eric reached over and took the strips that Cletus held out. He quickly wrapped the arm with one and knotted off the loose ends snugly with his teeth. "That should hold 'til I get that needle threaded."

"Let me do it for you…I gots both my hands free."

"Appreciate the help."

Nate fumbled around in the sewing kit and found a half dozen needles woven into a small patch of denim cloth. Finding a curved one used for whip stitching, he started looking at the spools of thread.

"Got a color you be partial to?"

"Black is good…Blood stains do not show."

"Get you fixed up in jiffy." Nate unrolled a two foot length and bit the thread in two. He licked the loose end, pulling it through his pursed lips to form a point and squinted to find the eye of the needle. On the third attempt, he found it and pulled half of the thread though and let it hang free before he knotted the ends together. "You want me to sew you up? I do not mind."

"Sure, it is kinda hard to do it yourself."

Nate untied the temporary bandage and pushed the two sides of the entrance wound together. "This is gonna hurt…"

"You are about ten minutes past hurt…just get 'er done."

He slipped the needle under the skin and pushed it through to the other side of the cut. He pulled it out and tied off the two ends and then repeated the process. He looked up at Eric who was watching the horizon, in case the Comanches decide to come back.

"Tell me, Eric what made you charge into that passel of redskins? I ain't never seen nothing as brave as that."

"Cain't say as it was all bravery…Being out in the open like we were is not a good place to survive an attack by defense alone. I took a calculated risk…it turned out it was a good strategy. At least for the first time…They will not be inclined to come at us the same way twice, I would wager."

Cletus spit out an amber stream of tobacco juice. "Learn't them injuns a thing or two, I 'spect. What kind of shootin' iron was that? Never seen me one like that."

"It is called a Spencer. The Union Army bought a lot of 'em."

"Spencer, huh? You do not talk like a Yankee..."

Eric grinned. "That is 'cause I am a Texan...born and bred, Nate...picked this one up on a battlefield when I served under the Stars and Bars."

"That so?" Nate glanced up at him for a second before he tied off the last stitch. "Turn it over...gimme the other side."

Eric complied and rolled his forearm until the exit wound was on top. "Just so you know...I never owned a slave. Got dragged into the war when a Yankee patrol killed my family."

Nate pinched up the torn skin once more. "Me...I was born a slave...Runned away when I got big enough...Headed out here to start me a new life."

"Funny...that is just what I thought I was doing...starting a new life."

"Where 'bouts were you headed? Ain't hardly nothin' out here for hundreds of miles," asked Cletus.

"I see that." Eric chuckled. "I was thinking about Wyoming or Colorado...Never saw real mountains like they have out west...You say you have been there?"

"You bet. My pappy drove for the Butterfield Stage Line. They had a contract to haul the US mail from Saint Louis to California. Closed down after the secession...anyway, he became a muleskinner for that there freight outfit. Hired me as his swamper...We covered a lot of ground before he died." Cletus let fly another glob of tobacco spittle.

"Sorry for your loss."

"Still miss 'im…He was a ring-tailed tooter, he was."

"What was your favorite part of Colorado? Is it all mountains?"

Cletus broke in a laugh. "Oh, hell no…the eastern half looks like this…" He motioned with his hand at the rolling plains. "…Bare as a baby's butt and colder than a witch's tit in the wintertime."

"Tell me about the mountains."

"Well, sir, they are real high, steep as all gitout and damned cold in the winter…kinda pretty and real nice in the summertime, though. Did you know they ain't got no skeeters in Colorado?"

"Nope, did not. Tell you what…back where I come from, in the piney woods…they must have kept all of Colorado's share. Those boogers could be seriously thick."

"Up in Arkansas, too," Nate said with a grin. "We used to slap each other as kids and holler 'skeeter, but I got 'im' just for the hell of it."

"They found gold and silver in the mountains…some beautiful places are filling up around the mines.

Eric looked down at the wound and saw the last stitch being tied off. The blood flow had stanched to a trickle, but his arm was already beginning to swell.

"That is all she wrote in the sewing department. Get it wrapped up and hope you do not got no infection," Nate said as he wiped the needle off on his sleeve.

"Appreciate the doctorin'…looks good…Excuse me, Cletus, you got any more of that tobacco?"

"Shore." He reached into his shirt and produced a leather pouch. "Hep yerself."

Eric opened the top flap, exposing a commercial twist of firmly compressed leaves. He cut off a small chunk and then handed the rest back.

"Take all you want. I got me lots more in my saddle bag."

"Only need a little bit." Using his teeth, Eric pulled the cork from his canteen let it fall to the end of the silver chain. He took a sip, and then popped the tiny chaw into his mouth. The flavor reminded him of the occasional cigar he tried to smoke to be sociable, but sweeter from the added molasses used to make the twist. The taste of tobacco was never one that he learned to enjoy.

The water helped soften it quickly. He fished the gooey mound out of his mouth and tore it in two. Placing a pat on each wound, he finished up with a new wrap of cotton bandage and held it out for Nate to tie off. "Hand me my shirt if you would."

Cletus reached back on the canvas cover over the cargo and retrieved the bloody garment.

"Be happy if you was quick about it...Already gettin' cooked by the sun...All I need to make a day memorable...Arrow in my arm and burnt up, to boot...Makes you wonder why the Indians live out here."

"They get purty dark...living out in the sun and all...Them and the Comancheros," Cletus said.

Eric slipped his buckskin over his head and pulled the drawstring tight in the front. "Who are the Comancheros? They part of the Comanche tribe?"

311

"Not exactly," said Nate. "They are a mixed breed...some Spanish, some Mexican and a little Indian throwed in...Hell, could be part Apache or Kiowa, for all I know. Sometimes they ride with the Comanches, sometimes alone. The thing to remember is you cain't trust 'em...no way, no how. If'n they try to stop you and try to trade with you, watch out. All they want to know is what you got, so they can figure if you is worth killin' to git it."

"I will remember that." He looked at the western horizon. "We best get moving, just in case they come back with reinforcements."

"Sounds good to me. Can you still drive that rig?"

"Hope so. I ain't plannin' to leave it here."

"Yo arm is startin' to swell...That just be nature takin' its course. Ain't gonna have you much of a grip on that left hand for a while. Some willow bark makes a mighty good tonic for the fever...make the pain more tolerable, too."

"Know where any willow might be?"

"You bet, we do. Me and old Cletus know this country purty dang good. 'Bout eight miles north is the Salt Fork of the Red...Plenty of willow up that way."

"All right, but I am gonna find my Remington six gun before we leave. Saved my butt too many times to leave it to rust out here on the prairie."

"We be glad to help you."

The three men walked the area line abreast and Cletus found it laying about thirty yards from one of the Comanche bodies. He snatched it up and dusted it off.

312

"Here you go, big guy. Still has a couple of shots left."

Eric fumbled with the flap on his left holster and then managed to get the tip of the muzzle inside and dropped in down. "Gentlemen, if you will indulge me for a few minutes, I want to check out the bodies of these Indians we killed."

His new friends exchanged nervous glances.

Nate forehead furrowed with a frown. "You ain't thinkin' 'bout scalpin' them redskins, is you?"

"Nope...Not my style. All I want to do is collect all their weapons and check 'em for anything of value. Not leaving it for the rest of their tribe to pick up and use against us later."

"Never figured it that way. I cain't shoot a bow, so I look at it as purty useless," Cletus replied.

"I never shot one of these little Comanche bows, but my papa built me one as a kid. Even hunted rabbits and bagged a few."

"This one had a shotgun on him. Musta took it off some unlucky settler."

"See, Nate, now that is what I was talking about. Over here, I found a knife, a bow and full quiver."

Back at the wagon, the three loaded up the salvaged weapons, knives and the ornately beaded bone breastplate worn by the band's former leader. It was designed something akin to an armored apron with a fixed loop around the neck and leather thong ties in the back. Its closely spaced bones could defeat an enemy arrow or even a knife. Eric figured it would be worth something in trade at the next settlement. He climbed back up to the buckboard seat and sat down.

"Lead off, Nate. I will follow ya'll to the river…Keep your eyes peeled."

"Preachin' to choir, white boy," Nate said before he broke into a hearty laugh. "Preachin' to the choir."

SALT FORK OF THE RED RIVER

Eric looked up and down the strip of sand winding up and down the wide valley. *They call that a river?* Sure enough there were scattered patches of willow trees along the edges. He could see the pair of horses belonging to his compatriots along the edge of one clump.

He reached for the binoculars and made a slow deliberate scan of the horizon before he clucked Dollar to head down the shallow slope. Finding a smooth gradient near the hobbled mounts, the set the brake and hopped down. A piercing shot of pain up his arm reminded him why they were stopping. He held the arm up above his heart and the throbbing seemed the ease slightly.

"Ya'll finding what we need?"

"Sure thing. Done got us an armload of young branches cut. Cletus is stompin' 'round trying to locate a waterhole. The Salt Fork do not run much in summertime."

"Saw that right off. Where do the cattle get their drinkin' water?"

"Here and there…" he said, motioning both up and down stream. "When the storms come up a frog strangler, this will run bank to bank. They's some deep holes, but this here spot is good one to cross in a wagon."

"Appreciate your thinkin' 'bout me."

"Not as much as I 'preciate you helping me keep my scalp." Nate lifted his hat and showed off his thick nappy head of hair.

"Indians could mistake that for black wool."

"I would make them pay 'afor I let 'em take it, I guarandamntee."

"Bet you would at that."

Nate waxed philosophical. "You know, it would be a better world if peoples would just let everybody live and let live. They is lots of room out here."

"Maybe so, but that is not the way most people are. Folks just seem to get territorial as all get out. That is why wars are fought…over bits of land and who has say-so over it."

"People hatin' people cause they look different or talk different…Cain't make heads or tails of it."

"I was not brought up to think like that…You know, folks do not have a choice who their parents were…Why hold that against somebody like you are some sort of God in judgment?"

"Then theys the ones who use God to fight for their religion against other religions…Cain't stand them holy rollers."

Eric nodded and glanced upstream. "Yep…hey…Looks like Cletus has found some water."

The two cowboys grinned at each other as Eric took a sip of the boiled bark.

"Whoa…this give bitters a run for its money."

315

"You got honey…a couple dollops might take the edge off it."

"Coulda told me that before, Nate…ya know?"

"Come on, blondie…It will do you good…drink it up."

Eric held his nose and drained the tin cup. "Happy now?" He set the cup down beside the fire. "Either of you read maps?"

Nate shook his head. "Cain't read a lick."

Cletus beamed. "I done map reading. Pappy learnt me real good."

"Then you are elected by default."

"Fault?…what fault?"

"Never mind." Eric smiled to himself as he walked back to the wagon and pulled out the three foot long metal tube and popped off the friction cap on one end. He rolled the handful of maps out and selected the Texas panhandle one first, grimacing as he spread it out on the dry sand. "Here is where I think we are," he said pointing at the river.

Cletus studied the sheet for a moment. "Maybe so…but, my gut tells me we are ten or fifteen miles west of there. See, we rode past the edge of the Palo Duro a few days past. Our corral is about right there." He pointed at a confluence of two canyons. "We keep 'em watered and the plan was to drive 'em to market and split the money…Like I said, that was the plan."

The topographic maps were some those supplied to the United States Army and taken over by the Confederates in San Antonio after Texas seceded. Basically, they showed terrain, roads and rivers with small annotations as to settlements and towns. In 1865, much of the west was very sparsely populated.

"With a buckboard loaded like it is, yer best bet is head due north. Got two rivers to cross...the Canadian here and the Beaver here in the Cherokee strip."

"Not too steep?"

"Naw...you come this far, you can make it. Do not go and break a wheel, 'cause they ain't no blacksmith in two hundred miles."

"Figures."

Cletus picked up another chart. "New Mexico is like five hundred miles of bad road. Ain't much out there, 'cept Santa Fe and Albuquerque. Some places out there, the water is alkali to boot. Got a map of Colorado territory?"

"Uh huh." Eric fingered through the stack and pulled out a sepia-colored chart. "All I have is on this one." It was marked Kansas Territory, but extended all the way west to the border of the Utah territory.

"Gotta make due..." Cletus said and he leaned in closer. "This is the Arkansas river down south. Most of the people follow it west, cause water is scarce once you get north of there.

"Git yerself up on the mountain section of the Santa Fe Trail and you got it whipped...Army's got forts and they's more people traveling that route."

"Safety in numbers?"

"When it come to fightin' off redhides, I say so."

"So, where are some good places to find work or set up a business?"

"Depends...What kind of work do you do and what kind of business?"

"I studied to be a gunsmith with my father and I grew up on a ranch. Not afraid to get my hands dirty…if you know what I mean."

"Figured that right off when I saw you lay into that war party. Anyway, things kicked off big once gold was found back in fifty-nine. Denver City is the biggest town, I reckon…kinda dirty in the winter, as I recall. See, its set up next to the mountains in kind of a bowl and smoke from all the chimneys just hangs over it if the wind is low."

"Anywhere else?"

"Lotsa places…Colorado ain't like Texas, but it is a still a big territory. There is Colorado City…now it is closer to the mountains, instead of being out on the flats like Denver City and Auraria. They discovered silver and gold in the mountains all over from here to here." He made a swath across the front range of the Rockies.

"This map does not show any towns there. It was made back in fifty-four."

"Well they's little mining towns all over now…Oro City…where the ore is rich and the girls are pretty."

Eric's eyes lit up and he grinned. "Did you make that up?"

"Nuh uh. Heard it a lot last time I was there. Got a big mine and a booming town building up. We hauled dry goods and liquor up to Leadville and Oro City. You can always get a job in the mine."

Eric shook his head. "Do not think I would like digging in a hole for a living." He handed Cletus a pencil. "Can you mark that Oro City place on the map?"

318

"Is a bullfrog waterproof?" Cletus laughed.

"That place sounds kinda good to me. You say there's a lot going on up there?"

"Hope to shout…They's got new buildings a going up 'bout ever day in the season. Pappy and me musta took purt near twenty-five or thirty loads up there. You name it, we hauled it. Lumber, windows, beans, whiskey and beer…If they needed it we brung it."

"The season?"

"I keep forgittin', you ain't been there yet…Not much gets done outside after the snow moves on down the mountain. Folks kinda hunker down 'til spring, like a grizzly bear…'cept in the mine. That rich Irish bastard keeps everybody working every day but Christmas."

"One guy owns the biggest mine?"

"Yeah, old man Malone," Cletus spat a stream of tobacco juice into the fire, causing it to sizzle and hiss. "Lucky booger hit it rich on the mother load four or five years ago…Now he owns half the town, I reckon."

"Is there still land to be bought?"

"Down the mountain a ways, there sure is. Most of the placer gold claims are way down in the creek bottoms…Nearly all the hard rock claims are up near the timberline. They got some nice looking meadows…a man could fatten cattle there real easy in the summertime…Lotsa water and grass up to yer belly."

"Sounds mighty invitin'. Think I will give it a look-see first thing."

319

Buck Stienke

"You should be there by early October, if yer luck holds out. Plenty of game in them hills, too. Mule deer, black bear and even some elk...they are starting to get pushed off the plains and into the mountains by sod busters...Good eatin', them elk."

"Cletus, my friend, you are wealth of information. Sure you boys do not want to ride along with me to Colorado?"

Nate shook his head. "No, sir...Truth is, I gets plenty 'nuff cold right here in Texas. Me and my partner is gonna take our cattle way down to the hill country north of San Antonio."

Eric grinned. "I am not sure which of us is the craziest...you or me. Want to wish you luck, though." He glanced west as the sun began to drop lower. "Ya'll join me for dinner? Got salt pork, speckled butter beans...and some canned peaches for desert."

Nate and Cletus exchanged grins and nodded vigorously. "Pilgrim, you got yourself a deal!" Nate smiled.

The fifth day on the Santa Fe Trail's northern section—called the mountain route as it passed over Raton Pass situated on the New Mexico and Colorado territorial borders—presented Eric with his first view of the distant Rocky Mountain peaks. "Looky there boys! Can you see 'em?" he hollered as he topped a long, gradual rise.

Neither Thunder or nor Dollar seemed impressed.
After passing a string of small outposts—Fort Aubry, Grenada, Bent's New Fort, Fort Lyon Number One—he came upon one called Fort Lyon Number Two. Designed to protect the route's travelers, provide a source of supplies and water, the small

320

military base was a branching-off point for those hardy souls still seeking fame and fortune in the years following the great Pike's Peak Gold Rush of 1859.

Persons wishing to continue on to New Mexico or California turned south, staying on the Santa Fe trail, crossing the Arkansas river and heading toward the tiny speck of a town called Trinidad—starting place of the Uncle Dick Wooton's twenty-seven mile toll road over Raton Pass. Others including Eric Schmidt, bought their provisions and headed west northwest along the northern banks of the Arkansas and toward the 14,000' tall snowcapped peaks.

COLORADO CITY
Sept 1865

Pike's Peak dominated the skyline west of the rough and tumble town that would later be known as Colorado Springs. A stiff west wind blew off the higher plateau and whistled down the canyon surrounding the majestic mountain on its north side. Eric turned the collar up on his sheepskin jacket as he looked over the horses and mules for sale at the livery. One—a large black mule—caught his attention. He watched it for a few minutes, before he walked back inside the log cabin used as an office next to the clapboard barns and corrals. An older man was seated near a wood burning stove, whittling a corn cob into a smoking pipe bowl.

"What you gents asking for the mules today?"

"Depends on the mule...You paying cash or trade?" The proprietor said as he wiped the dribble of tobacco juice off his lower lip with his sleeve.

"Got a horse to trade...he's five years old, sound and well cared for. He brought me up here from Texas. Figured I need me a bigger animal to pull the grades with my buckboard."

"They are fixin' to get snow up in the mountains...you plannin' to haul freight?"

Eric shook his head. "Just want to get me and my gear up there to Oro City."

"Gonna work in the mine, are you?"

"No, sir...Gonna set up a gunsmith shop there."

The old man eyed him suspiciously. "Ain't no reason to do that, boy. Everybody already has a gun that wants one."

Eric shook his head and grinned. "You may be right, but I am still going up there and check it out for myself."

Topping out the ridge, he gave the mule he had named Rufus a breather. "Whoa on up there, big boy. You done good on that long grade." He stopped for a second to take in the view. Aspen trees lined the edges of the meadows and had turned a yellow gold color.

The howling west winds died down overnight and were replaced by a gentle breeze from the south. To his left, the massive summit of Pike's Peak was not visible, only the flanks—covered with evergreen fir and blue spruce—rose up another 2,000 feet above what would in later years be known as Woodland Park.

He took in a deep breath. The air felt different—lighter, drier and fresher than he had ever experienced. Eric set the brake and stepped down off the wagon. He dumped a couple handfuls of oats into the feed bags and tied one on Rufus and the other his stallion. "Here you are, Thunder. After lunch, I'll give you a little workout...Ain't been earning your keep lately."

He cut a couple of thin slices of ham he had purchased in Colorado City and slapped them between two slices of dark pumpernickel bread. The hickory-smoked pork tasted really good and reminded him of ones his father had cured each fall.

Off in the distance, the second range of the Rockies loomed up, crystal clear in the early fall air. *That should be where Leadville and Oro City are, if those folks in town knew what they were talking about. Ute pass is only twelve miles west and then I can cut to the northwest.*

After he finished his sandwich, he wandered over to the creek and checked out the water. Clear and cold, he scooped up a handful and tasted it. *Nice...really nice.* He went back to the wagon and muscled down the small water barrel and carried over to the creek bank. Once it was refilled, he toted it back to the wagon and hefted it over the sideboard. He stood there panting, almost out of breath. *What the hell? It can't be any heavier...*

The words of the old horse trader he had met in Colorado City came back to him. *Take it easy flatlander. It will take time to get used to the altitude.*

"So that is what he meant. Flatlander...Never been called that before." Eric caught his breath and reached for the map

323

canister. He unrolled the Kansas Territory map and checked the elevation contour. *8,200 feet! No wonder.* He stowed the chart and climbed up onto to the buckboard seat. "Break is over, Rufus. You can finish your lunch on the move."

The hustle and bustle of the Oro City didn't come as a surprise. He expected the gangs of construction workers engaged in building a series of new businesses and homes. A huge mansion dominated the skyline slightly uphill of the main street. It was three stories high and reminded Eric of an European castle. Made of native granite and resembling a famous one in Belfast, it was the home of the wealthy Angus Malone.

Wagons laden with gold ore or rock overburden pulled out of the major mines trekked over to the stamping mills or tailings dumping area, depending on quality of the load. He passed a saloon with a dozen horses tied to the hitching posts. The sign painted above the entrance proclaimed its purpose.

MULDOON'S
Drinking and Gambling Mecca

Kinda early in the day for that, I would think. Eric pulled into the wagon yard beside the Whitman livery stable and climbed down. Entering the livery, he found an old man pumping a bellows and preparing to heat a horseshoe in the forge. "Excuse me, sir."

The old man never looked up. "Not now...cain't you see I am busy? I told you guys...no deliveries before three o'clock."

"I am not…"

"No…the answer is still no. Not 'til after three."

Eric shook his head. *Are all the horse people in Colorado naturally grumpy?* "Do you treat all your customers this way?"

The old man finally looked up over the top of his Benjamin Franklin wire rimmed glasses. "Oh, hell fire. You ain't the man from Denver City…"

Schmidt laughed. "Never been there in my life. Just need a shoe for my mule and some advice."

"Well, sir, you come to the right place. I will be with you soon as I get the sorrel shod…Do not eat yellow snow."

"Yellow snow? What does that have to do with anything?"

"You said you wanted advice, so I gave you some," he replied with a sparkle in his eyes.

"I get it," Eric said when had a chance to think about the suggestion. "Pretty funny."

"Where are you from? I have not seen you or that rig you are driving…must be new to town."

"Just got in from Texas."

"A little late for the gold rush…All the easy pickings are done played out."

"So I have heard. I am looking for a small building to set up my shop and a place to live."

"Not a miner?"

"Nope. I am a gunsmith by trade…studied under my father."

"Ever work with horses? I would imagine you know your war around a forge."

"That is a big part of gunsmithing...heat treating, making springs and small parts. Rode with the cavalry for three years in the war...You could say I know my way around horses. Why do you ask?"

The old man removed the horseshoe from the fire, dipped it in a nearby bucket of water causing a great cloud of steam, and then set it on the tapered end of the anvil to let it cool. "A man who is good with metal can do well as a farrier. You are big enough to do some of the work of a blacksmith as well."

"What is your point?"

"I'm gettin' too old to do some of the hard manual work and horse trainin' 'round here. Take me longer to get back up after I get throwed if you know what I mean..."

Eric nodded as the man wiped his hands off on his leather apron and then extended his right. "Name's Wallace Whitman. I own this place and the blacksmith shop next door."

"Pleased to meet you Mister Whitman. I am Eric Schmidt."

He took the older man's hand and was impressed by the strength of the grip.

"Come on in the office, son. Got some coffee on the stove...boiled it up fresh this mornin'."

After a half hour, the two shook hands again. Eric agreed to take over for Earl, the late blacksmith—a burly hothead killed four days earlier in a knife fight over a woman in Muldoon's saloon. He could set up his gun shop inside the unused storage space and provide needed muscle over at the livery when Wallace was not up to the job. Whitman also agreed to lease him the small cabin and barn between Oro City and Leadville that he had traded for when he first came to town.

He unloaded his bellows, anvil and tools and set them inside the wood frame blacksmith building. Looking around, he saw steel rims and hubs for wagons, a stack of oak wood—already cut for spoke blanks—and another whiskey barrel stood on end with longer ones already turned on a lathe for surreys and lighter wagons. The forge was larger than he was used to, but certainly capable of handling anything he planned to do in the area of firearms. It had a big bellows mounted to the floor and a hemp rope running up through a six inch pulley made from hickory.

On the end of the rope was a burnished wooden handle. The operator could pull down on the rope, lifting one side of the bellows. When he released it, the weight of the wooden frame would cause the side to drop, sending a fresh supply of oxygen to the bottom of the forge to increase the heat. Eric tugged on the handle, released and listened to the steady hiss of the out-flowing air. *That is nice. One thing less for me to build.*

He turned the buckboard around in the crushed rock street and drove up to Malone's Mercantile store. Parking behind two other wagons, already lined up to load their purchases, he tied off the reins and hopped down. The sidewalk was burgeoning with customers moving to and fro. Eric tipped his broad-brimmed black hat at the ladies, as did most of the other gentlemen. He noted the styles in Colorado differed from those he was used to down in Texas, with many men sporting bowlers with almost no brim. *Huh...What good is a hat like that? Will not keep you dry or shade you from the sun.*

He made his purchases and walked to the door with the nearly full apple crate. *I cannot remember when I had a fresh egg. Things are a whole lot more expensive up here in the mountains. Guess I will just have to get used to that.*

He loaded the crate beside him in the seat, being careful not to jostle the eggs too much in the cardboard box filled with shredded newspaper.

***

CHAPTER SEVENTEEN

ERIC'S CABIN

The log cabin was some forty yards off the road up to Leadville, nestled between a handful of towering blue spruce. It had a great view down the mountain and across a small fenced-in five acre meadow that went with the property. Like many of the places found at higher elevations, the soil was fairly thin and the fence itself consisted of aspen tree trunks that had been nailed to small A-frame supports that rested on top of the ground. Each section of fence had three rails on the inside and another on the outside for strength and stability. A small creek ran through the pasture and also provided water to a wooden storage tank beside the house. A one hole privy—often called the convenience—was set behind the house some fifteen yards.

Eric pulled in front on the cabin and parked. After untying the black stallion, he walked him to the barn. "Think you'll like it here boy? Plenty of room to run, and we have a barn for you when the weather turns cold."

Eric pulled the saddle and set it and the blanket on to the rail beside the storage bin. After he removed the headstall and opened the door to the pasture, Thunder raced off to check out the perimeter of their new digs, kicking up his heels like he was a colt.

Guess I would celebrate a little after following behind for six weeks. He returned to the wagon and began the process of getting moved into his new home.

The majestic bull elk bugled as he rounded up his harem of cows and moved them down the mountain. Snowfall at the higher elevations had already begun to cover the grass they grazed upon, and they were headed lower to keep themselves fed.

Hair on the back of Eric's neck stood up as the high pitched whistle echoed off the far side of the canyon. He could feel his heart pumping faster as the anticipation of a shot at the bull began to effect him. *Calm down, dang it. You have killed deer before. This ain't much different.*

He stepped slowly and deliberately as he silently moved over to a cluster of aspen trees, their white bark gnawed away in dark oval shaped patches where elk had eaten it off the previous year when they were trapped by heavy snow. The ground was already covered with four inches of new fallen white powder, muffling his footsteps even more. Tiny icicles formed on the hairs of his mustache, turning it to a shroud of ice that hung below his lips. Eric spotted a cow elk moving out of the dark timber above him. She was wary of entering the clearing and looked nervously about before she continued downhill. Another cow, and then a pair of yearling calves followed her as his heart beat even faster.

Thirteen…fourteen…how many are in this herd?

His unspoken question was soon answered. The patriarch of the herd, an imperial elk with seven polished white tines on massive mahogany colored beams eased out from behind a clump of young fir trees. The distance was almost ninety yards, but the bull's path would bring him much closer if the cows did not spook before that happened. Eric slipped the fingertips of his right leather glove into his mouth and bit down, allowing him to slide his hand free.

Putting his index finger on the trigger, he pulled it as he thumbed the hammer back on his Sharps rifle. That simple action prevented contact between the sear and the hammer as the two hardened steel parts moved silently past each other under the sideplate. The matriarch of the herd was only forty-five yards across the narrow meadow. Eric could see her warm breath forming tiny gray clouds as he stared through the snowflakes that lazily drifted down. *No wind at all. That is a good thing.*

With practiced precision, he released back pressure on the trigger just in time for it to catch the sear in the full cock notch.

Eric felt the two parts make good contact as the lead cow looked directly at him. He held his breath.

All she could see was a nondescript clump of white in between two aspen trees and determined it was no threat. How could she have known that the white canvas parka he had custom-made looked like a snow covered boulder? The cow turned her attention down the trail and continued moving forward.

Eric took a shallow breath and pursed his lips together and let it out slowly. He could feel his pulse throbbing in his temples as the bull walked slowly with this head held high, sniffing the air.

He turned his head and appeared to look directly at Eric—his horns flared out almost four feet wide from beam to beam. The animal's thick fur was a deep chocolate brown from his nose to his broad chest, but the elk's body itself was light tan in color—the rump almost white.

He lined up the brass front sight with the front leg and centered the top of the blade low on the shoulder and squeezed the trigger. The shot echoed up and down the canyon and the bull crumpled where he stood. Eric operated the Sharp's lever and slipped in another paper-wrapped cartridge as the remaining members of the herd bolted away. He automatically cocked the hammer once more for a follow-up shot, but it was quickly apparent that the second one was not needed. From fifty yards away, he could tell the bull was no longer breathing. He eased the hammer down to the safety notch, slipped back on his glove and stood up from his place of concealment.

Eric approached the downed bull from the rear. He had a lot of respect for the horns the elk carried. A wounded bull could still pin a man to the ground and the massive animal outweighed him over five to one. He touched the muzzle to the bull's unblinking eye and then said a silent prayer, giving thanks for the animal's life and providing him food for many weeks to come.

He leaned the Sharps against a nearby aspen trunk and moved back to the bull. *My God...each quarter weighs more than an east Texas whitetail.* He tried to roll the animal over on its back to begin to dress it out. *That is not gonna happen. Guess I will have to gut it out on its side and cut it up into quarters. Old Rufus will have his work cut out for today.*

As night fell, a weary hunter, his horse and mule made it back to the barn after two trips hauling back the meat. Eric hung four large quarters up by ropes dangling from the hay loft. A week of aging would help tenderize the bigger cuts. The back strap and tenderloins were already wrapped in cheese cloth and would fry up nicely as they were.

Eric buckled woolen horse blankets onto both of his animals to keep them warm as the snow continued to fall outside. He fed them an extra ration of grain for the hard day's work and put them in their stalls for the night before he went inside himself.

In the dark, he fumbled around for the tin of matches for a few seconds as he moved around the table. The coal oil lamp lit off and filled the icy cold cabin with enough light for him to get a fire going in the cast iron wood stove.

Eric stood by the stove and slowly stripped off the layers of clothes he had worn all day. He pulled a stick of jerky out of a side pocket on the parka and gnawed off a piece and slowly began to chew the peppery beef. *Shoot...I am too dog tired to cook tonight. Think I will finish this off and crawl in the sack.*

ORO CITY
JULY 28TH, 1866

The summertime Colorado sun beat down through the clear mountain air as the fifth wagon laden with freshly cut hay rolled into the livery wagon yard and pulled up behind the open barn door. Wallace Whitman motioned to the driver of the previous one. "Take it on out, Lester. Last one is waitin' on you."

"Yessir," the skinny fourteen year old said as he climbed back aboard and snapped the reins on the mule's rump. "Git on up, Sam...git a movin' now." The old mule with a gray muzzle responded begrudgingly and leaned into the harness.

Eric used the hay fork to toss the last of the previous load piled up in the drive-through over the six foot plank wall into the forage bin. The air was filled with dust and pollen from the hay—it danced in the tiny beams of sunlight shining through holes in the roof and cracks in the weathered boards on the barn wall.

"Got it in you to do one more load?" Wallace asked.

Eric was filthy, covered in sweat, and had bits of grass stuck in his shoulder length hair. His trapezoids, shoulders and arms were a little sore from the repetitive motions with the wooden fork. "Figure that maybe one more will not do me in. Now I see why you were so eager to get me to help you out."

Wallace grinned. "That, my friend is a young man's job. Once it dries completely, we can use that block and tackle overhead to move it into the loft."

"We have to move it twice?" Eric wiped the sweat from his brow on the sleeve of the faded red undershirt.

"It gets whole lot easier when it is dry...I made me a platform that can raise up half a wagon load at once. All it takes is a stout draft horse or a mule."

"Wondered how you got it up there...Bit too far to toss it."

"When you finish up, I will buy you a beer, son. You deserve it."

"Starting to get a little dry, now that you mention it. What do you think the temperature is?"

"Reckon it's in the low nineties. About the hottest day all summer I would think."

"I expect you are right." He moved over to a glazed pottery canister, lifted the lid and dipped the ladle in. He took a drink of the cool water and wiped his lips on the back of his hand. Eric had shaved off his handlebar mustache in the spring. The constant presence of ice on it was such a nuisance that he decided he could live without *snotcicles* as he called them. His clean-shaven face made him look much younger than his twenty-three years.

Eric had not talked much at all about his wartime experiences and had told no one of his former rank. Folks in town knew he worked with Wallace training horses and was a talented blacksmith who dabbled in guns on the side. He kept to himself most of the time and seldom drank in the saloon.

Once the last of the hay wagons was unloaded, he hung the pitchfork on the hooks he had forged from two worn-out horseshoes. "Ready for that beer, Wallace?"

"I will be right along. Got a couple things to finish up here first." He dug in his pants and flipped a quarter over to Eric. "First couple are on me."

He grinned as he snatched the coin out of the air. "That is a deal, two is better than one…see you over there." He turned and walked through the adjoining door to the blacksmith shop. He started to put on his light blue cotton long sleeve shirt that was hanging on the back of the office desk chair, but changed his mind. *I am already too danged dirty and the shirt is still kinda clean. That would just be one more thing for me to wash.*

He picked up his gun belt with the matched pair of Remingtons and the stag-handled knife and buckled it over his pants, just below the waist where his suspenders fastened to buttons near the waistband. Belt loops did not exist on men's trousers in the 1860s and almost every man still wore suspenders—called braces or galluses—to hold them up. He brushed off the big pieces of hay on his chest. The steady supply of food during the long winter helped Eric regain his body weight he had lost in the cavalry—particularly in the last year when supplies were scarce.

His muscles were well-toned like many other blacksmiths who labored with heavy wagon wheels and hand tools. He picked up the black broad-brimmed hat that had become his signature headgear and slipped it on before he flipped the shop's *open* sign over to the *closed* position and locked the door behind him.

"Hey big fellow...Did you miss me?" Eric patted Thunder on the neck and untied the lead rope from the pitching post. He snugged the cinch, stepped into the saddle and then made the sixteen-hand horse side-pass to a nearby water trough and slake his thirst. "That is plenty, boy. We will be home soon enough and you and Rufus can see who is the fastest all evening...How does that sound?" He reined the stallion east on Center Street past the small city marshal's office and jail, the assay office and a half dozen merchant stores that were closing for the day.

As he approached Muldoon's Saloon, a man walked out of the building and mounted a horse almost tied almost directly in front of the swinging doors. *Hey, how is that for timing? Got us a spot in close for a change.*

He rode up to the hitching post and tied off between a white gelding and a black appaloosa with a white blanket. Sounds from the rinky-tink piano and the raucous laughter of bar patrons in various stages of inebriation spilled out the doors. Eric stepped up onto the boardwalk from the sun-baked street, pushed the doors wide and walked in.

Sawdust covered the rough plank floor. A dozen round tables—each with four round back bow chairs—were set around the room and a long bar—standing four feet high and boasting a polished brass foot rail—shipped all the way from St. Louis—dominated the west wall. On the east side of the room was a stairwell that led to a series of small rooms called cribs, where the girls of the line that flitted around the menfolk could ply the oldest profession for a dollar. The piano player was not the caliber of the ones who played in bigger towns, but he tried to keep things lively.

Eric looked for an empty seat at one of the tables, but there were none available. *Crap...I should have got here before the day shift left the mine.*

Miners wearing navy blue canvas pants and shirts filled many of the seats. Others were taken by storekeeps and a couple by cowboys who worked on one of the bigger spreads in the valley below. He glanced over at the bar and spotted an opening between several men dressed in fine clothes.

Well, if I have to stand next to those prissy peacocks, so be it. The only claim to fame those O'Toole brothers has is to being born to Angus Malone's sister. For the life of me, I will never fathom why they act as if they discovered that vein of gold themselves. Hell...they were not even in the territory when that happened, that is what the old timers tell me.

He worked his way past several tables where miners were playing stud poker and drinking the watered down house bottles of what was called bourbon whiskey. He caught the attention of one of the three bartenders working behind the polished counter. He held up his index and middle finger. "Marvin, two beers, if you would."

The skinny man with a black pencil-thin mustache hollered back, "You got 'em." He pulled a pair of mugs out of a wash tub filled with dingy dishwater and let them drain for a second.

He filled them both from a spigot driven into the bunghole on a wooden barrel of beer that had been brewed down in Denver City and set them down on the bar. "That will be ten cents, mister."

Eric slapped the quarter down and picked up one of the glasses of amber colored liquid. It was still relatively cold, after being stored in the basement on top of huge blocks of ice that had been harvested from a frozen mountain lake in the wintertime and then covered with a bed of sawdust. He blew off the two inch head of foam and took a sip. *Whew…That will sure wet your whistle.*

Big Mike O'Toole sniffed at the working man's body odor. *Jesus…what in tarnation is that smell?* Standing six-feet-six inches tall, the giant from Boston turned around and glared over at the younger customer standing at the bar next to him. He turned back, looked at his brother, winked and then leaned over and whispered in his ear, "Let us have a wee bit o' fun…what do you say Paddy boy?"

Patrick nodded and looked past his slightly bigger older brother. He reached down behind the bar and picked up a pitcher of water and set it in front of Michael. He then elbowed an attorney buddy of his standing beside him. "Ye gonna want to see this…Me brother is feeling his rye, I am thinking."

Eric took a second, much longer drink of his beer and let his eyes drift up above the mirror behind the bar to the large oil painting of a nude Fatima relining on a couch. For a brief second the redhead's image triggered a memory of a much more beautiful red-haired woman he still loved very much. A sharp pang of regret and loneliness set upon him. He forced himself to push the memory away, as he had many, many times before and grit his teeth in resolution not to let the bittersweet thought come back—at least that is what he hoped. He looked in the mirror as the notorious braggart and bully turned to face him with a metal pitcher in his hand. *What the hell?*

In a booming Irish accent, O'Toole bellowed out, "Hey everybody! Looks like our local stable boy could use himself a bath! Whatcha think?" His left hand snaked out and snatched the black hat from Eric's head as he held the pitcher high.

Eric felt himself stiffen as his eyes narrowed. "Do not do it," he said in a firm voice.

The crowd began to roar with laughter as the nephew of the territory's richest man dumped the cold water on him. The water cascaded down, soaking his head and shoulders and making a puddle on the bar top.

Almost in a blur, Eric pivoted and threw a crushing left hook to O'Toole's face. The crack of the impact was heard throughout the bar. The laughter died out instantly and even the piano player stopped banging on the slightly out-of-tune standup.

Big Mike staggered back, bleeding and stumbled into his brother, knocking him into the next two men at the bar before he went down. He got back to his feet and spit his two front teeth into his hands. His nose was pushed over to the right and flowed crimson all over his ruffled silk shirt and brocade vest as he pointed an accusing finger at Eric and bellowed, "Ye ignorant hayseed bastard! See what ye went and done?"

"Told you not to do it, but you would not listen…Irish prick." Eric locked eyes with the bigger man and took a another sip of beer. He saw O'Toole yank back the front of his frock coat, exposing the pearl grip of a handgun in a shoulder holster.

Behind him, his brother Patrick went for a nickel plated Smith & Wesson Model 1½ he had stashed in his coat pocket. Eric's fingers loosened instantly and let the beer mug fall from his lips. His hands were like twin rattlesnakes striking at his two cavalry flap holsters on his gunbelt.

In the blink of an eye and a flash of blue steel, his gunsmoke filled the air. Eric was the last man standing, looking down at the fallen pair.

An errant shot from Patrick's .32 rimfire had shattered the giant mirror behind the bar. Big Mike had managed to pull his Colt Navy .36 caliber revolver and accidentally shot a miner seated at a nearby table in the leg when a .44 caliber ball from Eric's Remington shattered his wrist and then pierced his heart.

"Keep your hands where I can see them!" Eric yelled out at the stunned crowd. "You three…move out from behind the bar." The bartenders held their hands high and moved to the swinging cutout, lifted it and stepped out onto the sawdust floor.

"Never seen nobody fast as him," one of the patrons whispered to his buddy. The other man nodded as he kept his hands firmly planted face down on the card table.

The bartender who had served Eric the beer leaned over and looked at the bodies of the ill-fated brothers lying face up side-by-side on the floor. Each had a single gunshot lined up dead center in their chest. He shook his head and looked up at

Eric. "Old man Malone will pay to have you dead...even if it was in self defense...You know that?"

Eric nodded. "Ya'll can put your hands down...This ain't no robbery." He put his back to the bar, both Remingtons held waist high at the ready with their hammers fully cocked. He took in a deep breath and spoke in a booming voice so everyone could hear. "The only reason I came in here was to have a beer or two after a long, hot day. I did not start this fracas...Ya'll saw that." He looked around the crowd, making mental notes of the faces.

"Here is the best advice you will ever get...Do not come gunning after me for killing scum in self defense...Dying is a hard way to make a livin'." He knelt down to retrieve his hat and put it back where it belonged and the set the gun in his left hand down on the bar. With his free hand, he picked up the beer he had bought for Wallace and quickly drained the glass as he keep his eyes on the crowd.

Eric set the empty mug back down on the wet bar with an audible *thud*. He picked up the sixshooter and then made his way to the front doors as his gaze darted from person to person.

Most of the patrons could not bear to look him straight in the eyes and stared blankly down at their table. He turned around at the swinging doors, and backed out of the barroom, closely watching the crowd. He lowered the hammers of the sixguns and then, using the muzzles to flip open the flaps on the holsters, dropped the pair of deadly shooters back inside. He jumped off the boardwalk, quickly untied Thunder, swung up into the saddle and galloped up the street.

He slowed down to a lope as he passed Wallace leaving the livery.

"Where's the fire?" the old man called out to him.

"Watch over the store. I will come back when I can."

Wallace reined up and watched him disappear around the corner at the next street. *Danged young 'uns. Never can figure 'em.*

Eric whistled up Rufus from the pasture as he slid to a stop outside the barn. As the mule responded to his call, he sprinted to the front door and snatched up his old Confederate saddle bags he had kept stocked for any long distance trip. He pried a rock loose from the fireplace, retrieved a leather pouch with his last few gold coins from a hiding hole he had created, and stuffed it inside his pants.

Moving to the cupboard near the stove, he began to rapidly choose what little provisions he would take—some canned fruit, beef jerky, a side of bacon, coffee, flour, salt and pepper. He took a tote sack from under the counter and tossed the items in before he grabbed the open end and spun it closed. On his way out, Eric stopped and snatched the Sharps rifle from its normal resting place over the door.

He had the saddle blanket and panniers on Rufus in a matter of minutes, with his food and a sack of oats for the two animals. He covered the gear with a tarp and cinched it down with a hemp rope before he removed the southwestern style saddle from Thunder and replaced it with the McClellan he had ridden during the war. He knew that Angus Malone would be offering a reward for his capture or killing. He owned the mine and half the town and the sheriff worked for him at his beck and call.

Eric snapped the slots of the saddlebags over the brass U shaped fittings on the short skirt behind the cantle and locked them in place. He attached a second scabbard to the brass rings on the rig, moving the Spencer from his other saddle to the deeper McCellan. He climbed aboard the stallion and walked him out of the barn leading Rufus with a short rope.

Looking down the mountain road, he half-expected to see a posse galloping up the hill. He started to cross the road going north, when a thought hit him. *Damn it! It's hot right now but weather in these mountains can turn on a man in hurry.* He trotted back to the cabin, swung down and ran inside. In a few seconds, he reemerged with his sheepskin coat, a poncho and gloves. Eric rolled them up and lashed them in front of the saddle. He wasted no time in getting mounted again.

North of the road between Oro City and Leadville, he headed downhill to a rocky patch of open loose shale. He slowly descended the area for fifty yards and then cut left and rode parallel to the ridge line for a several hundred yards before he circled back and climbed up to the road to Leadville. He stayed off the dirt roadway itself and traveled back to his barn and entered his pasture. *That should give me another hour or so. By the time they figure I did not go north, they will play hob tryin' to follow tracks through these two animals' own pasture.*

When he got to the back fence, he dismounted, pulled the top two rails off the fence and walked the horse and mule across before he set the rails back in place. He picked up a heading of south. He knew in a few hours it would be getting dark. His plan was to make for Colorado City and he would turn east for Fairplay. If he made it down to the main road, he could still travel at night, but the deep woods and steep terrain made it almost impossible to do so in the area near Oro City.

"Get the lads off the floor and take them over to the undertaker." The old man eyes were filled with tears as he gazed down at his nephews. "What am I to tell their mother Maggie? Me sister sent them here for me to look after. 'Tis a fine mess we have on our hands now."

"Mister Malone, what can I do to help?" the sheriff asked with his hat in his hands.

"Lonnie, me boy, ye are a little late in askin'…Ye know who done the dirty deed, do ye?"

"Everybody knows it was that blonde blacksmith fellow, Eric Schmidt. They all seen him plain as day…he knocked Big Mike's teeth out and then shot him down in cold blood."

"That ain't the way I seen it," one of the bartenders said.

"Nobody asked you, Marvin. Shut yer trap."

"But sheriff, I was standing right…"

"How long you been working here?" Angus asked with a cutting edge to his voice.

"Almost a year, Mister Malone."

"If you want to be working in my saloon come the morning, I suggest you heed the Marshal's advice."

"Yes, Mister Malone." He turned around and began to pick up empty shot glasses off the poker tables.

"Five thousand in gold," Angus said in a low voice.

"Excuse me, sir?" Sheriff O'Donnell asked.

The old man glared at him. "Do not play dumb with me, Lonnie...I hired ye and I can fire ye just as quick. I want posters made up tonight...Five thousand dollars in gold...Dead or Alive." His eyes narrowed. "Make sure to put some hard men on the job. Anybody that can manhandle me nephew Michael is no slacker. Now get yer useless arse out of me sight 'fore I lose me temper."

"Yes, Mister Malone." O'Donnell bowed lightly and backed into a table behind him as a half dozen local miners lifted the bodies by the feet and hands.

Big Mike's head fell back, his open mouth exposing the two missing teeth and his face streaked in partially dried blood. Angus forced himself not to stare as the sight nauseated him greatly. *Damn you to hell Michael O'Toole. How many times did I tell ye that bull-headed temper was gonna be the end of ye? Big lummox. Not so funny now is it?*

***

CHAPTER EIGHTEEN

FAIRPLAY, COLORADO TERRITORY

Three miles west of the small town, Eric cut off the main road and circumnavigated the village by over a mile. The terrain was a relatively flat mountain plateau with deep grass in many places. No one had fenced any of the surrounding area as the invention of barbed wire would not occur for another year.

He planned to make following him as difficult as possible. One thing he knew, he didn't look like the average man. His size, blond hair and blue eyes made him a distinctive person to remember sighting and his detour left fewer persons to possibly see him pass by. What he did not know was a Ute Indian named Bear Claw was tracking him as part of the ten man posse that Sheriff O'Donnell had assembled out of the forty volunteers who responded to the reward.

He reached down for the bullseye canteen tied to the saddle. It was only a third full and the hot water tasted like the metal container, but it helped wash down the leathery deer jerky. Eric ran his tongue back and forth and eventually dislodged a jagged piece of cracked pepper that had stuck between his teeth. He sloshed a tiny sip of water around, swallowed and then placed the cork back onto the canteen's mouth. With the heel of his hand he tapped it home, sealing the unit tightly.

He noticed the stallion's head began to droop slightly as they neared the top of a ridge east of Fairplay. "Boy, I know you are tired. Been movin' all night and all day. Promise we will get some rest tonight." Eric reined back to a halt and turned around to study his back trail. In the haze, he was not quite sure what he saw. There was something dark in the wheat-colored grass just to the north of the road from Fairplay, but the distance was around eight miles. He lifted the flap on his saddlebags and pulled out the binoculars. Four quick breaths cleared most of the dust off the lens. He adjusted the eyepieces to bring the view into focus.

Son of a bitch...there they are. He counted the ten riders in single file along with a pack animal. They were following his trail around the village and soon would rejoin the road. *An hour behind me. Their mounts have got to be wearing out, just like mine.*

He spun Thunder around and urged him into a trot. "Come on, son. Top this ridge and we will see where to go next."

Two minutes later, he could see the trees and the west approach to Ute Pass in the distance ahead of him. He looked at the sun slowly setting back behind him. He remembered seeing a steep canyon off to the north of the road through the pass. Wagons could not make it through, but a rider possibly could. He would rest the animals there and set up a little surprise for the posse.

He woke up a good half hour before the sun came up, rolled the blanket up snugly and tied it off behind the cantle before he checked the security of the hobbles. Eric filled the two feed bags and fed his animals their daily ration of grain before he filled the canteen from the creek in the bottom of the canyon.

He yawned once, shook it off and slipped the strap of the full canteen over his head and across his chest. The saddle bags carried all his ammunition, binoculars, fire starter, venison jerky, compass and maps. He tossed them over his shoulder, picked up the two rifles and began the arduous task of ascending the steep side of the canyon. Thirty minutes later, he was ensconced in a clump of fir trees that had lower limbs almost reaching the ground. He had a clear view of a half mile long *U* shaped bend in the canyon. The sun was rising at his back and a light summer wind was in his face—all he had to do was wait.

Bear Claw followed the pair of animal tracks as they crossed over the creek upstream of the first of several abandoned beaver dams in the canyon. Trappers in the earlier part of the century had cleaned out the fur bearers in many of the Rampart Range valleys and this one was no different. Aspen and willow trees previously decimated by the hungry beavers had recovered on the hillsides and he was looking cautiously at every shadow in the canyon as the sun rose higher above the far ridge line. Sheriff O'Donnell banged his heels against the gray mare he rode to catch up with the scout.

"What is the hold up, Chief? Let get a move on it, before he gets a chance to beat us into Colorado City. We will lose him for sure if he does that."

The forty year old warrior cut his eyes at the lawman. "Maybe so, but if man we follow want to trap us…be good place."

"That blacksmith lit out like a turpentined cat after he laid those two Malone nephews in their graves…Think we will be in a tail chase all the way to the plains."

Bear Claw gave him a hard look and put his moccasin heels to the ribs of his paint horse. The gelding broke into a slow trot down the trail.

From his vantage point, Eric could see every one of the bounty hunter's and counted as number ten rode around the far bend in the canyon. *That is all of them. Guess they were not smart enough the send anybody up on the ridge lines to check for a rifleman waiting to take 'em out.*

He had pulled a short section of deadfall timber underneath the fir tree to use as a rest. The last two possemen, including the one with the pack horse were riding closely in trail of each other. Eric slipped the ladder sight on the Sharps up to the 200 yard notch and stood it up vertically. His saddlebag was beside the log and had a handful of paper cartridges already set for easy reach. The small circular tin of primers was open and next to it.

I wonder if... His question was answered when the last two bounty hunters lined up in a section of the well-worn game trail. He put the front sight on the closer of the two men's head and took in half a breath and let it out as he squeezed the trigger. The Sharps bucked back into his shoulder. Smoke temporarily blocked his view, but soon drifted up into the tree branches above him and dispersed.

The report of the big rifle echoed off the canyon walls again and again as the slug ripped through the first rider's head and then tore into the last man's sternum. Both toppled backward out of the saddle without a word.

Bear Claw lifted his old muzzle loader from across his thighs to his shoulder and scanned the hillside for a target. Sunlight glinted off the round headed brass tacks he had driven into the buttstock for decoration. His heart beat quickly for only a second before a heavy bullet from a Spencer rifle yanked him off the hand-woven saddle blanket and into the still waters of the beaver pond.

"Where the hell are they shooting from?" called out one of the men in the middle of the string of riders. He watched the sheriff point up in the direction of the far hillside and then his body slumped backwards on the horse's rump.

He spun around and started to ride the other direction when the last man in the column ahead of him fell from his horse. Not one of them had fired a shot and the awful sounds of big-bore rifles kept thundering up and down the canyon.

Eric methodically operated the lever and cycled another round into the chamber. He could hear the men yelling at each other as he lined up another man in his sights. He thumbed the hammer back and squeezed off another round, sending the sixth bounty hunter to his maker. Traces of gunsmoke began to work their way though the boughs of the tree above him. He jacked the lever down and brought it back up smartly, then pulled the hammer back again.

"There he is, up in the tree!" one man hollered and took a shot at the smoke with his Henry .44. The smallish rimfire sounded quite puny compared the big-bore Sharps and Spencer rifles. He worked the lever feverously and fired three rounds at the fir before a bullet from the Spencer caught him. It entered though the left side of his chest, taking out the lung and clipping the spine on the way out. He couldn't even manage a death scream as he slid off the right side of the startled horse.

Two of the remaining bounty hunters bolted back the way they came. Eric dropped the farthest one first, the bullet killing the rider and horse as well. The bay mare went down hard and somersaulted end over end, terrifying the rider right behind him.

The man thought of the words he had heard the big man say inside Muldoon's Saloon. "Dying is a hard way to make a livin'." Suddenly the thought of a share of a $5,000 reward seemed like the stupidest idea he had ever had. He reined south and made for a clump of aspen only eighty yards up the steep hillside. Another shot from a distant repeater tore into his leg, ripped though the horse and into his other leg. He dropped his rifle as his mortally wounded mount collapsed underneath him and then rolled over on its side. Unimaginable pain racked his body as he and the horse slid back down the rocky slope, his shattered right leg pinned beneath the dead animal.

Dammit. That one was a little low. He glanced to the sole remaining rider galloping down the canyon. He laid the empty Spencer on the log and picked up the Sharps and flung the operating lever down. Eric stuffed one of the waiting cartridges into the chamber. He fumbled with the first primer he tried to pick up. *Calm down. Be deliberate.* He took hold of another and pressed it firmly on to the waiting nipple. The rider was close to two hundred and fifty yards away when the hammer on Eric's rifle fell. He felt good about the shot, but when the smoke cleared, the rider was still in the saddle. *Damnation...he jumped the creek.* He could see where a small rock slide had blocked the old game trail and remembered having to cross the stream himself before darkness fell on the previous night.

He reloaded and slid the ladder sight up to 325 yards. Watching the man's rhythm as he was accustomed to do after so many encounters in the war, he led the chestnut a full body length and squeezed the trigger. His shot echoed off the canyon walls again, but the sound of a distant *whop* told him his bullet had made solid contact with flesh. He waved his arms to help disperse the smoke and could easily make out the horse galloping away alone.

Eric scanned the trail for movement, but could find none. He watched for a full minute before he reached for the saddlebags and grabbed a fistful of .56-56 cartridges for the Spencer and twisted the magazine tube cap in the buttplate to begin reloading. He allowed the empty magazine plunger assembly to drop free and loaded a couple of rounds. He checked the rocks and pushed another three rounds in before he looked up again. He saw a man rise up and move a few yards behind a larger boulder before he fell or lay back down. *Christ...he ain't dead...yet.*

He loaded the two last rounds into the magazine tube well and cycled the lever to bring one forward into the chamber. He quickly added the final cartridge and pushed the mag tube with its internal spring and plunger over the stubby copper-clad rimfire rounds and locked it firmly in place. He laid the repeating rifle down on the log, and then watched the rocks for about three minutes before he reloaded the Sharps.

Eric studied the vegetation on the canyon sides for a while before he made his decision. *I can back out of here, move on up into the dark timber and come down on the other side of him. Never give a man a shot at you if you can help it. Some son of a bitch just might get lucky.*

Using his glasses, Eric could see a young cowboy, maybe in his late twenties, leaning up against an eight foot tall boulder. His hat and double barrel shotgun lay some fifteen yards away where he originally landed after he was hit. The man had a visible wound in his right shoulder—his tan colored shirt was soaked in blood all the way to the waist and he was holding his bandana on the exit wound trying to stanch the flow of blood.

Maybe I can get some information out of him before he croaks. Eric slipped back into the woods and moved another two hundred yards downstream where he could descend out of view of the wounded bounty hunter. He jumped over the creek and—staying low in a crouch—eased up the trail until he could rise up and get a drop on the man. He set the Sharps down against a boulder, cocked the hammer and lifted the Spencer to his shoulder as he stood up only ten yards from the only member of the posse that was still breathing.

The luckless cowboy's eyes were already beginning to glaze over and his color was fading from the blood loss. Eric had seen that same sad condition hundreds of time before. "Keep your hand away from that shooter, mister. No way in hell could I miss from this distance."

"Go ahead…finish me off, you bastard."

Eric grinned. *Salty little shit.* "Hey…I saw you in the saloon yesterday, did I not?"

"Me and my brother Bart. He is around here somewhere and will kill you for sure."

Schmidt shook his head. "Not likely…I suppose there is some reason you all were following me."

"Hell, five thousand reasons…old man Malone wants you dead. You murdered his two nephews." The cowboy tried to spit, but his mouth was just too dry. "Got any water in that canteen?"

Eric nodded and lifted the strap over his head. Holding the Spencer with one hand, he tossed the canteen underhanded to him.

The cowboy tried to catch it with his good hand but missed—it landed against his chest with a thud. He winced a bit and then lifted the stopper to his teeth and pulled it open. He drank heavily, took a breath and drank some more before he dropped the canteen into the crook of his left arm and replaced the cork. "Many thanks…Got a question for you, Eric Schmidt. Where in hell did you learn to shoot like that?"

"Texas…What is your name, cowboy?"

"Billy…Billy Matthews…from down in Saint Louis town."

"Sorry you did not take my advice back in the saloon."

Billy tried to force a grin. "Me, too. Easy money, the sheriff said."

"Yeah? Well, he is laying back up the trail next to the Indian."

"Bear Claw had a bad feelin' about this canyon. Shoulda listened to him…He told me last night the Spaniards had a name for this place…Cañón Del Diablo."

"Canyon of the devil…Devil's Canyon…Guess that is appropriate."

"You gonna kill me now?"

"Nope…already did."

Billy leaned his head back on the rock. "Suppose dyin' is not that hard to do…Everybody does at one time or an…" His voice faded away as his chest sank slightly lower. His head tilted and his tongue hung out a bit as his jaw fell slack—he gave his final death rattle.

Eric sighed and lowered his rifle. He shook his head slowly. *So unnecessary...So damned unnecessary...all these people dead because one man could not control his kin and now he thinks he has to kill me to somehow make it even.* He walked closer and poked the man in the face with the muzzle of the Spencer. There was no response. He retrieved his canteen and stripped the gunbelt from the dead bounty hunter. *Never got a chance to use this shooter, did you, cowboy?* He rifled through the man's pockets and found four silver dollars and some change along with a folded up piece of paper. He unfolded the hastily printed poster and found to his dismay his name emblazoned near the top of the page.

WANTED

DEAD OR ALIVE

ERIC SCHMIDT

FOR THE MURDER OF
Michael Malone O'Toole
Patrick Angus O'Toole
REWARD $5,000 IN GOLD

Contact Angus Malone
Oro City, Colorado Territory

That about cuts it. No way in hell can I keep running with a price like that on my head. Some weasel bastard would back shoot me for that kind of money. He made up his mind about what he had to do. Eric followed his usual custom of collecting the armament of his fallen foes as well as their horses and gear. He roped the herd together as he had four years earlier and headed down the mountain.

By nightfall, he was through Woodland Park and back down the Ute pass road into Colorado City. He checked into a new building downtown called the Mountain View Hotel and got himself a bath and a good night's sleep. The next day he sold off the livestock, the tack and the firearms. With those two tasks completed, he stopped by the local tonsorial parlor next to the hotel.

A forty-five year old man with dark brown, slicked back hair greeted him. "Have yourself a seat, sir. You be needing a haircut and shave, I assume?"

Eric sat back in the black leather lined chair. "You assume correctly. I could use a trim…Getting a little long over the ears. But I would like to leave the mustache. Looking for a change, you know?"

"Of course, sir." The barber surveyed the two day old stubble. "Been on the road long?"

"A couple of days…I am looking for a tailor as well. I have been out doing some prospecting and made myself a small strike. Not enough to get rich, mind you, but I want to talk to some investors and need to get dressed for the part, you understand."

"Certainly…Believe I know of a few reputable places I can send you." He took a towel and poured hot water on it from a tea kettle sitting atop the cast iron stove. He wrapped the steaming towel around the young man's face and began to strop the straight razor against the strap hanging beside the mirror on the wall. He added a few drops of hot water to the shaving cup and stirred the hog bristle brush against the small disc shaped bar of soap resting at the bottom. In a few seconds, the cup was filled with suds. He carefully unwrapped the towel and made sure that Eric's beard was sufficiently softened before he deftly applied the foam and began the work with the straight razor.

Afterward, the barber handed him a small mirror and spun him so that his back was to the wall. "Does the cut meet with your satisfaction, sir?"

Eric studied the results in the oval framed mirror. "Looks fine. Much less of a mountain man look, now…Do you agree?"

"Of course, you look like a man of distinction if I do say so myself…That will be four bits for the haircut and shave."

Eric reached in his pocket for his money and then held up one finger. "One more thing…If a man wanted to change his hair color to black or brown. How could he go about it? I really like the color of your hair."

"Well sir, if you can keep a secret…" He looked around the empty shop. "I, myself, have some gray hair coming in at the top right here." He pointed at the distinct widow's peak. "I do not find it attractive in the least and I use a bottle color to match the rest…keeps me looking younger for the ladies." He winked at Eric.

"I never would have guessed," Eric lied. "Where could I buy such a bottle?"

"Why, I have a couple extras I could let do for a pittance. Only twenty cents extra, including the applicator brush."

"Sounds like my lucky day." Eric pulled out a silver dollar and handed it to the man. "Great job, mister, Keep the change."

Oro City
Colorado Territory

A dapper looking young man in a long burgundy frock coat rode up to Wallace Whitman's house on the last day of August. The sun was low in sky and casting long shadows across the yard. He dismounted from the California sorrel and tied off at the single wrought iron hitching post. He opened the swinging gate, walked across the lawn to the front door and knocked firmly.

Wallace, had been watching the man ride up from his parlor window. *Who in blazes is that slick peacock with the top hat? The last thing I need is a snake oil salesman.* He walked to the door, but didn't reach for the handle. "Go away…I ain't in the buyin' mood."

A familiar voice responded from the other side. "Wallace, open the door."

He grabbed at the handle and yanked it open. "Eric, is that you?" he said in a muted voice. The smile and the eyes were the same, but the dark hair and waxed mustache threw him.

"Shhh…do not just stand there. Invite me in."

Wallace stepped back and grabbed him by the arm. "Boy, you got a lot of nerve coming here! Malone put a bounty on your head and probably has fifty men out looking for you right now."

"Forty," Eric said with a sly grin. "That's why I am here. Mister Malone and I are gonna have ourselves a little talk."

"You are plum crazy…He will never agree to see you…"

"I did not say I was gonna ask to see him. He does not have a choice."

Without street lights like many other more established towns, the roads in the Oro City boom town were dark after the sun set. Eric rode the magnificent palomino up to one of the many hitching posts outside the iron fence surrounding the Irish mansion. He dismounted, tied up and then took an attaché case from his saddlebags and let himself in the gate.

The lawns surrounding the mansion were well manicured with formal flower beds. Oil lampposts shipped from back east lit the brick walk and were also used on either side the ornate entrance way where a single guard stood duty with a Henry repeating rifle cradled in his arms. The mansion interior was almost pitch black—only a few scattered candles and lamps provided enough light for the staff move from room to room. The guard stiffened at the sight of a stranger approaching at

10pm on a week night. He brought the rifle to a port arms position across his chest.

"Hold it right there, mister. Nobody gets in without an invitation."

The man in the top hat flashed a million dollar smile above a dark brown handlebar mustache, waxed to sharp points. He held up his index finger as he spoke in an Irish Accent. "Archibald McAllister, barrister, at your service. I have come from Boston to represent the estates of Mister Michael O'Toole and his late brother Patrick at the behest of their greatly bereaved mother. May I present me card?" He fished his hand into a tiny pocket inset into the paisley lining of his frock and produced a business card which he offered to the guard.

The guard released his left hand from the rifle and took hold of the card. As he raised the engraved card closer in an attempt to read it in the flickering coal lamp light, a lightning fast right hook came crashing against his jaw and his whole world turned black.

Eric lifted the rifle off the unconscious man's body and rolled him over his belly. He set the attaché case on the steps and snapped the brass locks to the side allowing the lid to open. Inside were several lengths of rope, three bandanas, a pair of iron wrist shackles and a small brown bottle with a glass stopper. He took the shackles and fastened them the guard's wrists, securing them behind his back. Moving quickly, he slipped one the bandannas around the man's head as a gag, made a pair of loops in one of the rope and pulled them over the guard's boots and securely lashed his feet and hands together.

That should keep him from moving around when he wakes up. Eric snapped the lid closed, stood up and briefly admired the architecture of the heavy oaken door with metal bands across it. The top was rounded and fit nicely inside the curved stone archway. He grabbed the wrought iron handle and gave the door a firm tug. It didn't budge. *Crap. Guess they do not trust people.* Thinking fast, he rolled the guard on his side and checked his pant's pockets. Sure enough, a large skeleton key was in one of them. *At least I do not have to break a window.* He carefully inserted the heavy iron key and turned it. A satisfying click told him the dead bolt was clear. He pocketed the key and pushed the massive door open and stepped inside.

No one else was awake in the house. Its stone walls were covered in Irish and Flemish tapestries. Heavily carved baroque furniture filled the rooms. He set the case down and stepped back outside. He grabbed the guard's legs by the bindings, picked up his rifle and dragged him inside and into a shadowy part of a side parlor off the foyer. Returning to the entrance, he closed the door and locked it.

He headed to the twin staircases and padded silently up the one to the right and on to the second floor. Wallace had told him which bedroom belonged to Angus Malone. It was the largest one, of course and faced west with a wonderful view of the town and the Rockies.

Eric took in a deep breath as he approached the twin doors to the bedroom. They were eight foot tall walnut ones with deep bas relief carvings of mounted knights dressed in armor. Everything in the mansion bespoke of the money the old man possessed. He leaned the rifle against the wall, set the briefcase down and opened it. Taking a bandanna out, the twisted the stopper loose in the brown bottle and covered the opening with the cloth. He tipped the bottle upside down for a few seconds until he could feel the chloroform dripping through his fingers. He held his breath and then turned the bottle erect and tamped the glass stopper firmly closed.

Eric held the soaked bandanna at arm's length as he turned the handle on the bedroom door and slipped inside. *Jesus! The bedroom is bigger than our whole house back home.* He stepped quietly, toe and heel, across the hardwood floor and moved to the area covered by the hand-knotted oriental carpet. The bed was gigantic, a European half-canopy style made using walnut with intricate rosewood and satinwood veneer inlays. A rococo walnut heraldic shield was carved into the footboard. The gracefully executed semicircular canopy featured a gold silk fabric gathered in a rosette and starburst design above the old man.

Malone was sound asleep, his head enveloped by a huge down pillow and his mouth open wide. His snores were reassuring to Eric as he moved closer and placed the drugged bandanna over the multimillionaire's mouth.

Malone awoke abruptly, his eyes filled with terror for a few seconds. Schmidt kept the cloth over the older man's face and restrained his flailing arms. Suddenly, his eyes rolled up in the back of his head and his lids fluttered a few times.

Eric removed the bandanna and tossed it on the floor. He walked to the door, grabbed up the rifle, reentered the bedroom.

When Angus Malone awoke, he found himself bound to the four corners of his palatial bed—his mouth gagged with some unseen cloth and the room lit by one of the lamps on the matching night stands. He glanced to his right and saw the heavy silk curtains had been drawn closed. He looked left and there was a well dressed stranger seated beside him, staring at him intently. His heart began to race and he strained at his bindings.

"That will do you no good, I am afraid. Try to relax," the stranger said. "I am not here to rob you...I am here to make a trade."

Eric could see the fear in the old man's eyes as he smiled at him. "Suppose an introduction is in order...My name is Eric Schmidt."

Malone's eyes flared wide at the name. Eric was not sure whether it was caused by hate or fear and it really didn't matter much. He knew he didn't have all night, so he got right to the point.

"Here is the deal...I am a business man, and so are you, so I will make this simple. A trade...my life for yours." Even without words being spoken, Eric could tell that the mine owner was confused by the offer. He took a copy of the wanted poster out of his inside frock pocket, unfolded it and held it for Malone to see. "You had this printed, correct?"

Angus nodded nervously.

"See, now we are getting somewhere. Five thousand dollars reward…Dead or alive. That is a lot of money…almost ten years labor for most folks."

Angus nodded again.

"And that is my predicament, you understand. I cannot live my life knowing someone might, at any moment, kill me without provocation for that reward money."

Angus glanced away for a second and then looked back into the intensely blue eyes watching him.

"Look, you know as well as I do that your nephew Michael was a drunk, a liar and a bully above all," Eric said coldly. "He thought he could make sport of me in front of the whole damned town. I warned him not to, but he did it anyway."

Angus' eyes showed a sadness that Eric could detect.

"I broke his damned nose and then he and his kid brother tried to kill me…They were not man enough or fast enough to get it done…" Eric said with a hint of steel to his voice. "…and that is the honest to God, gospel truth…whether you believe it or not."

Angus tried to talk, but the gag worked as expected.

"Look, I know I will never have enough money to buy my way out of this, so I will not even try." He fished in his pocket and pulled out a silver star. Engraved professionally on the front were the words *Sheriff* and *Oro City*. He held it up for Malone to see. "You sent him out with a bunch of cutthroats to track me down, did you not?"

Angus swallowed nervously.

"You gave him five hundred in gold to pay for expenses as well...I found it on his body...Ten fifty dollar gold pieces." Eric voice turned hard.

Malone could feel his heart beginning to beat faster.

"They are dead...all of 'em. That is why you never heard from them again." Eric stood up and leaned over the bed. "There has been enough killing...It stops tonight...One way or the other...Either you rescind that wanted poster and agree that it was self defense, or I will cut your throat here and now and be done with it...What is it gonna be?"

Malone tried to talk again and then nodded his head.

Eric pulled a stag-handled knife from his boot. "I am going to take off that gag, but try anything stupid and you will never leave this room. Understood?"

Malone nodded and turned his head so that Eric could untie it. Once it was free he took in a couple of deep breaths. "I agreed to rescind the reward."

"You made the right choice. I want it in writing on this copy and I want another five hundred copies printed up and distributed around the territory."

"I will do as you ask."

"Here is a pen and ink well I borrowed from your desk. You can use the attaché case to write on."

Several minutes later, Malone stood looking out the bedroom window. He watched as the lone rider disappeared in the moonlight—*Death rides a pale horse*—He clutched the silver star in his hand and trembled as he remembered the words of warning the young man said before he left: "Do not try to double-cross me…nothing in heaven or earth can save you if you do…I promise you that."

***

CHAPTER NINETEEN

DENVER CITY
SEPTEMBER 1866

Rounding the bend in the road, Eric looked down on his first view of the burgeoning city that had recently been named as the new capitol of the Colorado Territory. The mountains were again changing colors for the fall season with the aspen trees sporting gold doubloons for leaves. Farther below, oaks were beginning to turn orange—not quite ready to go fully red—and willows had taken on a bright yellow hue.

Cool winds of autumn put a little chill in the mountain air as the higher peaks wore a new mantle of snow. Descending though the foothills of the front range, Eric wished for a minute that he was wearing the heavier sheepskin coat that was packed in a trunk in the back of the wagon with all his other earthly belongings.

Buck Stienke

"Whoa up there, Rufus. Let me get a look at the layout down there. I hear tell they cannot keep the maps caught up, what with the towns all growing so fast."

He pulled the field glasses out of the saddlebags riding in the buckboard's seat beside him. Hundreds of small mining claims, with a mixture of small cabins and tents strung out lining the area's creeks were visible. Three more defined towns were laid out in the distance. *Aw hell...I cannot tell which one is supposed to be Denver City. Guess we will have to drive on down and ask somebody who lives there.*

Angus Malone had followed through on his promise to rescind the $5,000 bounty. His late-night encounter with Eric had left him shaken and utterly convinced that he had no other choice if he wanted to keep on breathing. He would never know how right he was.

Eric had bid a sad farewell to his friend and business partner Wallace Whitman. Both men had agreed that the town of Oro City was far too small for a man like him to try to live down a reputation as a fast gun, and he wanted no part of that albatross anyway. Once the final forage crop was cut and stacked in the barn loft, he packed up and headed northeast.

Crossing over the South Platte River on a wooden bridge, he hailed a man riding the other way. "Excuse me, sir, Can you direct me to the nearest wagon yard in Denver?"

The man reined up. "Sure enough, mister. Keep headin' east like you are doing. In about two miles, you will cross over Cherry Creek and it will be on your right. Cain't hardly miss it."

"Thank you kindly," Eric said and touched the brim of his hat. Half an hour later, he pulled into Larimer's Wagon Yard and climbed down from the buckboard, stretched and rubbed his backside. *That old seat sure ain't getting any easier on my behind.* He was greeted a young boy who worked at the livery.

"Howdy, mister. Gonna need to stay overnight?"

"Yes, indeed, son. Ya'll have a decent hotel hereabouts?"

"Uh huh…The Cattleman's is next door to the Golden Nugget and right close to downtown. It is over on Seventeenth Street." He pointed north toward some four story buildings.

"Thanks. Rub 'em both down and give 'em a quart of oats apiece. I will see that there is an extra quarter in it for you if you keep an eye on my wagon for me."

The boy's eyes lit up. "You bet, mister. I will pull it up close to the office for you."

Eric grabbed his saddle bags, the Spencer and a carpet bag with a change of clothes and headed for the hotel.

The sun rose over a cloudless sky on the Colorado plains. Light shining in the window of the third story hotel room bounced off the mirror above the wash basin and woke him. The brass bed squeaked a bit as he rolled over to get the bright light out of his eyes. *Boy howdy…Slept like a log. Kinda nice sleeping indoors for a change.* He stretched and reached over for the timepiece on the small table beside the bed. *Seven thirty! Gotta get a move on…cain't stay in bed all day. Got things to do.*

He filled a shallow china bowl from a matching pitcher and then began to soften his beard with handfuls of the room temperature water. Using a shaving cup, he whipped up a lather and then pulled out the folding straight razor that had belonged to his father and began to shave. *Glad that old boy in Colorado City sold me the hair die that washed out with lye soap. I was beginning to look like one of them thespians in a minstrel show.*

He lifted his chin to shave on the underside of the jaw and leaned down to see himself in the mirror. The cameo on the tiny gold chain swung free from his undershirt, but he could not see it dangling there behind his hand. It caught over the ebony handle of the straight razor and caused his upstroke to jerk slightly. He reacted involuntarily to the resulting nick and pulled his hand away quickly. The delicate chain broke at the clasp, allowing the precious memento to fall into the china basin. "Damn it!"

He stuck his hand into the soapy water and retrieved the cameo and chain, blew the excess water off it and set it down on the white cotton towel. *Clumsy move there, Eric. Now you have got yourself a dang razor cut to deal with.*

A small trickle of blood appeared where the blade had nicked him. He wiped it off on the back of his hand and finished shaving. Using another towel, he rinsed off his face, wiped it dry and dabbed at the cut, grabbed his styptic pencil and held it to the cut until it stopped bleeding. *Damn, that burns.*

He dried the razor and carefully stuck it back into its case before he could bring himself to study the damaged gold chain. The clasp was bent and the tiny loop that attached it to the end of the chain was gone. The cameo was all he had to remember Angelina by.

He took in a deep breath as a penetrating sadness overcame him. It had been over a year since he stopped looking for her and the lack of closure was something he thought he would never quite get past.

Looking out of the corner room's north window, he had a magnificent view of the Rockies up near Boulder. The snowcapped peaks looked picture-perfect in the early morning sunlight, but the spectacular view reminded him that he could not share the experience with the only woman he had ever loved.

Eric thought for a moment about tossing the cameo into the waste basket. It only seemed to serve as a remembrance of days long past and a hurt he had learned to push aside with considerable effort—almost like the painful recollections of finding his family killed. He stared at the graceful profile for a full minute, trying hard to make the colors come alive again. He closed his hand and shut his eyes tight.

The memory of her coming to him that night when he had asked for her hand in marriage flowed over him and touched him to his soul. He opened his eyes and glanced at his reflection in the mirror. Tears were streaming down his face and a lump formed in his throat. He put the cameo and chain in his brocade vest hooked on the back of a chair and wiped his tears away with the tips of his fingers. *Not today...Someday maybe, but I am not ready to toss it yet.*

After a breakfast of ham and eggs with biscuits and honey, Eric paid his restaurant bill and stopped by the front desk for some information. "Pardon me, sir. I am in the market for some property. Can you direct me to a reputable local land office?"

"I would be most happy to assist you. Just a few blocks east from here is title company who specializes in all sorts of land and buildings for sale. Frontier Title is their name. It is on the corner of Seventeenth Street and Stout, about two doors the other side of Pavillion Bank and Trust."

"Appreciate the help." Eric turned and started to walk away, but he spun back around. "One other thing…Is there anyone who can do jewelry repair in town?"

"You are in luck, sir. With all the gold mining going on in these parts, there is a Jewish fellow from New York who moved here a couple of years ago. He does a big business in smelting gold dust and nuggets and fabricating jewelry. The name is Goldstein and his place is even closer. Four blocks down on your right, next door to Gart Brother's Mercantile."

Denver City's sidewalks were bustling with people and surreys and wagons filled the streets as Eric made his way up the hill. *Looks like that gold rush has things jumping 'round here well. The town had a different feel to it than Oro City—more cosmopolitan and a lot less raw.*

He passed the mercantile business and spotted the neatly painted sign on the front window of Goldstein's. Behind the glass were a set of heavy steel bars to keep burglars at bay. He pushed open the door and heard a small brass bell mounted on the jam announce his entrance.

"Be right vit you," a voice came from behind a partition. Eric recognized the New York accent immediately. A small dark-haired man wearing a black silk *yarmulke* rounded the wooden wall. He wore thick glasses—a small jewelry loupe mounted to the dark frames—and a heavy leather shop apron. He sized up Eric's social and financial status in an instant, looking at his bare wedding finger and noting the fine cloth of the frock coat he wore. "Vhat can I do for you today, young man? A ring, a gold watch, a diamond stick pin?"

Eric smiled at the man's staccato speech pattern. He was obviously a salesman and a persistent one at that. "Nothing big today, just a little repair, if you do such a thing."

He waved his hand. "Oy vey. You came to ze right place. If Goldstein cannot fix it, it cannot be fixed...and ze day is still young...no? Maybe you vill change your mind...I have a special this week on..."

Eric grinned as he dug the cameo and chain out and laid them in the jeweler's delicate hands. "The clasp broke...right where it attaches to the chain."

The owner of the shop flipped the loupe down and studied the clasp. "I see...Very nice quality...Needs a good cleaning, of course. Vee do zat, too...For a slight additional charge."

The man's Yiddish accent amused Eric. "But you can fix it, is that right? Or, will I have to buy a new chain?"

"No, no...I fix good as new...maybe better. You see...save your money for a new ring or vatch."

"Fine." He smiled at the man's salesmanship. "Should I just leave it with you?"

"It vill take a while. You can come back." Goldstein slid the chain through the large hoop at the top of the cameo and caught sight of the engraving on the back. "Elouise...Is zat you lady friend's name?"

The smile faded from Eric's face. "No...That was actually her mother's name."

"Oh, I see." Goldstein flipped the cameo over. His eyes grew wide as he studied the carving in detail. "Now zat is the verk of a master...Is very, very nice."

Eric nodded his agreement.

"You know something funny, young man? Zis woman looks exactly like zat banker lady in town."

"Really? What a coincidence."

"I mean to say exactly...Except for the red hair, of course."

Eric's breathing stopped for a second. "Did you say red hair?"

"Long red hair. Very striking voman...I tell you, if I was not already a married man...Oy...vould I..."

Eric's heart began beating like crazy. "Her name...do you happen to know her name?"

"Of course...Miss LeBlanc is a regular customer."

My God. Eric tried to contain his excitement. "Mister Goldstein, what bank does she work at?"

"Pavillion Bank and Trust...Have you heard of it?"

Eric snatched the cameo from the surprised jeweler's hand and bolted from the store, leaving him wondering what on earth had got into him.

The downtown sidewalks were far too crowded to barrel through at full speed. Eric dodged a pair of elegantly dressed women carrying frilly parasols, jumped off the boardwalk, vaulted over a water trough and then turned up the street in a dead run. He sprinted past a man on a bay mare and it shied away—almost dumping the rider.

"What?…Are you crazy or something?" the man yelled and shook his fist.

Eric paid him no heed. His focus was on the businesses on the right side of the street. A new brick building caught his eye. It had a classic Greek broken pediment arch with Corinthian columns fashioned into a formal entranceway above the twin doors. Raised wooden letters, gilded in 24 carat gold leaf spelled out the name of the bank and left no doubt as to its financial stature. *She works in there?* He slowed to a brisk walk and stepped quickly onto the boardwalk.

Slightly winded after the two block sprint, he went through the ornately paneled front doors and looked around the lobby. Several tellers manned stations behind a wall of richly lacquered veneers with round openings though which the customers could conduct their business. Narrow steel bars provided protection for the tellers, with only an eight-inch-tall free space above the marble counters. He found a teller that was unoccupied and approached him quickly.

"Pardon me, sir. Do you have a Angelina LeBlanc that works here?"

The teller looked back curiously at the question. "Why yes we do…May I help you?"

Eric was relieved but nervous nonetheless. "Thank God...I need to see her."

"Sir, Miss LeBlanc is quite busy, I am afraid. Do you have an appointment, sir?"

"No...no, I do not have an appointment...I have been looking for her for quite some time." The sense of urgency in his voice gave the teller some concern. "I can take you to her personal secretary. Perhaps he can arrange something."

Secretary? She has a secretary? A thousand questions started to race through his mind. "That would be splendid," he replied as he caught his breath.

"Follow me, sir." The man walked over to a hidden door inset into the teller wall and stepped out into the lobby. "Right this way."

Eric fell in behind him, clutching the cameo in his hand. *What am I going to say to her? How did she end up here?* He watched as the teller entered a doorway marked *Executive Offices* and held the hallway door open for him. An awful thought crossed his mind. *What if she refuses to see me? Mayhaps she does not love me any more.*

Ten paces later, the teller stopped at a side door and knocked once before pulling it open for Eric. They stepped inside and approached the immaculately dressed thirty-year-old man seated behind a cherry desk. He wore wire-rimmed glasses and a charcoal colored three piece suit, complete with a bow tie. His slicked-down brown hair was parted neatly in the middle. A brass nameplate on a triangular shaped piece of varnished mahogany let visitors know he was Williston Bigsby III.

Something about the man's look told Eric he didn't go by Willy or Will.

"Williston, this gentleman would like a word with Miss LeBlanc."

Bigsby, frowned and glanced at the day's event calendar. "I do not believe we have you on today's schedule. Your name please, sir?"

"Eric Schmidt."

"No, you are definitely not scheduled. May I ask the nature of your business?"

The teller headed to the door, but turned to eavesdrop when he heard Eric say, "It is a personal matter. I have a something that once belonged to her mother and would like to know if she wanted it back."

The teller decided that was not worth hanging around to hear the rest of the man's tale. He stepped out into the hallway and gently closed the door.

Eric felt his throat growing drier by the minute. He couldn't bring himself to tell the secretary that he and his boss were once engaged to be married. His burning desire to see her again was dampened by a gnawing fear of rejection.

"I see," said Mr. Bigsby. "It may take a while. She is in conference with our head of acquisitions and our chief mining engineer. Have a seat and I will do what I can, but I am afraid she is booked solid today."

"Thanks," he replied and a turned around and spotted a high backed Chippendale leather chair. He sat down and glanced around at the oval coffee table and morning's newspaper on top of it. Looking at the office door, he finally noticed the engraved plaque upon its central raised panel. He leaned over to get a better look, as the coal oil lamp on the man's desk did not illuminate the windowless office very well.

A. LeBlanc

President

Chairman of the Board

Eric was stunned. He had never heard of a woman banker before. *Surely she must have married into money. Perhaps she chose not to change her name.* Insecurities grew inside him and he sank back into the chair. For the first time in his life, he felt truly defeated. He opened his hand and stared at the cameo.

"Sir...Mister Schmidt? Are you all right? Can I get you anything?"

He looked at the secretary and nodded. He got to his feet, stepped over to the desk and handed him the oval keepsake. "Angelina gave this to me for good luck during the war. Thank her and tell her that it worked well." A single tear ran down his cheek as he slowly turned around and headed for the door and left.

"Oh my," Williston said as he looked closely at the cameo. He sprang to his feet and entered the inner office without knocking.

Angelina was seated behind a huge Louis XIV desk with gilded ormolu figurines mounted on each of the four cabriolet legs. A matching bronze candelabra, also coated in gold, held six long-burning candles for illumination. Her hair was done up in a French twist and she wore a long sleeved dark hunter-green dress that had small raised ivory buttons all the way to her slender neck. She and her two colleagues were reviewing plans to expand another gold mine in which her bank had previously held a minority position and recently bought out the other owners.

"Something important I would hope, Mister Bigsby."

"Yes, ma'am. He said to thank you and tell you that it brought him luck."

She shrugged, looked curiously at her coworkers as she opened her hand and received the mysterious gift from her executive secretary. He mouth fell open as the familiar cameo came to rest face down. She read the name engraved on the gold back. Hurriedly, she flipped it over and saw her mother's profile. "Where did you get this?" she asked breathlessly.

"A gentleman brought it by and then left. He said his name was Eric..."

Walking across the marble floors of the lobby, Eric tried to push away the feeling of failure, without any success. To lose her a second time was almost too much to bear. He wiped a tear from his eye and reached for the polished brass door handle.

"Eric!"

The sound of her voice froze him instantly—he spun around.

All the patrons in the bank turned to watch as she leapt into his open arms and the two kissed with unbridled passion.

When they broke apart, both began speaking at the same time while trying to catch their breath.

"I thought I would never see you again…"

"They told me that Comanches killed you in the panhandle…"

"I assumed you got married…" he blurted.

"No one could ever replace you…No one."

He dropped to his knee, holding both her hands in his. "Angelina LeBlanc, I love you with all my heart and soul. I cannot imagine another day without you by my side. Will you do me the great honor of becoming my wife?"

Tears of joy rimmed her eyes as her lower lip trembled. She squeezed his hands firmly. "I have every material thing woman could desire but the one thing I cannot buy…is the love of a man who truly wants me for who I am. You were my first and only love…Yes…The answer is still yes, yes…a thousand times yes."

Eric rose back to his feet and they kissed again as the lobby broke out in applause.

****

TIMBER CREEK PRESS

PREVIEW FROM

TIMBER CREEK PRESS

HELL HOLE

by

Ken Farmer

CHAPTER ONE

MARIETTA, IT
CHICKASAW NATION

Felix Griffin twisted the young retarded man's own galluses around his neck and hoisted him to the top of the iron bar wall that formed one side of the cell. The small area reeked with body odor and the smell of stale urine from the white porcelain thunder pot in the corner. Nineteen-year-old, Abner Daly, kicked, struggled and clawed at the leather strap while it slowly choked him to death.

In the next cell, two other members of Griffin's gang, Harlan Walker and Martin Haynes, quickly secured the other end of the hapless youngster's leather suspenders to a crossbar. Felix grabbed a small wooden stand in a corner of the cell near the dying boy's kicking feet, overturned it and the large white porcelain pitcher and washbasin that were on top fell to the floor with a crash. Martin and Harlan stepped to their bunks, slid under their blankets and pretended to be sleeping.

In the front office of the small jail, sixty year old Deputy Charlie Metcalf, awakened by the noise, jumped up from his bunk and rubbed his eyes to clear them of sleep. He looked around the darkened room in confusion at the sounds of something banging against the bars in the back. *What in tarnation is that racket?* He grabbed a coal oil lantern from the desk, turned up the wick, and then dashed toward the door leading to the cells in the back room.

Haynes and Walker acted as if they too had just been awakened. The two men sat up in their bunks as the elderly deputy ran in—the hanging teenager gave one final jerk.

"What the hell…" said Charlie.

"Looks like my cell mate done gone and hung hisself," commented Griffin—a burly, dark visaged man—as he sat up in his bunk, blinking the sleep from his eyes.

Charlie set the lamp on the floor, unlocked the cell and rushed in—still half asleep and unthinking. "What the deuce did the kid do this fer? I knowed he was a tad slow, but he was only in fer chicken stealin'."

Felix didn't respond.

The deputy looked up at the body hanging three feet off the floor, completely away from his bunk on the other side. "Now how in Sam Hill did he git hisself up…"

The skinny man's feet were suddenly jerked out from under him when Harlan and Martin pulled the rope noose that was lying on the dark floor. They had unstrung the rope webbing from one of the bunks and snaked it along the floor and over the top of the bars to the next cell. Charlie was slammed upside down against the bars, completely off the ground next to the dead boy.

"Jesus…" the deputy exclaimed as his head banged against the iron bars.

Felix calmly walked over, removed the deputy's Bowie knife from the sheath on his belt, swiftly plunged it into his stomach and ripped downward, cutting through the top of his pants. The deputy's legs jerked and twitched in death as his intestines plopped to the floor with a soft wet sound and were rapidly covered with blood from his own cleaved heart. Griffin removed the deputy's keys, walked out the cell door and over to the other cell and unlocked it.

"Hey, how about us?"

"Yeah, come on, here!" yelled two rapidly sobering cowboys in the third cell.

"You boys broke the law. Need to do yer time." Felix chuckled as he picked up the lamp from the floor and the three headed for the front office. "Grab them other lamps," instructed Griffin as he held his up high to better light the room.

Following his order, Harlan and Martin started sloshing coal oil over everything in the jail. Felix took two swings to break the lock on the gun cabinet with an ax and they armed themselves with their own Winchesters and sixguns. Griffin opened a tin of phosphorus matches from the desk, struck one on the side wall and tossed it into a puddle of coal oil, setting it ablaze. The fire crawled across the floor rapidly like a starving animal, its fingers seeking food.

"This oughta keep the town busy fer a spell."

The trapped cowboys screamed frantically at the Griffin gang as they moved down the hallway to the back door.

"Let us out of here!...For the love of God..."

"Please....let us out!"

"You gotta git us outta here!"

At the rear door of the jail, Harlan and Martin ran out into the night, each carrying a rifle in addition to the guns they had strapped around their hips.

"Let's go find some horses," Walker said as they watched Griffin walk unconcernedly down the hallway.

Felix paused a moment in the doorway to survey their devilish handiwork, grinning malevolently as the flames consumed the dry board-and-batt building like a swarm of locust devouring a corn field. Then, ignoring the desperate cries of the other prisoners, he sauntered calmly out of sight into the darkness as the flames popped and crackled behind him.

CREEK BANK
ATOKA COUNTY
CHOCTAW NATION

The escaped prisoners rode down to the creek bank—all were riding worn-out looking horses and Martin Haynes rode bareback. They dismounted and allowed the horses to drink as they moved upstream to do the same.

"Damn, that water tastes good," exclaimed Martin.

Harlan splashed water in his face after drinking, wiped it semidry with his shirt sleeve and sprawled back on the grass. "Might taste good to you, but by God I'm hungry. We ain't et since yest'dy mornin'."

"We'll git somethin' to eat," said Felix squatting down after he too drank his fill.

"When? My stomach is startin' to think my mouth's been nailed shut." He waved his arm at the spavined horses nibbling on the fresh grass near the water. "And these here crowbaits you and Harlan stole ain't fit to pull a gol-durn plow!"

"Shut up, Martin…Jest shut yer damn mouth," said Felix.

"And ya'll got the saddles, while I'm havin' to ride that razor spined sonofabitch bareback…Why is it I'm always the one gits the short end of the stick?"

Felix backhanded Martin, knocking him on his butt. "I said shut yer mouth. Yer constant belly achin' makes my ass want a dip of snuff!"

"Martin's right though, Felix. That marshal's been stickin' to our tails like a duck on a June bug since we left Love County… Unless we git some good horses…"

"Shhhh! Listen," cautioned Felix as he held up his hand.

They heard the sound of a small wagon pulled by a single horse approaching along the hard-packed dirt road. The gang rushed over to the road and hunkered down in the brush.

A small flat-topped road wagon clattered and rattled along, with two men in the seat. Dressed in business suits and bowlers, they were traveling brush arbor preachers Thomas Whipple and Wesley Portis. The rear compartment of the wagon was hidden by roll-down canvas side curtains upon which was lettered in bright red:

REVIVALS
BIBLES - HYMNALS
WEDDINGS - CHRISTENINGS - BAPTISMS
FUNERALS

Portis, an older man about fifty, was counting some paper money. He shook the sheaf of bills at Whipple, who was driving.

"Look at these greenbacks, Thomas, my boy. Prettier than spring grass, ain't they?"

"Yes indeed, they surely are. They surely are. How did we do?"

Splendid, I'd say. Splendid! Over one hundred and twelve smackers. Yesireebob. A real profitable prayer meetin'…I love passin' the plate. Praise the Lord."

The Griffin gang watched the wagon as it drew closer to their hiding place in the grove of cedar trees.

"Travelin' preachers," whispered Martin.

"I kin read…Now, shhhh." Felix put his finger to his lips.

As the wagon drew abreast of them, Felix calmly stepped out in the middle of the road in front of the bay horse. Martin and Harlan followed immediately with their guns leveled.

"Hold the wagon," ordered Griffin.

Whipple reined the wagon to a stop as Felix motioned with his rifle.

"What…"

"Pull her over in the woods…Yonder behind us."

"Now see here…" Wesley protested.

"Don't give me no sass, preacher man."

"Do as he says!" Harlan levered his Winchester.

Thomas pulled the wagon to where he was ordered and stopped. The gang surrounded them.

"Climb down," Griffin ordered.

Hesitantly and fearfully, the preachers obeyed.

"I think you gentlemen should reconsider this. We're men of God."

"And I think you better keep your lip buttoned. God ain't here to bail you out and Mr. Griffin kin git mean as a bee-stung bear."

"Felix Griffin?"

"One in the same...Martin find their luggage an' you 'men of God'...shed them duds."

"I beg your pardon!"

Harlan shoved his rifle into Wesley's face, bruising his lips, as Martin started rummaging through the wagon.

"You deef? Peel 'em off, I said! And be quick about it."

Hurriedly the two pastors undressed, down to their union suits. Harlan gathered up their clothing.

"Find 'nythin', Martin?"

"Boxes of Bibles, hymnals, some grub, couple changes of clothes an'...looky what we got here." He held up a nearly full bottle of whiskey.

"Well, now, I thought you sky pilot types only drank wine fer communion...'Pears as though you're only men of God on the outside...Don't it boys?" He motioned again with the rifle. "Now wait over yonder by the creek!"

The preachers apprehensively trudged over and stopped at the edge of the water.

"Martin, pitch me one of them hymnals."

Haynes fished in the box, grabbed one of the worn hymnals and flipped it toward Griffin. He snatched it from the air, put his rifle under his arm, opened the book and thumbed through the pages for a short moment, and then stopped.

"We'll now sing hymn number forty-two." Griffin began to sing out like a choir director, "'Shall we gather at the river, the beautiful'...I said sing!" He looked over at his men. "Ya'll too, sing out."

Haynes and Walker grinned at each other and sang along—badly—with Griffin.

The two men shakily began to sing also, "'Yes, we'll gather at the river, The beautiful, the beautiful river; Gather with the saints at the river that flows by the throne of God'..."

Griffin grinned and winked at his cohorts, cold-bloodedly raised his rifle and levered off a couple of rounds, shooting the two men of the cloth in the back. Harlan laughed and fired two more. They crumpled forward and fell in the creek.

Felix continued singing and repeated the chorus as the bodies floated slowly downstream, "...'Gather with the saints at the river that flows by the throne of God'...Let me hear a Hallelujah!"

"Hallelujah!" both Harlan and Martin responded.

"Praise God!...Now let's change clothes, Brother Walker and Brother Haynes. We got services to hold and tithes to collect."

LIMESTONE GAP
ATOKA COUNTY
CHOCTAW NATION

Deputy US Marshal Taylor Blackledge stepped out of the front of Jolley's General Store, letting the screen door slam behind him with a bang. He had an open can of pickled peaches and was eating the tart fruit with his pocket knife. He stood for a moment on the porch and then moved over and sat in a slat-back, calf-hide bottom rocking chair next to a grizzled, white-bearded elderly man reading the weekly newspaper. After stabbing the last slice, he turned the can up and drank the remaining juice.

"Damn...pickled peaches 'er almost good as fresh."

"Yep, I'd say so...specially when the fresh is outta season," the old man said without looking up from his paper.

"Seen 'ny strangers about lately, old timer?"

The old man looked up, spit a long stream of tobacco juice into a brass spittoon beside his chair and wiped his chin with his sleeve. "Got warrants fer some nabobs on the scout, do ye?"

"Escaped prisoners. Real curly wolves. Killed five men down to Marietta bustin' out of the calaboose...Three of 'em they roasted alive when they burnt the jailhouse down...Arrested 'em onct, now gotta do it all over agin...Griffin gang. Know of 'em?"

"Who don't...By ginger, bad as they come...Trying to make out like the Larsons er Martins...so's I hear tell."

"Purty close, I 'spect."

"Jest wonder..."

"What's that?"

"Seen me three men yesterd'y...One was a ridin' bareback...wormy lookin' feller he was, another was a big man, dark beard. They's goin' down a old loggin' road near my place...Headed in the direction of the Shawnee Hills...I'd say."

"Damnation! Sounds like them...If they make it to the hills I won't stand a snowball's chanct in hell of findin' 'em." The marshal got to his feet and dropped the empty can in a wooden nail keg that served as a trash collector. "Thanks fer the information. Better be on my way."

"Take a caution marshal...they's real highbinders and a scourge to good people."

"Preachin' to the choir, old timer. Preachin' to the choir."

Marshal Blackledge walked his horse slowly along as he searched the ground for sign. He had found where the three horses met up with a wagon and then found two wind-broke gainted horses running loose. He had since been tracking the thin iron wheels of the small wagon with one horse tied behind. *They crossed the stream here.*

Thinking he saw something, he dismounted at the edge of the water and knelt to examine the ground—then straightened up with a hand-rolled cigarette butt. He took out a plug of Brown's Mule tobacco, bit off a chaw and speaking to his horse in his raspy voice, he loosened the girth, "Damned saddle gets a might hard, ol' son…Think we both could use a short halt."

He sat down on a log, working up his chew, contemplating, while his chestnut gelding started to drink from the stream. The sound of a horse snuffling in the bushes caused him to react alertly. He got quickly to his feet and spun around to see Felix Griffin with his two cohorts step out in plain sight.

The marshal drew his .44-40 Peacemaker and fired, but his rushed shot only knocked Griffin's hat from his head. The gang fired three shots into him from their Winchesters. He dropped his gun and staggered back, bleeding from the holes in his torso.

He held up his hands, shook his head and whispered, "No more, boys…No more."

As they watched, he slowly stepped back to the log and sat down. "No use wastin' lead…You done a good job." He grimaced from the pain and coughed up blood along with his wad of chew.

The gang just stood watching him, betraying no emotions.

"You'as always a gritty old bull, Mister Blackledge. I'll give you that," said Felix dressed in the much too small suit from the preacher, Thomas Whipple.

Taylor coughed up more blood as he strained to speak, "Now that you've kilt me Griffin...do me...do me a favor."

"Name it, ol' hoss."

"Be decent enough to...to bury me...deep...so's the coyotes and buzzards won't feast on me."

"Shore. Wouldn't want nobody to find you no how...Guess I owe you that."

"'Bliged."

Blackledge crumpled forward, dead, Felix caught him and lowered him to the ground on his back. He picked up Taylor's pistol, looked at it and shoved it in his pants.

"Dig a hole."

"Aw, come on, Felix. We ain't got no time to..."

Griffin suddenly lashed out and viciously slapped Harlan. "Gawdammit, do what I tell you! This here was a man!...More of a man than you'll ever be." He knelt down and closed Blackledge's eyes almost reverently. "I give him my word...and by gawd, I'm gonna keep it...Now dig!" He got back to his feet and glared at the other two.

"What'll we dig with?" Harlan asked, rubbing the side of his face.

Felix took out Taylor's big Bowie. "Here, start with this." He tossed the knife to Harlan, stepped to the marshal's horse and discovered a picket pin attached to the saddle, which he tossed to Haynes. "You can use this here." He discovered another pistol in the saddlebags. "Martin."

Haynes and Walker were just beginning to dig. Martin looked up as Felix tossed him the Schofield. He caught it, looked at it, grinned and slipped it into his belt.

"It's better'n that wore out Remington you been carryin'…See that you take care of it."

OKMULGEE COUNTY
CREEK NATION

Abby Holliway, a petite blonde-haired fifteen year old, poured the slop into a trough and the pigs crowded around it to eat. "Ya'll was hungry, wasn't you? Yes you was…And I see you're 'bout outta water too…All right ya'll eat up…I gotta go gather eggs. I'll fill up your water trough after that."

She turned and headed around the barn toward the chicken coop.

Abby came back around the corner of the barn to the pig pen, set her basket of eggs on the ground and poured the water from the white porcelain bucket into the trough. As she straightened up, Martin stepped out from behind a nearby tree.

"Howdy, Missy."

"Oh!…You startled me!"

"Now, don't holler ner make 'ny noise, if you don't want 'ny of them brothers and sisters of your'n harmed," Harlan said as he stepped from the other side.

"Who...who are you?"

"Don't matter none...Git in the barn," ordered Martin.

"What?...Oh, please, Mister...no. Please, dear God." She started backing away.

"Shut up and do as he says!"

Harlan and Martin hemmed her in and started walking toward her, forcing her back to the barn.

"Please, Mister...Please...don't..."

Abby backed into the barn with the two leering men following slowly. Once inside, Martin's narrow-set beady eyes looked back toward the house, and then closed the big hinged door...

Twenty minutes later, Martin Haynes and Harlan Walker exited the barn—both were adjusting their clothing.

"I declare, don't believe I ever seen such cryin' and takin' on in my life. You'd thunk somebody had whupped her with a wet rope," said Martin.

"Yeah, ain't no pleasin' some women...Grab them eggs. Felix'll be pissed we don't bring some back fer breakfast."

Haynes picked up the basket and they headed toward their horses back in the trees.

Harlan made one last comment as he glanced back, "Yessir...boss man's never gonna know what he missed out on...and we got the eggs too." He looked in the basket Martin was carrying. "They's enough fer all of us, what with that fatback the preachers had in the wagon…Gonna be a good day, yep…gonna be a good day."

As they rode off, Abby, with her pretty corn silk blue calico dress nearly torn off and her face bruised and battered, staggered to the edge of the open door of the barn. She held on to the side for a moment, and then shuffled outside where she collapsed to her knees, shook and sobbed quietly.

FORT SMITH, ARKANSAS
COURT HOUSE

The *Prince of Hangmen*—the moniker the press had stuck on the small, wispy, frail looking man with white hair and a matching long goatee—climbed the thirteen steps to the twelve-man gallows outside the court house. He was in fact, George Maledon, the official hangman for the Ninth Judicial District Court presided over by the honorable Issac Charles Parker—the hanging judge. Maledon, in his sixties, wore twin ivory handled .41 caliber Colt bird's-head revolvers in reverse holsters around his waist over his coat—he always dressed in black.

US Deputy Marshals Bass Reeves, Jack McGann and Jed Neal passed the gibbet on the way to the courthouse. Reeves touched the brim of his black Boss of the Plains hat with his hand. The deceptively frail looking man came as close to smiling as he ever would and nodded at the trio.

The six foot two lawman also had his own press-induced identity—*The Indomitable Marshal*—'*so tough he could spit on a brick and bust it.*' It was said in the papers that '*Bass Reeves was never known to show the slightest excitement, under any circumstance and some say he does not know what fear is.*' Now whether he had that same opinion of himself is open to discussion, but his dedication to the law and his duty was never questioned. The one thing he probably would agree with the press on was the often quoted statement: '*Place a warrant for arrest in his hands and no circumstance can cause him to deviate.*' To the first black US Deputy Marshal west of the Mississippi, duty was not the first thing—it was the only thing.

The three marshals had left their horses with the hostler at the wagon yard on the other side of the gallows. It was widely known that whenever Judge Parker was particularly anxious to bring in an outlaw who was on the scout—he sent for Bass and his long-time partners.

Jack, the middle-aged stocky mustachioed white man of the three, knocked on the cherry-paneled door with gold lettering that just read:

JUDGE ISAAC C. PARKER
U. S. JUDICIAL DISTRICT OF WESTERN ARKANSAS

"Enter," boomed a voice from the other side.

Bass, Jack and Jed entered the judge's chambers, snatching off their hats as they came through the door.

"Hang your hats on that tree, gentlemen."

They did as instructed, walked over and stood in front of the Judge's carved rosewood desk.

"Sit down, sit down," the big barrel-chested man said. Even a simple invitation by the most powerful man west of Washington, DC, to sit could have an unnerving effect on many men, including his marshals. "Cigar?" He pushed an ornate hand-carved cherry-wood box across the top of his neatly kept and polished desk.

When Judge Parker took the bench almost twenty years earlier, he had been dark of hair as well as beard. After some nine thousand warrants had passed through his court and the over seventy men that had danced on his gallows, his full head of hair and beard had turned snow white. His countenance, however, in no way belied his continued dedication and commitment to his job.

Jed, also a black man like Reeves—just not as big and smooth shaven—got out of his chair, picked up the box and passed it in front of Bass and Jack. Parker indicated the cut crystal match holder next to his inkwell. In a few short moments a large blue cloud hung near the twelve foot high embossed tin ceiling of the judge's chambers from the four expensive cigars now being enjoyed by the men.

"Jack, how's that pretty new wife?"

"Fine, sir, fine. Think she's kinda glad to git me outta the house fer a while...Said one puppy underfoot at the time was enough."

"I expect Son is near grown by now, isn't he?"

"Yessir, purt near big as his daddy an' got them same gold eyes...One reason I left him there...He's good comp'ny for Angie and he's a bit touchy about strangers when I'm not around."

The judge nodded, took a draw and blew a cloud of smoke over his head. "I asked you three to come in specifically...You heard about Marshal Blackledge's disappearance, I'm sure."

"Yessir, Taylor was a good man and more than that...a good friend of mine," said Bass.

"Mine too, Bass, mine too..." The Judge paused, turned his head and stared out the window for a moment, and then continued, "He had been on the trail of the Griffin gang since they broke out of the Marietta jail and killed everybody in it. Then they killed two traveling preachers and that's about when Blackledge disappeared. He was last seen at Atoka...A fifteen year old girl was raped near Okmulgee...Got a pretty good idea it was them."

Bass got to his feet and walked over to a large pink and yellow map of the Oklahoma Territory and the Nations on the Judge's wall. In the yellow section which set aside the Cherokee, Creek, Seminole, Choctaw and Chickasaw nations, Bass traced the sightings from Marietta to Atoka in the

Chickasaw Nation to Okmulgee in the Creek. "Yep, what I thought...Headin' toward Catoosa."

"The Hell Hole?" asked Jack.

"That's what they call it. Catoosa, the Hell Hole. The gathering place for outlaws of every stripe. Some say it's worse than the Hole-in-the-Wall up in Wyoming and I wouldn't be surprised...I want that cess pool cleaned out gentlemen...Once and for all," added Parker.

"Don't guess you could send the US Calvary in?" asked Jack.

"Violation of the Posse Comitatus Act."

"Pardon my ignernce, Judge, but what's that?" asked Jed.

"A law they passed in '78, some three years after I took the bench that basically prohibits using federal military personnel to enforce civil law."

"I'm assumin' you want us to bring the Griffin gang in," said Bass.

The judge spun his chair around and stared out the window again at the gallows. Maledon was fitting a noose over the second of two men with black hoods over their heads standing in the center. "Griffin is a man without a moral compass. I want to see him and those bastards in his gang out there on my gibbet..." He spun back around and looked into Bass' eyes. "Don't care how you do it."

"Yessir, I understands."

"I'm keeping this quiet. The damn press is getting to be like a bunch of rabid dogs...They would ruin any chance we would have of getting this bunch of societal paragons of miscreants and malefactors by letting them know you're coming in...They would just scatter."

"I think we all agree with that, Judge. Be better if'n we go in unannounced," added Jack.

"They're going to ask since I'm sure someone saw you come in to my chambers...I'll tell them that Marshal Patrick at Sand Springs requested federal assistance on a string of rustlings and horse larceny that have been going on."

"Sand Springs ain't far from Catoosa anyways," said Jed.

Parker opened his top desk drawer, pulled out a stack of warrants and pushed them across the desk toward Bass, who handed them on to Jack. "Here are some warrants that need serving on the way along with some John Doe's, if you need them...They include the Stanton brothers. It will add credulity to you being out in the Cherokee Nation. You may leave your prisoners with the local sheriffs or town marshals...I'll send a Tumbleweed Wagon for them or, if feasible, a marshal on a train. He laid three more on the desk. "These are the new charges for Griffin and his gang on top of the ones they were in jail for...including the murder of a federal officer. Bring them in alive...or bring them in dead."

***

TIMBER CREEK PRESS